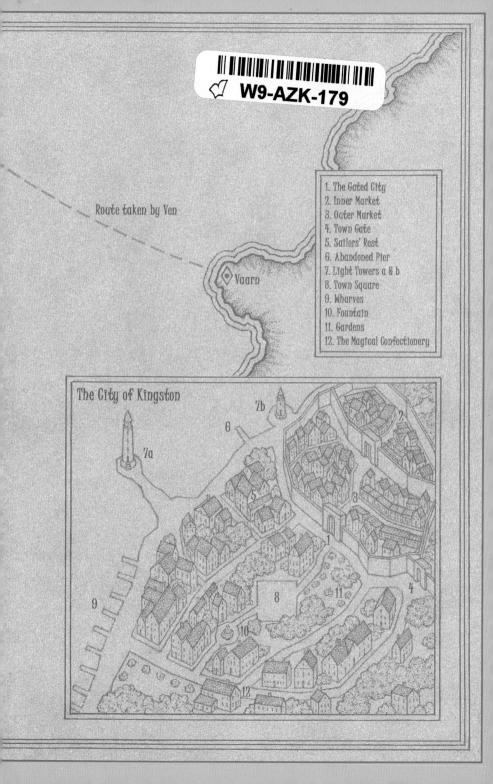

W9-AZK-179

Route taken by Ven

Vaarn

1. The Gated City
2. Inner Market
3. Outer Market
4. Town Gate
5. Sailors' Rest
6. Abandoned Pier
7. Light Towers a & b
8. Town Square
9. Wharves
10. Fountain
11. Gardens
12. The Magical Confectionery

The City of Kingston

— The Lost Journals of Ven Polypheme —
THE FLOATING ISLAND

Magnus
the
Mad

The Lost Journals of Ven Polypheme

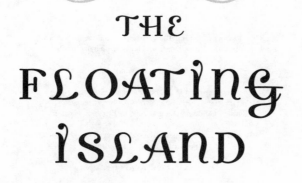

THE
FLOATING
ISLAND

Text compiled by

ELIZABETH HAYDON

Illustrations restored by

BRETT HELQUIST

A TOM DOHERTY ASSOCIATES BOOK · NEW YORK

STARSCAPE

THE FLOATING ISLAND

Copyright © 2006 by Elizabeth Haydon
Illustrations copyright © 2006 by Brett Helquist
Reader's Guide copyright © 2006 by Elizabeth Haydon

This book is printed on acid-free paper.

Book design by Nicole de las Heras

Endpaper map by Ed Gazsi

A Starscape Book
Published by Tom Doherty Associates, LLC
175 Fifth Avenue
New York, NY 10010

www.tor.com

Library of Congress Cataloging-in-Publication Data

Haydon, Elizabeth.
  The floating island / Elizabeth Haydon.—1st ed.
    p. cm.
  "A Tom Doherty Associates book."
  ISBN-13: 978-0-765-30867-2 (alk. paper)
  ISBN-10: 0-765-30867-3

2006005768

First Edition: September 2006

Printed in the United States of America

0 9 8 7 6 5 4 3 2 1

To my ever-so-very patient spouse and offspring,
who have endured many months of late nights
being ignored amid the house smelling of stale seaweed,
and many mornings scrounging for their own breakfasts
whilst I endeavored to restore this fragile manuscript.
I thank you for your understanding,
even if you *do* think I am crazy.

—E. H.

PREFACE

Long ago, in the second age of history, a young Nain explorer by the name of Ven Polypheme traveled much of the known and unknown world, recording his adventures and the marvelous sights he witnessed. His writings eventually formed the basis for *The Book of All Human Knowledge* and *All the World's Magic*. These were two of the most important books of all time, because they captured the secrets of magic and the records of mythical beings and wondrous places that are now all but gone from the world.

The only copies of each of these books were lost at sea centuries ago, but a few fragments of Ven's original journals remain. Recently discovered by archaeologists, some of those diary entries are reproduced in this book, in Ven Polypheme's handwriting, as they were originally written. Some of them are little more than a few words, or a sentence or two. A number of sketches from his notebooks also survived and are reproduced here as well. Great care has been taken to reconstruct the parts of the journal that did not survive, so that a whole story can be told.

A separate notebook containing only sketches of dragons, plus drawings of what appear to be cards made out of dragon scales, is still being translated. It was found, buried with the journals, in a waterproof chest lined with gold. It is as yet unknown what connection these dragons and cards have to the Ven journals, but their importance is clear.

These few scraps of text and sketches provide a map back in Time to hidden places, where pockets of magic might still be found.

Contents

— The Lost Journals of Ven Polypheme —

THE FLOATING ISLAND

Being thrown in jail to rot is not especially fun.

Being thrown in jail when you are innocent is worse.

Being thrown in jail to await having your head cut off is the worst of all.

All of this is even more depressing when you are far from home and everyone who loves you thinks you are dead.

It doesn't help to be of a different race than most of the people in this kingdom, who consider your kind to be odd at best and dangerous freaks at worst.

Nor is it a good thing to be a kid when all this is happening. People don't seem to listen much to kids.

But worse than all of that is being in jail, knowing that your fate will be determined by how well you can explain your innocence, and what has happened to you, in writing.

I wish I had paid better attention in writing class.

My birthday was a few weeks ago. I had hoped, and even expected, that this would be a good year. But I did something stupid on that morning, something that seems to have brought me nothing but bad luck.

So now I am sitting here, thousands of miles from home, alone in a smelly dungeon, with a few pieces of parchment paper and an inkpot. The king who will decide whether to keep me in prison, or cut off my head, or maybe even set me free, is away. Upon his return I am supposed to have finished the story of what happened, or at least my side of the story, in writing, so that he can determine my fate.

I hardly know where to begin.

I guess I will tell it as best as I can remember it. But I'm really not certain what to hope for. Having your head cut off is bad, but it's over quickly at least. Rotting in a dungeon seems a nasty way to spend your life. But it might be better than being set free. If they set me free, and then send me back to the crossroads, it might be worse than dying.

Because whatever is waiting for me at the crossroads can chase me to the other side of death.

THE JAILER BANGED ON THE GATE OF THE CELL.

Ven jumped at the sound, knocking over the inkpot. He righted it quickly, but not before smudging a good deal of what he had already written.

"Ya done with yer supper?" the jailer demanded. He was a short man with a skinny black beard that looked like the brushes chimney sweeps used to clean out gutters.

Ven nodded and hurried over to the small opening near the floor of the prison cell bars. He pushed the battered tin tray through while the jailer watched, then went back to his writing.

The burly little man picked up the tray outside the cell and turned away, then turned back, his ring of keys rattling loudly.

"If ya need more paper, I can get it fer ya," he said gruffly.

"Yes, if you please," Ven said gratefully. "Uh, do you know when His Majesty is returning?"

The jailer's black eyes glittered.

"I wouldn't be in a hurry for that, lad," he said darkly. "The king has no patience with thieves, and even less with murderers." He stared at Ven in the gloomy half-light of the dungeon. "Ya may as well enjoy whatever time ya got left."

He hurried back up the stone steps, leaving Ven alone again with his ink, his stained paper, and his thoughts.

✴

- 1 -

The Albatross

The morning of my fiftieth birthday found me, as the last twenty had, sneakily examining my chin in the looking glass, searching for a sign, any small sign, of a whisker.

And, once again, as on the previous twenty birthdays, I found nothing.

Absolutely nothing.

It may seem strange to you that I was able to reach the age of fifty years and still have my face remain as smooth and hairless as a green melon, and you would be right. Many lads of my race begin sprouting their beards by the tender age of thirty, and nearly all of them have a full layer of short growth, known as their Bramble, by forty-five. It is all but unheard of among the Nain for a boy to reach his fiftieth year without at least some sign that his beard is beginning to grow in.

But then, this is certainly not the first thing about me that the rest of the Nain in the city of Vaarn think of as odd.

If I were a human, by the age of fifty I would be entering the later years of my life, and my hairless chin would be of no consequence. In fact, it might even be seen as an advantage, since human men have the rather astonishing habit of removing their beards with a sharp knife known as a razor each morning, a practice that horrifies the Nain. This intentional sliding of knife over throat also permanently cements the distrust they feel for the race of humans. A man's beard is the story of his life to the Nain.

And on that morning it didn't seem as if I would ever have one—a beard, a life, or a story worth telling of it.

How quickly Fate turns things around.

Being fifty years old as a Nain is the same as being about twelve or thirteen in human years. We live about four times longer than humans, and grow more slowly. You might think that living four times as long as humans we would have special wisdom upon reaching those teenage years that humans do not have. I certainly thought so. On the night before my forty-second birthday I floated this theory past my mother, who looked at me doubtfully.

"Neh," she said, scorn in her voice. "It merely means you have four times as many years being pigheaded and stupid."

She had a point.

But while Nain can be somewhat pigheaded, I know they are not stupid. They are just uncomfortable in the air of the upworld, with the wind blowing and the bright sky and the commotion of those taller people walking about.

Nain much prefer the dark tunnels of the earth, the warm, solid feel of mountain rising around them, the clanging of anvils and the noise of digging that their deep world absorbs. Being out of the earth for any length of time bothers them. It makes them feel as if things are, well, <u>loose.</u>

So when my great-grandfather, Magnus Polypheme, chose to leave Castenen, the underground kingdom of the Nain, and make his way in the world of human men, it was considered more than strange.

It was a scandal.

Magnus the Mad, as he was known, was by no means the first Nain to leave Castenen. Nor was he the first Nain to choose to live among the humans that were the largest part of the population of the Great Overward, where I was born. Nain, in fact, lived in cities all over the vast continent. Oftentimes they were the merchants who sold the wares that were produced within the mountain kingdom of Castenen to humans in their towns and villages.

But not my great-grandfather. He chose instead to move to the city of Vaarn.

By the sea.

To work on building ships.

Even the upworld Nain couldn't figure that one out.

On the morning of his fiftieth birthday, as Ven Polypheme hurried excitedly to the docks, the light of the sun disappeared for a moment, as if it had been suddenly blotted out.

Ven shielded his eyes and looked up into the dark sky just in time to catch sight of the largest feather he had ever seen, wafting down toward him on the hot wind.

Momentarily blind as the sun returned, he reached out and caught it, an oily white feather tipped with blue-green markings.

It was as long as his forearm.

He had no time to wonder where it had come from. His father's voice filled his ears.

"Ven! *Ven!* Did you see it?"

Ven looked down the long wharf. Pepin Polypheme, a rather portly Nain of close to two hundred and fifty years, was hurrying toward him, puffing and wiping the sweat from his forehead with his pocket handkerchief.

"Did you see it, lad?" his father asked again.

Ven held up the feather.

"Not the feather, the bird!" Pepin gasped as he came to a halt beside his son. "The albatross—did you see it?"

Ven shook his head. "I saw its shadow as it passed overhead, but I was too busy trying to catch the feather to see the bird."

The older Polypheme shook his head as well, spattering drops of sweat into the hot air, and sighed.

"I fear that may turn out to be the story of your life, my boy," he said regretfully. "Catching the useless feather, missing the giant, rare, *lucky* bird. Ah, well. Come along."

Ven sighed as well, wondering if he would ever be able to do anything but disappoint his father. He slid the feather into the band of his cap and followed Pepin along the planks to the pier where the ship his family was outfitting was moored. Like all Nain he was stocky, but he was tall for his age, so he kept up easily with the old man.

"Have they decided what to name her yet?" he asked Pepin, who was waving to the head shipwright.

His father scowled at him. "You should know better than that. No one hears a ship's name until she is christened. It's bad luck."

"But someone must know what she is to be called," Ven said, mostly to himself, as his father was now talking to the shipwright. "Someone will have to paint the name on her prow before the christening ceremony."

"That won't be you."

Ven jumped at the sound of his second-oldest brother's voice behind him.

"Morning, Nigel."

"Morning, and many happy returns of the day, Ven. I'd say 'bless your beard,' but of course you don't have one yet. Now get your oversized fanny to the end of the causeway where the others are waiting. We're drawing straws to see who has to do the Inspection. Now that you're of age, you have to throw your lot in with the rest of us. No more free ride for you, little brother. Even if it is your birthday."

Ven nodded excitedly. He had long been aware of the need for the final check of the ship's fittings that was made on the open sea outside the harbor just before its christening. It was the last chance the ship's builders had to make certain the vessel was seaworthy before turning it over to the new owner.

His brothers dreaded Inspections. They feared the water and could not swim, so the eight-hour voyage on seas that were often rough was torture for them. Whenever it needed to be done, they had drawn hay straws, making the loser in the game undertake the Inspection.

Unlike his brothers, however, Ven could swim, and he loved to sail. His heart was always dreaming of adventure beyond Vaarn, the bustling seaside city in which he lived. So the opportunity to do an Inspection—taking a ship with a small crew out of the harbor and into open sea—made his skin prickle with excitement. *I hope I get the straw!* he thought, but he said nothing, following Nigel over to meet with three of his other brothers.

He could see them from quite a distance; his siblings, like Ven himself, had hair the color of ocean sand, and their heads stood out in the sea of darker-haired people milling about the docks, despite their being shorter than everyone else. Besides, most folks knew to give the Polypheme boys plenty of room in case one of their frequent scuffles broke out. Their good-natured horseplay had bumped more than one innocent bystander into the water.

Vernon, Osgood, and Jasper didn't appear especially happy to see him. They glanced up from the model of the ship's hull they were examining, then went back to arguing among themselves. Arguing was how the Polypheme family communicated.

Ven watched nervously as Jasper squatted down and pointed to a line of miniature lead rivets that fastened a small board to the keel of the ship's model. He grew even more anxious as his brother spat on the pier and continued to point at the model's hull. Ven had worked on that part of the model, and had forged many of the actual iron rivets for the ship himself.

Scale models of the ships they built were the Polypheme family's stock-in-trade. They fashioned whatever vessel they were crafting in perfect miniature detail, from stem to stern, in all its fittings, down to the last rivet and dead-eye, at one-tenth the size it would be when the ship itself was finished. In this way the Polyphemes could be certain the design was sound, and catch any problems before the vessel sailed into the harbor for Inspection.

At least that was the hope. It didn't always turn out that way.

On Osgood's first Inspection, a design flaw with the bilge pump caused the ship to start taking on water at alarming speed. By the time the leaky sloop returned to the pier, it was riding very low in the water, and Osgood was gibbering like a panicked monkey.

But for the most part, these models served to prevent problems in the enormous projects of building sailing vessels. Whether it was a frigate, a sloop, a galleon, or a fishing boat, before the first iron rivet or steel nail was forged to fasten it together, the Polyphemes had already built a smaller version of it. The model for this one was lying in great sections on the planks of the dock in front of their family factory.

Jasper pointed a stubby finger at Ven, then indicated the bottom of the model again.

"There's twice as many fastenings here as there needs to be," he said, scowling. "Ya think we're made of gold or something, Ven? Do you have any idea of the *cost* of this?" Jasper was in charge of the factory's finances.

"I know that the ship stands twice as good a chance of holding together if it hits a reef because of them, Jasper," Ven replied. "Since that might save the entire cargo and crew, by my reckoning it's cheap. Just looking after the family's reputation." It was his birthday, so he decided to risk a playful poke at his brother's stinginess. "Wouldn't want skimping on rivets to cause the loss of the ship and the business at the same time."

Jasper's face turned an unhealthy shade of purple. Even though he was half a head shorter than his youngest brother, he strode over to him angrily and bounced his belly off of Ven's.

Ven knew the belly blow was coming and braced himself. So when it came, Ven didn't move an inch, but it sent Jasper sprawling backwards, landing on his backside with a resounding thump.

"Stow your bickering," ordered Nigel, holding out a curled fist from which five straws popped. "Time to draw. Short straw inspects. Since it's your birthday, Ven, you can draw first."

Swallowing his excitement, Ven stepped forward to get a better look at the ends of the straws, trying to determine which of them was the shortest. He inhaled the salty air, hoping it would bring him luck. Then he took hold of one end, closed his eyes, and plucked the straw from Nigel's hand.

At first he thought he must have dropped the straw because of his eyes being closed. Ven opened them quickly, feeling nothing in his hand, then looked.

The straw between his thumb and forefinger was not even the length from his fingertip to the first knuckle.

Nigel opened his palm. Every other straw was at least the length of his hand.

"Tsk, tsk; hard luck, bucko," said Osgood in obvious relief, wiping the nervous sweat from his forehead with the back of his hand. "Your first draw, and your first short straw. Too bad."

Ven nodded but said nothing, knowing that any word out of his mouth would betray his jubilation. He turned away from his brothers and walked slowly down to the end of the pier, where the all-but-finished ship was moored, still waiting for its sails to be brought aboard.

As Ven moved beyond earshot, Vernon turned in disgust to Osgood.

"You sniveling baby," he said contemptuously. "Why are you sweating like a prisoner about to be keel-hauled? You knew all along the draw was rigged."

Ven was too far away to hear when Osgood tackled Vernon, too caught up in excitement to notice his brothers rolling around on the docks, pounding each other's heads into the planks. The sight was a common one anyway.

Instead, he was listening to the call of the sea wind, to the scream of the gulls, to the glad song his heart was singing of adventure beyond the harbor of Vaarn, where he had spent his entire life.

It was an excitement none of his family could possibly understand.

In the distance he could make out a tiny moving shadow against the sun, flying in great circles on the warm updrafts.

The albatross.

Ven touched the long feather in his cap.

"Thank you," he whispered into the wind. "Seeing you seems to have brought me luck this day after all."

He had no idea how much—or how bad.

-2-

The Inspection

"Ours is a working family," said my father that morning, again. My oath to Earth if he hasn't said it at least twice a day, every day, I have been alive. He probably says it much more often, out of my hearing, to my brothers and sister, since they actually run parts of his business. For me, "Ours is a working family" usually explains why I have to do as I'm told, rather than as I please.

My father inherited the factory from his father, who inherited it from his own father, Magnus the Mad. For Dad, manufacturing is a mission. Every one of his children works there, even my only sister, who apprenticed early in her career to a canvasmaker, and now runs the section of the shop that makes the sails. My mother is the only Polypheme who does not toil in the factory, but she is part of the mission, too. It is her job to manufacture the workers.

And she has. Thirteen of us.

I am the youngest, number thirteen, the last of the dozen sons of Pepin Polypheme. I am also by far the tallest, reaching the height at this early age of sixty-eight Knuckles, close to five feet in human measure, a half a head taller than all my brothers. I was named for my mother's father, and Magnus the Mad, and so bear the name of Charles Magnus Ven Polypheme, but have been known most of my life simply as Ven.

▇▇▇ is the Nain word for "and." It was my first word, and so was ▇▇▇ ▇▇▇ name ▇▇ the age of three, when I first spoke it. That is ▇▇▇ ▇▇▇ each child's first word becomes an official part of his or her name. As a result, three of my brothers are Petar Da-da Polypheme, Osgood No! Polypheme, and Linus Poo-poo Polypheme.

Personally, I think the Nain should rethink this tradition.

As for my name, I think perhaps there should be a question mark after it—"and?"—as if life is always posing the question of what I am to do next. I was born with more than my share of curiosity, and it gets me into a frightful amount of trouble. I want to know what comes next from the time I wake up in the morning, wondering what the day will hold, till the moment I fall asleep, imagining where my dreams will take me that night. It's like an itch; my skin or scalp hums with excitement whenever my curiosity starts to take over. _And? And? And?_ Scratching it does nothing to help; the itch doesn't go away, and I just look like I have dandruff or fleas.

On clear evenings I watch the sun dive into the sea, and wish I wasn't wishing my life away. Wishing I was older. Wishing that I was diving into the sea with the sun. Wishing my beard would grow in enough so that my mother would make a joke about washing the smudge off my chin, like I'd seen her do with my brothers when they each first came into their own beards. Wishing for adventure, to see the places in the world I've read about in human books—Nain don't write such tales—and the places no one has seen to write about yet.

Wishing to know all the answers to "and?"

But mostly I just wish to find the one thing that will finally satisfy my curiosity.

Otherwise it will surely drive me mad as Magnus.

THE POLYPHEMES' SHOP RESEMBLED A SMALL MOUNTAIN OVERLOOK-ing the port. It was set on the edge of the city, partly built into a ridge that defined the harbor. The brass bell clanged as Ven ran through the office doorway, puffing with excitement, slamming the door loudly behind him.

The shop had three sections. In the rear was the factory, the huge ironworks, where smiths and casters, many of them up-world Nain, smelted iron ore into steel fittings for the ships the Polypheme family built, as well as those that needed repair. The forges ran all the time, day and night, bright rivers of orange coals burning furiously, turning rock to steel. The steam that belched from the towers sometimes made the factory look like an active volcano.

Vaarn

In the middle of the complex were the woodworking tools and the drafting tables where the ships were designed and the smaller wooden fittings were crafted. From the time he was small, Ven had loved walking through the midsection, inhaling the fresh smell of planed wood, watching his father and brothers draw designs that would one day turn into ships that sailed the seven seas.

And in the front was the office, where the deals were made.

It was in this office that his father was now standing, trying to calm a very large man with a bulbous nose and bright orange hair.

"Just a few more moments, Mr. Witherspoon," Pepin Polypheme was saying when Ven came through the door. "He'll be here, I prom—oh! There you are, Ven! You lost the—er, *you're* doing the Inspection?" Ven nodded excitedly, and Pepin rolled his eyes. "He's here now, Mr. Witherspoon." Ven's father glared at him, his eyes smoking like the towers of his factory.

"This project is already three days late, Polypheme," Witherspoon said with a growl. "I wanted to be loaded by now, with plans to cast off tomorrow. You haven't even completed the Inspection yet."

"I know, I know," Pepin said soothingly. "The Inspection will begin in a moment, will only take eight hours or so, and then you can begin loading. The weather is much better for it today, anyway. Been raining all week."

Witherspoon's enormous nostrils flared as he inhaled.

"We have begun loading already, Polypheme," he said. "Couldn't wait forever for your silly Inspection. A child could see that the ship is sound, but the harbormaster won't release it until you sign off. So we took some of the stores aboard, some of the cargo, and a few of the weapons."

"Weapons? Which weapons?" Pepin asked, straining to keep his voice calm.

"Not the heavy ballista, if that's what has you worried," Witherspoon said quickly. "Just some bows and the like. Some of the lighter cargo, too. The major loading will have to wait until the Inspection is completed and the certificate filed."

Ven and Pepin exchanged a nervous glance. The ship was supposed to be inspected without any extra weight. The cargo could make it difficult to determine where a leak was, or a balance problem existed. Still, the chance of one of Pepin's ships being flawed was very slim. The Polyphemes produced the most carefully made ships in the known world.

"I'm ready to begin if you are, Mr. Witherspoon," Ven said. "Let me get the checklist, and I will meet you at the gangplank."

The orange-haired man looked Ven up and down.

"I've never sailed with this one before, Polypheme," he said to Pepin. "He looks young, even for one of you Nainfolk, though he's almost as tall as a human lad. Isn't he just a boy?"

"Ven is fifty years old today, Mr. Witherspoon," Pepin replied huffily. "He has a fine eye for detail. Get along, then, Ven. The Inspection sheets are in the top middle drawer." He pointed to a large cabinet of blue-gray wood with iron hinges shaped like butterflies.

Ven dashed to the cabinet and pulled out a hand-printed sheet of oilcloth. He grabbed a quill pen and inkpot, then hurried out the door behind his father and Witherspoon, who had already started down to the docks.

The ship loomed over the pier like a sea monster rising from the depths. For all the times he had seen it, Ven never failed to be amazed at the size and beauty of it, its towering wooden masts gleaming in the sun.

The ship was a three-masted schooner, fashioned of blond wood. A painter's scaffold hung in front of the prow. His brother Jaymes was perched atop the scaffold, putting the finishing touches on the figurehead. Ven shaded his eyes to get a better look at it.

The large wooden statue carved into the front of the ship was of a dark-haired woman in a flowing blue gown. Her eyes were closed, and she was smiling, her arms stretched out behind her, with watery-looking wings dripping from them. The figurehead looked as if she was enjoying the sun and the wind on her face.

"A beauty, isn't she?"

Ven glanced over his shoulder and saw old Max standing there, stirring a pot of pitch-paint.

"Good morning, Max," he said. "The ship, or the figurehead?"

"Both, lad," said the elderly Nain painter. "Hear you're doing the Inspection today."

"Yes, sir."

"And that it's your natal day as well?"

Ven looked at the ground. Old Max had one of the most impressive beards of any Nain he had ever seen, a long gray Thicket with ends that curled up pleasantly. There were always flecks of multicolored paint decorating the curls. Standing next to such a beard, Ven felt suddenly naked.

"Yes, sir," he mumbled again.

"Bless your—er—"

Ven winced. "That's all right, Max. I appreciate the thought."

The old Nain cleared his throat. "Well, then, seein' it's your birthday and all, I thought you might like to take a quick glance at this." He looked both ways, then furtively opened a rolled piece of oilcloth so that Ven could see what was written on it.

Ven's brow wrinkled. "What is this?"

Max looked behind him, then quickly rolled the oilcloth up again.

"Ship's name," he whispered.

"Of course," Ven murmured. "I forgot it was your job to paint it on the prow after the Inspection." His father had told him long ago that the task fell to Max because, besides being a master painter, Max could not read, and therefore even he did not know the ship's name until its christening.

But now Ven knew it.

In his head he heard his father's voice.

No one hears a ship's name until she is christened. It's bad luck.

A heartbeat later he could hear that voice in his ears.

"Ven! Get up here!"

Ven hurried up the gangplank and climbed aboard just as the major sails were hoisted. The sound of the cloth snapping almost sent him over the side.

Three huge sheets of canvas with many smaller sails rigged to them opened to the wind. The massive ship lurched on the water for a second, then settled back into the gentle waves, tugging impatiently at its moorings. Pepin took hold of Ven's arm and led him over to a group of men chatting on the deck in front of the mainsail.

Mr. Witherspoon was talking to the captain and three other crew members when the Polypheme father and son joined the group. Pepin waited respectfully until the conversation lagged, then pushed Ven forward into the circle of human men.

"Captain Faeley, this is my youngest, Ven. He's to do your Inspection today."

The captain, a tall, clean-shaven man with dark gray hair, regarded Ven thoughtfully, then smiled.

"Well met, Ven," he said pleasantly, holding out his hand.

"Thank you, sir," Ven answered, shaking it.

The captain turned to the other men in the circle. "I assume you know Mr. Witherspoon," he said, ignoring the ship owner's impatient snorting. "This is my first mate, Thomas Lavery." The mate nodded, and Ven nodded in return. "Lewis, the boatswain, and Krebs, the cook."

"A pleasure, gentlemen," Ven said, as he had heard his father say many times before.

"If you are ready, then, Ven, we're set to cast off," said Captain Faeley.

"Right. I'm ready," Ven said. His stomach tightened suddenly in a mix of excitement and nervousness.

"Have a good ride, my boy," said Pepin, loudly enough for the crew to hear. He took Ven's arm again and walked a short distance to the gangplank, then waited for Mr. Witherspoon to descend before turning back to his son. "Let's have no problems, now," he said tersely under his breath.

"No problems," Ven promised.

"The ship's already been completely checked; all you have to do is make sure she functions well in the water, which she will. You know what you're doing, Ven. Just keep all your lessons in mind, and you'll be fine."

"I will."

"I know you will, too." A twinkle came into his father's eye, and he reached into the pocket of his vest. "Maybe this will help."

He drew forth a flat wooden tool, only as long as his palm and about as wide as two fingers, and handed it to Ven.

"This was your great-grandfather's jack-rule," Pepin said, closing Ven's fingers around it carefully. "Now it belongs to you."

Ven couldn't speak. He had coveted Magnus's jack-rule from the first time he had seen it in his father's hand. Carefully he unfolded the thin wooden and metal measuring stick, which was fastened together with an intricate system of oddly shaped hinges and pins, allowing it to extend more than the length of his arm. He ran a finger carefully over the marks by which his father had always determined measurement, then looked up to see Pepin grinning at him.

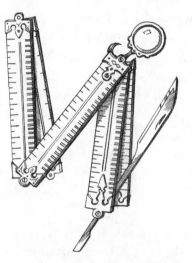

"Magnus was the youngest in his family, you know," his father said softly. "As was my da, as am I. So it's only right that his jackrule go to you now, Ven. The youngest may be at the end of the line for everything from shoes to supper, but often we are at the head of it for curiosity and common sense. Use it well—it was calibrated precisely to the Great Dial in the Nain kingdom of Castenen, and so it will always measure truer than any other instrument could. It also contains a small knife, a glass that both magnifies and sees afar, and a few other surprises—you will just have to discover those for yourself. Happy birthday, son."

Ven's grin mirrored his father's. "Thank you, sir."

Pepin cleared his throat. "Now, get the Inspection under way, get it over with as quickly as possible, and be home in time for tea. You know how cross your mother becomes when her tea is allowed to get cold."

"Yes." Impulsively, Ven threw his arms around his father and hugged him in full view of the crew.

Pepin clapped Ven's shoulder awkwardly. "Good lad. See you at teatime." He turned and disembarked, then waved to the crew as the dock hands untied the moorings and cast the ship off.

Having no vest, Ven slipped the jack-rule into the buttoned pocket of his shirt and watched his father scurry back up the pier without a backward glance.

On the dock, a dozen arms suddenly took to waving; Ven's eleven brothers and his sister, Matilda, had come forth from the shops and offices of the factory to bid him a good journey. Ven waved back, watching them grow smaller as the ship pulled away from the quay.

The movement of the ship below him changed. When tied to the dock it had tugged impatiently, straining against its bonds as if in a hurry to get out deeper. Now, freed from the mooring ropes, it almost sang through the water, skimming smoothly over the waves of the harbor, out toward open sea. Ven felt exactly the same way, though mixed with his excitement was a fair amount of nervousness.

He swallowed the knot that had tied itself in his throat, and nodded to the crew waiting on the deck before the mast. He watched them hurry to their positions, then rolled open the Inspection sheet and set about checking off the functioning of the moorings, the gangplank, and the sail structure.

What am I doing here? he thought to himself as he watched the sailors go aloft, climbing the shrouds, the checkerboards of interwoven ropes that attached from the decks to the top of the new masts, with little effort. *Shroud rosin good, no crew slippage,* he noted on the checklist.

Above his head, the sailors who had gone aloft stopped on the crosstrees to rest and check the main shroud. They cast shadows onto the sails that rippled as the ship plowed through the waves. Ven envied them; sometimes he dreamed of climbing the mast all the way to the crow's nest on the fighting top, where he could see the wide world before him, beckoning to him.

A beam of amber sunlight broke through the sheets of the upper sails, turning the ship's deck gold. The brightness stung his eyes; Ven closed them and suddenly became aware of the wind rushing over him, billowing his shirt like the sails, whispering along the decks, blowing salt spray before it.

The wind carried with it the feeling of utter freedom.

Behind him Ven heard a deep chuckle. His eyes snapped open in embarrassment and he turned to see Captain Faeley watching him closely.

"Don't drink too much of the wind, young Master Polypheme," the captain said, still smiling. "It's intoxicating; it will get you drunk more easily than you can imagine. And then you will be lost to it, as we are, and have no choice but to chase it over the sea for all your life."

Ven sighed. "If only I could," he said wistfully. "But I have to be home in time for tea or my mother will chase *me* over the sea for the rest of my life."

The captain laughed. "Well, then, we had best get on with the Inspection, so that you can."

He walked with Ven around the ship, checking the iron fittings, ropes and sails, the give of the wooden decks and the soundness of the rudder. They did a quick drill of the pump system, which would provide seawater to extinguish a fire if it broke out in the galley where the food was prepared. And they checked the six lifeboats, which hung three to a side.

Belowdecks in the hold they discovered some of the cargo Mr. Witherspoon had mentioned, barrels and crates that had been neatly lined up inside wooden slats and bolted so they would not slide around when the ship pitched. Ven examined the manifest, the list of the cargo, and circled a few things.

"I see you have quicklime aboard, Captain," he said nervously, eyeing the neat line of barrels bolted in place in the hold. "Magnesium, bitumen. These are flammable and explosive. We do use these in the ship's manufacture, but they should have been taken off before the Inspection."

The captain consulted his own list. "Must not have been removed yet. Mr. Witherspoon was in such a hurry to load that he may not have let your father's team remove all their tools and supplies before they began to bring the cargo aboard."

"They must have been bolted in by accident. I will make certain it all is taken ashore as soon as we put into port," Ven promised, making a note on his Inspection sheet. "Because it is flammable, and cannot be extinguished with water, quicklime is hazardous to have aboard, especially so close to the galley. Magnesium is even worse. We will get them off promptly after the Inspection."

"Thank you," the captain said. "Otherwise, all looks well down here, yes?"

"Yes, sir."

"Do you want to head closer to the harbor? Or a little farther out into open water?" the first mate asked Captain Faeley as they came out of the hold.

The captain considered. "How 'bout it, Ven? Are you feeling brave?"

The excitement roared through Ven, almost setting his scalp on fire. "Yes sir!" he shouted, scratching his itching head.

"Then give Lavery the order and let us return to checking the navigational instruments."

Now, get the Inspection under way, get it over with as quickly as possible, and be home in time for tea, his father had said. Ven pushed the words out of his mind and cleared his throat. "Take her out, Mr. Lavery!" he said, feeling both excited and guilty.

The first mate laughed. "Aye, sir," he said, and winked at the captain, as Faeley and Ven returned to the checklist.

Finally after more than four hours they came to the ship's wheel, where Lewis, the boatswain, had carefully guided the ship out of the harbor and now had taken her out onto the open sea beyond.

"She draws well in the water, smooth as glass," Lewis said admiringly. "Your father is an artist, Master Polypheme."

"Thank you," said Ven, consulting the checklist. "I will tell him so. Any problems with the wheel?"

"None whatsoever," said Lewis. "Have a go at it yourself."

Ven leaped forward in excitement and took the wheel from Lewis, running his hands over the smooth wooden handles that stood out like spokes. He marveled at the pull of it, and the strength he had to put into keeping it straight against the tug of the wind.

He glanced to his left off the port side at the coastline and was surprised to see it was entirely gone. All around them the horizon stretched for as far as he could see, with only a shadow at the edge where the land had been.

With a thud, Thomas Lavery landed on the deck, having just climbed down from the crosstrees of the mainmast.

"Everything look good up there, Lavery?" the captain asked.

"Aye, sir," the first mate replied. "Strong and tight."

"Good."

"That's quite the feather in your cap, Master Polypheme," Thomas Lavery said.

Ven's cheeks turned red. "Well—uh—in my father's cap, actually," he said in embarrassment. "I really had very little to do with crafting this ship."

Lavery shook his head. "No, I mean that one," he said, pointing to Ven's hat. "Albatross, isn't it?"

"Oh! Yes," Ven said. "It flew over me this morning and dropped the feather."

The sailors exchanged a pleased glance. "Well, then, surely our voyage is blessed," said Lewis. "Sighting an albatross before sailing is always good luck."

Ven opened his mouth to explain that he actually hadn't seen the albatross. His mouth remained open, but no words came out, as a black and orange streak blazed across the upper deck from the right and slammed into the mainsail.

The sail and all its riggings burst into flame.

Off the prow a ship appeared, a moment before hidden within the wind itself. It was a smaller vessel, dark and fast, that flew a flag of a skull in flames. Ven had never seen that flag before, but he had heard tales of it from his brothers, whispered stories that had given him nightmares for years.

The symbol of marauders who attacked mercilessly, and never left a single victim alive.

It was the flag of the Fire Pirates.

-3-

The Fire Pirates

If only my father had let Luther teach me to fight!

If only he had let me become good at anything at all.

My darkest secret is that I seem to have been a failure at everything I've ever tried in the shipbuilding business. My father never said so, but his disapproval was apparent in the fact that he wouldn't leave me in one place long enough to master the skill.

Just as I felt I was getting the hang of something, where I finally knew what I was doing wrong and how to fix it, he would pull me off and set me to studying in another place in the factory.

I started in sales as a small boy of twenty, trailing after my father or Petar, my oldest brother, lugging a model or a packet of numbers. At their heels I learned what Pepin Polypheme called "the hammered truth," facts that were not varnished or hidden, but shaped straight. "Tell people the hammered truth, and it will ring like steel against an anvil," my father would say.

But just as I got to know all the names and faces, just as I earned a greeting from the old men we dealt with, my father took me away from the public side of the business to the model shop.

My brother Alton was our master modelmaker, and he let me do everything in his shop but carve the actual molds. I thought I was getting fairly good at this, but just as Alton was having me choose the wood for my first try at the model of a fishing galleon, my father pulled me off and sent me to Alton's twin, my brother Dalton, in Drafting.

From there it became a depressing cycle: from Alton to Dalton, to making sails with Matilda, to Jaymes for painting, to Jasper in Accounts, where all the records were kept, every ounce of metal, every copper coin kept in order by my brother's careful recordkeeping.

Each one of my siblings was expert at something, and I was doing my best to learn from them. But no sooner was I beginning to feel that I, too, might be able to do a job well, or maybe even have a specialty, than my father would appear at the doorway, beckoning for me to pick up my leather apron and follow him. I was working with Vernon in the foundry, where Pepin's belief was that whatever iron we received from a supplier wasn't good enough, so everything needed to be resmelted and reshaped, when my birthday came around and I drew the short straw.

And so I never got to train with Luther.

Luther is the third-oldest Polypheme son. He had been dropped on his head as a baby by Nigel, who was using him as a ball at the time. Luther never really was able to be trained reliably to work in the factory. Like Old Max, he could not read, so he had little else to do but eat and grow muscles. When he came of age, my father sent him to a fighting school, where he excelled and soon became the best guard the town had ever seen. He was put in charge of security for the factory, and from the time he took over there was not a single break-in.

This might be because Luther had once bitten off the thumb of someone who was bothering Matilda. His reputation had quickly spread. He was the only one of the Polypheme boys who would not fight with the rest of us. None of us were crazy enough to provoke him.

So I was looking forward to learning from Luther. While my

other brothers got teased a lot growing up—our family is considered odd even by the Nain of Vaarn—no one ever bothered me, because I am very tall for my race. A little paunchy around the middle, too, but at least I look strong. And I am related to Luther, so everyone leaves me pretty much alone. The only people I had to worry about bothering me were my own brothers.

If only I had gotten the chance to learn how to fight like him, maybe it would have saved us from the pirates.

T HE SHIP FLYING THE SKULL-AND-FLAME FLAG HOVERED FOR A MO-
ment broadside before the prow of the new ship, forming a T in the sea.

There were so many pirates aboard the dark vessel that they looked like a swarm of ants scurrying about on the deck. They were busy loading three small ballistae, weapons resembling huge cross-

bows that flung objects great distances, while lines of archers took their places along the rail.

Ven could only stand and watch in horror as barrels of smoking oil were heaved overhead, onto the deck and into the sails, followed by a rain of flaming arrows.

Lewis the boatswain was the first to recover his voice.

"We're under attack!" he shouted to the sailors aloft, trapped between the deck and the crosstrees by the burning sail.

A gourd shattered at Ven's feet, spilling a thick, oily substance onto the planks of the deck, which ignited a moment later.

"Lavery, Ven, go belowdecks to the hold, and then to my quarters," Captain Faeley shouted, directing the sailors trapped above in the crow's nest to rigging ropes that were not yet burning. "Gather whatever weapons you find and anything else we can use—go!"

Blindly, Ven followed the first mate through the oily black clouds of smoke and into a dark doorway that led below to the hold, where the cargo of the ship was stored. Thomas Lavery grabbed a length of burning rope as he went by and held it up for light.

"Look around—what have we got down here?" he said, running to the dark recesses of the hold where lines of barrels and crates stood.

Ven's mouth was full of sour spit, and his stomach felt like it was being squeezed in a vise. Above him he could hear thumping on the deck as the sailors jumped down from the burning riggings and began to take cover, positioning themselves to defend the ship.

He grabbed hold of the nearest crate and lifted the top off. It was full of dry cloth sacks. He continued to tear through crates and barrels, finding apples, iron bolts, dried peas, pinecones, and water.

"Food and dry goods, nothing useful," he gasped, wading through the barrels to the next row of supplies, which was covered with canvas sheets. "Over there?"

Lavery had gathered an armload of rope. "Not much—I have to

go get weapons," he said. "Stay here, Ven. Find a place to hide, but stay away from the stores and the galley. They will ransack those places first once they take the ship." The first mate started back toward the door.

"I—I don't want to hide," Ven said shakily. "I want to help."

"Can you fight?" Lavery asked, still walking.

"I haven't been trained, but I can try," Ven said, still pulling tops off of crates. Now he was finding the materials he had seen on the manifest that had gone into the making of the ship: pitch-paint, the lacquer for the deckboards, quicklime used to clean the metal fittings and for signaling, and a full barrel of magnesium.

"You're better off hiding," Lavery said over his shoulder. "You'll just die quicker if you fight."

Ven slammed the barrel of quicklime shut. "I am going with you. If we don't fight, we're all done for."

Thomas Lavery stopped and looked back at Ven.

"We're all done for anyway, lad," he said sadly.

Then he stepped through the smoky doorway that led back up onto the deck.

Ven followed him up to the top deck, to the captain's quarters in the fore of the ship, where the few weapons that had been brought on board were stored. Lavery tossed him several swords and grabbed whatever bows he could carry, strapping on quivers of arrows and crossbow bolts. They hurried back to the main deck, steadying themselves as the pirate ship, now alongside them on the starboard side, fired another round from their heavy ballistae.

Instead of burning oil this time, however, the ballistae were firing grappling irons, metal hooks that looked liked giant claws attached to long ropes. They shot over the deck rail and onto the floorboards, then were pulled back, toward the pirate ship, anchoring themselves in the new ship's wooden rail.

The new ship lurched violently. The wood screeched as the iron fingers of the claws sank into it.

The pirates were pulling the nose of their ship closer to the bow of the new ship.

Ven, who was passing swords out to the dozen or so crew members, caught a glance between the captain and the first mate.

"They're grappling us—they just burned the sails so we couldn't get away," shouted Thomas Lavery above the noise of the screaming wood, tossing bows to the crew as well. "It's the ship they're after."

"Right," said Captain Faeley, fitting an arrow to his bowstring. "We can't let them have it. We have to scuttle her."

Ven heard the words thud against his eardrums as he fought back tears of dismay and panic. They were about to be boarded by Fire Pirates, who always killed their victims. Understanding this, the captain had decided to sink the ship intentionally rather than let it fall into the pirates' hands.

It's probably just as well that I am going to die now, he thought grimly, watching the wickedly grinning faces of the sea bandits draw closer as they tugged on the ropes, pulling the ships together side by side. *It's better than having to explain to my father that I intentionally sank his new ship. Especially since I'm the one who decided to go out into deeper water.*

He could hear his father's voice in his memory.

Let's have no problems, now.

I wonder if this counts as a problem, Ven thought.

"Tayne, loose the lifeboats," the captain called to one of the sailors. "That might draw their attention away for a moment or two. Krebs, get down to the galley and turn the fire pump system on full blast. Fill that kitchen with as much water as you can. Ven—help him; you know how the pump works. Lewis, go below to the galley and burst the seams of the hull with whatever you can find. The rest of us will defend the hold to give you all as much time as possible to scuttle the ship. Everyone into the stairway and close the hatch. Godspeed, gentlemen. It's been good to know you."

Amid a chorus of *aye, sir*, the sailors scattered to their posts.

Ven ran down the stairs behind Krebs, clutching a crossbow he barely knew how to fire, heading through the hold and into the galley. As he opened the large doors where the fire hose was kept, coiled on big hooks, he could hear the sound of the empty lifeboats hitting the water off the other side, the port side, of the ship.

With shaking hands he set down the bow and tossed the nozzle of the canvas-wrapped hose to Krebs, lowered the other end of it out the porthole, then began working the pump, drawing water from the sea into the galley.

"A lousy way to die," Krebs muttered, unwinding the hose and holding it where the water could flood the ship's kitchen most easily. "If we're gonna go down, at least we could go down fighting."

"There will be plenty of fighting, I'm sure," Ven said, pumping the handle as hard and as fast as he could. "But the captain is right. There is no way a skeleton crew can hold off a hundred pirates, or even run, since they burned our sails first."

"Bah," said Krebs grumpily. "We ought to stuff their bloody fire right back up their backsides, if you ask me. You gotta fight fire with fire. Instead we're drowning ourselves. Ain't right."

Ven stopped short for a moment, his father's voice ringing in his ears.

You know what you're doing, Ven. Just keep all your lessons in mind.

Just then the ship shuddered violently. Ven and Krebs were thrown to one side and slipped beneath the knee-high water that was now flooding the galley. Ven's head popped to the surface amid floating pots, pans, and vegetables. He struggled to get back to his feet, made his way to the porthole and peered out.

The pirate ship was now directly alongside them, its hull so close that Ven could have lobbed an apple into the nearest porthole. He could see the pirates on the deck above beginning to climb over the ropes from their ship to the new one.

Keep your lessons in mind.

Osgood had been the one who instructed him in chemistry.

Ven dropped the hose, startling Krebs.

"You want to fight fire with fire?" Ven asked, grabbing a meat axe and starting back into the hold. "Come with me!"

"Are you daft, boy?" Krebs demanded. "We have orders to flood the galley."

"And we will," Ven promised, beckoning to the ship's cook. "The hose is running on its own. But I have an idea. Come on!"

Reluctantly Krebs followed him back into the hold where the barrels and crates stood, secure in their wooden moorings. The sounds of fighting could now be heard through the hatch. The sailors were defending the entranceway, trying to buy Ven and Krebs as much time as they could.

Ven stopped long enough to dip the crossbow bolts Thomas Lavery had given him in the barrel of pitch, then went to the barrel that held the quicklime. He bashed the wooden mooring with the axe over and over until the barrel rolled free, while Krebs stood, dumbfounded.

"By my mother's ale-soaked drawers, what are you doing, boy?" the cook demanded.

"No time to explain—help me roll these back to the galley," Ven gasped, breathless from exertion. He grabbed hold of the barrel of quicklime, and, with Krebs' reluctant help, turned it on its side, followed by the barrel of magnesium.

Keep your lessons in mind.

In his mind Ven pictured the ship as the model his family had built. He knew every corridor, every hatch. He led the cook back to the galley through the port-side hallway, knowing it was wide enough for the barrels. The water had spilled over from the galley. They waded through the overflow until at last they set the heavy containers down next to the fire pump, which had flooded the galley almost up to Ven's hips.

"Help me stand the barrels up and pry off the tops," Ven said.

Once Krebs was working on getting the lids off the barrels, Ven found the end of the hose beneath the seawater that now filled the ship's kitchen and pulled it up to the surface. He looked around for a knife, but the block in which the ship's cutlery had been kept was now submerged.

He felt around in his shirt pocket. The jack-rule was still there.

Ven transferred the hose to beneath his arm, pulled out the jack-rule, and unhinged the small knife it contained.

"Hold the hose," he said to Krebs as he sawed away at the fittings that held it in place. Once the fittings were severed, he gave the hose a tremendous tug.

"Help me pull it from the sea!" he shouted to the cook.

Perplexed, the old cook hauled on the canvas tube with Ven until the end that had fed water from the sea came into sight.

"Now what?" Krebs demanded.

In response, Ven stuck the end of the hose into the barrel of quicklime. He looked quickly out the porthole into the porthole of the pirate ship alongside them. The shadows of dozens of pirates were passing overhead, landing with thumps on the deck above.

"Point the nozzle out the porthole!" he shouted to the cook.

Krebs' face changed as understanding took hold. He shoved the hose out the galley porthole, aiming through the open hole in the pirate ship.

Ven grabbed the pump handle and worked it with all his might. He could see Krebs struggling to hold the hose as the silvery-white powder sprayed forth, some of it splashing back into the galley itself.

"Spray it around their decks as well!" Ven gasped, working the pump.

Krebs only nodded, struggling to maintain control of the wildly flapping hose.

The sounds of fighting had now reached the hold outside the galley hatch.

"The quicklime's almost gone," Ven said. "I'm going to switch to the magnesium. Be careful not to get any on yourself."

"Too late for that, lad," said the cook. "The wind blows the stuff back like snow."

Ven looked up and saw that Krebs was right. The old cook was frosted with a dusting of quicklime.

He jammed the hose end into the barrel of magnesium and went back to manning the pump, struggling to ignore the terrible sounds from above and outside the hold.

With a great thundering *crack*, the hatch of the hold split open.

"All right, we've got to light it," Ven shouted, pushing Krebs away from the porthole. "Try and stay back—you don't want to go up in flames yourself."

He took one of the pitch-tipped bolts and reached out the porthole with it, waving the tip around in the attempt to catch a spark from the burning ashes of the sails that were falling like black autumn leaves into the sea. It took a very long moment, but finally the tip began to smoke, then spark.

"Get down!" Ven screamed to Krebs, then shakily brought the crossbow to rest in the porthole. He closed his eyes and pulled the trigger.

Nothing happened.

"You have to span it," Krebs shouted over the din beyond the galley door.

"I don't know how to do that," Ven stammered.

"Pull the string back against the nut, then load it and fire," said the cook.

Quickly Ven did as he was told, reloaded, steadied the crossbow, and pulled the trigger again.

This time the bolt fired, wobbling forth from the unsteady weapon, but the porthole of the pirate ship was near enough by to be almost impossible to miss.

A bright white flash exploded from within the pirate ship's hold, followed a moment later by a black plume of smoke.

Ven and Krebs watched as a rolling wave of black and orange fire poured out of the porthole and up over the deck of the pirate ship, burning with intense heat.

Suddenly the pirate ship, from the hold to the top of the mast, erupted in flame. Its skeleton glowed orange amid the black clouds of smoke.

"Get to the hold and direct the sailors to the port side!" Ven called, grabbing the meat axe and running for the back galley hatch. "I'm going to go chop the porthole to make a bigger escape route— we can abandon ship and swim for the lifeboats!"

Whatever Krebs answered was lost in the noise of the flames and the yelling from the pirate ship.

As he ran to the port side of the ship through the back hallways, Ven kept his mind focused on the memory of the ship's model. *Two turns here—there should be a porthole right across from me—*

Then the world exploded.

– 4 –

The Merrow

THE HARSH CRY OF A SEABIRD WOKE VEN.

Woozily he tried to sit up, but when he did, the world dipped crazily around him. He was aware enough to know that he was still on the sea, so he continued to lie on his back, feeling the sun on his eyelids.

When he finally could open his eyes, he saw nothing but blue sky. The sea beneath him was calm, rocking him in a slow, unhurried motion. A misty white barracuda formed of clouds floated overhead, its eyeball round and puffy in the middle of wispy scales and a long, jutting jaw with spiky cloud teeth. Before his eyes the wind blew on the barracuda, making it stretch into the face of a jester.

His throat was dry, and his lips cracked from the salt and heat. Ven tried to lick them but found he had no spit.

He tried to sit up again, but whatever he was lying on rocked violently the moment he moved.

"Lie still, or you'll fall in again."

The light voice to Ven's left startled him so much that he twitched, causing another loss of balance. He turned his head slightly in the direction it had come from, but all he could see was the green waves of the sea and, in the distance, something that was floating on it, still burning.

The voice seemed to come from the sea itself.

He tried to form a word, but no sound came out of his dry mouth. He swallowed, pain in his throat, and tried again.

"Thirsty," he croaked.

Ven heard an annoyed sigh come from his left.

"Oh, that's right. You can't drink seawater. A pity. Hold on."

For a long time Ven heard nothing more than the gentle splash of the waves. He continued to stare at the sky, watching as the jester cloud stretched into nothing but soft white sky-foam. He was just about to lose consciousness when something hard and cold was slapped into his hand.

"Here. Drink."

Ven brought his hand up before his eyes. In it was a metal flask.

Still lying flat, he struggled to remove the stopper, then gratefully lifted the flask to his lips, spilling a good deal of the contents over his neck. He swallowed.

The liquid burned down his parched throat inside and out like fire, causing him to sputter.

"Ack!" Ven choked. "This is rum!"

"You don't like rum?" the voice asked. It sounded amazed.

"Too young to drink it," Ven whispered, his throat still burning.

He heard another sound of annoyance. "Picky, picky, picky. Hold on again."

A moment later another flask landed next to his hand.

"Here. Try that."

Ven uncorked it and drank more carefully. It was half full of fresh water. He quenched his thirst and pressed the opening of the flask to his lips to moisten them.

"Thank you," he said gratefully, though he could still see no one.

"You're welcome. Goodbye."

"Wait!" Ven said quickly. "Please don't leave." He turned to his left and saw a pair of sea-green eyes staring back at him from just above the water. He leaned closer to get a better look, but once again whatever he was floating on tilted, and he almost slid off it headfirst into the sea.

A strong hand grabbed him by the back of the shirt and hoisted him back onto his perch. Ven could see he was in the grasp of a girl, his age or perhaps slightly younger, with dark, wet hair that floated around her on the waves. She tossed him onto the middle of the wreckage on which he had been floating, a piece of the hull from the ship his father had built.

"That wasn't very bright," the girl said. "You really should learn to hold still. You are heavy, and hauling you out of the water is getting tiresome."

"Sorry," Ven said. "Thank you for saving me."

"You're welcome," said the girl. "Goodbye."

"Please wait!" Ven said again, this time not moving.

"Sorry—have to be going," said the girl. "My mother won't let me talk to humans. We can rescue you if you're drowning—which you certainly *were*, by the way—but we're not supposed to talk to you. Goodbye."

"But I'm not a human," Ven said, fighting dizziness. "I'm Nain." He tried to remember what had happened after the explosion. There was a vague memory of falling, of sinking beneath the green waves, and all the world growing quiet. He thought he also remembered being grasped by a strong hand and hauled out of the depths, but it seemed more a dream than a memory.

The green-eyed girl moved closer. "Nain? What does Nain mean?"

"Not human," Ven said quickly.

"Hmmm," said the girl. She did not look like she believed him.

"What are you doing here in the middle of the sea?" Ven asked, trying to change the subject. "Were you on the pirate ship?"

"Don't be ridiculous," the girl said disdainfully. "Do I look like a pirate to you?"

Ven exhaled, trying to keep still. "I can't see you very well. I have no idea what you look like."

"Not like a pirate," the girl said. She swam a little closer to give Ven a better look. He could see that she was wearing a gown that seemed to be made of bubbles, or sea foam, beneath which he thought he could make out multicolored scales that went all the way up to under her armpits. From her shoulders a dark cape draped behind her, and on her head was a red cap woven in pearls. Her face, while plain, was pleasantly angled, and her green eyes held a gleam of curiosity, the same gleam Ven had seen in the looking glass in his own eyes.

"Are you a mermaid?" he asked in wonder.

The girl's eyes narrowed. "Are you *sure* you're not a human? Because 'mermaid' is a very human word."

"Completely sure," said Ven quickly. "But I might have heard the word from humans. Nain don't know much about the sea."

"The word you are probably looking for is 'merrow,'" the girl said, leaning back and floating away a bit. "And if you were to actually use that word, you would be half right. My father is a merrow." Ven watched, fascinated, as a fishlike tail of rainbow-colored scales flipped out of the water where her feet would have been. "And if you aren't going to drink it, toss me that flask of rum. He will appreciate it, even if you didn't."

"I appreciate that you gave it to me," Ven said, moving the flask carefully toward the edge of the wreckage.

"Hmmm," the merrow said. She reached out of the water and snagged the flask.

"What is the other half? Your mother, I mean."

"My mother is a selkie," the girl replied. "Similar to a merrow, but with a gentler nature. I got my cape from her—selkies can look like seals sometimes because of their capes." She rotated her arms in the water, making small ripples in the sea. "But I consider myself a merrow, because my nature is more like that of my father."

"Does that mean you like rum?" Ven asked.

"Goodbye," said the merrow.

"Wait! I'm sorry," Ven said quickly again. "I don't know how to talk to a merrow. I didn't mean to be rude."

"Maybe that's just *your* nature," the merrow suggested.

For the first time Ven smiled slightly. "Actually, you're probably right. Rude is a fairly big part of being Nain."

"Well, there you have it," said the merrow.

"So you live here in the sea?" asked Ven.

"No, I live in the *mountains*," said the merrow scornfully. "I'm just here on holiday."

"Forgive me," Ven said, embarrassed. "I'm not quite thinking clearly. My head is muddled from everything that has happened to me."

"Do you remember your name?" asked the merrow.

"Oh yes," said Ven. "My name is Charles Magnus Ven Polypheme, but most just call me Ven."

The merrow nodded. "Well, if you are going to forget your manners, at least it is good to be able to remember your name. Mine, by the way, is Amariel."

"Amariel," Ven repeated. The word rolled around in his mouth like the ocean waves. "Very pretty."

"It means *Star of the Sea*," said the merrow proudly. "My mom thought it up."

A wave of exhaustion rolled over Ven, and he felt his eyes begin to close.

"Hey! Wake up!" the merrow shouted, slapping her tail down sharply on the water. A cold salty splash hit Ven in the face, bringing him around again. "You can't afford to sleep, Ven. You have to stay awake, or you are going to die. What's worse, you are making me feel as if I am not good company. Stop being so Nain."

"Sorry, sorry," Ven muttered, shaking the water droplets from his face.

"So, since you obviously don't live here in the sea, why don't you tell me how you came to be here?" the merrow said. "I certainly have never seen anyone who looks like you around these parts. Tell me your story; maybe that will keep you awake."

"I didn't really have much of a story until today—at least I think it was today," Ven said, struggling to remember. He looked at the position of the sun and felt suddenly cold; it was rising, still before noon.

"The ships burned yesterday," said Amariel, floating on her back and watching him intently. "You have been asleep since then, all through the afternoon and night until now."

"Thank you for staying with me," Ven said.

The merrow shrugged.

"Did you see anyone else?" Ven asked hopefully, sadness beginning to take hold of him. "Did anyone else survive the explosion?"

The merrow shook her head. "I don't know," she said blandly. "I didn't see anyone but you by the time I got here. I came with my school because we saw the fire on the water. The merrow men have a great fondness for rum, as you know, and there are always a good many treats to be found floating when a ship sinks. Especially a pirate ship. Always makes for a good party. You were pretty far down below the waves when I found you. I don't think anyone else survived."

"I was afraid of that," Ven said sadly. "The explosion was my fault. I should have died, too."

The merrow splashed him with her tail again. "Well, you didn't. Obviously you weren't meant to. The sea could have taken you if it wanted to—and it still might. But at least now you have a few friends watching out for you."

"Friends?" Ven asked. "More than you?"

The merrow nodded and pointed overhead. "There's one. She's been flying overhead since I got here."

Ven looked up, careful not to upset his raft of wreckage, and saw the albatross gliding in great lazy circles above him.

"Oh" was all he could say.

"Yes, she guided me to you. Otherwise I would never have seen you amid all the flotsam and jetsam floating in the shipwreck area."

"Oh," Ven said again. His eyes were growing heavy, and his skin was starting to turn gray.

"So tell me your tale," the merrow said.

Ven explained about Magnus the Mad and his family's factory, about his birthday and the Inspection, and about the albatross. In the course of the telling, he noticed that his cap with the feather was gone, and fell silent for a moment. The merrow splashed him impatiently, and he took up the tale again, telling her about the Fire Pirates, the quicklime, and the explosion.

"That quicklime was a wise idea," the merrow said, drawing patterns in the waves with her impressive tail. "Fire Pirates are merciless; they never leave anyone alive. They can hide in the wind and appear as if from nowhere. I'm sure you all did the best you could. Just as well that you blew up both ships."

"I'm not exactly certain how that happened," Ven admitted. "I was only trying to set fire to the pirate ship, fire that wouldn't be put out with water."

"Well, you certainly managed to do that," Amariel said. "There are pieces of it scattered for leagues, still burning now, some above the surface, some below. It looked very pretty last night—lit up this whole part of the sea."

"Great," Ven said gloomily.

"Oh, do cheer up," the merrow said in exasperation. "Does Nain mean 'melancholy' as well as 'rude'?"

"Frequently," Ven said, trying to muster a smile. "There were good men on that ship—my father's ship. Which I destroyed."

"Sounds like you didn't have much choice," said the merrow. "And at least you took the Fire Pirates down with the ship. Even for land-livers, those pirates were really bad men. Hmmmm—that *does* mean there'll be less booty for us to find under the sea, now that they're gone. Maybe we should talk about something else."

"Why don't you tell me *your* tale?" Ven asked, struggling to keep his head up. "What is it like, being a merrow, living in the sea?"

"Oh, it's wonderful," said Amariel, swimming in long arcs at the edge of the drifting wreckage. "There are many splendid sights that you humans—er, you land-livers—never get to see, in your tiny and limited world."

Ven laughed. "Our world is limited? I always thought of it as enormous. Of course I've seen very little of it."

"That shows how little you know," said the merrow, smiling. "The tallest mountains on land are tiny foothills compared to the mountains beneath the sea. Your deepest canyons are only scratches in the ground compared to the deepest, darkest ocean trenches. There are creatures in the depths that you could never imagine, and colors you have never seen. Water fairies and nymphs, sea dragons with great hordes of sparkling treasure taken from shipwrecks— there is nothing like the excitement of the carnival that is held on midsummer's day, with the crowning of the sea king and queen, and the hippocampus races—"

"Hippocampus?" Ven asked.

"Horses with tails like mine, only bigger and stronger. They swim their races in great circles, and that sometimes causes a giant whirlpool to form." The merrow sighed. "Yes, the world beneath the sea is an amazing place." She sat up and looked brightly at Ven. "You should come see it."

Ven sighed as well. "I would love to," he said sincerely, "but I can't breathe under water."

"You could if you had gills."

"Well, yes," said Ven, "but I don't." He stole a glance at her neck, and saw, to his surprise, that there were small flaps of skin which must have served that purpose.

"There are fishermen who know how to cut them," said Amariel excitedly. "They become so expert with their filleting and boning knives that they can actually slice gills into a human's neck, and, until they heal, he can breathe under water, like one of us."

Ven winced, struggling to keep from clutching his own neck at the thought. "That sounds painful."

"It's not," the merrow said, an annoyed tone in her voice. "Or so my father told me, anyway. But you have to find a fisherman who knows how to do it, and they are very rare indeed."

"Is there any other way for a—someone who is not a merrow—to breathe beneath the sea?" Ven asked, his curiosity causing his skin to itch uncontrollably. "I'd love to see those sights."

The merrow shrugged. "You can kiss a merrow—if you can find one who is nearsighted or silly enough to want to kiss someone like you."

Ven was too interested in what she was saying to take offense. "What would kissing a merrow do?"

"It would enslave your soul to the sea," Amariel said, looking up into the sky at the albatross as it passed overhead again. "You could breathe, as we do, but you would never again want to return to the land. They say that sailors have all been kissed by merrows in their sleep, and that is why they are so restless, so unable to part from the ocean."

"Ah," said Ven, thinking back to something Captain Faeley had said. "And here I thought it was because they had drunk too much of the wind."

He lapsed into silence, trying to concentrate on his breathing, which was becoming more and more difficult. He was shivering from the cold and from being soaked to the skin for so long.

Amariel swam over to the edge of the wreckage and leaned across it. She put her hand on Ven's shoulder and shook him gently.

"Do you want to hear what happens to merrows who want to walk on the land?" she asked, trying to keep him awake.

Ven blinked. "Merrows want to walk on the land?" he asked shakily, his voice faltering.

"Oh, yes; it is a deep and sometimes irresistible desire. And they can do it, too, if they are foolish enough."

"How?" Ven asked.

"By giving their red pearl caps to a human man," Amariel said contemptuously. "If a merrow gives in to the desire to walk on the land, and finds a man to entrust with her cap, she will grow legs and be able to do so."

"That's wonderful!" Ven said, his tired eyes taking on the gleam of curiosity again.

"No, it's *not*," the merrow said firmly. "Because when a merrow gives in to that desire and gives her cap to a human man for safe-keeping, she sacrifices her freedom for her curiosity. In the course of growing legs, she forgets all about the sea and its wonders, and loses all the joy in life that came from living here once. She marries and has children with the man who holds her cap, forgetting every-thing about the merworld and the life she had there." She gave a disgusted snort. "I would never be so silly as to do that."

"I can see why you wouldn't—want to," Ven said, yawning. "You're too smart for that."

The merrow's face took on an amused expression.

"And why do you think I'm smart?" she asked.

Ven smiled wanly. "Because instead of wasting your time like the rest of your school, snarfing up every last flask of rum and what-ever treasure could be found in the wreckage, you retrieved some-thing really valuable—*me*."

The merrow threw back her head and laughed aloud.

Ven's eyes opened wide in shock, and he recoiled involuntarily. The merrow's teeth were oddly shaped, a little peglike and sepa-rated slightly from each other, like porpoise teeth.

Abruptly the merrow stopped laughing. Her wide eyes met Ven's. Then she disappeared below the waves.

It took Ven a moment to get over his shock. "Wait!" he called in the direction she had vanished. "I'm sorry! Please come back."

The tiny ring of ripples she had made as she left was caught by a swell in the water and swallowed into the vastness of the sea.

Ven let his head fall back against the wreckage in despair. Mentally he kicked himself for embarrassing her, for driving her off.

It doesn't really matter if the sea takes me now, he thought. *I've killed a group of men who were nothing but kind to me, disgraced my family, and now I've hurt the feelings of the merrow who saved my life and kept me from drowning. It doesn't matter. In fact, it's probably better.*

His ears were suddenly wet. Ven looked to the side and his eyes were splashed with salt water.

His floating life raft of wreckage was sinking.

Weakly Ven felt around in his shirt pocket. His jack-rule was still there, as was something else. He unbuttoned the pocket and took out the folded oilcloth Inspection sheet, water-soaked but still readable, its checkmarks smeared. It was almost complete; before the pirates struck, he had managed to certify all but one last step as complete.

The box that remained unchecked was next to the last item on the Inspection sheet.

SHIP'S NAME INSCRIBED AND SPELLED CORRECTLY, it read.

Determined to see to the last of his duty before he slipped back into the sea, Ven rolled slowly onto his side, clutching the wreckage with all his strength. He extended the jack-rule's folded knife and carefully set to carving.

The wreckage began to leak. Now that he was no longer on his back Ven noticed that what he was lying on was the hull seam with the extra rivets that Jasper had chided him about the previous morning. He laughed at the irony. The extra fastenings had kept this remaining part of the ship afloat longer than any other.

With the final letter carved into the boards of the hull, Ven used the last of his breath to blow the wet dust from the ship's name.

Angelia, it read.

Shakily he made a checkmark in the box next to the last item, tucked the Inspection sheet and the jack-rule back in his pocket, buttoned it, then put his head down to rest.

In the distance he thought he could hear his name being called. He shook his head, trying to drive the noise from it as if it were a mosquito or a buzzing fly, but as it got closer, he raised his head with the last of his strength.

Not far from him, over the crests of a few waves, Amariel was swimming, waving to him excitedly.

Behind her she was pulling an empty lifeboat.

Ven's heart leapt when he saw her, both because he knew she was bringing him a safe place to rest in the sea and because she had come back. He resolved to never again gape at anything about her that surprised him.

"Hoay! Ven! Stay awake!" she was calling over the sound of the waves splashing against the sinking wreckage.

"I'm awake," he called back weakly.

Later, when Ven tried to remember what happened after that, he could not recall it clearly. He had a vague recollection of the merrow helping him into the boat, and feeding him apples and parsnips she had found floating in the sea. She must have given him a blanket of seaweed, because when he woke up it was covering him. And distantly he seemed to recall that she had stayed with him all afternoon and through the long night, floating in the sea with her folded arms resting on the edge of the boat, singing him merrow songs and telling him fascinating tales of her folk, of the marvelous world beneath the waves, and all the wonders waiting there for him to explore someday.

All the while the albatross flew in great circles overhead.

When dawn broke, he thought she was there still, though the haze had set in, and his mind was no longer able to separate the real world from the world of dreams.

Consequently he did not see the ship until it was upon him.

~ 5 ~

The *Serelinda*

I was dreaming of grinning pirates with wicked-looking blades and burning torches. Their evil smirks changed into the look of disapproval on my father's face. His disappointed eyes became deep green, green as a merrow's. My face grew hot as the world exploded around me in my dreams.

Then I dreamed of the albatross, flying high above me.

And that I, too, was flying.

And then it suddenly felt as if I really <u>was</u> flying.

I opened my eyes. The sky was coming closer.

Then I realized the lifeboat in which I had been sleeping was being hoisted aboard a sailing ship, a huge, four-masted schooner.

Perhaps my mind would have been more appropriately fixed on the miraculous luck of my rescue, but instead all I could think about was Amariel. I struggled to look over the side, to catch a glimpse of her, but there was no sign of her, no sign at all.

The more I thought about it, the more I felt it must have been a dream. Did the explosion and the salt and the cold only make me think I saw her? Or wish I saw her?

V EN AWOKE TO THE THUMP OF GRAPPLING HOOKS. THE LIFEBOAT shuddered, then began to rise up into the air.

The sunlight blinded him for a moment as his eyes popped open. He tried to sit up, but he was too weak from the cold and the ordeal he had been through to do more than just lie still and watch helplessly.

I hope these aren't more pirates, he thought as he felt the lifeboat being lifted closer and closer to the deck of the ship. There were shadows of heads staring down at him from the ship's rail, and he could see the outlines of other figures hauling on the ropes that were pulling him aboard. *But it appears that there is nothing I can do about it anyway.*

He could tell that he was being brought aboard the ship at the bow, off the port side. Ven shielded his eyes to block the sun and saw the ship's figurehead. It was not a carving of a woman, as most figureheads were, but instead looked like a glistening silver star shooting from the prow. As the lifeboat cleared the portholes on its way to the deck, he could read the ship's name on his way past it.

Serelinda, it said.

Ven twisted, trying to see where the merrow had been, but all he could see was green waves splashing white against the ship's hull.

With a few more screams of the ropes, the lifeboat swung over the side and thumped down onto the deck.

A dozen faces looked down at Ven. They were the faces of men, sailors no doubt, in all sizes, shapes, and colors, but kinder than the grinning faces of the pirates in his memory.

Suddenly a chorus of voices all talking at once broke out. Ven's ears were ringing from the salt water, so he could hear only a few words of what they were saying.

"Blimey! I think it's a Nain!"

"Young 'un, too—no beard yet. Big fer his age, though."

"Gray from the sea. Pull those weeds from him and get him a blanket and some rum."

"No rum," Ven whispered. "B-burns."

"Are you *sure* he's Nain?" one redheaded man asked his shipmates doubtfully. "Never known a Nain to turn down a swig of rum before."

Several hands reached into the lifeboat and pulled a blanket of seaweed off him. Ven could hear someone shouting for the captain as well, but as he was lifted out of the lifeboat the world went suddenly dark.

When he could keep his head up and clear he saw he was in the galley of the ship near the small cooking fire, sitting in a chair, wrapped in a heavy blanket. A human boy about his own age with dark, straight hair was watching him from the shadows. Standing in front of him was a broad-shouldered man with a thick wave of silver hair and bright blue eyes in a dark blue coat with brass buttons, also watching him closely.

"Warmer yet, son?" the man asked.

Ven nodded, suddenly tired again.

"What's your name?" the man asked.

"Ven Polypheme," said Ven hoarsely. His full name would have taken too much effort.

"Well met, Ven Polypheme. I'm the captain, but you may call me Oliver, if you wish."

"Thank you, sir," Ven said.

"I was glad to see you were alive," said the captain. "Fire Pirates don't usually leave any survivors, and this looks to be their work. Didn't know quite what to expect when we got to you."

"How did you find me?" Ven asked, pulling the blanket more snugly around himself.

"Why, the albatross, lad. Saw it from a goodly distance away. Flying in great wide circles around something, so we came to see what it was. Turned out to be your boat. You are one very lucky young man—er, Nain."

"Yes," Ven said, thinking about being pulled from the depths by the merrow. "Yes, I suppose I am."

"Well, I never knew a lucky man who was not a good man as well. At least, not one who is lucky enough to have an albatross as a guardian. So you are welcome here, Ven Polypheme. You are aboard the good ship *Serelinda*, registered to His Majesty, King Vandemere, of the Island of Serendair, which is where we are presently headed. Where are you from?"

"Vaarn," said Ven. He was starting to feel better. "On the Great Overward."

The captain nodded thoughtfully. "Polypheme," he said, almost to himself. "You're not related to the shipbuilding family, are you?"

"Yes," Ven said, looking down. Now that he was safe, thoughts had already begun to come into his head about his family. Beyond thinking he was dead, his father was undoubtedly in very deep trouble with Mr. Witherspoon.

"Well, well, then," said Oliver, sounding pleased. "I've purchased many a ship from Pepin Polypheme. The best in the business, he is. You're one of his sons?" Ven nodded. "Then you are more than welcome to sail with us, Ven. We will be landing in Serendair in a few short weeks, if we have a fair wind, in the northwestern port city of Kingston. From there you can set about making arrangements to head home if you like."

"Thank you, sir," Ven mumbled.

"I have to be getting back topside," said Oliver. "Be sure you get a length of lanyard from the first mate and tie anything to you that you don't want to lose—like that folding ruler. On a ship, everything's tied down." He motioned to the human boy who had been hovering in the shadows of the fire. "This is Char, the ship's cook's mate. He'll look out for you while you recover. Try to rest, and eat something if you can. The sea takes a lot out of a man. It may take a while, but you will feel better." He patted Ven on the shoulder and climbed out through the galley hatch.

Ven thought about his father, Mr. Witherspoon, and the rest of his family. *I'm not so sure about that*, he thought.

He looked up to see that Char was staring at him.

"What are you looking at?" Ven asked crossly.

"I'm not sure," Char answered, wide-eyed. "Are you a ghost?"

"No," Ven said. "Do I look like a ghost to you?"

The boy shrugged. "Dunno. Never seen one. But I never seen an albatross neither, till today. They say an albatross is the soul of a dead sailor come back as a seabird, so I didn't know if there was a reason it was followin' you around the sea. Maybe it was an old friend of yours? Or a dead relative? Or maybe you were about to die yourself?"

"Ugh," said Ven. "That's a cheerful thought." He pulled his blanket closer to his neck and turned toward the fire.

The cook's mate filled a battered mug with stew and handed it to Ven. "You want some cider?"

Ven nodded. "Thanks."

The boy's brown eyes glistened with excitement as he gave Ven the drink. "Know what else I seen?"

"No," Ven said, taking a sip. "What?"

"A seal," said Char with wonder in his voice. "All the way down here—a seal following the ship. Been a truly odd voyage, it has."

Ven almost dropped the mug. "A seal? Where? Show me!"

Char shook his head vigorously. "Faith, no. The cap'n told me to keep you warm and feed you. He didn't say nothin' about letting you go topside. If you slip or somethin' and end up in the drink again, I'll lose my position."

"I won't fall in, believe me. And I won't tell him you showed me."

Char crossed his arms stubbornly.

Desperately Ven banged the mug down and threw off his blankets. "Show me!" he insisted, taking Char by the arm and pulling him toward the hatch.

"Why is it so important to you?" Char asked, bewildered. "It's probably not even there anymore."

Ven tried to wrestle the cook's mate over to the hatch. "If it's a seal, you're probably right," he said between grunts; Char was thin and stringy, but his stubbornness gave him extra strength, and Ven was weak from the sea. Finally, when it became clear that Char wasn't going to budge, he stopped pulling and looked the mate in the eye.

"All right," he said, breathing heavily, "if I tell you a secret—a really *special* secret—will you show me?"

Char's eyes narrowed suspiciously.

"Would have to be one *heck* of a secret," he said.

Ven swallowed hard, hesitant to part with the information. Finally he realized that he had no other choice. He looked in both directions and behind him, then leaned forward and spoke quietly.

"I don't think that's a seal," he said seriously. "I think it might be a merrow."

"What's a merrow?"

"A—er, mermaid," Ven said.

Char's eyes opened wide again. "A mermaid? Gah! Why do ya think so?"

"Because I *saw* one," Ven said impatiently. "Now, come on! Show me."

The two boys jumped through the hatch and ran up the steps to the aft deck, Char leading the way. They waited until two sailors passed, then hurried over to a line of barrels that collected rainwater and slid between them and the rail.

"Blimey, don't fall in, now," Char warned, grabbing hold of Ven's shirt as he leaned out over the rail. "I'd have to go in with you; there'd be no end to hearin' about it otherwise."

Ven steadied himself and stared out into the sea. It was a great, unbroken expanse of blue-gray water, dotted occasionally by floating driftwood or seaweed. In the distance he could see a few scraps of wreckage from the pirate ship, floating lazily over the waves, burning still.

"Where?" he said desperately. "I don't see it."

Char shrugged. "Dunno. Maybe it left." He pointed to a small flock of gulls swooping at the surface to the left of them. "Could be fish there; the seal's prolly feeding off the same school that the gulls are."

At the fore of the ship they heard the first mate shouting orders to hoist the sails. The *Serelinda* was preparing to go back to serious speed now that Ven's rescue had been accomplished.

"Sorry, mate," said Char. "Got you all worked up for nothin'."

"It's all right," Ven said, still watching the sea hopefully. He gripped the rail tightly as the sails opened to the wind and caught it, pulling the ship fast along with it.

"Let's go back now," said Char, stepping around the barrels. "I have to get the cornbread started for supper. The crew will be wantin' to eat soon."

Ven let out a sigh, then nodded. He turned to follow the cook's mate, but looked quickly back when something caught his eye.

He thought he saw a small dark shape following the ship for a moment, but then it dove into the depths and disappeared. Far out near the gulls he could see the shadows of many similar shapes arch through the water, then dive as well.

Quickly he pulled out his jack-rule and extended the glass that magnified from afar. He peered through it. Below the green waves he thought he caught sight of a multicolored fin as it slipped into the deep, but he couldn't be sure.

"Goodbye, Amariel," he whispered into the wind. "Thank you."

He turned around to follow Char. Suddenly the deck lurched below him. Ven grabbed the rail, dizzy and sweating. Char came back and took him by the arm.

"What's the matter? Seasick?"

"Maybe," Ven said, his face going pale. "I—I want to get off the ship." His forehead and hands grew moist, and panic was starting to creep over him. His hand shook as he closed the jack-rule and put it back in his pocket.

A voice spoke from behind him.

"What are you two doing up on deck?" It was a deep, gruff voice, which Ven recognized as the captain's.

"I—I was showing Ven where I thought I saw a seal earlier," Char stammered.

"You all right, Ven?" the captain asked.

"No," Ven answered shakily.

"Feel nervous, sort of green around the gills? Like any land beneath your feet would feel good right now?" The captain handed Ven his handkerchief.

"Exactly," said Ven, wondering how the captain could tell.

"He's seasick," offered Char.

"No, it's not seasickness. He's got the sea-shakes," said Oliver. "You probably never were afraid on the water before, but since the pirates and the ordeal of being shipwrecked, you've taken on a fear of the sea. Perfectly natural, under the circumstances. Come with me, and we'll cure you of that." He nodded to Char, who hurried back to the galley hatch, then took Ven gently by the arm.

"Close your eyes, lad, and don't open them till I tell you to," Oliver said. His voice was pleasant, but it had the ring of a sea captain's order.

Blindly Ven allowed himself to be led, his legs wobbly, his stomach queasy, until Oliver stopped.

"Hook 'im up," he heard the captain say.

Ven felt a rope being tied around his waist and something being slipped over his shoulder and between his legs. He suspected it was a harness for climbing the mast.

"Er—Oliver, sir?" he asked nervously.

"Quiet, lubber," growled the sailor who was knotting the rope. "You speak when the captain tells you to speak, not before."

The captain took both of Ven's hands and put them on the shroud. Ven recognized the smell of the rosin and felt his stomach flip like an acrobat.

"Climb," the captain said.

"Sir—"

"No talking, and keep your eyes closed," Oliver ordered. "You're a Polypheme; you should be able to do it with your eyes closed."

Ven's heartbeat was thrumming in his ears. He had climbed shrouds before, many times, but never on the open sea. He could barely breathe as he felt around the ropes until he caught handholds. Then, slowly, he hauled himself up.

He could sense the captain climbing too, somewhere below him; he could feel the ropes shift and sway with his weight as he moved. Ven concentrated on his breathing, trying to keep it steady, as hand over hand he made his way up the mast. The ropes were salty from the ocean spray that coated them with slime all the way to the top.

Each step of the way, the captain directed him with a calm voice. "Now, lean back and climb away, Ven. Good, that's right. Pull yourself over—the handhold's a little more to your right. Put your arm out—the mast is ahead of you."

After what seemed like forever, he heard the captain say, "Hold there, Ven. Step forward and let go of the ropes."

Hesitantly he put his foot down on solid wood, his eyes still closed, and walked forward until his hands felt the rim of the enclosed wooden platform ahead of him. A moment later he heard the captain step onto the platform as well. He gripped Ven's shoulder.

"All right, now, Ven, open your eyes," the captain said.

Ven obeyed slowly.

At first the pitching of the sea was made worse by the height. The mast swayed much more than the deck did, and Ven felt his stomach turn over again. He looked down at his feet, trying to focus on the wood planks that made up the floor of the fighting top, which was also known as the crow's nest.

Then his eyes adjusted to the light, and he looked up and out. The nausea was replaced with wonder.

At his feet the world stretched out before him, green and gold in the light of the afternoon sun. He could see the horizon bending away, the sea rushing over it, frosted in glistening white waves, into the blue of the sky beyond the land's end.

A great gust of wind came up, and it rattled the sails, making the riggings groan and creak. Instead of letting it scare him, however, Ven closed his eyes again for a moment and let it race over him, blasting his hair in every direction, rippling through his shirt. He remembered what Captain Faeley had said on that fateful day, his birthday.

Don't drink too much of the wind, young Master Polypheme. It's intoxicating; it will get you drunk more easily than you can imagine. And then you will be lost to it, as we are, and have no choice but to chase it over the sea for all your life.

"Whales," the captain said. Ven opened his eyes again and followed the captain's finger off the left side. From his perch high in the crow's nest he could see them, dozens, scores perhaps, a whole family of long, dark shapes, blowing fountains of spray into the air where it glistened in the fading sunlight. Ven thought he could see calves, too, swimming alongside their mothers, diving deep and flipping their tails, waving their flukes in the air as if to say goodbye.

The sky seemed wider than he ever could have imagined.

"From here you can see more of the vault of the sky, what sailors call the welkin, than any man can ever see from the land," said Oliver, watching him with a smile. "Look below you."

Ven glanced down at the deck of the ship and was amazed to see that it was already cloaked in darkness, while in the crow's nest they were still standing in full light. He watched, fascinated, as the line of the sunlight climbed up the side of the ship to the mast and sails, swallowing the ship little by little into night, while he and the captain remained in the last light of day.

The sunset burned in fiery colors, far more glorious than Ven had ever seen before. The arc of the sun blazed hot orange as it sank into the sea beyond the rim of the world.

They continued to stand in silence, smiling, as the stars began to appear in the vast sky above them, winking in between the racing clouds, brightening as the sky darkened from robin's-egg blue to cobalt to indigo, until finally it was inky black. As more and more stars appeared, it looked to Ven as if someone had scattered handfuls of diamond sand across the sky.

As they watched, one star streaked across the heavens, dragging a line of light with it that faded quickly.

"A shooting star," the captain said. "An omen, it is, of magical things. 'Twill be an interesting day tomorrow, I'd wager. Well, young Master Polypheme, do you have your sea legs about you yet?"

"Yes, sir!" said Ven enthusiastically.

"And how much longer would you like to stay up here in the crow's nest, then?"

"Forever, sir," Ven replied.

Oliver laughed and clapped him on the back. "A true sailor's answer," he said. "But a true sailor also heeds the call of his stomach, and I would guess that yours is grumbling loudly. In fact, I think it's making more noise than the riggings."

"Yes, sir," Ven laughed. He didn't remember if he'd finished that second mug of stew before his fitful nap, but even if he had, he'd been at sea without food for several days. Now that his sea-shakes had passed, he was famished.

"Well, then, let's be down from here. Char's cornbread is—well, let's just say the boy is well named—but at least it's filling, if a little burnt."

Coming down seemed to take no time at all, and when his feet thumped onto the deck Ven heard a merry cheer behind him. He unhooked his harness and turned to see the deck crowded with sailors, eating their supper from tin plates and mugs, a small fire in a barrel in the middle of their group that cast dancing shadows around the dark ship. The smell of the food made him feel hungry for the first time since he left Vaarn.

The captain banged his metal mug against the mainsail and called for the crew's attention.

"I'd like to propose a toast," he said in his pleasantly deep voice, "to Ven Polypheme, who this day has been pulled from the sea, gained his sea legs, and is the first Nain in my knowledge ever to climb the mainmast of a sailing ship at sea, and without question the first to summit the mast of the *Serelinda.*"

"To Ven!" the sailors shouted in one voice, followed by a host of other salutes.

"Hear, hear!" "Well done, lad!" "Takes a brave man to go aloft." "Here's to you, Ven!"

Ven sat back, warm and happy, as the sailors who stood the afternoon watch bade him good night and went to their hammocks belowdecks, while the night watch took up their positions. Oliver sat on an old sea chest near the fire barrel and started a round of storytelling that lasted most of the night, broken by the occasional singing of sea chanteys, tales of lost ships and great storms that thrilled Ven to the bone.

When dawn broke, Ven was still wide awake, watching the sky turn from black to gray to pink. Finally it exploded with color as the sun rose over the sea. The night watch changed, and the crew shifted again. Char stumbled, sleepy-eyed, out of the galley, a bowl of hot porridge dotted with globs of sweet black molasses in his hands.

"Mornin'," he mumbled, thrusting the bowl at Ven.

"Morning, Char," Ven answered, accepting the porridge gratefully. "Thank you."

"Been up all night?" the cook's mate asked in amazement.

"Yes, telling stories and singing songs," said Ven. "What a great life you have here on the sea."

"You only think so 'cause you don't have to work for the *cook*," said Char grumpily. "A couple of weeks of having *your* ears twisted every time you accidentally burn somethin', and you might be thinkin' otherwise."

Ven grinned, but his attention was drawn away a moment later by the harsh clanging of the ship's bell. The crew was beginning to muster, gathering to receive orders from the captain and the first mate.

He listened to the commands Oliver gave them, then watched as three sailors went aloft on the shrouds of three separate masts as easily as climbing a ladder into a hayloft. The captain, satisfied, turned to Ven.

"Off to the hold for some sleep, now, Ven," Oliver said, smiling. "You've had a long night, but every man needs his rest on board. Storms come up from nowhere, and sometimes the seas turn rough for no reason at all, so it's wise to take forty winks whenever you have the chance. You want to have your wits about you."

"Aye, sir," said Ven.

"A well-rested crew is a safe crew," Oliver continued jokingly, loud enough so that the crew could hear him. "But the captain, now, the captain can stay up as late as he wants, and drink as much as he wants, because it doesn't matter what kind of shape he's in. If something happens, a captain is supposed to go down with his ship anyway. Isn't that right, gentlemen?"

A chorus of voices swelled in reply. "Oh, yes, yes, sir." "Quite right, sir." "True, true." "Yes, indeed."

An amused look came over the captain's face. "But, of course, because of their sterling characters, undying loyalty, and superior capacity as human beings, I know that if I were to go down with the ship, my crew would insist on going down with me. Isn't that right, gentlemen?"

Once again, the sailors answered in chorus, this time with humor in their voices. "Oh, yes, yes, sir." "Quite right, sir." "True, true."

"Yes, indeed." "Indubitably." "No question about it, sir." It was clear to Ven that this was a standard joke between the members of the crew and their captain.

"Even if there was plenty of room in the lifeboats, to a man they would stay, every one of them, to the bitter end, right, gentlemen?"

"Oh, yes, yes, sir." "Quite right, sir." "True, true." "Yes, indeed."

The captain's blue eyes twinkled. "In fact, even if we were only a few steps away from the dock, and were sinking in water that was only knee-deep, since I would feel obligated to go down with the ship, they would all go down with me, rather than hop off and wade to shore, isn't that right, gentlemen?"

"Oh, yes, yes, sir." "Quite right, sir." "True, true." "Yes, indeed."

"Ah, what a great crew," Oliver said, clapping his hands together. "Can't beat that, Ven. The loyalty of good, true-hearted men. Men who would stand with you when your back is to the wall."

"Aye, aye!" the crew shouted enthusiastically.

"Men who would go overboard clutching your hand rather than let you fall in alone."

"Aye! Aye!"

"Men who would cut off a leg if you lost one of yours, to keep you from feelin' bad about it."

"Aye! Aye!"

"Men who would be willing to stand in front of my wife and tell her I forgot her birthday, facing whatever consequences might come about."

The sailors fell suddenly silent.

The captain threw back his head and laughed. "You lily-livered cowards!" he shouted, cuffing the first mate playfully on the back of the head. "You are willing to brave the storms of the seven seas, laugh in the face of impending disaster, sneer at death on a daily basis, and yet you are frightened of my wife?"

"Oh, yes, yes, sir." "Quite right, sir." "True, true." "Yes, indeed."

The sailors roared with laughter.

"Did I happen to mention that they are also *wise* men, Ven?" the captain said merrily.

Suddenly from the crow's nest above came a hoarse cry.

"*Megalodon!* Starboard!"

The laughter choked off and the crew fell utterly silent again, but this time with the tension of fear. The boatswain clamped a hand on the wheel and held it firmly, so that the rudder beneath the surface would not move.

Ven felt the captain's hand grip his shoulder.

"Don't move or speak, Ven," Oliver said quietly.

Ven stood completely still, but slowly let his eyes follow the eyes of the crew, all of whom were staring off the right side of the ship behind them.

For a moment he heard nothing but the flapping sails rattling against the *Serelinda*'s masts, saw nothing but the vast blue-gray expanse of the ocean.

Then, slowly, a little way behind them, the sail of another ship seemed to rise from the depths.

Ven watched in amazement that turned into horror as he realized that it was not a sail.

It was a fin.

The size of the ship's mainsail.

Then it slowly sank back into the sea again.

His stomach turned to ice as the ship floated along in silence, waiting. From where he stood near the rail he could see a long, dark shadow approaching from behind them.

Ven's eyes went back to the faces of the crew. Every one of them, from the slightest to the burliest of the sailors, was ashen. Most were sweating, and a few were praying silently, their lips moving with no sound coming out.

The shadow moved closer, gliding silently beneath the waves, shallow enough for the sunlight to catch it. It caught up to the ship quickly, passing beneath it. The sailors held their breath.

Ven's heart pounded as the monster's dark, tapered form continued forward, extending longer than the boat's length from bow to stern.

Suddenly it dipped deeper and vanished.

"It's diving," Oliver said softly. The grip of his hand on Ven's shoulder tightened slightly.

Ven's eyes met Char's. His new friend appeared to be frozen in terror.

The crew waited, tense and fearful, looking around, hoping that their next sight of the beast would not be as it reared out of the water with the ship in its teeth. They held their breath until a soft call came from above. All eyes looked up.

The sailor in the crow's nest pointed off the starboard bow, into the distance.

At the edge of his vision Ven could see the enormous fin, now small from afar, moving away, disappearing again into the sea.

The crew slowly began to breathe again, then went back to their posts, talking softly and seriously among themselves.

"What—what was that?" Ven asked shakily.

"Megalodon," the captain replied, releasing his shoulder and moving to the rail, staring out into the sea where the fin had been heading.

"It looked like the fin of a shark," Ven said.

"Aye, lad, it was. If you travel the sea long enough, sooner or later you will either see him, or meet someone who has. He's an ancient monster, a deep sea shark from the time before history. Each of his teeth is bigger than my hand, and he has a mouthful of thousands of 'em. He is possessed of a hunger that can devour a ship and all its occupants without a moment's difficulty, and he does from time to time. Vibrations or noise draw his attention, and so the only thing to do when he is sighted is to remain as silent as one can and hope for the best."

"Is—is there only one of him?" Ven asked hopefully, though inside his curiosity was itching again.

The captain grasped the rail and looked off in the direction in which the fin had been traveling. "Now, that's a good question, lad. Megalodon lives in the deepest part of the sea, where it is always night, along with more monsters and horrors than your nightmares could ever hold. He doesn't come up often, but you see him often enough to know he's not just a legend. Who knows how many are down there?"

Ven swallowed hard. "What kinds of monsters?"

"Oh, sea serpents, giant squid, clams the size of the hold of this ship. Dragons that own entire reefs, and defend them vigorously with fire more caustic than what burned that pirate ship of yours. Colorful fish with deadly poison in their quills. Eels as cruel and cunning as any man who ever lived. They're the worst, as far as I'm concerned; their bite causes pain that cannot be healed. Tiny plants that can paralyze a man with one touch. Yes, the sea is beautiful beyond measure, but her depths are filled with danger, Ven."

Ven thought back to the "wonders" that Amariel told him of and shuddered.

Oliver saw the expression of concern on his face and smiled. "We'll be in Kingston soon, lad. Once you've seen the spectacular Island of Serendair, you will most probably never want to leave. And then you will never have to fear what lies out there in the deep."

Ven said nothing, but continued to watch the horizon. He thought he saw the giant fin one last time, almost too small to make out, disappearing over the edge of the world. *No*, he thought, *I* will *see what lies in the deep up close one day.*

Because I've drunk too much of the wind.

- 6 -

The Floating Island

By day there was only work. There is so much to be done on a ship that I never had time to think. Mostly scrubbing decks and water barrels, helping the cook and cleaning the passenger cabins, and whatever other tasks I could do to make myself useful. It kept my mind busy.

But at night, I lay awake in my hammock and listened to the creak of the ship, the sea wind howling, the snapping of the sails, and the sailors snoring all around me in the dark. Then all I did was think. I was too tired to sleep, too worried to rest. Too guilty to deserve sleep or rest.

I wondered if my mother had taken my teacup off the table yet and put it away.

THE DAYS AT SEA PASSED, ONE INTO ANOTHER. THE *SERELINDA* sailed west, following the setting sun, through fair weather and rain, making its way homeward to the Island of Serendair.

Ven became good at reading the stars. The boatswain showed him and Char how to use an old sextant, the navigator's tool, so when there was time between tasks, they took turns mapping constellations and planets, plotting the course they were traveling and comparing it with the navigator's official one. After a few tries, they found they were right more often than not.

But there were other ways to read the stars as well. Oliver had said that the shooting star they had seen the night Ven first climbed the mast was an omen, a sign of magical things to come the next day. After seeing the giant fin of Megalodon rise from below the surface of the sea, then disappear into the horizon, Ven began to understand what he meant.

On clear nights, when the world seemed like nothing but endless moving darkness, he stared up into the black sky, watching the brightest stars wink in the sparkling diamond dust. He saw thin streaks of light fall almost every night. But on the night when one lingered in the sky again, leaving a shiny trail glittering behind it, he was fairly certain he would see something amazing, either magical or monstrous, the next day. The shooting star burned in his dreams that night, pushing away his worries of home, and making his curiosity itch fiercely.

He was still dreaming of what would come when just before daybreak he heard a shout from the crow's nest.

"Cap'n! *Cap'n!* The island! To port!"

Char's head popped up from the pile of blankets to Ven's right.

"Can't be," the cook's mate murmured sleepily. "We got at least a week's sail left till Serendair."

"Maybe that's not the island he's talking about," Ven suggested, rolling out of his hammock. "C'mon!"

Abovedecks the crew was scrambling faster than Ven had seen. Oliver stood at the rail, a spyglass to his eye, staring out into the hazy blue dawn. Ven and Char shielded their eyes and looked in the same direction.

The morning mist seemed to form clouds in the water. Rising from the middle of the clouds was the peak of what looked like a small mountain. The wind spun around it, making the heavy vapor dance in thick waves.

"Blimey!" Char whispered. "Would ya look at that! I don't remember seeing an island like that anywhere on the navigator's maps."

"Nor do I," Ven admitted. His gaze went back to the crew, who were preparing a longboat and hurrying around the decks at the captain's command.

Oliver looked up and saw him. He beckoned for Ven to come near.

"How's your sense of adventure this morning, Ven?" he asked. He sounded in a hurry.

"Strong and well, as always, sir," Ven replied.

"And if you could do but one thing today, anything without limitation, what would it be?" the captain asked.

Ven thought for a moment. His sense of adventure dimmed as his guilt returned.

"I would get a message to my family, to let them know that I am alive," he said.

The kindly blue eyes of the captain twinkled.

"Well, perhaps you will get the chance," he said. Then he turned to the first mate. "What did we decide last time, Bill? Scroggins's turn?"

"Aye, Cap'n," the mate said. "He's waitin' for word on his wife."

"Well, get him down here, then. And go ask among the passengers if anyone wants to pay to go over. There was a line of them last time—including Maurice Whiting." Oliver looked back at Ven. "You want to see the Floating Island? It's a chance you may never get again in this lifetime."

"Oh, yes, sir!" Ven blurted. He had never heard of the Floating Island.

"Could be dangerous. Do you care?"

"Not a bit, sir."

"Good," the captain said. "Climb into the longboat; we'll be rowing out shortly. Have to get out there before it drifts away."

Ven didn't understand what Oliver was talking about, but he checked his pocket for his jack-rule and, finding that to be safe, went up to the first mate. He was instantly helped over the rail and aboard the longboat.

He sat for a few moments alone in the boat, amid coils of rope and bundles of oilcloth, until Scroggins, a thin sailor with curly black hair, climbed aboard, carrying a small sea chest.

"You goin' too?" Scroggins asked, taking a seat next to him. Ven nodded. "Well, good for you, lad."

Ven strained to see the island in the distance through the swirling clouds. He kept his eyes fixed on it as Oliver appeared at the rail again, two men, both passengers on the ship, standing next to him.

"Payment will be due upon your return to the ship," the captain was saying to one of the men, a soldier. The man nodded curtly and climbed into the longboat, causing it to sway a little in the air. Oliver looked the second man up and down, then shook his head. "I'm sorry, Mr. Whiting," he said regretfully. "We have to consider the weight; another man would be just a little too much."

"Throw the boy out, then," Mr. Whiting said crossly. "I am willing to pay handsomely."

"I've already promised him," said Oliver. "I'll give you first preference next time. I'm very sorry."

"You've *promised* him—a Nain whelp—and that *matters?*" demanded Mr. Whiting. "Toss him out—let him go next time. I have thirty gold crowns right here." He dangled a red cloth bag in front of the captain.

The look of regret disappeared from the captain's face. He turned his back on the man and climbed into the longboat, then signaled to the crew to lower it and loose the ropes.

"Away," he said, taking his seat. "Take your oars, gentlemen."

Ven looked up at the side of the ship as the longboat was lowered into the water. The passenger Oliver had left behind, Mr. Whiting, a tall man with a hawk nose dressed in elegant clothes, glared down at him with undisguised rage from the deck. Ven swallowed and picked up the long, flat paddle and set it into the iron oarlock opposite Scroggins. The soldier took up his oar as well while the captain steered the boat with the rudder.

"What is this place we are headed to, Captain?" Ven asked excitedly, his back to the island as they rowed.

Oliver smiled. He reached into his pocket with his free hand and pulled out a small conch shell, then placed it on the seat beside Ven.

"Once we are well clear of the ship, take a look at that," he said. "Ever put one of those to your ear and listened to the sound of the sea wind?"

"No," Ven said. "Shells like that are rare in Vaarn. My brother Jaymes has one in a cabinet that a sailor gave him, but he nearly twisted one of my fingers off when he found me with it when I was little. So I never did get to hear the sea."

"Ah, but you tried, didn't you?" the captain said. "If he hadn't caught you, you would have put it to your ear, yes?"

Ven thought back. "Yes," he said, pulling on the oar.

"Interesting how folks just know to do that, even when they've never seen a conch shell in their lives. You can keep that one, by the way. Now you have one of your own." The captain stared over Ven's head, into the morning light, but said nothing more.

The excitement in Ven's stomach expanded like soap bubbles, making him feel light-headed. He continued to row with all his strength until finally Scroggins told him to ease up; they were almost to the shore.

Ven picked up the shell and turned his head to see what was behind him. The sight took his breath away.

The Floating Island must have been drifting toward them while

they were rowing nearer to it. It loomed ahead, the pink sand of its beaches gleaming in the sun, ringed with seaweed. The clouds that circled it were rolling still, the thick mist beginning to surround their longboat. In the center was the mountain, though Ven could not see it very well in the mist. From what he could glimpse it appeared to be covered with trees of every imaginable color.

He looked down at the gray-white shell in his hand. It was wide at the top, with a spiral of pointed horns that curled down to the narrow base. Inside the shell was smooth and pink.

The mist was thicker now. Oliver nodded to Scroggins. The sailor put down his oar, stood up in the longboat and took hold of the anchor rope. He leapt out of the boat, landing in water up to his waist, and hauled it to shore, anchoring it in place.

The captain turned to his passengers.

"First, some rules and a story, before we go ashore," he said, his voice soft and serious. "This island is a ship of sorts. More than that, it is an *ancient* ship. As such, it is to be respected and treated with utmost care. This place is the home of the sea wind. You are about to enter the wind's garden. Anything that grows here remains here. Do not pluck a single flower, or pick a single piece of fruit. You may take nothing from this place that belongs here, even a grain of sand that can't be shaken from your boots. We are sailors, and we cannot afford to have the wind angry with us. Is that understood?"

Ven, Scroggins, and the soldier nodded.

"There are many stories about how the world was made," Oliver continued. "Whether any of them are true, only the one who made it knows for certain. But it has long been said that five things were used to make it: fire, water, wind, earth, and the light of the stars, which is called ether. These five things, these elements, were called the Paints of the Creator.

"It is said that when the Creator made the world, it began as a piece of a star that broke off from its mother and sped across space, until it came into orbit around the sun. So ether was the first element to be born. Fire burned on its surface, the second element. Then the fire died back into the center of the world, where it still burns to this day, and the world was covered with water, the third element. The wind, the fourth element, rose up from the water and blew it back, revealing the land, the earth, the last element."

Oliver began buttoning his jacket. "I don't know if there is any truth to the tale—as I said, only the one who actually did the creating knows that. But legend says that when the wind blew back the sea, revealing the land, a tiny piece of earth floated to the top of the waves, like a pebble or a clod of dirt in a river. That tiny piece of earth was this island.

"This island, then, was born when land was born, at the very beginning of the world, and is the child of both wind and water. So it is a very old place, a magical place. It floats about the sea at the pleasure of the wind. A man may see it once in his life, or many times—or never. Each time a man is given a chance, he should be respectful of it. So walk carefully—this is a fragile place, and unlike other islands, it is not connected to any ground below the sea. We don't want to up-end it, now, do we?"

"No, sir," Ven and the two men whispered.

"Good. All right, then, out you go, and take care to be quiet. Scroggins, hold the rope fast. You first, Ven."

Ven nodded and stood up. Carefully he climbed over the board that had served as a seat, then stepped over a coil of rope onto a clump of oilcloth, preparing to climb over the side.

"YAAOW!" the oilcloth screeched.

Ven's feet flew out from under him, his backside went up in the air, and he fell backwards out of the boat with a loud splash.

"What the—" Oliver said angrily. He grabbed the oilcloth and jerked it from the floor, revealing a dirty face, dark hair, and wide, dark eyes.

"Char! What are *you* doing here?" the captain demanded.

"Er—followin' your orders, sir," Char said sheepishly. "You told me to look out for Ven. Couldn't do that from back on the ship."

Ven stood up in the surf, dripping seaweed from head to foot.

"Thanks," he muttered.

The anger in the captain's eyes softened into amusement.

"Well, I can't very well discipline a crew member for following my orders," he said. "Good thing you don't weigh much, Char, or I'd have to leave you in the boat. But seeing as you and Ven add up to a man between you, I suppose we can risk taking you ashore. Get out of the boat."

The moment they set foot onto the pink sand of the beach, Ven understood what Oliver had meant about the Floating Island being the wind's home. Inside the swirling clouds of mist a stiff breeze blasted, warm in some moments, cold in others. The forest they had seen from the boat seemed just beyond their sight in the haze of moving vapor. Ven's heart pounded as they crossed the sand, his hair blowing wildly around his face and in his eyes.

"It's like we're in the sky," he whispered to Char. "Like that mountain's rising out of the clouds."

"Blimey, I hope there's not a giant around here somewheres," Char whispered back nervously. "Don't giants live in mountains in the sky?"

"Nonsense." The soldier snorted. "Fairy tales. I cannot wait to be in port, so that I can get back to the real world, and no longer have to endure all the superstitious talk of sailors, all the silly tales of mermaids and albatrosses and giants in the sky."

Scroggins rolled his eyes. "If you don't believe in the magic of this place, why did you pay a hefty price to come here? There was a line of others that wanted your seat in the boat, and couldn't have it."

The soldier paused, then turned around and stared at them through the billowing mist.

"The legend of this place is known to every man who spends his life as a soldier," he said tersely. "It is said that if you put your name on the wind here, it will be carried far and wide, across the whole world, even to places that are unknown. Into the ears of everyone the wind touches."

"So you are willing to believe superstitions as long as they can make you famous?" Scroggins said disdainfully. "You'd never make it as a sailor anyway; you're too selfish."

"Enough talk," Oliver said sternly as the two men glared at each other. "In this place, one should listen, not speak."

Char and Ven exchanged a glance, relieved the argument was over. All around them the wind roared, whipping their clothes, making them flap like sails on the sea. The boys put their hands over their brows to keep the sand out of their eyes, which were stinging from the bite of the wind.

Finally they came in sight of greenery. Ven recognized the scent of the forest, but it was sharper, richer than he was used to. Once every few years his father made a trip away from the city streets of

Vaarn to the country where the timber for their ships was harvested. Ven had gotten to go with him once, and was in awe of the sight of the forests, the sounds and smells and the feeling of peace that he had never felt in Vaarn.

Here, that feeling was even deeper, not just peace but silence, to the point of being a little bit frightening.

He put his head down and followed Oliver into the forest.

Suddenly the wind died down to a whisper. Ven looked up. All around him was the most remarkable collection of plant life he could imagine. Lush tropical plants with wide leaves and brilliant flowers were everywhere among the tall, thin trees with shaggy bark and green fronds reaching into the mist above. Mixed in with those strange trees and plants were evergreens and trees with leaves, some in the earliest budding of spring, others partially turned to the shades of autumn. Birds of all colors of plumage twittered in the branches of the trees.

"In no other place in the world would these sorts of trees and plants grow together," Oliver said, leading them along a thin trail through the forest. "Everything you see here came from a seed that is carried by the wind, or that floated to shore from places the island has drifted near to."

"Are there any animals?" Ven asked, looking around him in wonder at the glorious blossoms of deep purple and red that were the size of his head.

"Specifically, any animals that eat people?" Char added nervously.

Oliver shook his head. "Only birds. Seals and other sea mammals rest here occasionally, but the island's travels are too random to allow it to serve as any kind of a home for them."

The birdsong was growing louder. Ven held his breath and listened; the music of the birds blended perfectly with the song the wind was singing.

The group walked through the odd forest toward the center of the island where the mountain stood in silence, no sound at all but that of the wind. Shafts of dusty sunlight broke through the trees as they began to climb the outer edges of the mountain. Finally Char stopped in his path and pointed ahead of him.

"Look!" he shouted. He voice was dulled by the noise of the wind.

In the upper branches of a pine tree a hat was hanging.

Oliver smiled. "Ah, yes, we must be on the windward side of the island, where the breeze comes in from the land. You'll see a lot of hats in the trees through here, along with scarves, crumpled letters, and all sorts of other litter. The wind is a bit of a pickpocket. Every sailor I know has lost at least one cap to it."

They walked beneath the branches, marveling at the multitude of caps, top hats, and ladies' headdresses stuck in the trees. Char stopped and pointed again.

"A kite!" he shouted. Ven followed his finger and saw it as well, a red and blue box kite with its tail tangled around the branch of a shaggy-barked hickory tree. It was battering itself against the trunk, twisting and tugging in the wind. Char turned to Oliver, desperation in his eyes.

"Can't we save it, sir?" he pleaded. "It will be smashed to bits if we leave it up there."

"You remember what the captain said about not takin' stuff from here," Scroggins said sternly.

Oliver watched Char intently. "Yes, that's true, but I was talking about the things that belong here. The kite is only here by accident—if anything, it's trespassing." He exhaled. "You want to save the kite, Char?" The cook's mate nodded eagerly. "Then I suppose it's all right. Scroggins, get it down."

The sailor's eyebrows went up to his hairline, but he said nothing. He turned and scaled the tree as quickly as he might summit a mast, then crawled out onto the branch and carefully unwound the kite from its tangles.

"It's wrapped good and tight," he called from the treetop. "I don't think I can break the cord."

Ven saw the excitement on Char's face turn to dismay. He reached into his pocket and pulled out his jack-rule, staring at it for a moment. Then he walked to the foot of the tree and called up to Scroggins.

"Here," he said. "You can use this—it has a knife in it. But please be careful; it was my great-grandfather's."

Scroggins nodded and leaned down from the branch, reaching out a hand. Ven tossed him the jack-rule, watching nervously as the sailor extended the blade, then sawed through the string. He lowered the kite down to Char and climbed down again.

"You probably should keep it, Char," the captain said as the cook's mate turned the kite over in his hands, his eyes shining with glee. "A gift from the wind. Now, let's get on." He started up the side of the mountain once more.

Scroggins handed the jack-rule back to Ven, and they turned to follow the captain.

-7-

The Hollow Mountain

THE REST OF THE CLIMB TO THE MOUNTAIN'S SUMMIT WAS MADE IN silence. The mist was thinning as they neared the top, and Ven could see that the peak narrowed as it got taller. The winding hillside seemed to twist in ever-smaller circles as it got higher. Oliver was leading them up a spiraling path that headed toward a dark cave at the mountain's summit.

The birdsong grew quieter the closer they got to the top, while the wind grew stronger. The more tropical plants of the forest began to disappear, leaving only the tougher trees, evergreens and low, brushy bushes that bent in the whipping breeze. Scroggins finally had to tie Ven and Char to himself with a length of rope to keep them from blowing off the mountainside.

Struggling to remain standing, they hurried inside the cave.

As soon as he got inside, Ven understood why Oliver had shown him the conch shell. The whole island was shaped like one. The inner walls of the mountain curled downward, widening, the same way the shell did, smooth and translucent, winding down into darkness. Trees and plants grew inside, but fewer and farther between. A twisting path led down into the belly of the mountain.

"Listen," Oliver said, untying the rope that bound the boys to Scroggins.

At first I didn't hear anything but the endless roar of the wind. Then, upon listening more closely, I heard voices all around me. They spoke in many languages I did not understand, as well as the common tongue that I did. There were voices of men, of women, of children, some whispering, some shouting, all muted and fuzzy in the sound of the breeze whirling down through the cave inside the twisted mountain. It was a symphony of noise—prayers, wishes, arguments, promises, and threats, all sorts of words that people had spoken into the wind, all caught here now in this cave that curled like a conch shell. All remembered by the wind alone.

The captain turned to the soldier. "Now's your chance," he said. "As we go down inside the mountain, speak your name in each place that you take a breath. The wind will catch it and take it all over the world—that is what you desire, isn't it?"

"Yes," said the soldier.

"Then go to it," Oliver said. He gestured to the others. "Come along."

Slowly they descended into the dark tunnel in circles that grew bigger and bigger. The soldier cleared his throat and followed them.

"Marius," he said. "Marius, Marius, Marius." He chuckled uncomfortably. "Marius is the greatest warrior who ever lived! Marius. Marius. Marius."

"What a bloated head," Char whispered to Ven, who nodded.

Oliver continued down the twisting tunnel, until he came to a place where the light was dimmer and trees had stopped growing, leaving only low bushes and flowers that bloomed in shade. He stopped, then gestured for the others to stop too, and for Marius to be quiet.

He listened carefully, the voices on the wind chattering all around him. Finally he smiled.

"It's a boy, Scroggins!" he said cheerfully. "Stand here."

The sailor excitedly took his place and listened, his face glowing happily. Ven and Char looked at each other in confusion.

Oliver leaned over and spoke softly. "Think of this hollow mountain as a flute. Each place in the world is like a hole in the flute, so somewhere along this wind tunnel there is a tie between that place and here. This is the place where the wind blowing from Serendair can be heard. Scroggins is hearing the news of his newborn son. And he might like a little privacy, as I believe he is going to send a mushy message back to his wife. None of us want to have to witness *that*, now, do we?" He nodded farther down the tunnel, and the boys followed him until he stopped again.

"This is where the wind from Vaarn blows, Ven," he said quietly. "I don't know if your father is one to stand out in the wind and listen to what it says. You can try and send a message. The odds are against it getting there, like throwing a note in a bottle into the sea. But it can't hurt, now, can it?"

"No," Ven said excitedly. "It can't hurt."

"Good. Keep it short, about as long as a gust of wind takes." He nodded farther down the passageway. "Let's move out of the way, Char."

Ven closed his eyes, listening to the voices on the wind. He cleared his throat nervously and spoke.

"To Pepin Polypheme—Father, this is Ven. I'm alive." He coughed. "Er—sorry about the ship."

The soldier had begun chanting his name again, and Scroggins appeared.

"All right if I head up now, sir?" he called to Oliver.

"Aye," the captain replied. "Take Mighty Marius back with you and get the boat ready. We'll be up in a minute." He turned and tromped quickly down the tunnel into the dark.

Char tugged at Ven's sleeve. "You wanna go back up? Or down with the captain?"

"Is there any question?" Ven said. "Down! C'mon!"

They hurried after the captain, into deeper places where only ferns and moss grew now.

At the very bottom of the cave was a small pond filled with moving silver water, surrounded only by glowing moss. Ven thought back to the conch shell and realized that this was where the crown of the shell would be. Oliver was crouched over it, looking down into the water.

"This spring is fed by ice deep below," he said softly. "Ice left over from the earliest days of the world." He reached into his vest pocket and pulled out a small flask, carved from what looked like crystal. He pulled out the stopper and poured a thin stream of blue water into the moss, then dipped the flask into the silver spring. He drew it back quickly, stoppered it again, then put the flask back in his pocket, rubbing his hands together to warm them up.

"All right, gentlemen," he said briskly, "let's get back to the ship."

"Captain," Ven said as he and Char followed Oliver up the pathway into the light again, "I thought you said we weren't to take anything from the island."

"This is a trade I've been making with the place for a long while, lad," the captain replied, not looking back as they headed down through the odd forest toward the shore. "This place needs the water I bring it. It comes from a well that the wind cannot reach, a well from before history. A form of water that is as rare as the water of this spring. That water helps keep the island alive, in some respects. In return, I take a small amount of water from the silver spring, for my own purposes."

"What do you do with it?" Ven asked.

The captain stopped for a moment and looked back at him, then smiled.

"Enough questions for today, Ven."

Ven was bursting with questions, but it was clear that the captain wasn't going to answer. Instead, they walked silently, listening to the millions of voices on the wind until they reached the entrance of the tunnel at the top of the hollow mountain.

Once they stepped out into the light again, Oliver raised a hand to his eyes and looked down to the beach.

"Now, I see that Scroggins is ready to cast off. Once we're under way, there is some lunch to be had in the sea chest he brought with him. So I hope your rowing arms are good and ready."

Ven was trying to catch sight of the longboat, when something white hanging from a low branch of a tree caught his eye.

It was an albatross feather.

His albatross feather, with the familiar blue-green markings and a stain at the base where his hat had discolored it.

"Impossible," he murmured, staring at it. "I lost that in the sea weeks ago."

"By now you should realize that nothing is impossible, Ven," Oliver said. "Though some things are unlikely. But it looks like all of us are going back with a gift from the wind." He plucked it from the branch and helped Ven stick it back into the new cap the sailors had given him.

When they had rowed halfway back to the ship, Ven turned around to catch one last glimpse of the Floating Island, the home of the sea wind.

It was gone.

Ven did not see the captain for the rest of the day once they were pulled aboard. A crowd of passengers and some of the crew were waiting there to greet them. Or, more correctly, they were waiting to greet Marius, whom everyone suddenly remembered hearing of as the greatest soldier in the world. Ven and Char watched in amazement as one by one the men shook the soldier's hand, awe on their faces—all except one.

Mr. Whiting, the man whose seat Ven had taken in the longboat, was staring not at Marius, but at Ven, the afternoon sun glinting off his diamond tie-tack and crisp white shirt. Ven felt the hairs on the back of his neck prickle.

"Unbelievable," he muttered, trying to ignore the man's stare, watching the passengers swirl around the newly made hero. "All he had to do was say he was famous, and now it's so."

"Yeah, next time we find that bloody island, I'm gonna whisper in that cave that it's lucky to give me money," Char said in disgust. "I suspect I will have a king's fortune right quickly."

They returned to their chores until sunset. The boys sat together on deck in a friendly silence, watching the stars appear one by one in the deep blue of the sky. A very bright one hung low over the horizon, rising as the evening passed.

"That's Seren," a deep voice said behind them. They looked up to see Oliver standing there.

"Seren?" Ven asked.

"Aye; the star the island of Serendair was named for. When it comes into view it means that it is only a short matter of time before we are home."

Ven nodded and watched the blue-white star, the brightest he had ever seen, twinkle at the edge of the sea. A star that wasn't even visible from his old home, so very far away.

If only I had any idea where home was now for me.

-- 8 --

The Island of Serendair

Most Nain get very nervous on the water. When forced to take to the sea, they cannot wait to get back on dry land again. I once saw Dalton kiss the ground after he returned from an Inspection. I never understood this until I caught my first sight of Serendair.

Then I got nervous.

In the time since my rescue, I had come to feel at home on the sea. Climbing the mast had shaken the sea-shakes out of me, and now I felt like I could happily spend my life on a ship's deck, sailing the wide world. So when the peaks of the northern islands came into sight, purple in the morning sun, instead of enjoying their beauty, all I wanted to do was be sick over the side.

Because we were coming to land. And once on land, I would have to face going home.

And face my father.

B ALATRON! HO, TO PORT!" CAME THE SHOUT FROM THE CROW'S nest.

Ven looked quickly off the left side of the ship. It was still just before daybreak, and the sky was still gray. He couldn't see anything in the morning haze, so he took out his jack-rule and extended the glass. He peered through the side that magnified objects far away.

In the distance he could see a mountain peak, the palest of purple, frosted with snow.

"That's Balatron, the largest of the three northern islands off Serendair," Bill, the first mate, said as he passed Ven on the deck. "There are two others, Briala and Querrel, a little to the south and east of it. We should be landing in Kingston day after tomorrow."

Ven nodded, struggling to not throw up.

He scurried around the deck, finishing his tasks, until Oliver finally came to the rail. Ven paused in his mopping.

"Captain," he said, "are we sailing north now?" The captain nodded. "I thought Serendair was to the south."

"It is, lad," Oliver said, "but we have to sail north a bit to avoid the grave of the Sleeping Child."

Ven's eyes popped open wide. "Grave? Sleeping Child?"

Oliver pointed into the distance. "Do you see how there is steam over the sea yonder? That's the grave. Long ago, a burning star fell from the sky. The Lirin, the race of people who live in the forests and fields, called her Melita. When she fell, she hit the sea with such force that the resulting tidal wave swamped the island, taking almost half of it to the bottom with her. For a long time, Serendair was known as Halfland. The purple islands you saw this morning were mountains before the Sleeping Child fell."

"Why is it called the Sleeping Child?" Ven asked, curiosity starting to twitch inside him.

"Because it lies there, deep beneath the waves, quiet, but burning still," Oliver said. "Sometimes the sea above it is still as glass, so that you would never know it's there. And sometimes it boils with angry heat. But it has been there a thousand years now, and still it shows no sign of awakening." The captain glanced back at the sea again. "Of course, if it ever does, now—" He shuddered. "Well, that's why we sail around it. Out of respect."

"I understand," Ven said, staring at the steam disappearing in the distance. He returned to his chores.

By nightfall the *Serelinda* had turned southeast, and when the sun came up again, land was in clear sight.

"There she be, Ven," Oliver said in a hushed voice. "The island of Serendair, one of the most beautiful places on earth. Look well, lad; you may see her many times in your life, but this is the only first glimpse of her you will ever have."

Ven watched as the ship sailed ever closer to the island. The first thing he saw was a brilliant beam of light circling slowly in the gray haze of dawn, high in the air. A moment later he saw that it was from a giant tower that stood at the end of a long sandbar at the outer edge of the harbor. It was the tallest building he had ever seen, as high as the mast of the *Serelinda*, or higher. He looked up and down the coast and saw two more towers, not quite as tall, their lights circling as well.

Beyond the light towers was the harbor. Ven swallowed in amazement. The harbor was easily ten times the size of the wharf in Vaarn, with hundreds of docks lining the shore. Brightly colored flags flew from the end of each pier, flapping merrily in the ocean breeze. There were so many people scurrying about on the docks, loading and unloading ships, that it reminded Ven of an anthill with thousands of ants carrying crumbs.

The land beyond the dock seemed to go on forever. "I thought Serendair was an island," Ven said.

"Aye, lad, it is. A right *big* island. It's almost a continent all by itself," Oliver answered. He handed Ven a wooden box. Ven looked at him questioningly.

"Sir?"

"In here you will find parchment paper, ink, a quill, and some sealing wax. Find a corner out of the way while the crew is making ready, and write whatever letter you wish to your family." The captain's blue eyes twinkled. "Of course, you might want to just wait a few days and take it to them in person." Ven stared down at the letter box. "You do understand you will need to stay in Kingston at least a few days, Ven?"

"Why?" Ven asked.

"Well, I have to report your rescue to the authorities," Oliver said calmly. "It's just a matter of procedure. Most likely the harbormaster will sign off on it himself, but just in case he wants to send it onward, you need to wait around before you can get passage back on a ship home."

"Onward?" Ven asked nervously. "Where might he send it?"

"Oh, nothing to worry about, lad. It might go to someone in the naval office, or even the Secretary of the Navy. In theory, it could go to the king himself, but I would doubt it. You never know, so until the report has been signed off on, you will need to stay in Serendair." He inhaled deeply. "I'm sorry. I imagine you want to be getting home as soon as possible."

Ven looked out over the rail, watching the bustling city wharf come ever closer.

"I'm not certain what I want, sir," he said honestly. "Or, more rightly, what my father will want."

"Why is there a question?" Oliver asked, his silver brows drawing together. "I cannot imagine any father not wanting his lost son to come home as quick as the wind can carry him."

"Not a son who has destroyed the family business," Ven said sadly. "Among the Nain there is no greater disgrace. Each ship we build is very expensive, and costs my father a lot of money in materials and labor. He does not get paid until the harbormaster signs off on the Inspection. I didn't bring the ship back—in fact, I blew it up—so my father will never get paid. And he will be out so much money that it might cost him the business. My family might even have lost their home. They could be living in the street by now. And me being around would only embarrass him on a daily basis."

"Be that as it may," Oliver said pleasantly, "whatever loss he might suffer can't begin to compare to how much I'm sure he misses you." His face grew serious. "Trust me on this."

Ven said nothing, but suddenly realized that there were more differences between Nain and humans than he had ever realized.

The sea captain reached into his coat pocket. "Until you are cleared to go home, you should probably go to the Crossroads Inn and ask for lodging in the youth hostel there. That's where young folk stay when they have nowhere else."

"How do I get to the inn?" Ven asked.

"Once you get to Kingston, go to the main gate at the eastern edge and follow the road until it comes to a crossroads. It's about three miles to the inn. You can usually catch a ride with a farmer or merchant's cart, or you can walk. You will know when you have reached the inn, you can't miss it. The innkeeper is a lady named Mrs. Gertrude Snodgrass. She's a—hmmm. Well, she's a fine woman, yes, indeed. Tell her I said that she would be happy to put you up, and she will be."

"Thank you, sir," Ven said, his stomach turning over sickly.

"But don't go today." The captain glanced up at the sky. "It will be afternoon at least before we make port." He looked intently at Ven. "You do not want to go to the Crossroads Inn at night. Do you understand what I am saying?"

The firmness in his voice made Ven shudder, even while his curiosity was tickling the back of his mind.

"Yes, sir," he replied. "But why?"

The captain's face hardened. "*Don't start out on the road after the sun begins to go down.* Do you understand?"

"Yes, sir," Ven said quickly.

"Good," Oliver said. He looked around to make sure no one was watching, then reached into his vest pocket and pulled out the crystal flask he had filled from the spring on the Floating Island.

Ven's eyes opened wide as a beam of light caught the bottle. It sent rainbows flashing around the deck.

"I would be most grateful if you would deliver this to Mrs. Snodgrass for me," the captain said quietly. "It's extremely important that it gets to her."

"I'd be happy to," Ven said, taking the flask in his hand. It was cool to the touch, and hummed as if it were singing. "But why don't you deliver it yourself, sir? Surely it would be safer with you."

"Because I ship out in the morning, lad," the captain said. Ven thought he saw a touch of sadness in Oliver's eye, but when he looked again it was gone. "And as I already told you, one does not go to the Crossroads Inn after the sun begins to set. But I must get this water to Mrs. Snodgrass. Can I trust you to make certain of that?"

"You can count on me, sir," Ven promised.

The captain clapped him on the back. "Good. Now, excuse me. I have to get the sailors' pay ready. Go write your letter. You may use the desk in my cabin." He turned and went belowdecks. Ven carefully put the flask into the pocket where he kept the jack-rule and buttoned it.

Then he went to the captain's quarters and sat down at the small desk in the corner of the room. He took out the parchment paper, ink, and quill, and, after a good many squiggles and blots, began his letter.

Dear Father,

On that day the ship was lost at sea, as far as I am aware, all other hands were lost, but I was saved by a merrow.

Ven stared at the page, then shook his head, scratched out a few words and started again.

Dear Father,

On that day the ship was lost at sea, as far as I am aware, all other hands were lost, but ~~I was saved by a merrow~~ I was rescued. I write to you now from just off the coast of the island kingdom of Serendair, in the Southern Ocean. I was pulled from the water by the captain of the good ship Serelinda, and brought here to a hospitable welcome.

Ven fiddled with his quill, suddenly out of words. Despite what Oliver had said, he had no idea if Pepin would want to hear from him again once his father was assured of his safety. He took a deep breath and continued writing.

I am terribly sorry about the loss of the ship, Father. I did try to remember my lessons, as you instructed me. I fear I may have remembered them too well. I will need to remain in Serendair until the records of my rescue have been reviewed by the authorities here. Until that time I expect to be housed at the Crossroads Inn under the supervision of a Mrs. Gertrude Snodgrass.

He blotted the ink dry, then added one more sentence.

Please give my love to Mother, and tell my siblings that I miss them and am very sorry.

Respectfully,
Ven

The ink in which he had signed the letter suddenly smeared and ran. Ven blotted it quickly, then dried the eye that had dropped the tear onto it, looking around hastily to see if anyone had noticed.

Everyone on the ship was moving furiously, hurrying to get the last of their gear ready to off-load when the *Serelinda* was anchored in port. No one had seen him crying.

He quickly sealed the letter with wax and went back to work.

From then on everything happened in a blur. The passengers and crew darted hastily around the decks, lugging baggage up from the holds, getting ready to leave the ship as the docks came closer into sight.

Finally they came into port. The passengers and all their baggage were off-loaded. Then the captain came to the gangplank with a sea chest full of envelopes, and handed them, one by one, to the sailors as they left the ship. He shook each of their hands. Char and Ven were the last in line.

Oliver handed Char the second-to-last envelope. "Here you go, Char—ten gold measures of scrip. Pay for a mate, third class." The captain patted Char's shoulder. "It was good sailing with you. And if you decide you want to go back to sea, you're welcome to serve on any of my ships."

"Any except the *Serelinda*, unless you're changin' cooks," Char said gloomily. "I need to keep what little of my ears is left un- twisted."

The captain laughed. "Aye, good enough," he said, shaking Char's hand. He turned to Ven and handed him an envelope of the same size, the last in the chest. "You, too, Ven. Ten gold measures."

"Sir?" Ven asked, staring at the envelope in Oliver's hand.

"Go on, take it, lad," the captain said, pushing it at Ven. "You served as a deckhand. Deckhand's pay is also ten gold measures of scrip, which is paper money that sailors use."

"I—I know about scrip," Ven said haltingly as Char tromped

down the gangplank, his kite over one shoulder, and disappeared into the crowd of people. His father's shop accepted scrip as payment for small things, like rope. All the other shops on the docks did as well. "But I don't deserve to be paid. I was rescued."

The captain's blue eyes crinkled at the corners. "We put you to work as a deckhand, Ven. I have to pay you, and I have to pay you scale—what every deckhand makes—or I'm in violation of the sailor's code. And that I won't do. So take it, and good luck to you."

"But I only served for a few weeks. Char was on the *Serelinda* for six months. And we made the same amount of money."

Oliver exhaled. "Doesn't seem fair, does it? But that's the code of the sea, and we are bound to it." He cocked his head as Ven looked down at his feet. "You goin' to be all right, Ven?"

Ven nodded. "It just seems unfair. Char has it so much harder than I ever did."

The captain regarded him seriously. "Aye, it may seem that way now. But actually, in some ways Char has it much easier than you will, Ven. Unlike you, Char is human. In most places in the world, no one will look at him twice. You, now, you are Nain. While you were home, in the protection of your family, that may not have been a problem. Your father is a very well-respected man, and a family your size—well, there is safety in numbers. But now you are on your own. Alone you may find that there are a few people who are not friendly to Nain, or anyone from a different race."

He looked out to sea, where the sun was beginning to set into the western horizon, red-orange above the blue water.

"Now, Serendair is a friendly place to people of all races most of the time. The king himself insists upon it. But people come here from all around the world. You find all types of folks, especially in a port city, and not all of them have the same attitude as the king. Do you understand what I am saying?"

Ven nodded. His family had discussed the problems of being different many times, but as Oliver said, he had never felt in danger because of it.

Until now.

Oliver smiled, and Ven's worry lessened. "Just remember, Ven, you're as good as any other living soul on this earth. Whether other people know that or not doesn't really matter as long as you do."

"Yes, sir," Ven said, smiling slightly. His father had often said the very same thing.

"Good man," Oliver said. He put out his hand, and Ven shook it. "Now, give me your letter. Be sure to get that flask to Mrs. Snodgrass safely, and as quickly as you can. But not till morning."

"I will," Ven promised, handing him the letter. "Thank you for everything, captain. I owe you my life."

Oliver shook his head. "You owe me nothing, lad. If you ever find yourself in the position to rescue someone, be sure to do it without expecting anything it return. It all evens out in the end, believe me." His eyes twinkled. "But you *do* owe that albatross, don't you think?"

"Yes, sir."

"Good enough. Best of luck to you, Ven. I expect we will meet again." The captain tipped his hat and headed back up the gangplank.

Once Ven got down to the dock, he had to walk through a huge swarm of people pushing and shoving their way to get closer to the ship. They were talking among themselves.

"Do you suppose he's gotten off yet?"

"I didn't see him. He must have been kept for last, to get the less important people out of the way first."

"Unless he came off *first*, and we missed him!"

"Oh, no!" a young girl wailed at the thought.

"Er—who are you looking for?" Ven asked a heavy human man who had stepped on his foot, trying to get a better view over the heads of the crowd.

"Marius," the man said impatiently, still straining to see. "The greatest warrior that ever lived, boy. He was said to be traveling on this ship."

At the name, the crowd grew even more excited and anxious. "Marius, yes, indeed, the greatest warrior who ever lived, everyone knows that."

"Oh, brother," came a familiar voice behind him. Ven looked over his shoulder to see Char pushing his way through the people.

"Hey, Char," Ven greeted him, taking him by the shoulder and steering their way out of the crowd. "Where are you off to now?"

"The Sailors' Rest," the dark-haired boy replied. "Gotta find a place for the night."

"What's the Sailors' Rest?" Ven asked.

Char shrugged. "Sort of an inn for sailors, a place to sleep for a night or two, down by the docks. They let you pay in scrip, o' course."

"Hmmm," said Ven. "Do you think I count as enough of a sailor to stay there?"

"Sure," said Char, shifting his duffel to the other shoulder. "It's not a great place, lots of men who have had too much rum to drink. I was gonna go get a space on the floor, wander around Kingston for a while until the last minute, then go to sleep quick. We can go together if you want."

"That sounds great," Ven said.

Char led Ven off the docks and up into the cobbled streets of Kingston, where more people than he had ever seen were milling around in the afternoon light.

Above them they heard a harsh cry. The boys looked up to see a dark shadow of an enormous bird pass overhead, circling twice, then fly out to sea.

"That albatross must *really* like you," Char said, starting down the street again.

Ven wasn't sure. *I wonder why that bird is following me?* he thought. *It seems to be looking out for me, but every time it appears something ter-*

rible happens. He watched the shadow until he could no longer see it, then followed Char.

Neither of them saw the other shadow, this one lurking in the streets behind them, following them silently through the alleys of Kingston.

- 9 -

Kingston

THE MAIN STREET OF KINGSTON WAS LINED WITH PRETTY SHOPS that sold roses and bread, arrows and armor, meats, lamp oil, fruits, vegetables, and everything else imaginable.

Ven followed Char around women buying fabric, men trading leather, and children playing, to the center of the street where a great fountain stood. In the center of the fountain was a large copper sun, and from its metal rays water sprayed in seven different directions, each reflecting a different color of the rainbow.

"You hungry?" Char asked.

"Yes," Ven said, staring at the fountain.

"Well, then, let's hit the Confectionery," Char said, nodding across the street.

Ven followed him to a large stone building with a glass window across the front. The smell of freshly baked cookies and other sweets billowed out of the shop every time the door opened. A sign above the window said:

The Magical Confectionery

Ven stared in the window.

"Whoa," he whispered.

"Don't just stand there," Char said, pulling open the heavy door. "C'mon."

The shop was full of every kind of pastry and candy, all fashioned in amazing shapes. On one side of the shop were pieces of castles made entirely out of cookies—guard towers, gates, walls, and shields, and even a portcullis made out of pretzel sticks. On the racks next to it were chocolate figures of mythical beasts, some of them tinted with colors—strawberry-scaled dragons, white chocolate unicorns with horns glazed with golden sugar, winged horses rendered entirely in dark chocolate.

A completely assembled confectionery castle stood in the shop window, beautifully detailed, from the cobbled walkway of tiny sugared jellies in front to the garden of spun-sugar trees and beds glittering with gumdrop flowers in the back.

"Don't just stand there," Char said, picking up a gingerbread drawbridge. "Buy something."

Ven stared at all the castle pieces, finally choosing a guard tower formed of boiled caramel sugar dipped into hardened chocolate.

"Good choice," said the gray-haired man behind the counter, smiling.

Ven smiled awkwardly in return. "I've never eaten a guard tower before," he said. "Makes me feel a bit like a giant, a rare feeling for a Nain indeed." He fumbled in the envelope Oliver gave him for his scrip. "You—you do serve Nain, don't you?"

The confectioner's face lost its smile. "Of course we do, lad," he said seriously. "Your money's as good as anyone else's. That'll be a copper for the guard tower."

"I'll pay for his, too," Ven said. He handed the man a gold measure of scrip.

"I wonder if they make ships," Ven said to Char as the shopkeeper made change.

"Of course we make ships, lad," the confectioner said, handing him back nine silver pieces and eight copper coins. "This is a port city." He pointed to another table on which stood edible ships of every size and shape, with marzipan sails and gingerbread hulls, their riggings made of spun sugar.

Ven continued around the shop, walking past a table spread with crowns, rings, and necklaces, the jewels all made of candy, and paintings of pretty places all done in colored sugar on a gingersnap canvas.

I could not believe all the marvelous things before my eyes; it was like something from a fairy-tale world. And the smell! I wanted to eat everything in the shop. And if Char had not opened the door at that moment and left, I think I would be there to this day, doing so.

"Don't do that again," Char said crossly as they stepped out of the cool shade of the confectionery shop back into the bright light of afternoon.

"Do what?" Ven asked in surprise, his mouth full of caramel sugar and chocolate.

"Don't pay for me. I pay my own way." Char popped the last of his gingerbread drawbridge into his mouth and wiped his hand on his shirt.

"Sorry," Ven said, embarrassed. "I guess I'm still bothered by us getting the same amount of money, when you served all that time on the *Serelinda*, and I just got pulled out of the sea and mopped the deck for a couple of weeks. It isn't right." He wrapped the remainder of his sugar guard tower in his handkerchief and stowed it in his duffel for later.

Char shrugged. "It *is* right," he said agreeably, heading down the street past a store full of colorful quilts and another filled with exotic birds. "Cap'n didn't have any choice in that. It's right, though it may not be fair. But then, life ain't fair. It ain't fair that some kids got no parents and others get two."

"What about you?" Ven asked. "Do you have parents?"

"Naw," Char said. "No one who had parents would have to work as a cook's mate. At least, no one with parents who didn't *hate* him."

Ven felt even worse now.

"But I got two legs, and two arms, and two eyes," Char said as they passed a bakery where the bread was sitting in the long front

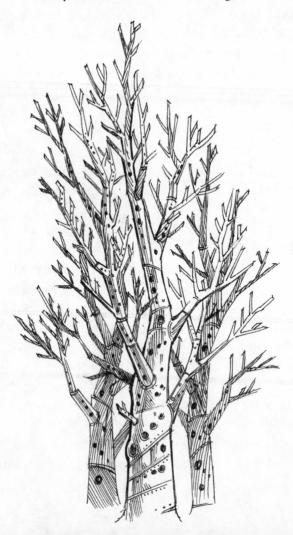

window, cooling. "And lots of folks don't—you'll see a bunch of them in the Sailors' Rest. So I reckon I'm doing all right."

Ahead of them they heard music, and Ven looked around for the musicians, but none were in sight. The farther up the street they walked, the louder the music grew, until finally they stopped in front of a garden in the center of the road, brimming with red and yellow flowers.

In the middle of the garden was an enormous sculpture of polished metal that was carved to look like a glade of trees, but in each branch and leaf were holes through which the breeze was blowing, playing a random melody of wind music. Char broke into a grin and pointed.

"Look!" he said to Ven.

In front of the garden Scroggins, the sailor they had traveled to the Floating Island with, was standing with his arm around a smiling young woman, a squawking bundle at his elbow.

"This must be the place she sent the message from, the one he got on the island," Ven said, walking closer to get a better view of the sculpture. "The holes in those metal trees make it play like a giant flute when the wind blows through."

"Criminey," Char murmured.

Ven noticed the breeze was tugging at Char's kite. "Do you want to see if we can find a place to fly that before the sun goes down?"

"Sounds like as good a plan as any," Char replied.

Together they hurried through the streets, heading toward the north end of town.

Along the way they passed all kinds of people, rich families in splendid clothing, ordinary folk chatting among themselves, poorer people pushing carts and calling to their children, all of whom seemed comfortable walking the same streets. Most of them were human, but occasionally Ven saw a few other kinds as well. They passed two slender, dark men he recognized as Lirin, the people who lived in wide fields and forests. And across the street he thought he saw some smaller folk, but he was not certain, as they darted into a nearby store before he could catch a good look at them.

As the sun was starting to go down, they passed an enormous section of the city that was walled off by a barricade, a stone wall more than a dozen feet high, with guard towers atop it. Soldiers patrolled the top of the wall, armed with crossbows. In the center of the barricade was a huge set of doors, bound in brass, beside which a gatekeeper sat.

"What is this place?" Ven whispered to Char.

"The Gated City," Char answered, pulling his kite and duffel a little closer. "The Market of Thieves—you want to stay as far away from there as you can. Some folks go in on Market Day, the middle day of the week, to shop for all kinds of weird stuff that you can't buy in a regular store. Me, I'd never need to buy anything so bad that I'd risk being stripped of everythin' I own."

"Why is there such a place right here, at the north end of the city?" Ven wondered aloud.

Char shrugged. "I guess a long time ago it was a prison or somethin'. Dunno. But keep moving; I don't want to lose my kite or my pay." Ven followed him, staring back over his shoulder at the Gated City, his heart pounding with excitement.

Out of the corner of his eye he thought he saw movement from one of the towers on the wall. Ven turned, and as he did, the setting sun cast a beam of golden light across the street, lighting the cobblestones and glittering in a rainbow flash. He lifted his hand to shade his eyes.

For a split second he thought he saw someone beckoning to him.

Ven squinted in the afternoon brightness, and came to a halt in the street.

He imagined, for as long as it took him to catch his breath, that the figure was summoning him, its long shadow stretching behind the wall of the Gated City. He took a step toward it, and when he did, he could swear that the figure nodded and beckoned to him again, but it was impossible to see who or what it was with the glittering sunlight in his eyes.

Char tugged impatiently at his shirtsleeve.

"C'mon," the cook's mate urged. "Let's get away from here—last time I was in this port, I heard seven sailors went into that place an' never came out again."

Ven tried to see past the afternoon shadow, but whatever he thought had been there was gone now.

"All right," he said finally, turning back toward the wharf. He pushed Char's pinching fingers away from his shoulder and followed him through the streets again.

They continued walking north and west until they came back to the docks, where the traffic and activity was beginning to shut down for the night. In the distance Ven thought he saw an abandoned pier, and he pointed it out to Char.

The wind along the water was stronger, and the two boys hurried to the end of the pier, which was solid but had holes in some of the boards, where it led out into the harbor.

"Here, I'll hold it and you run with it," Ven suggested, reaching for the kite. Char nodded, and within a few moments the kite was dancing over the blue-gray waves, dipping and nodding in the changing wind.

Char offered Ven the string, but he shook his head, preferring to watch the sun sinking into the waves where the sea met the sky. Great dusty shafts of sunlight, burning brightly gold, stretched upward from the horizon behind the dancing kite. It was enough for him to just stand there and watch as the sky grew darker, the horizon fading from gold to fiery orange.

Once it was gone, and dusk was beginning to set in, Char reeled the kite back in and sighed.

"It's getting late," he said wistfully. "I think we'd better go get our places on the floor at the Sailors' Rest."

Ven nodded, and turned to follow him, casting one last glance back at the darkening sea.

In the distance, not far beneath where the kite had been flying, his eye caught movement again.

Ven squinted and looked harder. Something was sticking up in the water.

It was a tail.

And it was waving at him.

Then it disappeared.

"Uh—Char," he sputtered, "go on ahead and I'll catch up to you."

The cook's mate blinked. "You all right?"

"Yes, I just want a few more minutes watching the sea," Ven said. "Go on, and I'll be right there." Char nodded and headed back toward town.

Once he was out of sight, Ven went all the way to the end of the abandoned pier, crouched down and spoke over the tops of the waves cresting under the dock.

"Hello, Amariel," he said, trying to contain his excitement.

The merrow's face broke the surface, water streaming from her hair and nose. She looked off in the direction where Char had gone.

"What were you doing?" she asked curiously. "Fishing for birds?"

Ven swallowed the laugh that came into his throat. "I can see how it might have looked that way, with the string and such, but no, we were just playing. It's so good to see you. How did you find me?"

"Followed the ship," said Amariel. "And guess what?"

"What?"

"I found a fisherman who knows how to cut gills!" she said, smiling but not showing her teeth. "His name is Asa, and he lives in the fishing village to the south of that big city. He sets out each day at dawn, but if we go to him early enough, he will do your neck, and then you can breathe underwater, and come with me to go exploring."

Ven winced. "I'd love to," he said, fighting back his curiosity, which was itching so hard that his brain felt like it was burning. "But I have to wait for my papers to clear with the harbormaster. And I really should find a way to go home."

The merrow floated back in the water, confused. "Do you want to come into the depths with me?"

"Yes," Ven said sadly. "But I can't today."

The merrow's face took on a look of displeasure. "Hmmph," she said. Then she floated back in the water, looking like she was preparing to dive.

"I do want to go exploring with you," Ven said quickly, trying to keep her from leaving so soon. "There's just a few things I have to do first."

"Oh, that's all right," said the merrow testily. "I understand."

"Will you come back?" Ven asked desperately.

The merrow shrugged in the water. "Maybe," she said. "Maybe not. Goodbye."

"Wait!" Ven called, but he was speaking only to waves.

He watched for a while, hoping to see her, or where she went, but it was getting dark, and the sea was too vast and too choppy to notice anything. Finally he gave up and started back to town.

The lamplighters were busy lighting the oil streetlamps, climbing ladders that rested against the poles with a long tallow candle in one hand, when he returned to the main section of Kingston. Ven noticed how different the city looked in the dark. There was still a lot of foot traffic, as people made their ways home, or stopped by taverns for supper, but the shops were either closed or closing, and there were many shadows cast by the streetlamps.

He decided to cut through an alley to get to the Sailors' Rest more quickly. He was only a few streets away when someone grabbed him from behind by the shoulder.

Ven felt the air rush from his lungs as he was slammed up against a brick wall in the alley.

A face he had seen before appeared over his. The eyes were red and gleaming angrily. The stench of rum filled Ven's nostrils. He blinked, trying to remember where he had seen the face. Then it came to him. It had been glaring down at him from the deck of the *Serelinda*, the same anger twisting it into a mask of hate.

It was Mr. Whiting, the passenger Oliver had turned away from the boat to the Floating Island.

"You're a brave young man, walking alone in the alleyways of a port city after dark," Whiting said angrily. "Or maybe you're just foolish."

Ven tried to twist his arm free of the man's grasp, but it was no use. He stared back into Whiting's dark eyes, the way he had seen his brother Luther do, but his heart was pounding too hard to be convincing.

"Listen to me, you Nain brat," Mr. Whiting hissed. "You cost me what may have been my only chance to visit the Floating Island. And that loss cannot be measured, do you understand?" Ven nodded. "You can never make up for that loss." His face twisted. "But you will pay for it, mark my words. You will pay."

"Ven?" Char's voice rang out in the cobblestone alley, a street or so away. "Ven, where are you?"

Mr. Whiting's eyes narrowed. "You had best hide, boy," he said softly. "Dogs are fond of Nain meat. And I own a *lot* of dogs."

He stepped aside, then melted back into the dark shadows of the alley.

A moment later, Char appeared around a corner.

"Ven! There you are. I got us some room on the floor at the Rest," he said. He looked at Ven oddly. "Are you all right?"

"I'm fine," Ven said, trying to sound calm, though he was trembling and confused. "Let's get out of here."

He followed Char the rest of the way to the inn for sailors. Both boys kept their heads low and their eyes on the floor as they passed tables of grizzled men, many missing legs or eyes, as Char had said. Ven did not recognize anyone from the *Serelinda*, and the realization made him nervous. He and Char found a corner near the fire in the main room of the Rest, pulled thin blankets from their duffles, and settled down to an uneasy sleep.

His dreams were plagued by Fire Pirates and shadows that lurked in alleyways.

Somehow he was certain that he had not seen the worst of what remained hidden yet.

- 10 -

The Crossroads Inn

THE NEXT MORNING, AFTER A LOUD AND SLEEPLESS NIGHT IN THE Sailors' Rest, Ven and Char walked to the south gate of town, looking for a ride to the Crossroads Inn.

When they got to the gate, there was no one there except the gate guard and the town crier, who was polishing his bell.

"Oliver said it was only three miles or so," Ven said, looking down the road. "We could walk."

"Let's wait for a little while," Char grumbled. "My feet hurt."

"Were you born in Kingston, Char?" Ven asked while they waited.

Char shrugged. "Dunno. I've been passed around a lot. Only been here once that I remember. Never been to this inn before, but I hear it's the place kids without parents go."

A few minutes later the crier began ringing his bell, announcing the morning's news. The sleepy streets seemed to waken. Shopkeepers opened their doors, fish and flower sellers appeared with carts, and the children of the city hurried from door to door, laughing.

"A merchant or farmer should show up soon, and then maybe we can catch a ride in his wagon," Char said.

As if by magic, the boys heard a clopping sound coming down the street. A wagon came into sight, driven by a man with a thick beard. It was filled with spools of wire.

"I'll go talk to him," Char said.

Ven nodded, then turned back to watching the wakening city. He saw a group of women greet each other at the well as they drew water up in the bucket, and townspeople begin to visit the store fronts.

"Her-aaaaa-chhoooOO!"

Ven leaped straight up in the air at the harsh, violent sneeze behind his ear. He turned quickly around to see a young girl with dirty blond hair wiping her nose.

Her hand had been in his pocket.

Ven reached out and grabbed her arm as she turned to run. "HEY!" he shouted. "What do you think you're doing?"

The girl twisted her wrist, broke free of his grasp, and ran away down the street. Once she got out of reach, she turned and thumbed her nose at him, then hurried around the corner out of sight.

"Ugh," Ven said. The back of his neck was wet.

Grimacing in disgust, he brushed the snot off of his shoulders and back, then took off his cap and shook it. The albatross feather fluttered in the wind.

"Well, well," he said to himself, running his finger over the feather, "the thief must have had her nose tickled. I guess the luck from the albatross is still with me. It saved my wallet."

"Ven!" Char shouted from down the street. "Hurry! I've got us a ride!"

Ven put his hat back on and jogged over to the gate, where Char was standing beside the wire wagon.

As he approached, he saw the bearded man's face change.

"Not him," the man said quickly to Char. "There's no room for him."

Ven froze in the street. Char looked at Ven, then back at the driver.

"Whaddaya mean?" he demanded. "I told you I had a friend."

The driver's expression turned sour. "There's room for one. You can ride, but not him. Get in."

Char's face held a similarly sour expression. "All right then," he said. "He can ride, and I'll wait."

"Char—" Ven started to say, but the driver angrily snapped the reins, and the wagon started away without them.

"That's all right—I'd rather walk," Char shouted after the wagon. "Somethin' stinks *bad* in that wagon."

"Hope the demons at the inn get ya," the driver shouted back. "Nain scum."

The boys stood in silence for a moment in the dust from the wagon wheels.

"Demons?" Ven asked finally.

Char shrugged. "The sailors in the Rest are afraid to go to that inn," he said. "They think it's haunted. But you know sailors. They think *everything's* haunted. They're very superstitious."

"Well, they aren't the only ones who think that about the inn," Ven said. "The captain didn't want us to go there in the dark." His scalp started to itch.

They watched as the wagon drove out of sight. "You didn't need to do that, by the way," Ven said quietly after a moment. "You should have taken the ride—your feet hurt."

"Not as much as my conscience would have if I'd ridden with that snob while you waited," Char said.

Ven shrugged. "My father says you have to ignore that sort of thing," he said, watching the human population of the city mill around in the streets. "When you're of a different race, people distrust you because they are afraid. If you don't give them reason to dislike you, it becomes their problem, not yours."

Char looked both doubtful and disgusted. "I dunno. Seems ta me that his fear means sore feet for you an' me. That makes it *our* problem. Come on. We may as well get started. If we leave now we might make the inn by noon-meal."

They started down the dusty road heading south. Just beyond the ivy-covered gates it was cobbled like the streets of Kingston, but once it got away from the city the road became little more than a dirt path, with deep ruts carved by wagon wheels over time.

After a little while they heard another wagon approaching, this one pulled by two red-brown horses. The wagon was piled high with summer squash, and as it came near to them it slowed. The driver, an older man with gray hair, waved them over.

"You on your way to the inn?" he asked.

"Yes, sir," Char answered.

"Well, hop in, boys, and I'll drop you there," the old man said. Ven looked at him questioningly, and the driver nodded and pointed toward the wagon bed. "Hurry, now."

Ven and Char scrambled to the back of the wagon and climbed aboard. The driver whistled to the horses. The wagon gave a lurch, and then began to roll down the road again.

In the back amid the squash a thin girl with a sharp face, pointy chin, and dirty blond hair was sitting. She scowled at the boys, thumbed her nose at Ven, crossed her arms, and settled down more comfortably in the vegetables.

It was the pickpocket.

Ven coughed, then leaned closer to the driver. "Uh, sir," he said, "did you know there's a—a girl back here?"

The old man chuckled. "That's no girl, lad, that's Ida. She's a wildcat. Don't get too close, now—she's got claws."

"Ida?" Char asked. "You got a last name?"

"No." The girl sneered.

"Ida No," Ven said. "That's precious."

"Shut up," Ida said. She hurled a squash at Ven and hit him in the forehead.

The boys looked at each other and exhaled deeply.

After a short while a white building appeared in the distance. As the wagon got closer they could see it was a large inn with a tall stone fence around it and iron gates in front. The stone from which it was built had been whitewashed so that it shone brightly against the green fields and trees, many of which were white-trunked birches. All the flowers blooming in the gardens were white as well. The lawn was perfect and green. It was beautiful, and fancy, and not very welcoming at all.

A sign out front read:

The White Fern Inn

"Is this the inn at the crossroads?" Ven asked the driver.

The old man shook his head. "No, we have a ways to go still. This here's the White Fern. You could never afford to stay there, lad. And even if you had all the money in the world, they still wouldn't take you—no children allowed."

"Hmph. Probably just as well," Char said. "Who'd want to stay in an all-white place anyway? You'd go bonkers tryin' to keep from getting everything dirty."

Ven said nothing, but continued to look down the road, watching the girl out of the corner of his eye.

A little farther down the road on the same side as the inn was a large pen. He could hear the sound of barking from a long distance away. As they got closer he could see that it was coming from a dog compound.

Ven looked at Char, whose eyes were wide as saucers. Inside the huge pen were dozens of dogs, all black as the night, with thick shoulders and necks, barking angrily as the wagon passed. The driver clicked to the horses to make them pick up the pace, which they did willingly, passing by the noisy compound as quickly as they could.

"What—what is that?" Ven asked the man nervously.

"Mr. Whiting's guard dogs," the driver answered, slowing the cart down as the barking faded away in the distance.

"Mr. Whiting?" Ven's face went suddenly pale.

"Yes, he owns the White Fern. Raises killer dogs and sells them to people who have places they want guarded. I suggest you stay far away from there."

"Don't have to tell me twice," Char muttered.

Ven noticed that the girl's face had turned the color of milk, too, but she merely pulled an apple out of her pocket and began to munch on it.

The three children sat silently among the squash in the back of the bumping wagon until at last on the other side of the road a small cemetery came into sight. The road widened, then came to a point where it crossed with another road that ran north to south.

And there, at the far corner to the north past the crossroads, was an inn.

The building was larger than the White Fern, but not as fancy. It had two wings, both with two stories, and was built of stone with a thatched grass roof. An enormous chimney rose from the center of the two wings. Behind the inn, two smaller buildings could be seen, one round, one rectangular, each about a hundred yards away from the main building. A small girl kneeled outside one of them, tending a bed of brightly blooming yellow flowers.

A large green sign stood out near the road, painted with gold letters and a strange symbol that looked like a circle with a spiral inside. The sign read:

The Crossroads Inn

"All right, lads and—er, Ida. This is it, out you go," said the driver pleasantly. He climbed down from the wagon and patted the horse, then grabbed a bushel basket and made his way to the door, which was standing open. "Good morning, Trudy, love," he called into the doorway. "Got some nice squash fer ya."

Out of the doorway came a small, stout woman with red hair that was turning gray near her ears. Her face was lined, her eyes tired, but her cheeks were rosy. Even though she looked a bit pale and haggard, Ven saw something in her that seemed strong and reassuring, something that reminded him of his own mother.

"Mornin', Jeremy," she said, drying her hands on her apron. "Will you take it 'round back for me?"

"Of course, darlin'," said the old man. "Bye the bye, I brought you some new guests." He nodded at the boys and Ida.

The woman walked closer to the wagon. "Well, well, Ida, back so soon? Did the constable send you?"

The girl nodded curtly.

"All right, then," said the red-haired woman, "but if so much as a spoon disappears from my inn this time, I will reach down your throat and dig around inside until I find it, do you understand?"

Ida nodded again, then strolled into the inn. The woman turned to the boys.

"And who might you fine gentlemen be?"

"Ven Polypheme, Mrs. Snodgrass," Ven said, putting out his hand. "Captain Oliver of the *Serelinda* told me to come see you." His voice faltered. "He, um, said to tell you that you would be happy to put us up."

The red-haired woman shook his hand. "Oh, he did, did he?" she said with mock severity. "Well, now, wasn't that nice of him? He's very free with offering my hospitality. Next time I see that Oliver Snodgrass I shall have to remember to thank him with the toe of my shoe in his backside."

"Oliver—Snodgrass?" Ven asked, amazed. "The captain is your husband?"

"Ah, he neglected to mention that, did he?" said Trudy, pulling herself up straight and trying to look stern. "Yes indeed, I am the legendary wife of the great Captain Snodgrass. I hear there are stories about me from here to the edge of the Seventh Sea."

"Yes, ma'am," whispered Char. "There surely are."

"And who might you be?" Mrs. Snodgrass asked. "Oh, wait! I do remember you. You're the mate of the *Serelinda*'s cook, are you not?"

"I'm Ch-ch-ch—ch-ch-ch. Char. Yes, ma'am."

I was afraid that he might faint. At any moment I expected his eyes to roll back in his head, he looked so frightened.

Trudy's face softened. "Well, then, Char, you surely have suffered enough; that cook's the grumpiest sailor that ever drew breath. Get your things, come inside, and we'll find you boys something to eat."

She led them into the inn, which was warm and inviting inside.

The front door was made of heavy wood on which a golden griffin was painted. I wanted to touch it; I'm not certain as to why, but I had to struggle to keep my hand from reaching out and brushing it as we walked past. In the center of the inn stood an enormous fireplace, wide enough to roast an ox whole, with a large stone hearth at its base. Some chairs were clustered around it, none of them occupied. The only person in the area I could see was a man who sat on the far edge of the hearth, playing a strange-looking stringed instrument and singing quietly, as if to himself. Next to the fireplace a wide stairway led to the upper floor.

On the left side of the hearth was a large bar with stools in front of it. A tall, roundish bartender with a bald head was drying glasses with a white cloth. Two men in traveling clothes were sitting at a nearby table, arguing quietly.

To the right were three long tables and an open door that led

into a large kitchen. Ida sat at one of the tables, eating some bread and cheese and running the bread knife over the sole of her boot. She did not look up when we came in, but ignored us and continued to sharpen the blade, munching away.

Other than that, the inn was empty, except for a large orange tabby cat that was eyeing us seriously.

Mrs. Snodgrass scratched the cat behind the ears. "This is Murphy," she said fondly. "He's an old ratter from one of the captain's ships—the best he ever had, in fact. Retired from the sea now, he lives in the inn. Murphy knows everything that goes on around here, though he rarely tells." She patted the cat again, and looked up as two rough-looking men tromped down the stairs, nodded to her, and left the inn.

The argument in the bar was growing louder. Ven looked over to see that the men were now glaring, occasionally jabbing each other in the chest with their pointed fingers.

It reminded me of my brothers discussing business, actually.

Ven coughed politely.

"It must be very hard to be alone here, with all the strangers that come through," he said.

"Ah, yes, 'tis a very scary thing, a poor woman like me, all alone, without a husband to protect her," Mrs. Snodgrass said. She looked over her shoulder. The noise from the argument at the table had gotten very loud. "Excuse me a moment."

She walked over to the two bickering men, both a head taller than she, seized them each by an ear and slammed their heads together with a resounding thump. Then she returned to Ven.

"So sorry," Mrs. Snodgrass continued. "Yes, it's a very frightening thing, to be a poor, weak woman all alone out here."

Ven grinned. He glanced over at Char, who looked even more terrified than before. Then he remembered the crystal vial in his pocket. His skin started to itch; from the moment he had seen the crystal vial, his curiosity had been nagging at him. He stepped forward and spoke softly to the innkeeper.

"Er—may I speak to you alone a moment, Mrs. Snodgrass?" he asked, his curiosity itching so fiercely that his palms were sweating.

The red-haired lady nodded, then gestured for both boys to follow her. Char clutched his hat as they made their way to the kitchen, where Mrs. Snodgrass gave them both apples and cheese.

"Why don't you sit down, Char?" she said, pointing to a stool at a long table. "You look like you're about to faint." Then she led Ven back into the hall.

"What did you want to say?" she asked.

Ven unbuttoned his shirt pocket and carefully removed the vial. He handed it to her as gently as he could.

"From the captain," he said.

Mrs. Snodgrass exhaled, and Ven noticed she looked even more tired and drawn than he had first thought. She took the bottle.

"Thank you," she said simply. "If you and your friend are still hungry, there are biscuits in the crock near the fire." Then she turned and walked away down the hall, deeper into the inn.

Ven watched until he could no longer see her, then looked around the inn once more. It was clear that at one time the place had been very grand, and could hold enough guests to be a small town all by itself. Whatever it was that Oliver had warned them about, whatever was wrong with the Crossroads Inn, had left it standing all but empty.

Music caught his ear again, and he looked over at the fireplace, where the man was still playing his strange instrument, singing softly to himself. Ven listened as the song came to an end. Then he thought he could hear soft applause coming from the corner near the hearth. The singer smiled and nodded, but didn't say anything.

"Who is he singing to?" Ven wondered aloud, looking closely but seeing nothing.

"The Spice Folk," a scratchy voice said behind him.

Ven turned quickly around, but there was no one there. No one new had come into the inn, and the two men whose heads Mrs. Snodgrass had bashed together were still in the bar, looking a little dazed, too far away to have spoken.

"Who is speaking to me?" he asked, feeling a little foolish but more curious.

There was no answer.

Ven turned around again and looked back at the singer. "Spice Folk?" he asked. "What are Spice Folk?"

He heard a rumbling sound, like a throat clearing.

"A kind of Meadow Folk—little spirits who tend to the spices and flowers of the fields. You know—fairies."

"Fairies?" Ven asked excitedly. "I thought they just existed in stories."

"They think the same thing about Nain," the voice said, sounding amused. "They will certainly be intrigued by you. I advise you to keep your room door securely locked."

"And may I ask who is speaking to me?" Ven said. "I don't want to be rude, so I'd like to look you in the eye and not have my back to you."

"Certainly," the scratchy voice answered. "Turn around again. You must have missed seeing me the last time you did."

Ven spun around quickly, but still saw no one there. "I would like to make your acquaintance. My name is Ven," he said, his eyes scanning the empty inn. "May I ask what yours is, sir?"

"You've already made my acquaintance," said the voice. "And my name is Murphy."

- 11 -

Hare Warren

I had never imagined that a cat might be able to talk.

But then again, I had never imagined that fairies might really exist, or merrows, or giant ship-eating sharks. I had never imagined that a Nain might summit a mast on the high seas, or walk on a Floating Island, or fight pirates.

I was quickly learning how limited my imagination had been up until now.

I DO BEG YOUR PARDON," VEN SAID, BOWING POLITELY TO THE CAT. "I didn't mean to overlook you."

Murphy seemed to shrug. "Not a problem. I'm used to it."

"So you used to sail with the captain?" Ven asked, feeling a little foolish.

"For ten years," the cat said. "Caught rats for him on three different ships. But those days are over. Now I stare at the guests until it bothers them, and sleep by the fire a lot. It's my job to catch any mice that come into the inn, but none ever do. Saeli has warned them about me, so they stay away."

"Who is Saeli?" Ven asked, sitting down in a chair in front of the cat.

"She lives in Mouse Lodge," said Murphy. "I suspect you will meet her sooner or later."

"What's Mouse Lodge?"

The cat rose slowly, then stretched. "That's more than enough questions," he said a little crossly. "Curiosity killed the cat, you know. I take that rather personally. Trudy told you I don't like to tell what I know that much. If you want answers, ask her. If you are looking for insights, ask McLean. He's the one who taught me to talk in the first place."

"Er—who is McLean?" Ven asked quickly as the cat ambled away.

Murphy stopped, looked back over his orange shoulder, and rolled his eyes. Then he strolled over to the hearth, curled up at the feet of the singer, and went to sleep.

Ven watched the cat for a moment, then slowly made his way to the hearth. The man Ven believed to be McLean was in between songs, twisting the wooden knobs on the neck of his strange instrument to tune it. Ven stopped at a polite distance.

"Good afternoon, Ven," the singer said, not looking at him but continuing to adjust the instrument.

Ven's eyes opened in shock. The man had addressed him in the language of the Nain, which he had rarely heard spoken outside of his own home before.

And he had called Ven by his name without being introduced yet.

"Erk," he said. It was the only sound he could make.

McLean looked up at him. His eyes, which were dark as night beneath dark brows and dark curly hair, sparkled with amusement. "I apologize if my pronunciation is bad," he said, still speaking Ven's language. "You are Nain, are you not?"

"Yes," Ven said, his surprise changing to delight. "But, if you will forgive me, you are clearly not. So how did you learn the language? And how do you know my name?"

"I'm a Singer by trade," McLean answered, strumming the strings softly and switching back to the common language. "That's with a capital 'S.' The actual title is Storysinger. I make it my business to know as many languages as possible, so I can sing most songs. And you told Mrs. Snodgrass your name. Once you speak your name, it's on the wind. Singers know how to listen to what the wind hears."

Then he went back to his work, plucking the strings of the odd instrument and singing a strange song very softly. Ven listened, spellbound. After a moment he realized the tune McLean was singing was one he had heard in childhood from his own grandmother, a song that told of a place in the mountain kingdom of the Nain on the continent of the Great Overward, where Vaarn was.

Where Ven's family was from.

It was the story of the Great Dial, an ancient clock of sorts that worked like a sundial, only lit by the shadows of the fires that burned in mines within the earth. The tale was about the history of the world, as measured by the Great Dial, and what sorts of things had happened at each of the hours.

The story was fascinating, but Ven was more entranced by the sound of McLean's voice.

I have been trying to think of the right words to describe the way he sang, but none of them will come into my head. It was a pleasing sound that he was making, but when he ended a song I realized I couldn't remember what his voice itself sounded like— whether it was high or low, rich or thin, sweet or harsh. It seemed, in fact, to be all of those things, as if all the sounds of the world were present in it at once. I felt I was listening to the universe singing in one man's voice.

"So you know a lot about the Nain, then," Ven said when the song was finished.

McLean was tuning his instrument again. He smiled.

"Not particularly," he said. "Just the songs I've learned, and some of the stories. Being of another race myself, I have a fondness for the non-humans of the world."

"You're of another race?" Ven asked in amazement. "You look human to me."

"My mother was human," McLean said, plucking one of the strings and listening for its pitch. "But my father was Lirin, and a Singer, so I learned the secrets of the trade from him."

Ven sat down in one of the comfortable chairs before the hearth. "What are the secrets?" he asked, scratching his head absently.

McLean chuckled, still not looking at him. "Perhaps you don't know the meaning of the word *secret*, Ven?"

Ven blushed. "Sorry," he said. "I didn't mean to be nosy."

"That's all right," McLean said, starting to play another tune. "I understand that secrets, by their nature, really want to be told. Everyone has a secret or two. Some secrets I tell, but most I keep."

"What makes you willing to tell one?"

"Whether or not by doing so I can help someone."

Ven grinned. "Well, that seems a good way to decide," he said. "Do you have a secret, McLean?"

The singer smiled. "Of course."

Ven leaned closer. "What is it?"

McLean chuckled again. "You'll just have to figure that out yourself, Ven."

"Murphy said I could ask you for insights," Ven said. "And that you taught him to talk."

"That's true," McLean acknowledged. "On both accounts. What insights do you want me to provide?"

Ven thought for a moment. There were so many things he wanted to ask, tumbling over each other in his mind, fighting to be the first. Finally a big one made it to the front of the line.

"Why do people think the inn is haunted?"

McLean strummed his instrument. "Because they don't know the truth."

"Ah. So the inn's not haunted? Good," said Ven, relieved.

"That's right, the inn's not haunted, Ven," said McLean. "It's the crossroads."

"Erk," was all Ven could manage to say. He waited until he could speak again. "The crossroads is haunted?"

McLean shrugged. "Perhaps not the right word. There is something wrong there. Since I am a Singer, I am able to only tell the truth, because the power of a story is in the truth of it. Lying, or being inaccurate, can take the power right out of a tale, and so Singers are sworn to always tell the truth. I don't know if what disturbs the crossroads is a haunting, so I will not call it such. But there is something wrong there.

"Now, the inn on the other hand, the inn is a wonderful place, a magical place. A safe place—as long as you are inside it. There are many more rooms than there appear to be, each of them with a unique magic or story behind it. It would be a fascinating place to explore, I would imagine. You might want to follow Clemency around sometime when she's cleaning and have a look at some of them."

"I haven't met Clemency yet," Ven said. "Or Saeli."

McLean smiled. "I'm sure you will meet both of them shortly," he said. "All the children from Hare Warren and Mouse Lodge generally eat together. And it's almost time for noon-meal."

At his words the sound of soft footfalls came down the hall, and Mrs. Snodgrass appeared.

There was something different about her that Ven noticed immediately, but could not put his finger on. She seemed healthier and younger, perhaps, her face fuller than it had been a few moments before, as if she had been a drying apple that was suddenly full of juice again. She had more vigor in her step, and all traces of gray in her red hair had vanished. She strode into the kitchen, calling for someone named Felitza.

McLean stopped fingering the instrument. He looked off toward the kitchen and broke into a grin. "Did you bring it?" he asked.

"What?" Ven said.

"The Living Water," McLean replied. "I didn't hear it come in—it must have been in a diamond bottle."

"I—er—"

The Singer waved a hand at him. "That's all right, Ven. You don't have to confirm it. I'm just glad to know the captain managed to find some more of it. She was getting pretty tired."

"Is Mrs. Snodgrass ill?" Ven asked worriedly.

"I don't discuss a person's health with another person without his or her permission," replied McLean. "But I'm sure you can see she is better after drinking the water."

"I was with the captain when he obtained it," said Ven.

The Storysinger looked up at him again for only the second time. "Where did you get it?" he asked. "The Floating Island?"

"Yes," Ven said, and he told McLean about all that had happened there. The Singer listened very carefully, as if he was memorizing what Ven said.

"Thank you for telling me the tale," he said quietly after Ven was done. He smiled. "That sly fox, Oliver Snodgrass! He certainly made good use of you, then, didn't he?"

"Yes, he put me to work on the ship. And I learned a lot there." He saw McLean's smile grow broader, but the Singer said nothing more. "Is that why Oliver spends his life on the sea?" Ven asked.

"Why he couldn't take even a day to come visit Mrs. Snodgrass, after being away for so long? He needs to keep finding that water for her, to make her better?"

McLean looked away again and returned to plucking a melody out on his instrument. The sound was harsh, and Ven realized a moment later that while they were talking, the music was keeping their words muffled so that no one else could hear what they were saying.

"Captain Snodgrass makes his living as a ship owner and sailor, it's true, but he is really searching for the places in the world like the Floating Island where he can find the Living Water for his wife, who needs it," he said. "You'll never find two people more in love than those two, even though they are almost always apart. And that's the truth—since that's all I am allowed to tell."

"Why doesn't she just go with him?" Ven asked, perplexed. "That way they could always be together."

"She has her reasons for staying here," McLean replied.

The kitchen door banged open, and Mrs. Snodgrass emerged, followed by Char at a cautious distance.

"So, do you boys want to go see Hare Warren now?" she asked briskly.

"What is Hare Warren?" Ven asked, stepping casually between Mrs. Snodgrass and Char to give him more distance.

"That's the building where the boys stay," Mrs. Snodgrass replied, untying her apron and hanging it on a peg near the kitchen door. "The girls live in Mouse Lodge. They're both out back of the inn."

"We saw them on the way in, I believe," Ven said. "The round and square buildings?"

"Yes. The round one is Mouse Lodge—rectangular's Hare Warren, where you both will be housed. I have only one room left—you'll have to share." The boys nodded.

"What's the rent for the room?" Ven asked, taking out his wallet. "And do you take scrip?"

Mrs. Snodgrass drew herself up. "I'm the wife of a sea captain. Of course I take scrip," she said severely. "But whatever Oliver paid you won't last long if you have to pay for your room and board. On top of that, you won't be able to get passage home."

"I hadn't thought of that," Ven admitted. "When the harbormaster releases my papers, and I work up the courage to go back, I can always work as a deckhand again on the way back, I suppose."

"Well, a better idea is that you hang on to your money and work for your keep here," said Mrs. Snodgrass. "That's what all my young tenants do. You help around the inn, and in return, you get your meals and stay in Mouse Lodge or Hare Warren for free. Does that seem reasonable to you?"

"That seems more than generous, thank you," said Ven. Char nodded.

"All right, then, follow me and I will show you the accommodations," said Mrs. Snodgrass.

She led them through the kitchen and out the back door to a stone pathway that led through the gardens and across the field behind the inn to the place where the two smaller buildings stood.

"What sort of work needs to be done, Mrs. Snodgrass?" Ven asked as they walked past flowering bushes and trees with lacy green leaves.

"All kinds," said Trudy. "What sort of work are you good at?"

"Char can cook," Ven said quickly.

"Oh, can he now?" Mrs. Snodgrass said, eyeing the cook's mate. "Wait till you taste what my Felitza can do. Perhaps he can help her; we'll see."

"Is—Felitza your—daughter?" Char stammered.

"No," said Mrs. Snodgrass. "I—I don't have any children of my own. Felitza is the kitchen girl."

Ven cast an eye around, noticing that the lawn was full of dandelions. "I can weed," he offered. "I could set to clearing out all these dandelions, if you'd like."

From over near the round building he heard a strangled gasp.

The little girl they had seen tending the flower beds when they first arrived turned around with a look of horror on her face. Ven could see she was of a different race as well. She was tiny, only coming up to just beneath his ribs, with a heart-shaped face, large green-gray eyes, and caramel-colored hair that hung in a long braid down her back. She looked like she was about to cry.

"It's all right, Saeli," Mrs. Snodgrass said quickly. "He just doesn't know. It will be all right." She turned to Ven with a look of displeasure. "You don't want to be messing with the Spice Folk's sun harvest, now, do you?"

All the blood left Ven's face. "Uh, no, ma'am, I most certainly do not."

"Have you ever noticed," said Trudy, "that one day a field will be green, and then the next day, it's completely covered with dandelions?"

"I live in a city," Ven said. "I only see dandelions rarely, and then one or two at a time, in between the cobblestones of the street."

"Ah. Well, trust me, out here, one day they appear like a gold blanket in the grass. And that's because the Meadow Folk gather the sunlight when the light is ripest—they alone know the day of the Harvest. Light is their source of power. Dandelions are what they use to collect that light. They use what's left of the last year's crop of light-power to grow the dandelions, which are almost colorless. Then they open them, like umbrellas, and the clear blossoms absorb the sunlight. That's why they appear so quickly, and so bright yellow. When the Folk are done collecting the power, the dandelion flowers lose their color, dry up and blow away. That's why you can wish on one before you blow on it—it's got a little magic left over from the Harvest."

"Oh," said Ven. "Well, then, I guess I shouldn't pull the dande-lions, then."

"No," said Mrs. Snodgrass. She walked up to the door of the rectangular building, which had neatly whitewashed walls and a thatched roof, and rapped sharply.

"Females are not allowed in Hare Warren, and males are not al-lowed in Mouse Lodge," she said. "One of the posted rules. Of course, this does not apply to the innkeeper."

A moment later a tall young man opened the door. He was hu-man, and thin, with a shock of dark hair and the very beginnings of a mustache. Ven guessed he was about fifteen years old.

Even a fifteen-year-old human can sprout a mustache, which is at least the beginnings of a beard. I found my hand going to my own chin, which was still as smooth as glass, and sighed.

"Vincent, I have two new charges for you," said Mrs. Snodgrass. "Ven Polypheme and Char, this is Vincent Cadwalder, the steward of Hare Warren. He's responsible for your obedience of the rules, so pay attention to him. He works at night as the watchman and stablekeeper, so he sleeps through breakfast. Try not to disturb him in the morning, if possible."

The older boy extended his hand.

"Polypheme," he said briskly. "Char. Welcome." He opened the door wider and beckoned for them to come in.

Inside the building was a tidy center corridor with a table and two chairs, a woven rug, and a small fireplace. Off the center hallway were five doors. A wooden sign was posted above the table.

HARE WARREN HOUSE RULES

Make your bed daily.
Keep your room clean.
Lock your door.
Do not touch anyone else's belongings.
Report all infractions to steward, even your own.
No females in Hare Warren.
No food in the rooms.
Likewise no spirits.
No teasing the cat or Spice Folk.
Mind your own business.
Behave like gentlemen.
NO EXCUSES!

"You'll take your meals in the inn itself—no food in Hare Warren, as you can see," said Mrs. Snodgrass, pointing to the list of rules. "Business at the inn has been off for a while, so the meals are not as plentiful or as fancy as they once were, but the food is healthy and filling. Breakfast is served whenever it's ready—usually shortly after sunrise. Noon-meal is served promptly at noon. Tea is available at quarter past four, and supper is served in the summer at seven o'clock. In winter, tea is the last meal of the day and is extended to a more generous portion, so that you can get back to Hare Warren immediately after the meal is over."

"Why?" Char asked nervously.

Mrs. Snodgrass looked at him seriously. "So you can get to bed before it gets dark."

Ven and Char exchanged a glance. The look on the innkeeper's face was as solemn as the one on her husband's had been when he warned Ven not to start for the crossroads at night. Ven's itch returned.

"Well, at least we'll be safe from the ghosts at the crossroads," said Char jokingly. "After all, no spirits are allowed in Hare Warren."

"Amusing," said Mrs. Snodgrass dryly. "Well, then, I will leave you with Vincent to get settled. See you at noon-meal—which is in precisely fifteen minutes."

She turned on her heel snappily and strode back to the inn.

"Glad to see she's feeling better," said Cadwalder. "All right, then, lads, this will be your room." He pointed to the first door on the left. "Next door is Jonathan Conroy and Lewis Craig, then the door to the privy closet outside. Please make sure that door's always closed, especially since my room is the one next door—I can get very cranky if I wake up smelling sewage. And finally, the last door is Albert Hio and Nicholas Cholby. The cleaning of the privy closet rotates from room to room by week, and aren't you lucky—this week the duty falls to your room."

"Great," muttered Char. "I miss the heads on the ship, where you can do your business, it disappears into the sea, and you never have to think about it again."

Cadwalder did not smile. "Well, things are very different here," he said. "If any of us had anywhere else to go, we would." He went to his room and returned a moment later with two keys. "Keep these safe at all times—I have a master key, but these are the only other copies. The room should be stocked with blankets and such. If you need anything, let me know."

"Thank you," said Ven and Char simultaneously.

"You're welcome," said Cadwalder. "See you at noon-meal."

The boys waited until Cadwalder had gone back into his room. Then Ven went over to the door and slid his key into the lock.

He turned the handle and opened the door.

The room was small and tidy, with a window near the ceiling and two beds on short wooden legs topped with mattresses stuffed with hay and a blue and white quilt. A washstand with a basin stood between them, and each bed had a small sea chest at the foot of it for personal belongings. Under each bed was a chamber pot for emergency use, should the weather be too cold or the night too dark for a run to the privy closet outside.

"Not bad," Ven said, looking around the little room.

Char was wide-eyed. "It's a bloody *palace*," he said.

*I remembered once again how spoiled I have been all my life.
I was thinking that it was somewhat smaller than the room I
shared at home with Brendan and Leighton, the two youngest
Polypheme brothers besides myself. Our room is crowded, or maybe
it just seems that way because both of them work in smelly parts
of the business. Brendan is the head of Pitch, the department
where bitumen, tar, and resin from trees is boiled down to make
the pitch, a thick, oily substance used to waterproof the ships.
The odor of Char's cooking sometimes reminds me of the hideous
smell from his enormous cauldrons. And Leighton works in Varnish.
So there is very little fresh air in a room when either or both of
my brothers are there.*

*Char, on the other hand, has no brothers to stink up his room.
He has no room. He doesn't even have a last name.*

I suddenly felt luckier than I ever had before.

"Which bed do you want?" Ven asked. "Left or right?"

Char considered for a moment. "The right," he said, walking into the room and tossing his duffel onto the bed. "Closer to the privy closet, at least technically."

Ven unbuttoned his pocket and untied the lanyard that had anchored the jack-rule to his shirt.

"It's nice to have a place where we can finally put our things and not have them slide or go over the side when the ship pitches," he said.

Char chuckled and nodded in agreement. "I lost a sock once into the drink," he said. "I'm not sure which is worse—having a single sock, or no socks at all. Well, now at least whatever we have will stay put—since touchin' other people's belongings is against the rules."

The boys unpacked their few belongings quickly. They were too busy laughing and joking and putting things away to notice the shadow that fell over the room from the window, then disappeared as quickly as it came.

- 12 -

The First Night

NOON-MEAL SMELLED WONDERFUL.

Ven opened the back door to the kitchen, and immediately his mouth began watering at the aroma that filled the air. It was working on Char, too. Both of their stomachs growled in unison.

They walked through the kitchen to the table, where a number of children, including Ida, had already gathered, awaiting their food.

Ven nodded politely to Saeli, the small girl he had seen in the garden. She turned red and looked away. So he sat down next to Cadwalder and another boy, a human with brown hair and light eyes who was stringy like Char but more muscular.

"Polypheme, meet Nicholas," Cadwalder said. "Nicholas is the inn's messenger. He's quite a runner, if you ever need to deliver something quickly."

Ven shook hands with Nicholas. "Pleased to meet you," Nicholas said.

"Likewise," said Ven, trying to close his ears to the sound of Ida belching.

He looked across the table, where Char had plopped himself down next to Saeli, and was talking to her. The small girl was listening silently and smiling as Char gabbed away.

The door opened again, and a short human girl, solidly built with skin the color of chocolate, came in. She wore robes like those Ven had seen in the churches of Vaarn, and an odd collar. Suddenly the inn was alive with the sound of soft whispering.

"What the heck?" Char asked, turning his head all around.

"Good afternoon, yes, yes, choir practice is on, will be right before supper," the girl was saying to the floor as she walked to the table. She pulled out the bench with a slight squeak and sat down next to Saeli, then blinked when she noticed Char and Ven. The girl extended a hand.

"Good afternoon," she said brightly. "My name is Clemency, but you can call me Clem if you want to. I'm the steward of Mouse Lodge. You must be Ven and Char."

Char banged his hand on the table as Ven shook Clemency's hand. "Everyone in this bloody place knows our names before we even tell them," he said crossly.

"Well, my congregation tells me *everything*," Clemency said knowingly.

"Who are your congregation?" asked Ven.

"And why do you have one?" asked Char.

"I have one because I am a curate-in-training," said Clemency proudly, sitting up a little straighter. "I am studying to be a helper to my pastor back home. Part of my missionary work is to go out and tend to a small congregation who needs services, blessings, healing, weddings, and the like. My congregation is the Spice Folk."

"Oh, great." Char groaned. "So the inn's fairies are your spies?"

Clemency looked displeased. "That's an unpleasant way to put it," she said. She picked up her spoon as the three girls who were working at the stove carried over a large pot of soup and baskets of rolls and began spooning the soup into the dishes and passing out the bread. "The Spice Folk lived in these fields long before the inn was even built, and that was hundreds of years ago. This is their place, and they are very interested in what happens here. They don't gossip—well, most of the time, anyway. They just like to keep me informed."

"I'll keep that in mind," muttered Char.

Clemency introduced them to the three girls serving lunch duty, Lucinda, Ciara, and Emma, and a fourth girl, Bridgette, who had long red hair in pigtails and freckles.

"Saeli, do you think you could ask the moles to stay out of our privy?" Bridgette asked the small girl next to Clemency. "They've dug a hole right behind the dunny so the wind blows right up your—well, you know what I mean." Saeli nodded and continued eating her soup.

"Saeli is a Gwadd, in case you didn't know that already," Clemency said. "Gwadd are an ancient race, like Lirin and Nain, and they are a little shy around bigger folk. Saeli can speak in words, though she doesn't generally like to. Instead she tends to use flowers to communicate. She can make them grow. And she can talk to mice and moles and other kinds of small animals."

"Very nice," said Ven. He wanted to hear more, but Clemency had returned to her lunch. He gestured to Saeli to encourage her to tell more, but she turned red and continued eating her soup hurriedly.

"We are going to have services later this evening, and I am going to go out to bless the cemetery in a little while," Clemency continued, carefully brushing the bread crumbs from the table in front of her into her hand. "You are welcome to attend if you want to."

"Thank you," said Ven, curious as to what a fairy church service might be like, and more—his ears had perked up at the word *cemetery*. "I believe I will."

"Yeah, maybe you can add Hen Polywog here to your congregation," said Ida snidely. Everyone at the table jumped; up until then she had been silent.

"Pipe down, Ida," Clemency said pleasantly, "or I will keep you up all night listening to me sing battle hymns again." The girl shuddered and went back to eating her bread and slurping her soup.

After lunch was over Char went to investigate the kitchen, and Ven accompanied Clemency out behind the inn to the fields.

The curate-in-training was a friendly girl and an easy talker. Ven asked her everything he could think of, and she chattered away during their walk, about the inn, the fairies, Mouse Lodge and Hare Warren, and all the strange happenings that had occurred since she began her missionary work a few months back.

"The wind blows wild here at night sometimes," she said, stepping carefully around patches of herbs and wild strawberries growing in the field grass. "It can howl pretty fiercely. But when the happenings occur, the howling sounds different."

"Different how?" Ven asked curiously.

Clemency thought for a moment. "Demonic," she said finally. "There's a harsh and evil sound to it. And sometimes you can see things—spirits that flit about in the darkness, ghosts of wolves or some other beast I've never seen before that hunt, seeking whatever they can find to tear to pieces. It's very frightening. I don't even look out the window anymore when it happens—I'm responsible for the girls in the Lodge, and so I spend my time comforting them and reassuring them that as long as they stay inside, they will be safe."

"Are you certain there is really anything there?" Ven asked. "At sea, the wind howls something fierce, and rattles the mast and makes the ship shudder. You sometimes think you're being eaten by a sea monster, it sounds so horrible. But it's just the wind."

He looked around, at the wide fields with forests in the distance, and the place where the two roads intersected. It seemed a perfectly harmless place, peaceful and pretty. And yet there was something underneath the peace, something darker and frightening, that he could not see or smell or even understand. All he knew was that it made his skin itch and his hands tremble at the same time.

Clemency stopped as they came to the crossroads.

"Listen to me, Ven," she said, her voice quiet and serious. "It is definitely *not* just the wind. Over the years, a lot of people have died here, or disappeared. The steward of your very own house, Hare Warren, lost his parents here."

"Cadwalder?" Ven asked. "Cadwalder's parents died at the crossroads?"

"Yes," said Clemency. "He was really little then, way too little to remember, but he was left orphaned when his parents were killed just traveling through here. No one knew who they were, or if he had any other family—he was just a baby, so he didn't even know his own name. Mrs. Snodgrass felt so badly for him that she took him in, gave him a place to live and a job, and has promised to let him stay until he is old enough to go out on his own in a few years. No one has ever found out what happened to his parents, or any of the others, even though there have been many investigations into their deaths."

"How horrible," Ven said. He had found Cadwalder pleasant but not particularly friendly. Maybe this explained why.

Clemency folded her hands in prayer, chanted a few words, and was silent for a moment, then started out into the roadway toward the cemetery.

"Come on," she urged. "The blessing only lasts for a little while."

"What does the blessing do?" Ven asked as they ran across the northern roadway into the green fields on the other side. He could see the cemetery, the same little one he had seen on the way in, in a small grove of trees not far from the edge of the road, ringed by a fence.

"Makes me feel safe, I guess," Clemency said. "Don't know what else it *can* do. I'm only a curate-*in-training*."

"That's good enough for me," Ven said, hurrying to keep up with her.

When they reached the burying ground, Clemency sighed sadly.

"Look at this," she said, pointing to a bunch of dry weeds at the base of one of the gravestones. "These were the most beautiful forget-me-nots. Saeli just made them come up this morning."

"What happened?" Ven wondered, crouching down and running his finger over the dry stems and withered leaves.

"I don't know, but it happens all the time now," Clemency said. "Saeli's ability to speak in flowers is affected by how much magic is present. At least that's my theory. Everything she causes to grow from the ground here looks lovely for a short time, then withers and dies before a whole day has gone by. Something seems to be taking all the goodwill out of the land around the inn. I told you, the Spice Folk have lived here a very long time, but even they are afraid of what's happening. We're especially worried about the Harvest this year. Even Mrs. Snodgrass seems to be getting sicker and sicker all the time. I don't know what is doing it, and why, but it must be something highly powerful. And highly evil."

Ven looked around the graveyard. It was a small family burying ground, only a handful of stones, neatly tended and tucked away in the little grove of trees for shade and privacy. The stone in front of which Saeli had planted the now-dry flowers read:

PRICE

He respectfully brushed some of the dirt from the carvings. It seemed to be a family stone for a husband and wife. He could make out the first names of the people listed:

STANISLAUS AND WINIFRED

"I wonder who these people were," he murmured. "Maybe if we knew their life story, we might find out if they are why the crossroads are haunted."

"Doubtful," said Clemency. "Those are Mrs. Snodgrass's parents. They were very nice old people; he was a toymaker. Her whole family is buried here. I don't think this is why it's haunted. It may be close to the crossroads, but it's not that close."

"Still, doesn't it make you feel, well, uncomfortable being here?" Ven asked. The small hairs on the back of his neck were standing on end, and his body was bathed in a cold prickly sweat.

"Not at all," said Clemency. "This is a restful place, a peaceful place. There is great love here. All the people who are buried in this cemetery had good lives, did good deeds, and were cherished all the while they were alive. They were born, they lived, they died—that's the cycle, as the Creator wills it. I find nothing but happy memories here." Her brow wrinkled for a moment. "Well, perhaps in all cases but one."

"Where's that?" Ven asked, his curiosity burning.

Clemency led him over to a slightly older stone, a white rectangle that had an urn of dead flowers in front of it.

"This one," she said. "Gregory Snodgrass."

"Is this Oliver's father?" Ven asked.

"No, it's Captain and Mrs. Snodgrass's son."

"They had a son?" Ven kneeled down and brushed the dirt from the face of this stone as well. He read the inscription.

The date of his death was eleven years before. He had been fourteen at the time of his death.

"Oh," said Ven. The sound came out of him without him meaning for it to, like a breath after being hit in the stomach. "Oh," he said again.

He thought back to what Oliver had said to him on the *Serelinda* about his own father.

Whatever loss he might suffer can't begin to compare to how much I'm sure he misses you. Trust me on this.

Now he understood why the captain was so sure.

He stood looking at the headstone for a long time while Clemency performed her blessing and pulled weeds. Finally when she was finished and ready to go back, he turned to her.

"Clem," he said, "how did he die?"

"I'm not certain exactly," said Clemency, "because Mrs. Snodgrass becomes quite sad if you mention it. From what McLean has told me, I think he was killed by brigands, bandits of some type."

Like pirates, Ven thought. "He was one of those people you mentioned who died at the crossroads?"

"I think so. But whatever is sucking the life out of the earth here was doing it long before Gregory died. Cadwalder's fifteen, so it's been going on at least that long. Mrs. Snodgrass comes here every day to take care of his grave, and leave him flowers in summer and spring. She sits and talks to him, I think; it makes her feel better." She pointed to a bare spot in the grass beside the grave.

"Well, thank you for bringing me here," Ven said as they headed back to the inn. "It's sad, but it helps me understand better why Mrs. Snodgrass doesn't go to sea with her husband. McLean said she had her reasons for staying. Now I know what one of them is, at least."

The Spice Folk were waiting impatiently for Clemency when the two of them returned. Ven couldn't see them, but he could hear a good deal of fluttering and whispering as soon as they walked in the door.

"All right, all right, calm yourselves, please," she said, bending over and speaking to the floor. "I will meet you in the chapel in a few moments. Get along, now."

Ven met up with Char over supper. He had spent the day exploring the storehouse and the kitchen pantry.

"I don't know how they do it," he said. "There's really not much on hand. If they get a whole crowd of people, I don't know what she'll serve 'em. We had better provisions on the ship, and you *know* that means there's nothing here."

"I don't think there much of a worry that the inn will be full anytime soon," Ven said. His mind was still burning from all he had learned, and his excitement started to build. "Maybe we can help, though. If we can solve the mystery of what's going on at the crossroads, maybe people will start coming here again, and Trudy will have a full house."

"Yeah, that's a good idea," Char said as they sat down to supper. "By the way, I tried to fly my kite today."

"Tried?" Ven said, sipping his hot cider. "Not enough wind?"

"Oh, there was plenty of wind to keep it aloft most of the time," Char said gloomily. "Until it got too close to the crossroads. The minute it did, the wind died down totally. And it plummeted like a bloody stone."

Ven finished his supper in silence.

THEY PASSED A PLEASANT EVENING IN FRONT OF THE FIRE, LISTENING to McLean sing and talking with the other children. Suddenly in the middle of a song, the Singer stopped the music and looked up.

"Good night," he said quietly.

Immediately the other residents of Hare Warren and Mouse Lodge rose, gathered their things, and headed for the back door.

"The sun is setting?" Ven asked. McLean nodded. "All right then. Good night, McLean."

They hurried quickly to the door, where they were joined by Trudy, who was holding a lantern.

"I'll walk you," she said, holding the door open for them. "It's your first night—I want to make certain you've settled in all right." Ven glanced anxiously out into the dark, searching for some sign of what might be haunting the crossroads, but saw nothing but the twisting shadows cast by the lantern.

The boys walked across the back field to the door of Hare Warren, where Cadwalder was standing, counting his charges.

"Good evening, Mrs. Snodgrass," he said as she came through the door.

"Good evening, Vincent. Is all as it should be?"

"Yes, ma'am."

"Very good." Mrs. Snodgrass waited while Char opened his room door with his key, then held out her fist to the boys.

"Here," she said. "Hold out your hands."

Ven and Char opened their palms, and Mrs. Snodgrass gave them both a tiny handful of very fine seed, tiny and soft as silk.

"What's this?" Ven asked.

"Flax seed," said Mrs. Snodgrass, walking over to the beds and plumping their pillows. "You want to scatter it on the floor tonight before you go to sleep to keep the Spice Folk busy. They are very neat beings, and they can't stand mess—so while they are busy tidying up, they won't be bothering you."

"Thank you," Ven said doubtfully.

"All right, then, boys, good night," said Mrs. Snodgrass. She handed them the lantern and closed the door behind her.

"Well, what do you think?" Ven asked, sitting down on his bed.

"I think I'd best visit the privy now, before night falls," said Char.

"Good idea. I'll wait till you get back and then go, too," Ven said. When Char returned he hurried into the privy closet and pulled back the curtain at the window. He couldn't see anything, so he carefully opened the latch and stuck his head out, spying all around for any sign of haunting, but he saw nothing but the warm lights of the inn, the distant lantern of the stable, heard nothing but the sound of crickets and the night wind. He shut the window quickly.

When he returned from the privy, he hesitated, then knocked on Cadwalder's door to say good night.

"He's at work," Nicholas said on his way into his own room.

"Oh, that's right," Ven said, remembering. "Good night."

"Don't count on it," Nicholas replied, closing the door behind him.

Ven went back into the room and found Char already in the bed on the right, snoring away. His handful of flax seed was scattered on the floor. Ven scattered his own on the rug between their beds, took off his trousers and put on his nightshirt, then put out the lantern.

The moon shone in the window, lighting the room in an eerie shade of blue. Ven crawled into bed, but could not sleep. Instead, he lay awake and listened to the wind as it began to pick up, gusting at first, then growing in intensity, until it was howling and rattling the shutters outside the windows.

It was loud, but it was nothing he hadn't heard before.

At least at first.

For a long time Ven drowsed, his head on the pillow beneath the high window, in a state of half-sleep, listening to the bumping and moaning of the wind.

Then in the distance he heard something different.

It seemed far away at first, a sharp note in an otherwise melodious symphony of the rising and falling voice of the wind. His body went numb for a moment, but then the moment passed, and he relaxed, waiting for the tiny prickles of heat to fade from his limbs. And they did.

Until he heard it again.

There was a different voice in the wind, a harsher, higher howl than he had ever heard before. He heard it once, then again.

It seemed to be coming closer.

And worse, it seemed to have been joined by more such voices, more harsh moaning, growing in intensity.

It sounded angry.

"Uh—Char?" Ven said. His voice came out in a thin squeak.

The sound of snoring answered him.

Ven cleared his throat and called again.

"Char?"

"Hmmm?" Char answered sleepily. "What's wrong?"

In answer, a new round of screaming howls rent the air.

Char shot out of his bed like an arrow on the string and leapt onto the end of Ven's.

"What—what's that?" he asked shakily.

"I don't know," Ven said, not moving. "But remember Megalodon? How you're not supposed to move or make any sound?"

"Oh. Yeah." Char slid slowly off of Ven's bed and back into his own.

They lay there, frozen with fear and the hope not to make any noise, as the sound grew closer.

"It's coming for us," Char whispered.

"Ssshhhh," said Ven softly.

The wind died down, and along with it the harsh noise. The boys lay still, listening intently to the silence. The occasional gust blew through, the shutters rattled lightly, but otherwise all was still.

Until suddenly there was a violent bang on the door of Hare Warren.

And the screech of splintering wood.

"Cripes!" Char gasped, too frightened to remember to remain silent.

Something was dragging what sounded like claws down the front door.

Ven sat up quickly and put his feet on the floor.

"There's a fireplace poker in the hall," he whispered. "I'm going to get it."

"Don't go out there," Char said in a strangled voice.

"You think we're safer in here?" Ven retorted, heading for the door.

"Yes! There's an extra door between it and us," said Char urgently.

"I'd say it's *them* and us, Char," said Ven. "And I'm not going to take this lying down. If I'm going to die, I'm going to die on my feet, and not cowering in bed." He fumbled on the bedside table and grabbed his jack-rule, extending the tiny blade with trembling hands.

Just then a low growl came from outside their window.

At first it sounded like the rumble of a wolf, but then, a moment later, as it moved, it began to whistle weirdly, then scream in a demonic wail. The unearthly sound of sniffing could be heard, hot breath clouding the glass pane high above the floor.

A shadow fell across the floor, blotting out the light of the moon.

Ven froze where he was.

The beast waited, too.

In the distance they could hear others coming, rooting around Hare Warren, their shadows crossing in the blackness of the room.

He heard a voice above it all, carried on the wind, soft and toneless.

Ven.

Every hair on Ven's head stood up. *How—how does it know my name?* he wondered, his sense of nervous excitement giving way to fear. He tried to remember what McLean had said about names on the wind, but his heartbeat was thrumming too loudly in his ears, drowning out all sensible thoughts.

Suddenly a scream of shrill, harsh voices built to a caterwauling wail, then faded into the distance, along with the panting breath.

Silence returned.

Ven remained frozen, motionless except for the tremors that were running through his body from head to toe. He waited for what seemed like an eternity in the silence, then let his breath out and whispered Char's name.

"Are you awake?" he asked.

"Nope," came the sarcastic reply. "I'm sleepin' like a baby. Why do you ask?"

Ven turned slowly to see his roommate hunched up in the bed, the covers pulled up to his nose.

"I think it's gone," Ven said.

"Good thing I went to the privy before bed," muttered Char.

Ven steeled his nerve and went to the window. The night was clear, with thin white clouds racing in front of the full moon.

In the distance, near the crossroads, he saw mist swirling, rising from the ground in the hot steam of the summer night. He opened the lens of his jack-rule and peered through it.

At first he thought he could make out the filmy shapes of white wolves running through that mist, but as soon as he had fixed his eye on them, they had turned into something else. He stared into the mist until he could no longer see anything in it.

Hanging low in the sky was the bright blue-white star he had seen on the deck of the *Serelinda*, the star Oliver had called Seren.

When it comes into view it means that it is only a short matter of time before we are home, the captain had said.

I had always thought of home not as a house, or even a place, but a feeling of safety and acceptance, a warm light when the rest of the world was a dark, forbidding place.

Whenever my family was around, wherever we were, I felt like I was home.

When my mother scolded me for being late, I knew she was worried because she loved me. And we both were relieved that I was home. Even when two of my brothers held me down while a third tickled me until snot came out my nose, I knew I was home.

You know you're home when your name is called out, sometimes in welcome, sometimes because you are in trouble, and it rings like a bell. Not spoken on the wind outside your window, hollow, with an unmistakable threat.

Home was where I was safe.

At that moment, I never felt farther away from home in my life.

~ 13 ~

The Next Day

THE FOLLOWING MORNING VEN SLEPT LATE. HIS DREAMS THE NIGHT before had been full of nightmares, and his body was exhausted from his long journey.

Char must have been having nightmares of his own, he thought sleepily, because instead of his normal snoring, he was moaning wordlessly on the other side of the room. He kept making strange sounds in his sleep, finally causing Ven to turn his back to him and pull the pillow over his head.

The pillow remained there until a violent, strangled sneeze erupted, loud enough to be heard even through the goose feathers against his ear.

Ven rolled over quickly and sat up.

Char was tied to his bed, several lengths of rope around his upper arms and middle, leaving only his head loose. His mouth had been stuffed with cloth, and his nose with glitter, judging by the sparkling spray of color that was floating down in the air all around his bed.

A soft chorus of tiny *ooooooooooo*s and *ahhhhhhhhhh*s could be heard, followed by a smattering of polite applause.

"Yikes!" Ven exclaimed. He leapt from the bed and dashed over to Char just as his roommate exploded again, sending puffs of glimmering red, blue, green, and gold skyward.

Char struggled in his bonds as Ven scrambled to untie him, making ugly sounds through the gag. Once his mouth was cleared, he spat angrily and blew his nose, causing a round of high-pitched disappointed sounds of *awwwwwwwwwww* from the floor of the room.

"That's it, the fairy fireworks are *over*," he snarled, his nose still glowing pink and purple.

Amid soft injured sniffing and irritated fluttering, the sparkles disappeared from the floor and blankets, and it was quiet in the room again.

"Can you *believe* those little blighters?" Char demanded. "They tied me down, gagged me, and stuffed my nose with glitter so they could have fireworks! The little pests. I thought the mess on the floor was supposed to keep 'em busy."

"I guess we'll need to ask for more flax seed tonight," Ven said, handing Char a handkerchief and trying not to laugh.

"Maybe we can borrow Murphy," said Char grumpily. "I'll bet those Spice Folk aren't so cheeky when he's around."

"Come on, let's go to breakfast," Ven said. "I want to find out if anyone else heard what happened last night."

"I think they hear it *every* night," muttered Char, struggling to get into his socks. "That's why Nick told you not to count on it when you wished 'im good night."

"Maybe," said Ven, pulling his shirt quickly over his head. "But I bet they've never heard *my* name outside their windows—and if they have, that's even *more* of a mystery."

The two of them dressed quickly, locked their room door, and hurried out into the bright morning sunshine.

There were scratches on the front door of Hare Warren, deep gouges that rent the dark wood and exposed a lighter layer beneath, like a wound. Both boys gulped.

They had gotten halfway down the path to the inn when Ven stopped in his tracks.

"Rats! I forgot my jack-rule," he said, smacking himself on the forehead. "It's under my pillow from last night. You go on, Char, and I'll meet up with you there." Char nodded, and Ven jogged back to Hare Warren.

He stepped into the common hall and waved to Nicholas, who had just emerged from his room, dressed and yawning, then slid his key into the lock and opened his door.

He reared back in surprise.

Ida was stretched out on his bed, filing her toenails with the knife in his jack-rule.

"What the heck are *you* doing in here?" he demanded angrily. "You know the rules. No girls in Hare Warren. In fact, you've just broken about every rule that's posted."

"Hey, Polywog, can I borrow your knife?" Ida said, ignoring what he said and continuing to prune her toes.

"NO! Get off my bed," Ven shouted, snatching the jack-rule out of her hands. He glared at her as she rose lazily and stretched, then ambled toward the door. "How did you get in here, anyway? The door was locked."

Ida just snickered and walked out of the room.

Ven waited until she had left Hare Warren, then crossed the common hall and rapped sharply on Cadwalder's door.

"Just a minute," came the muffled reply. A moment later the door opened, and Cadwalder appeared, his hair ruffled, in his nightshirt. The older boy blinked. "Polypheme. What's the matter?"

"Ida No was in my room," Ven said. "And I *do* know the door was locked when we left."

"What do you want me to do about it?" Cadwalder said, rubbing the sleep from his eyes.

"You're the steward," Ven said impatiently. "I thought you should know."

"I'll report it," Cadwalder said in a bored voice, and closed his door. A moment later Ven heard the sound of a hay mattress crunching as Cadwalder went back to bed.

Ven gave up and headed to the inn. The morning wind was fresh, and the grass sparkled with dew. The air was sweet with the smell of summer, and not too warm yet. He looked around at the green fields and distant trees and sighed, excitement, nervousness, and fear jumbling inside him.

When he was almost to the kitchen door he met up with Clemency and Saeli on their way into breakfast.

"Morning, Ven." The girls' steward saluted him cheerily. The small Gwadd girl beside her smiled shyly and nodded but didn't say anything.

Ven touched his cap politely, making the albatross feather dance merrily in the wind. "Good morning, Clemency. Saeli, how are you on this fine morning?"

Saeli blushed, looked away, and hurried into the kitchen, her long caramel-colored braid bobbing nervously behind her. Ven sighed, hoping he hadn't frightened her, then started into the inn himself when he noticed that he was standing in a patch of bright yellow buttercups that hadn't been there a moment before.

"She says 'very well, thank you,'" said Clemency, holding the door open for him.

"Clem, do you think you could keep your congregation out of our bedroom?" Ven asked as he sat down at the kitchen table.

"Or, failing that, you might want to prepare for dozens of tiny funerals," muttered Char. "Murphy's sleepin' on my bed tonight. It's open season on fairies in our room."

"The cat gets along fine with the Spice Folk," Clemency said, sitting down between Bridgette and Emma. "It's the mice that have to be worried around him."

Ven saw Ida at the far end of the table, picking her teeth, and looked away in disgust.

The children of Mouse Lodge and Hare Warren continued to

gather, greeting each other with varying degrees of enthusiasm. Ven questioned each of them about the events of the night before, but the children had grown so accustomed to the strange sounds at the crossroads that they all slept through the night without hearing anything, even Nicholas and Albert, who lived next door in Hare Warren. When his questioning seemed to be making them uncomfortable, Ven fell silent. Finally Mrs. Snodgrass appeared, carrying pitchers of milk and syrup, followed by Felitza, the scullery cook, a thin, plain girl with buck teeth and almost colorless hair who was carrying a plate of steaming pancakes.

Ven watched, amused, as Char stared at the kitchen girl, his eyes following her back to the stove once she had served the table and set the plate down. He nudged his roommate.

"Gah," Char murmured, entranced. "What a girl. Beautiful."

"Er—what specifically are you referring to?" Ven asked.

"Her timing on the stove," Char said, still smitten. "Look at the brown crust on those griddle cakes—not too dark, not too pale. What an artist."

Ven grinned and glanced around the inn. No guests had arisen yet, if there were any, but the fire on the hearth was going, chasing away the cold of morning. And McLean was there, in his usual spot, singing wordlessly. Felitza handed him a steaming mug in between songs, which he took with a smile. Murphy lounged in front of the fire, asleep.

This could feel like home if it had to, Ven thought. The strange happenings of the night before still bothered him, but he felt a certain comfort that they had survived without anything other than a scare, and all seemed normal now.

That normalcy was shattered a moment later. The front door opened abruptly and a man with a haughty face and piercing eyes strode in.

It was Mr. Whiting.

"Oh, great." Ven groaned, his appetite disappearing.

Mr. Whiting was followed by another man wearing eyeglasses, whose gray hair matched his clothing and the bag he carried. In his hand was a sheaf of papers.

"Constable Knapp," Mrs. Snodgrass said, glaring at Mr. Whiting. "What are you doing here on this fine morning, with this—*fine* gentleman?"

"I'm looking for one of your guests, Mrs. Snodgrass," the constable replied.

"Why? We've had no trouble," Mrs. Snodgrass protested.

Mr. Whiting tapped the constable on the shoulder, then pointed over to the table where Ven was sitting.

"The one on the end," he said.

Ven's heart lurched into his throat as the constable walked toward him. He turned around and looked nervously at Char as the man approached the table, and saw that his roommate was staring, glassy-eyed, as were the rest of his new friends. Murphy was now awake, his tail twitching, crouched on the hearth next to McLean, who had stopped his song in mid-note.

"Ven Polypheme?" the constable asked, looking at his papers.

"Yes," Ven replied, struggling to keep his voice from cracking.

The man looked up from behind his glasses, and his eyes met Ven's. He took a set of heavy iron chains out of his bag and held the thick cuffs up in front of him.

"You are under arrest," he said.

~ 14 ~

The Arrest

Mrs. snodgrass set down her heavy pitchers with a re-sounding *thump*.

"For what?" she demanded, striding over to the constable with an expression on her face that made Char slide quickly down the bench and out of the way.

"Thievery, to begin with," the constable said, unlocking the wrist irons on the chain he was holding. "Possibly more."

"I—I didn't steal anything," Ven protested, his stomach turning to ice. "I don't *have* anything, except a jack-rule, a seashell, and my scrip. These are the only clothes I own."

"What is he supposed to have stolen?" Mrs. Snodgrass asked, stepping between the constable and Ven.

"A ring," said Constable Knapp, looking uncomfortable. "A very valuable ring."

Mrs. Snodgrass turned to Mr. Whiting, who was smirking. "Oh, and let me guess—that ring belongs to you?"

"Well, as a matter of fact, it does," said Mr. Whiting smugly. "It's quite distinctive—pure polished copper, very heavy, with a picture of a white fern enameled in the center. It was made specially for me, of course, and was very expensive." His grin dissolved into a darker expression. "And that Nain brat stole it from me on the *Serelinda*, either when he was cleaning my cabin, or perhaps off my finger while I slept."

"What makes you think Ven would even know you had such a ring, let alone want it?" Mrs. Snodgrass asked.

"He saw it on my hand every day we were at sea. I noticed him staring at it, but I never thought he would actually steal it." Whiting's smile oozed over his lower face, and his eyes shone with cruel enjoyment. "Apparently I was wrong. He did."

"That's a lie!" Ven shouted angrily.

Whiting came closer to him, and the smell of soap and expensive cologne filled Ven's nostrils, making him ill.

"Careful, boy," Mr. Whiting said softly. "You are a child, even if you are Nain. A Nain child accusing a human man of lying? You could be thrown in jail forever if you are not careful. Or worse."

A screeching sound rattled everyone's ears, making them wince. They all looked over to see Ida, who had pushed her wooden chair back from the table, dragging the legs loudly over the stone floor, making a noise that sounded like giants grinding bones.

She stared rudely at the constable and Mr. Whiting, then ambled slowly over to the middle of the room. She stopped in front of Whiting and gazed at him, an insolent look on her face.

"Well, I'm a human child, so *I'll* say it instead—your story's a load of manure," she said. "Polywog is way too butterfingered to steal a ring off someone's hand without him noticing, and way too clumsy to sneak it out of someone's cabin without dropping it. You're lyin'."

Whiting's hand jerked back behind his ear, preparing to strike Ida across the face.

Ven lunged in front of her just as the man's hand came down, and in so doing caught the blow squarely across his jaw. The force of it made his head snap back, but even though his body rocked to one side, he remained standing. He thought woozily that Ida would have been thrown across the room by the slap.

Sometimes it's not a bad thing to be on the stout side.

"Mr. Whiting," the constable said, a warning tone in his voice.

"If we search his room, his belongings, I have no doubt we will find it," Mr. Whiting said. "Stand aside, Mrs. Snodgrass, and show us to his room."

"Who do you think you are, Maurice Whiting, ordering me about in my own establishment?" Mrs. Snodgrass demanded angrily, her face turning red as a tomato. "You'll not set foot in the rooms of my inn, thank you very much. And if you touch another one of my guests, I'll slap you myself." She motioned quickly to Murphy, who was poised to bite Mr. Whiting on the leg; the cat looked disgusted and slunk away.

"*I* need to search the room, to determine whether there is truth to these charges or not," the constable said regretfully. "I do apologize, Mrs. Snodgrass."

Trudy exhaled loudly.

She looked over her shoulder. Cadwalder had just come into the kitchen, looking sleepy.

"There's his steward," Mrs. Snodgrass said. "Vincent, go back and check Ven's room in Hare Warren. Search for a ring, and if you find one—which I'm sure you won't—bring it here."

Cadwalder rolled his eyes, then turned around and went back out the door.

"Felitza, get a wet cloth," Mrs. Snodgrass ordered. She took Ven by the shoulders and looked worriedly into his face. "You all right, Ven?"

He nodded, a little dizzy and the side of his face throbbing. Felitza hurried over with a dripping towel and Mrs. Snodgrass pressed it against his face, then turned to the constable once more.

"Evan, think on this for a moment, please," she said. "You used to be able to look into someone's heart and see if he was of good or ill intention. What do you see in this boy?" She pointed scornfully at Mr. Whiting. "And in that man? He uses ugly words, and Ven's race, against him."

The constable looked uncomfortable. "I don't know what I see, Trudy, except that it's my duty, as a warden of the king's law, to investigate any criminal charge that is filed with me. The king is a tolerant man, but he don't tolerate stealing, even by Nain. Their laws may be different where he comes from—"

"They're not different," Ven interrupted angrily. "Nain do not steal, either."

"Well, then, you must understand why I'm here," the constable said.

"Yes, I do," Ven replied. He looked over at the other children, who were staring, wide-eyed, at him and the adults. "It's all right," he said, trying to sound reassuring. "They'll be gone in a moment, as soon as Cadwalder gets back."

Just as the words left his lips, the kitchen door opened, and the Hare Warren steward came in. His face was pale and his mouth set in a tight line. He held out his hand.

In it was a heavy copper ring, enameled with the image of a white fern.

The whole inn, from the center hall to the hearth through the upstairs wings, was silent.

For a long, hollow moment, no one moved. Then Mrs. Snodgrass's eyes went from the ring in Cadwalder's hand to his face.

"Vincent," she said softly, "where did you get that?"

"Hare Warren, ma'am," Cadwalder answered flatly. "In Ven's room."

All the eyes in the room went immediately to Ven.

Constable Knapp opened the wrist irons again.

"Let's go," he said to Ven.

All the times I had ever been scared in my life suddenly disappeared from my memory. There is nothing in the world more terrifying than a constable opening a pair of heavy shackles in front of your wrists and expecting you to put yourself inside them.

I thought of my mother, and how much I had been missing her. Suddenly I was glad she was so far away, and couldn't see me like this, about to be arrested.

"Wait!" Char shouted as Constable Knapp locked the irons around Ven's wrists. He turned to Cadwalder. "Where did you find that ring in our room?"

"In one of the beds," the older boy said. "Under the mattress."

"Which one?" Char insisted. "Left or right?"

Cadwalder considered for a moment. "Left," he said.

"Ha!" crowed Char. "That's *my* bed. So I guess *I'm* the thief, not Ven. Even though you know it's all a bloody pack of lies."

"Very well," said Whiting smugly, "lock that one up, too, Constable."

Evan Knapp scratched his head. Then he sighed, reached into his bag, and took out another set of irons. He fitted them around Char's wrists and chained the two boys together.

"I'm going to let the judge sort this out," the constable said.

"Brave of you," said Mrs. Snodgrass contemptuously.

The constable opened a third set of irons. "You too, Ida," he said, nodding to the girl.

"What did I do?" Ida demanded.

"There's a line of folks in town waiting to tell me what they're missing this week," said the constable.

"She's been *here*," protested Clemency. "She only went to town for a short time on an errand yesterday—otherwise she's been in Mouse Lodge the whole time."

"She works fast," said Evan Knapp, locking the irons on Ida and chaining her to Ven and Char. "All right, let's be off, now. The judge is waiting."

"I'm going with you, Evan," Mrs. Snodgrass said, untying her apron.

"Sorry, Trudy," the constable said regretfully. "You can't see 'em until they come before the judge. You're not their mother."

"None of them have mothers, at least in this place," Mrs. Snodgrass said. "Let me go with you. They're only children, for goodness' sake."

"That one's older than you are, Mrs. Snodgrass," Mr. Whiting said, pointing to Ven. "He'll be made to stand trial as an adult. Adult thieves face a much more serious punishment than little pickpockets. You might want to write to his family and tell them the bad news—gently, of course—that they'll never see their son again outside of a prison cell."

"That's all for the judge to decide," said the constable, nodding toward the door. "Let's not get ahead of ourselves. There are a number of other charges pending as well, very serious ones."

"What other charges?" Ven asked shakily.

"Move along," said the constable, pointing to the door.

"I'll be right there, children, don't you worry," said Mrs. Snodgrass angrily. "By the time I'm finished with that judge, he'll need a new pair of ears, because I'm going to chew off the ones he has."

"What are you doing?" Ven whispered to Char as the constable opened the door and led them outside in the bright sunshine. "You got yourself locked up for nothing. You know there was no ring under that mattress. And you have the *right* bed, not the left."

Char shrugged. "The cap'n told me to watch out for you," he said, glaring at Ida as she trod upon his heel. "I can't very well do that if you are in the brig, and I'm in the inn."

"That was on the ship," Ven said. "I think you are released from that order now."

Char shook his head. "Cap'n didn't say that. So until I hear it from him, I'm followin' orders."

They stopped short as they reached the roadway, the men and Mrs. Snodgrass behind them. A large wagon with high wooden sides and bars on the window and a padlocked door stood, pulled by a team of four heavy black horses. A burly driver sat on the buckboard, a long whip in his hand. All three children swallowed hard.

Mr. Whiting stopped behind them. "The jail wagon," he said with dark humor in his voice. "I hear it can get hotter than fire inside that wooden box, with no water and little air. Sometimes prisoners don't make it all the way to the judge. That's just as well— they use the same wagon to take the bodies away from the gallows when they hang criminals."

"Stop it, Mr. Whiting," Evan Knapp said sharply. "His Majesty don't hang children. No need to scare 'em any more than they already are."

"Ah, but that one's a *Nain*," Mr. Whiting said, pointing to Ven. "He's fifty years old, I hear. That counts as being a man in Serendair. And who knows what other crimes he may be guilty of? I hear one fellow went over the side of the *Serelinda*, and was never found. That Nain probably pushed him. He may look like a child, but he's a man—an evil man. Mark my words—he'll swing for sure. Or lose his head."

"Well, at least that means there's *one* man here, then," said Mrs.

Snodgrass scornfully. "You certainly don't count as one, Whiting. And until this day I thought you were more of one, Evan Knapp, a good man who would never be deceived by the likes of this—this snake." She pointed at Mr. Whiting. "But if you think I'm going to allow you to bully my guests, Maurice Whiting, you had best think again."

"Guests?" Whiting said nastily. "You have guests? That's odd, Mrs. Snodgrass—from what I've heard, barely a soul comes here anymore. Most of your rooms stand empty. Folks have heard your place is cursed, and they want nothing to do with it—or you."

He climbed aboard a beautiful white horse that was hitched near the wagon.

Constable Knapp opened the doors of the jail wagon, and pulled down the ramp.

"Get in," he said.

The children looked at each other. Ven sighed, and climbed up the ramp into the musty, airless wagon, the other two following behind.

The door slammed shut behind them, taking most of the light with it.

Through the wood walls they heard a heavy metal *clunk* as the constable locked the door.

Then the wagon began to slowly roll down the bumpy road toward town.

~ 15 ~

The Reprieve

INSIDE THE JAIL WAGON IT WAS AS HOT AS A FURNACE, AND THE AL-most nonexistent air was musty and stale.

Ven slumped down in a corner, the chain between him and Char rattling on the planks of the floor.

"I'm sorry I got you into this, Char," he said gloomily.

"There ya go again," said Char crossly. "How many bloody times am I gonna to have to tell you? I make my own decisions. Stop it."

Ida yawned and reached up to scratch her ear. Both boys were pulled forward as the chain went up behind her head.

"Hey," Char said, annoyed. "What are you doing?" He gave the chain a sharp tug and settled back against the moving wall of the jail wagon.

Ida yanked the chain as hard as she could, causing both boys to lurch forward on their faces.

"All right, stop now," Ven said to Char as the cook's mate rose up on his knees, fury in his eyes, preparing to drag Ida across the floor on her nose. "This is a fight no one can win."

"And a very fine morning to you all," they heard Mr. Whiting say outside the wagon. It rolled to a stop in the road.

"Shhhhhh," said Ida, inching closer to the barred window.

Ven got to his knees and struggled over to the window.

In the road was an open carriage with two men and two women, finely dressed, heading the other way.

"Good morning," one of the men said. "What's going on here?"

Mr. Whiting sat up taller on his horse. "We've arrested a thief and a murderer," he said smugly. "A Nain. And we're bringing him to justice."

"A Nain?" one of the women gasped. "Horrors! I had no idea there were *Nain* around here."

"Calm down, Carolyn," said the man.

"Well, they do travel through from time to time," said Mr. Whiting. "Where are you folks headed?"

"The Crossroads Inn," the other man said. "We are heading east to Hope's Landing, on the Great River, and are in need of a place to rest."

Mr. Whiting leaned forward on his horse. "Oh, you don't want to go *there*," he said ominously. "That's where this unsavory lot was arrested just a few minutes ago. Besides, have you not heard the stories?"

"What stories?" the nervous woman asked, clutching her throat.

"Calm down, Carolyn," the first man said again.

"The place is haunted, cursed," said Mr. Whiting. "Howling spirits that walk the crossroads, searching for blood to drink and souls to steal. Many people who have gone to that inn have never returned. That's the problem with being so close to a crossroads. They used to bury criminals at crossroads, gypsies and murderers, and most especially those they thought might be vampires, who might rise from the grave at night and walk the world again. That way, if those monsters did reawaken, they would be confused, and not able to find their way back to town. Small wonder the place is cursed."

Ven, with his face wedged against the tiny barred window in the jail wagon, could see the woman's eyes pop open wide, then she fainted.

"Are there any other lodgings around here?" the first man asked nervously. "Far from the crossroads?"

"Well, by chance, yes, there are," said Mr. Whiting. "About a mile back you might have noticed an inn called the White Fern. It's a lovely place, and very safe. I'd be happy to show you where it is."

"That lowlife," Char muttered angrily, as the carriage turned around. "No wonder Mrs. Snodgrass has no guests."

"Well, there is some truth to what he says," Ven admitted sadly. "We saw it for ourselves—there's something wrong going on there. McLean said that it wasn't the inn that was haunted, it was the crossroads. And Captain Oliver was very specific that we weren't to go to the inn after the sun had begun to set, remember? So even if Whiting's a heel for stealing her business, he's not lying."

"Not about that," Char agreed. "But he's a liar nonetheless."

Mr. Whiting yanked on his horse's reins.

"I will be available to testify whenever you need me, Evan," he shouted up to the constable. Then he rode away, leading the carriage out of sight from the barred window.

The jail wagon lurched, then started to roll again.

Ven settled back down onto the floor, dispirited.

I had finally found something that made my curiosity go away—being arrested. All the excitement I had felt at the top of the Serelinda's mast was gone. The stories that Amariel had told me to keep me awake of the summer sea festivals and dragons of the deep unwound themselves from my mind and vanished. The desire to explore the Crossroads Inn, to see the Spice Folk, to listen to the talking cat, had disappeared. I had no interest to go adventuring anymore.

All I wanted to do now was go home.

Char leaned back against the black walls of the wagon and sighed.

"You must have ridden in here a lot, Ida," he said.

The girl shook her head. "Naw. This is the first time. Usually the constable just drags me by the ear or lets me ride in front of him on the horse. This is the first time I've been in enough trouble to get to ride in the jail wagon."

"Good for you," Char said sourly.

"Stow it," Ven said as Ida jerked the chain. "No point in fighting amongst ourselves."

The three of them sat in silence in the stuffy heat of the jail wagon. They banged into the walls and floorboards every time the wheels hit a bump in the road, leaving their bones rattled and sore. Char drifted off to sleep between bumps, tired from his night of terror and fairy fireworks, but Ven remained awake, wondering what the judge would decide to do with him.

After a while, they heard approaching hoofbeats, and felt a rumble on the road. The jail wagon rolled to a halt again.

"What's goin' on?" Char asked, half asleep.

Ven got to his knees and peered out the little barred window again.

"Soldiers," he said. "Six of them, on horseback, with a carriage of some sort."

"Prolly just want us to move out of the roadway for someone important," said Ida.

The wagon rocked from side to side as the constable climbed down. The children waited while Evan Knapp spoke with the soldiers, unable to hear anything. After a few moments, they heard a scraping of metal and the *thunk* of the lock opening.

The door of the jail wagon swung open with a creak, flooding the dark space with bright sunlight. All three children winced.

"Come over here," the constable said to Ven.

Ven crawled forward on his knees, pulling Char and Ida behind him.

"Hold out your hands," the constable said.

He unlocked Ven's irons, then took him by the shoulder and helped him climb out of the wagon.

"What's happening?" Ven asked nervously.

"You've been granted a reprieve—at least from your charges with me."

"What's a reprieve?"

"A temporary pass, a stay—but don't be too happy about it," said Evan Knapp. "Seems your paperwork has made its way through all the channels. The harbormaster sent it to the admiral in charge of the port of Kingston. The admiral sent it on to the Secretary of the Navy. The Secretary of the Navy sent it on to the king. And apparently the king wants to see you."

"*What?*"

"Yes, I suppose his charges are more serious than the ones Mr. Whiting filed with me. You will have to be judged by the royal court first."

"Can't I just go to jail in town with my friends?" Ven asked. "I mean, you arrested me first and all."

"Go on, get moving," the constable said, pointing to where the six soldiers waited on horseback in front of a plain black coach. Atop the coach sat a driver, who gestured impatiently.

Ven looked back into the wagon, where Char and Ida were staring at him, still chained together.

"What about them?" he asked anxiously.

The constable looked over to the head soldier, the captain of the guard.

"He has two friends who were arrested with him. He wants to bring them."

The soldier shook his head.

"Just him. This is a summons, not a social call."

"I'll have to go with him," the constable insisted. "He's under arrest, accused of thievery and possible murder. The king will need to decide the punishment for those charges, in addition to his own." The soldier nodded, and Evan Knapp turned back to Ven, who was staring at Char and Ida in a panic.

"Sorry, lad," the constable said regretfully. "They'll be all right, don't worry. It's you Whiting wants, and you who are in the most trouble." He pointed to the burly driver of the jail wagon. "Cedric will see to it that your friends are taken care of. Just try and save yourself if you can."

Ven nodded, then looked back into the wagon.

"I'll get you out, I promise," he said to Char.

"You shouldn't make promises you can't keep," Char replied uneasily.

"Ida, thank you for standing up for me back at the inn," Ven said as the constable started to close the door.

"Fat lot of good it did me, Polywog," the girl said as the doors slammed shut. The constable turned the key in the padlock and gave it to the driver.

"Into the coach," said the captain of the guard.

Ven hurried over to the coach and climbed aboard. Evan Knapp followed him in, then closed the door behind him. Ven watched sadly as the jail wagon pulled away.

The captain of the guard signaled the driver of the coach, and they started off east again.

Ven sat back against the seat cushion and stared out the window, rubbing his wrists to ease the soreness from the irons. His stomach was sinking by the moment.

What have I gotten myself into now? he wondered sickly. If Oliver's report had been too much for the harbormaster, the admiral, and the Secretary of the Navy, the depth of trouble he was in was very great. He thought of the explosion and the destruction of the two ships for which he was responsible. *Maybe the king is going to try me for multiple murder,* he thought, his stomach cramping violently.

He watched sadly as they passed the Crossroads Inn, where the flowers that Saeli had caused to grow the day before had already shriveled, along with many of the dandelions. *What is withering the inn and its people?* he wondered.

Perhaps the place really *was* cursed.

The constable settled comfortably against the cushions and fell immediately into a deep sleep, snoring in time to the quiet hum of the carriage wheels.

After a while Ven dozed off too, still tired from the night before. He woke with a start when the smooth-rolling carriage began to rumble loudly.

He looked out the window.

The carriage was crossing a bridge, the largest he had ever seen, over a river wider than he could have imagined.

"The Great River," the constable said, yawning. "It flows north to south and divides Serendair into two parts, Westland and the lands beyond to the east. All north of here are great mill towns, where the harvest of grain is brought to be ground into flour and meal. Lots of excitement in those towns, you might want to visit them someday—er, if you ever get out of prison, that is."

Ven said nothing. The constable cleared his throat, then settled back into sleep.

Ven continued to watch out the window for a while, but finally the unbroken landscape of wild green fields reaching to the horizon lulled him to sleep as well.

He woke to the sound of trumpets. The coach was being greeted by the barracks of soldiers that stood guard at the base of the battlements leading up to the castle Elysian, where the king of Serendair lived.

～ 16 ～

The Castle

THE CASTLE ELYSIAN WAS PERCHED ATOP A TALL, ROCKY CLIFF AT THE northern edge of the island. More steps than Ven could count were carved into the crags, zigging, zagging, and winding all the way up to the gleaming white palace at the top.

At the bottom of the rocky cliff, and growing up its face, stood an immense forest of trees, all taller than he had ever seen. They seemed different from normal trees as well, as if they had been carved from stone, except that they were green and purple and blue and brown, and hummed sort of like the Living Water.

Jutting from the front of the cliff was a giant irregular rock formation that seemed to be naturally formed in the shape of a man's face, craggy and bearded.

"What's that?" he asked the constable, who was just waking up.

"Hmmm? What? Oh, that's the Guardian of the Mountain," Evan Knapp said. "It's been there ever since the castle was built. The current king, His Sovereign Majesty, King Vandemere, decided he didn't want to live in the castle his forefathers had always ruled from, because it was far away from the people and the places where most things were happening, so he built this one—Elysian's brand new, and is still unfinished. The day the king moved in, people noticed that formation in the rocks they had never seen

before. Some say it emerged when the king arrived, and stands watch for him."

Ven felt his curiosity stir deep within him, then flood back through his entire body again, leaving his head and scalp itching like wildfire.

The coach rolled to a halt behind the soldiers at the outpost. The guard changed, and a new group of soldiers marched over to the coach. Their captain opened the door.

"Charles Magnus Ven Polypheme?" he asked briskly.

"Yes, this is him," the constable replied.

"Come."

Ven was led to the base of the cliff, and up more stairs than he could count, past the huge rocky outcropping that formed the face of the Guardian of the Mountain. He had to stop several times to catch his breath, not just from the climb, but also for the view.

Once they were almost to the top of the crag he could see the sea again to the south, rolling in great white waves to the shore. To the north was the darkly beautiful forest of stone trees, stretching up the cliff face. Behind him, the green fields and forests spread out to the ends of the world, it seemed. He felt a little like he did atop the mast of the *Serelinda*, the world again at his feet.

I may as well take a good look now, Ven thought wistfully. *Who knows if I will ever get to see the open world again?* For all he knew, he might be living the rest of his life in the dungeon of this beautiful white castle.

He and the constable were led through checkpoints and guard stations, past splendid gardens blossoming in the summer heat. Finally his escort of soldiers came to a door in the side of the castle, and he was handed over to the guards who were waiting there for him. He followed them to a massive stairway that had flights going both up and down. Bright light was shining through the windows above the upper flight, but down the lower flight Ven saw the light give way to darkness beyond.

One guard waited as the other started down the stairs. He gestured to Ven to go ahead of him. Ven looked at the constable, whose face wore a very grim expression.

"You're putting him directly into the dungeon?" Evan Knapp asked.

The guard nodded curtly and pointed down the dark staircase into the gloom.

Gray beads of sweat popped out on Ven's forehead.

"Please, I didn't steal the ring," he said, his voice faltering.

The constable looked at him with what seemed to be sympathy. "Now, now, buck up, lad," he said, taking Ven by the shoulder and starting down the stairs with him. "I thought you Nain liked it underground."

"I've never been underground in my life," Ven replied, trying to keep his heart from flying out of his throat. The second guard took his position behind, following them down the stone staircase.

"Well, we all end up there eventually," said the constable, trying to sound cheerful. "Mind the step—you don't want to fall, now."

The sound of dripping water could be heard as they descended. The guards stopped at the bottom, where a dim lantern was burning. The first guard picked it up and led the group down a dark passage that smelled of mold and misery, until they came to a large archway.

Beyond the archway was another stone stairway and a series of cage-like cells, each the size of Ven's room in Hare Warren, with a cot, a chair, and a small desk on which a washbasin sat. He saw a chamber pot under the cot.

I actually felt a little better at the sight of the cell. I know that sounds strange, but what I had been expecting was worse. And from what I could see, there were no rats. I had grown accustomed to them on the Serelinda, but the thought of sharing a dungeon cell with them made me start sweating. At least there was a chamberpot. It was pretty grim, but it could have been worse. And I'm not just saying that to make points with the king, knowing he is reading this.

A glowing light approached. A short man with a wiry beard came out the darkness, clanking as he did. A massive ring of keys hung from his belt. Without looking at Ven or the constable he went to the bars of the cell, slid a long brass key into the lock, then pulled on the barred gate. The door screeched as it swung open.

"In ya go," the jailer said. Ven swallowed hard, then walked into the cell, trying not to shake.

The jailer slammed the gate shut. The noise made Ven's teeth rattle and his throat feel like it was closing up.

"Are you certain His Majesty wants to imprison a young boy in the dungeon?" the constable asked, looking around in the smelly gloom. "These dungeons are usually only for the worst type of criminals."

"His Majesty is away at present," said the first guard, checking the gate after the jailer locked it. "The order of imprisonment was signed by Galliard in his stead. The charges against him are serious enough. If they are true, he *is* one of the worst type of criminals." He turned to the jailer, who was eyeing Ven suspiciously. "Galliard has ordered that he is to be given ink and parchment, and light to write by. He may make his plea in writing, and it will be reviewed by the king when he returns, before sentencing."

The constable sighed.

"Who—who is Galliard?" Ven asked Evan Knapp nervously.

"The king's Royal Vizier—or one of 'em, at least." The constable took hold of the bars and leaned as close as he could to Ven. "Now listen, lad; don't panic. Just write down your story, and tell the whole truth. The king will know if you are lying; he is said to have a way with that, and it makes him very angry. I will come back for your trial and tell him what I know of your case—though I can't really say that will help you much." He smiled awkwardly, then followed the guards back into the blackness, leaving Ven alone with the jailer.

The bristly man continued to stare at him for a while, then walked away. A few moments later he returned with a stack of paper, an inkpot, and a feather sharpened into a quill pen for writing. He pushed it through a small grate at the bottom of the bars and motioned toward it.

"Mayhap ya want ta use yer own quill," he said, pointing at the long feather in Ven's hat.

Ven squatted down to pick up the writing supplies. "Uh, I don't think so, thanks," he muttered. "It hasn't exactly brought me the best of luck so far."

The jailer shrugged. He set a lantern outside the cell for light and hurried back up the stone stairs.

At that moment all I could think was how much I wish I had gone down with the rest of the crew of the Angelia.

~ 17 ~

A Friend in the Dark

Ιτ took a long time for the echoes of the jailer's bootsteps to die away.

When at last they did, the first thing Ven noticed was how loud the sound of silence could be.

Then all he could hear was the distant sound of water dripping.

Except for him, the dungeon was empty.

The fierce itch of curiosity that had lived below the surface of his skin all his life gave way to a sickening tingle of numbness. Ven's eyes, however, adjusted quickly to the dim light. He realized after a moment that it was because of his Nain heritage. Even if he had never been below ground for more than a few moments in his life, his ancestors had lived for thousands of years in caves and mountain tunnels and underground cities far darker than this jail cell. The thought brought him little comfort.

In the back of his mind he remembered Amariel's voice, sensible and calm above the splashing of the waves in his memory.

There are places that are truly dark in the world, Ven, but this place here is not one of them. It's not really dark here—it's just night.

The lantern the jailer had hung outside his cell gleamed a little brighter in the gloom.

Ven glanced at the table, then at the quill, ink, and parchment in his hands. The voice in the back of his mind changed from Amariel's to his father's, speaking the words he had heard almost every day of his life.

Ours is a working family. Get to work, Ven!

He sat down at the table, staring at the blank paper for a long time. Then finally he began to write.

He continued to do so, stopping only when he was so tired that he could no longer keep his eyes open, or when the lantern burned out and the cell was plunged into total darkness. Whenever the light vanished, the thoughts of his home and family took over his mind, leaving him as lonely and homesick as he had been on the floating wreckage of the *Angelia*. Eventually the jailer would return with a burning wick and relight the lantern, watching him suspiciously the whole time. As soon as the light returned, Ven went back to work.

Most of the time he was undisturbed. The jailer stayed upstairs, coming only to deliver food or more ink and paper. The spiky-bearded man shoved the quills, inkpots, and parchment scrolls through the same opening in the bars through which food was passed, then disappeared again, usually without saying a word.

If the custom in the palace was that prisoners were fed twice a day, I was there for three days. I think.

It's very hard to tell how many days have gone by when you are underground, without windows or daylight, with nothing to mark the passing time but the appearance of a jailer, whose name you do not know, who shoves a tin tray of food through a grate in the cell door and vanishes again.

For all I know, it might have been thirty days.

It felt like three hundred.

After a long and very draining session of writing describing the battle with the Fire Pirates, Ven heard footsteps approaching. He kept working, waiting for the familiar sound of the floor grate opening behind him, but the footsteps stopped outside his cell, followed by silence.

Ven looked over his shoulder.

A figure in a long gray cape stood outside the barred gate, its head cloaked in a hood.

Ven put down his quill and rose from the chair, rubbing his tired eyes. He walked nervously over to the gate and stared up into the hood, but could make out only the shadow of a face. He waited for the person to speak, but the cloaked man just stood, watching him, in the flickering lanternlight.

"Who—who are you?" he asked finally, his voice cracking. "What do you want?"

"A friend," came the whispered reply. "And I want to help you."

"How?" Ven blurted. His heart began to beat thunderously in his chest.

"I can get you out of here," the man answered softly, his words masked by the sound of dripping water. "I can take you back to your home—your real home."

"How?" Ven asked again, his face flushing.

The man in the hooded cloak stood silently for a moment. He glanced over his shoulder toward the staircase, then turned back to Ven and leaned closer to the bars of his cell.

"Do you want to go home, Ven?" he asked, his voice low and scratchy.

"More than anything," Ven replied.

The hooded man nodded. "I can arrange that. I can get you out of here right now. Get your things."

Quickly Ven checked his pocket for the jack-rule, then ran to the cot and pulled his hat out from underneath it. He ran his fingers over the albatross feather, wondering if it had brought him this newest round of good luck. Ven smoothed his rumpled hair and pulled his hat onto his head.

"Thank you," he said gratefully to the hooded man. The man nodded, then walked over to the staircase and shouted up to the jailer.

"Guard!"

The word rang against Ven's eardrums, and the voice, no longer soft, now sounded unpleasantly familiar. "Wait," he demanded. "Who are you?"

The man in the hooded cloak walked back to the cell.

"I told you," he said. "A friend." With that, he reached up and pulled down his hood.

It was Maurice Whiting.

Ven jumped away from the bars, sputtering in surprise. Mr. Whiting reached toward him, a look of concern on his face.

"Be calm, now, my boy," he said quickly. "You don't understand."

"I understand that you are no friend of mine," Ven said. "Go away and leave me alone."

"Hear me out," Whiting urged. "You will change your mind when you hear what I have to say."

"I doubt it."

"I'm sorry you had to suffer the hardships that brought you here," Mr. Whiting said. His eyes grew bright in the light of the lantern. "You are in this place because it was the only way I could save you from the terrible danger you were in—and will still be in if you don't leave this island and get back to your home as soon as possible."

Ven continued to back away, eyeing Mr. Whiting distrustfully.

The man inhaled deeply, then exhaled and let his hand come to rest on one of the iron bars.

"I know you think that I am your enemy, but that was all for show," Mr. Whiting said, his voice dropping to just above a whisper again. "I had to get you into the custody of the king, and make certain that people at the inn and in town knew you were there, so that you would be safe from the enemies who are really after you."

"Who—who are those enemies?" Ven asked suspiciously. "Someone worse than *you*, who lies about me, insults me for being Nain, and has me arrested and thrown in a dungeon for something I didn't do?"

Mr. Whiting's other hand came to rest on the bars of the cell. He stared thoughtfully at Ven for a moment.

"Sometimes things are not as they appear, Ven," he said, his voice soft. "Sometimes the people who seem to be your enemies are trying to help you, and those who seem the most friendly are using you for purposes of evil. Great evil." Ven eyed him stonily but said nothing. Whiting leaned a little closer, so that his hawklike nose was protruding through the cell bars.

"You were attacked by Fire Pirates, were you not?" he continued. "So you know that they are among the most vicious killers roaming the world, but what you may not know is that they need people to help them, to buy the chemicals to make their terrible fire, to sell the spoils of their conquests, to keep them supplied—they need support. Do you know where they get that support?" When Ven did not answer, Whiting's eyes grew even more bright. "They get it from legitimate ship owners and sea captains. People in the sea trade. Seemingly honest men—like the good Captain Snodgrass."

Ven's mouth dropped open in shock. "That's a lie!" he shouted. His words echoed off the underground chamber, punctuated by the sound of dripping water.

"I wish it were so, boy. I know you want to believe it, because the captain seems a kind man, a good man—but as I told you before, not everything is as it seems. How do you suppose he found *you*, hmmmm? What is the possibility that a ship will sight a single young boy in all the vastness of the sea? How did it happen that the *Serelinda* was passing through when you happened to need it to be?"

Ven's eyes narrowed. "It just was. They saw the albatross."

Maurice Whiting sniffed. "Oliver Snodgrass was there to see the albatross because shortly before that, he was *meeting* with the Fire Pirates, delivering the catapults they used in their attack. The ships came abreast of each other in the dark the night before; I watched myself as goods were unloaded from the *Serelinda* into the longboats and rowed over to the pirate ship in the darkness."

"I don't believe you," Ven said.

Whiting smiled sadly. "I know you don't, but you must, my boy. The people who seem to be your friends, who smile at you and make you feel at home in a place you don't belong, are using you in ways you could not imagine, unholy ways that would make you fear for your life, and your soul, if you had any idea of them."

In the back of his mind, Ven suddenly remembered something McLean had said to him on his first night in the inn.

That sly fox, Oliver Snodgrass! He certainly made good use of you, then, didn't he?

"Using me how?" he asked Mr. Whiting uncertainly.

Whiting looked over his shoulder at the sound of the jailer's footsteps as he approached. He waved dismissively at the man, who glared at him in annoyance at being summoned for nothing, then turned away and headed up the stairs again. Mr. Whiting waited until the sounds of the footsteps died away, then turned back to Ven.

"Do you know the stories of how the Floating Island was made? The wind blowing back the sea to reveal the earth for the first time?" Ven nodded grudgingly. "Well, what do you suppose comes to pass when something so rare and improbable as what you did aboard the *Serelinda*—what the captain *had you do*—happens?" He smiled. "Think about it, lad—you're a Nain. For all that some humans consider people like you to be freaks, the truth is that you are of an ancient race, a race that still has a lot of old magic in it. You are a creature of the earth, like the rest of your race. Nain are never found on the sea, are they? Nain don't swim; they're afraid of the water, never travel on the sea. But there you were. And what did the captain do, upon pulling a Nain from the sea? Almost as soon as you could stand upright, he made you *climb the mast*. Why?"

"To—to help me get over the sea-shakes," Ven stammered.

"Nonsense," said Whiting. "A Nain, a creature of earth, traveling on the sea, at the top of a mast in the wind? Don't deceive your-self, lad. By sending you up that mast, he was re-creating the birth of the Floating Island—earth, wind, and water. He was *calling the is-land.*" His eyes narrowed, and his voice dropped to just above a whisper again.

"And a few days later, it came. Didn't it?"

Slowly Ven sat down on his cot.

That sly fox, Oliver Snodgrass! He certainly made good use of you, then, didn't he?

Ven thought back to standing atop the mast with Oliver, watch-ing a light streak across the sky, then hitting the deck to the cheers of the crew.

I'd like to propose a toast, the captain had said. *To Ven Polypheme, who this day has been pulled from the sea, gained his sea legs, and is the first Nain in my knowledge ever to climb the mainmast of a sailing ship at sea, and without question the first to summit the mast of the* Serelinda.

Whiting was watching him closely.

"It's easy to trust people who seem kind, isn't it?" he said softly. "And to distrust those who seem cruel or harsh, like me. But one thing you learn as you grow up, Ven, is that many things are not as they seem." He let go of the bars of the cell and began to pace slowly back and forth in front of the gate. "Oliver Snodgrass pulled you from the sea, saved your life, made you feel welcome, when you probably have never felt welcome outside your own family before. He gave you a job and treated you as if you were an adult. That must have been a heady feeling. How could you have known you were being used in an unholy purpose?"

"How—how is it unholy?" Ven asked nervously. "So what if he used me to call the Floating Island? Nothing evil or bad was done there."

The sad smile returned to Whiting's face.

"You think not?" he said, continuing to walk back and forth in front of the cell. "Did you take anything from there?" His smile grew wider as Ven's eyes did. "No need to deny it—there is only one purpose for going to the Floating Island, and that's to obtain some of the Living Water."

Ven could feel the rough stone of the dungeon wall scraping his back through his shirt as he inched farther away.

"No," he said, trying to keep his voice from shaking. "That soldier, Marius, went to put his name on the wind, nothing more."

Whiting's smile faded and he rolled his eyes.

"That fool," he said, contempt in his tone. "That is like being a starving man who finds a great feast spread out by the banks of a rushing stream, stops to take a sip from the stream, and then crawls on, leaving the food untouched. The Living Water is the most precious substance in this world. It has powers that you cannot imagine. It is more valuable than diamonds, than gold, than any treasure you can name." He stopped, and looked sharply at Ven. "And you, my boy, *you* have the natural ability to find it. The Floating Island is not the only source of the Living Water, but the others are said to be even harder to find, and almost impossible to reach. How simple it was, really, to have you climb up into the wind on the high seas, duplicating that same combination of earth, water, and wind that the island is made from, and, by doing so, summon the Floating Island itself. And you can do it anytime you want."

Ven's head was spinning. The walls of the tiny cell seemed to close in, making it harder to breathe.

"Nothing evil was done with the water," he repeated, his voice wobbling.

Mr. Whiting stopped suddenly. "You think not? You are wrong. Snodgrass gave it, no doubt, to that harpy wife of his." His voice turned cold. "Didn't he?"

"She—she needed it," Ven said, hating how shrill and squeaky his voice sounded.

Whiting's face hardened.

"Well, that's true, boy," he said, "but I don't know if you want to be the one giving it to her."

"Why?"

Mr. Whiting looked above him into the dripping darkness, and when his eyes returned to Ven, they were shining with what seemed like fear.

"Because Trudy Snodgrass is a Revenant," he whispered.

‑ 18 ‑

Upon Closer Examination

WHAT IS A REVENANT?" VEN ASKED NERVOUSLY.

The endless dripping seemed to stop, the light in the lantern to dim, as Maurice Whiting considered his words.

"A Revenant is a person or thing that has died, but who lives on in an unnatural and unholy way after death," he said. "Something that returns from the grave—usually because there is something in their lives that remained unfinished when they died. They are called by many names the world over, but in the end it comes down to the thwarting of nature so that someone who should be gone remains on the earth. It is evil, and unholy—and what they do to remain in this state of undeath is even more so."

Ven was trembling as violently as the sails of the *Serelinda* in the wind.

"You're lying," he said.

"No, lad, I'm not," Mr. Whiting said darkly. "Did you have the chance to observe the woman before you gave her the water, and then after? Did you notice a difference?"

Beneath Ven's feet the floor of the dungeon began to shake. A heartbeat later, he realized it was not the floor, but his own body that was shaking.

He remembered thinking how Mrs. Snodgrass had improved

once he had given her the diamond vial, how her face had filled out in places that before had seemed withered, how her energy had returned.

Like a drying apple suddenly full of juice again, he thought.

"You did, lad, I know you did," Whiting said softly. "You saw the life actually return to her, because the life within that woman is *artificial*. She actually died long ago, when her son did, but her husband was not willing to lose them both. He had enough of the Living Water with him to save her—but their boy was too far gone to be brought back. They buried their child, but Trudy remains, ruling that tawdry inn with an iron fist by day." His voice dropped. "Walking the crossroads by night—with the other undead buried there. She haunts the crossroads because she can't find her way away from it—just like the other Revenants."

"Stop it," Ven whispered. "Stop it."

"She sends you to bed as the sun goes down—doesn't she?"

"Stop, please, stop." Ven clapped his hands over his ears.

Whiting shook his head. "The captain warned you not to go there at night, didn't he?"

You do not want to go to the Crossroads Inn at night. Do you understand what I am saying? Don't start out on the road after the sun begins to go down.

Ven turned his back and leaned his head against the damp dungeon wall behind his bed.

"Leave me alone," he said weakly.

Behind him he heard a sympathetic sigh.

"I know this is distressing, lad, but you must be strong and hold to your courage. The Snodgrasses have been kind to you, but for an evil purpose; they want you to live in their shoddy inn where they can keep you at the ready to call the Floating Island whenever Trudy's unnatural health begins to fail. Doubtless you would have been happy to do so until the day when the first of your friends disappeared, the victim of that Revenant's evil hunger. That's what happens to the travelers who stay at the Crossroads Inn. Sooner or later they become food for the Revenants. Or they become Revenants themselves—which is why they cannot leave, like that Singer who is always on the hearth. The sailors on his ship all know this—why do you think they are all so afraid of her?

"Fortunately for you, I was traveling on the *Serelinda* with you; I can save you from this path of death, and undeath that you are unwittingly on. I will get you out of here today—though it's dark in here, it's only noon now. I alone have the power to drop the charges and have you released. We will hide at the White Fern Inn until night falls. Under cover of darkness we will hurry to Kingston Harbor and set sail away from this place." Mr. Whiting inhaled deeply. "And I will take you home."

Home. The word rang in Ven's ears above the dripping water and the harsh tones of Whiting's voice. In his mind he was suddenly back on the wharf in Vaarn, trailing along behind his father, watching his brothers and sister in the course of their work building ships, hurrying home to his mother in order not to be late for tea.

His chest squeezed so tightly it ached, bringing the sting of water to his eyes.

Home.

Slowly Ven turned around.

"You'll take me home?" he asked shakily. "Home to Vaarn?"

Whiting nodded. "Yes. All the way to Vaarn."

"My friends, too?"

The man nodded again. "We will stop on the way to the harbor and have them released from Kingston jail. They can sail with us." He smiled at the grateful light that was beginning to shine on Ven's face, then his expression became serious. "But they will need to remain on the ship while we are on the Floating Island, of course. We can't risk too much weight."

Ven felt his ears pop.

"The Floating Island?" he asked. "We are going to the Floating Island? Why?"

The warm look on Whiting's face faded, and he blinked.

"We should check on it, don't you think?" he said quickly. "Who knows what might have happened to it when Snodgrass was there? For all we know, he might have even *poisoned* the water."

Ven took hold of the bars of the cell, trying not to think about the sight of Oliver bending over the tiny silver stream. There had been respect in the sea captain's gestures as he poured blue liquid from the diamond vial into the moss, then refilled it with the Living Water.

His own voice rang in his memory.

Captain, I thought you said we weren't to take anything from the island.

Oliver had walked away, not looking back.

This place needs the water I bring it. It comes from a well that the wind cannot reach, a well from before history. A form of water that is as rare as the water of this spring. That water helps keep the island alive, in some respects. In return, I take a small amount of water from the silver spring, for my own purposes.

What do you do with it? Ven had asked.

Enough questions for today, Ven.

Down the hallway a jangling of keys could be heard.

Mr. Whiting looked quickly over his shoulder.

"All right, now, Ven, time to go. I will have the jailer release you, and then we must hurry if we are to make it to town in time to free your friends before we sail. We don't want the sun to go down before we get through the crossroads, now, do we?"

Ven said nothing.

I didn't want to believe him.
At the same time I was afraid not to believe him.
I wanted to go home. I wanted to go home now more than

*anything. Even if it meant facing my parents. Even if it meant
my brothers and sister resented me and didn't speak to me for
the rest of my life.*

*From the moment I met the captain, he had been nothing
but kind to me. Mrs. Snodgrass, too—the other kids at Mouse
Lodge and Hare Warren might have found her to be a little
frightening, but my mother is the same way, stern, bossy,
insistent that everything be done just so, and even a little bit
scary. But my mother is a good woman.*

Mrs. Snodgrass seemed like a good woman.

*Whiting had been nasty to me, but it was hard to deny what
he was saying.*

I didn't have any idea what to believe.

*I felt like a Revenant at the crossroads myself—unsure which
path would take me home. Lost in the dark.*

*I missed my family. I wished any one of them was there to
help me. I wished my father was there to help me tell what the
hammered truth of the situation was.*

My head was spinning so fast that it made me dizzy.

"Ya gonna talk to Galliard, then?" the jailer with the bristly beard
demanded. "How many bloody times do ya expect me to trot those
stairs, man?"

Ven's hand went to his pocket. He pulled forth his grandfather's
jack-rule, remembering what his father had said on Ven's birthday
as he gave it to him.

It will always measure truer than any other instrument could.

Slowly he opened the measuring tool and extended the magnifying glass.

"Yes," Mr. Whiting told the jailer. "I'm going to drop the charges and take custody of this prisoner as soon as I can speak to the Vizier."

Ven raised the magnifying glass to his eye.

At first he could see little in the dim light of the jail cell, and what he could see was out of focus. Then he tilted it a little and caught the lanternlight, and the image sharpened.

The magnifying glass was pointed toward the jailer's coarse beard, and tucked within the folds Ven could see pipe ashes and the crumbs of the man's breakfast. He moved the glass to the left as Whiting continued to talk to the jailer, and examined the hawk-nosed man a little more closely.

Ven started at the top of his head, then moved down until the glass caught a sudden glint in the folds of Whiting's gray robe. He turned the jack-rule carefully to enhance the image.

A rainbow sparkle gleamed within his pocket. Ven recognized the colorful pattern of the light.

Whiting had a diamond vial of his own.

Before he knew what he was doing, a word formed in the bottom of his throat and shoved its way up his neck until it came out his mouth.

"No," he said quietly.

Both Whiting and the jailer fell silent, then turned to him, shock on both of their faces.

"What did you say?" Whiting asked, disbelief in his voice.

"I said *no*," Ven replied, louder this time. "I'm not going with him."

Through the glass in the jack-rule he saw the veins pop out in Whiting's forehead, and beads of sweat emerge as the man strode over to the cell bars again.

Ven quickly folded the measuring tool and put it back in his pocket.

"Are you daft, boy?" Whiting demanded. "Haven't you heard a word I've said?"

"Every one of them," Ven replied, a tone of bravery that he didn't feel ringing in his voice. "And I disbelieve every one of them as well. You aren't here to help me; you are certainly *not* my friend. You want the Living Water for yourself, nothing more. You have since that day on the ship when I got your place in the longboat. I'm not going to help you get it. I will take my chances with the king's justice."

Whiting's eyes darkened with rage.

"You're a fool," he snarled, his mask of pleasantness gone now. "Look around you, Nain *brat*. Do you like this place? It may very well be your home for the rest of your life."

Ven shrugged. "Well, we Nain like it underground," he said. He stepped away from the bars of the cell as Whiting jammed his fingers through them.

The hawk-nosed man laughed sharply.

"This cell is not the only *underground* you will see before I'm done with you, boy," he said. "When the king returns, you will be tried for your crimes as the fifty-year-old Nain that you are, not the idiot boy you appear to be. Thievery of my ring aside, the king will hold you responsible for the deaths of all those sailors you blew to smithereens on the *Angelia*. You will hang for sure, and then they will plant you underground forever. With any luck, they will bury you at the crossroads, with all your Revenant friends. What a joy that will be, now, won't it? You can haunt the night with them for eternity." A cruel smile spread across his face at the look on Ven's.

Ven had gone white, but from shock, not fear.

"How did you know the name of that ship?" he asked. "An unchristened ship, in *Vaarn* Harbor? No one was supposed to know that."

Whiting's smile faded. He leaned as close as he could to Ven through the bars.

"You truly must be stupid, even for a Nain," he said disdainfully.

"I would have thought you might have noticed by now that I know many things that no one is supposed to know."

He turned on his heel and strode up the stairs into the darkness, leaving Ven and the jailer behind, both blinking, one on each side of the bars of the cell.

- 19 -

The King

After that, I lost all track of time.

I wrote until I couldn't think of anything else to write, and then I gave my papers to the jailer, who nodded at me and went back up the stairs again. I assumed he gave them to whoever would give them to the king. Now he only returned to feed me.

Leaving me, most of the time, alone in the dark, with little to do but sleep, and worry, and wonder how Whiting and McLean, and everyone else, seemed to know things that they shouldn't.

I did a lot of all three.

V EN WOKE TO THE SOUND OF HEAVY FOOTSTEPS APPROACHING.
He sat up quickly, rubbing his eyes, hoping to make them better able to see in the dark. The lantern had gone out, as it frequently did, and the jailer had not returned to relight it. The dim glow appeared in the distance as the footsteps moved closer.

Ven ran his finger over the cold stone wall of his cell. On his first night there he had followed the custom and carved his name into it, along with the names of the other condemned inmates who had been imprisoned there.

I realized from the moment I saw those names why men would carve them into the wall. It was their only way of remembering who they were in this place of endless darkness, where time didn't exist. I used my great-grandfather's jack-rule, which they hadn't taken away from me. My father probably would have thought it a disgraceful use of an honored tool, but I think Magnus would have understood.

As the sound of the boots grew closer, I wished I had been able to write a last letter to my mother. I had been trying to do so since they put me in the cell, but the words just wouldn't come.

With a jangling of keys, the jailer appeared, hurrying down the stairs. He got to the cell just as the contingent of four guards came around the corner, the constable with them. The bristly man looked at him for the first time with what Ven believed might have been sympathy.

Struggling to keep his last meal in his stomach, Ven rose from the cot. The soldiers had come like this once before, but they had only retrieved the sheets on which he had written his account and marched off into the darkness again.

This time he suspected they would take him as well.

"Good luck, lad," the jailer whispered as he unlocked the cell door.

"Thanks," Ven mumbled. The guards came to a halt outside the cell, and the leader gestured to him.

"Oh—excuse me," Ven said over the angry screech of the rusty metal hinges as the jailer pulled open the door. "I didn't think to ask your name."

The jailer blinked. "Nobody ever does," he said as Ven stepped out of the cell.

"May I know it?"

The bearded man blinked again. "Harumph—well, yes, I guess," he said awkwardly. " 'Tis Henry. Why do ya want to know?"

Ven smiled weakly. "Just curious."

The lead guard signaled to the constable, who held out the iron manacles for Ven's wrists.

"Thank you, Henry," Ven said. He fell in line with the constable and marched away with the soldiers, all the while trying to keep from throwing up.

They followed the soldiers back up the dark staircase and down a tremendously long hall lined with rich tapestries and marble statues to two towering doors, which were opened by two guards in full uniform. Ven's eyes stung from the daylight.

The doors led into a mammoth room with a towering ceiling and a long blue and red carpet leading up to a wide carpeted platform in the middle of the room. In the center of the platform was a magnificent throne, made of carved wood that had been leafed in gold and inlaid with blue lapis in a channel down the arms.

The throne, like the room around it, was empty.

Ven's escort led him to a doorway in the side of the throne room, then stopped.

"You are to go in here," the lead soldier told him.

Ven nodded.

The soldier opened the door.

The room into which Ven was led was huge, round, lit with lanterns, and filled with puzzles.

There were many small tables and benches around the smooth marble walls that held chess and checker boards, and games Ven recognized—Wari, Parchisi, Hounds and Jackals, Ferses, Fox and Geese—and many more that he didn't. Most of the tables, however, held puzzles of all kinds, in varying degrees of completion. Some were made of stones, some of glass, some of wood, some of metal, some of jewels, and other materials he didn't recognize. Many of them stood taller than Ven, and were shaped like buildings, or trees, or strange animals, or mountain ranges, or shapes he had never seen before. One was shaped like a globe with a side missing.

A tall, thin man with a sour expression, dark eyes, long hair bound back with a tiny gold chain stood at the windows. His face was shaped differently than Ven had seen in a human before, making Ven wonder if, like McLean, he was of another race. He was dressed in midnight-blue robes that were embroidered in all kinds of shapes, and in his hand was a long staff of dark wood on top of which was carved an eye.

In his hands were papers Ven recognized, the top one smudged with ink.

He was the most regal person Ven had ever seen, and he turned as Ven and the constable entered the room, then walked forward until he came to a large table in the room's center.

At the table sat a young human man in a plain cloth shirt and dark blue trousers tucked into boots. He had long dark hair and bright blue eyes, blue as the sky. Ven guessed that he was about twenty years old.

"Bow, you idiot," the constable whispered.

Ven bowed to the tall man. The man's eyebrows shot up into his hair, and his hooked nose wrinkled in disdain.

The young man at the table chuckled.

It was then I realized I was in the presence of the king. But I had been foolish enough to bow to the wrong man.

I could not have been more surprised—or more stupid. I remember turning and bowing again, or trying to. The constable whomped me on the back when I didn't assume a respectful position fast enough. I fell forward, thumping my head on the table and sending puzzle pieces flying in every direction.

I wanted the earth to open up and swallow me whole.

The young king smiled pleasantly at Ven.

"Perfectly natural confusion," he said politely. "Happens all the time." He rose from his chair and extended his hand to Ven, who shook it, much to the horror of the king's man and the constable.

I took his hand gratefully, and shook it firmly, a handshake that was all business, just as my father had taught me. "A man's only as good as his word and his handshake," he used to always say.

I heard the constable gasp behind me, and the king's man looked ready to light me on fire with his eyes.

I learned later that I was supposed to either bow over the king's hand, as a foreigner, or press my forehead against it, if I were a native of the island. Shaking it was terribly bad manners. I was doing everything wrong. But at least I was consistent.

Ven quickly let go of the king's hand.

"I'm Vandemere, high king of Serendair," said the young man. "This," he said, pointing to the older man, "is my assistant Vizier and adviser, Galliard. My chief Vizier, Graal, is away on an extended trip. I am certain he would have liked to meet you. He has a fondness for Nain."

Ven blinked, but said nothing. His curiosity, which had disappeared while he was in the dungeon, was beginning to spark back to life. He wanted to examine every puzzle and game in the room, to ask what a Vizier was, where the chief one had gone, and why the king wanted to see him, but he settled for bowing again.

"I hope you were not mistreated in the dungeon. It was not my intention for you to end up there, but there was some confusion while I was away." The king looked at the Royal Vizier.

"No, Your Majesty," Ven said quickly. "Henry looked after me very well."

"Henry?"

Ven coughed awkwardly. "The, er, jailer."

The king's eyes gleamed with interest. He looked down at a different set of papers.

"You've been accused of some serious crimes," he said. "Some of them punishable by death."

Ven swallowed hard. "Yes, Your Majesty—though I don't know what, exactly."

The king consulted the papers. "Thievery at sea, which carries a higher penalty than on land. Multiple murder in the deaths of the crew of the ship that sank. Do you understand these charges?"

"I—I think so," Ven stammered. "But—"

"Answer His Majesty's questions and do not speak otherwise," snarled the Vizier.

"I ordered you to be summoned here because I found the report from the captain of the *Serelinda* very interesting," King Vandemere continued, returning to the table and sitting down again. "In it he states that you were found floating in the sea because an albatross marked your position. This is a very important sign, perhaps an omen of something about to happen. I must know what it means, how you happened to come to my island, and whether or not you are a danger to the people of my kingdom. I've read your account, but I wanted to see you for myself, and hear the tale in your own voice."

The young king opened a wooden box the size of a loaf of bread on the table, then turned it over. Inside were many oddly shaped pieces of glass, in every color Ven could imagine. He carefully spread the pieces out on the table in front of him, then looked up at Ven and smiled.

"Tell me your story," the king said.

So Ven took a deep breath and told the king the tale of his birthday and everything that had happened since. He started with the falling of the albatross feather, then told about the Inspection, how all was going well until the Fire Pirates appeared.

The king listened intently, with no expression of disapproval or disgust on his face. He was very easy to talk to, and Ven found himself telling him naturally all the details of what happened, including his own role in the sinking of the ships. He hesitated for a moment, realizing he might be confirming the charges against him, but Vandemere just continued to listen, moving the shapes of glass around, fitting them together like pieces of a puzzle.

Ven told him about the merrow, Megalodon, and the Floating Island. He told him about Char, and Marius, and everything that befell him since he arrived in Serendair. He told him about the Singer who could see the Spice Folk, and the Gwadd girl who could make flowers grow and talk to mice. He even told Vandemere about Ida, how he had been spared from losing his money to her by the albatross feather, and how she had tried, in her own ugly way, to spare him from arrest. All the while he talked, the king played absently with the puzzle pieces on the table in front of them.

Ven's voice shook as he talked about the hauntings at the Inn, but the king only nodded, spinning a black piece of glass around until it fit into the puzzle. Finally he told the king about Mr. Whiting and his arrest.

When Ven finally came to the end of his tale, he felt winded, as if someone had knocked the breath out of him. Once his story had come to an end, the king stopped moving the pieces of the puzzle. While many of the shapes lay unused on the table, the design the king had been fashioning was almost complete. It was a swirl of what looked like blue and white waves beneath a shining sun, with two pieces missing.

Silence filled the room.

The king sat quietly for a long time, with his elbows on the table and his hands folded in front of his mouth. Finally he spoke.

"The barrels of magnesium and such that you used to blow up the Fire Pirate ship—were they full?" he asked.

Ven thought for a moment. "Yes, Your Majesty."

The king nodded. His hand went to the pile of shapes. He selected an orange one, then fitted it into the almost-finished puzzle. He stared at it for a long time, then looked up at Ven.

"Who, besides your father, knew that you were undertaking the Inspection that day?"

Ven blinked. "My brothers did," he said uncertainly.

"Well, of course," said the king, smiling slightly. "They rigged the draw so that you would have to go."

"They did?"

"Yes. But other than your family, who knew? The harbormaster?"

Ven shook his head. "The harbormaster is extremely busy," he said. "An Inspection is scheduled when the shipbuilder thinks the vessel is ready. The harbormaster only hears about it after the Inspection is done, and then he signs off on it so the new owner can take possession."

"And the new owner of the ship that sank—that was Mr. Witherspoon?" the king asked.

"Yes, Your Majesty."

The king smiled. He selected a last puzzle piece, a white one, and fit it into the picture, completing it.

"Witherspoon was in on the attack, I'd wager," he said.

Ven's mouth dropped open. "How can that be?" he asked. "What possible reason would he have to have his own ship stolen?"

Vandemere sat back in his chair and crossed his hands over his stomach.

"If it hadn't passed the Inspection, he hadn't paid for it yet, am I right?"

"Yes, Your Majesty."

The king's smile grew broader, as if he were enjoying a particu-

larly rich dessert. "And Witherspoon told you they had already begun loading goods onto the ship, even though he knew that might
cause a problem with the Inspection?"

Ven thought back to that morning in the office. "Yes, he did," he
said.

"So those barrels of explosives, which you said were bolted into
place, were put there by Witherspoon—not forgotten by your
brothers when they were making the ship," the king said. "They
were full; if they had been used in the manufacturing process, they
would have been partially empty."

Ven's head felt like it was about to explode. "You're right," he
said, his mind teetering wildly. He remembered what Whiting had
said to him that day in the dungeon, about Fire Pirates needing
support, and getting it from people in the sea trade, like sea captains.

And ship owners.

"Witherspoon must have made a deal with the pirates," the king
said. He ran a hand over the completed puzzle. "He must be one of
the people who supply them with the ingredients to make their fire.
I'd bet that he had an arrangement with them—they were to attack
the ship, burn the sails, kill the crew, then take it and sell it—or
perhaps they just paid Witherspoon for it to use themselves. Witherspoon would not have to pay your father for it, since it never
passed Inspection. So he made money on the deal, and your father
lost his ship, his son, and maybe even his business. That's an evil
man, to be sure."

Ven's face flushed red with anger. "I have to go home," he said
before he thought better of it. "I can't stay here—I have to go home
and deal with Mr. Witherspoon. When I get done with him—"

"You could be a very old man," the Vizier said dryly. "You seem
to have forgotten that you are under arrest, and about to stand trial
for thievery and possibly murder. You won't be going anywhere for
a long while, young man."

The king exhaled and looked over at the constable, who nodded. He gathered up the puzzle pieces, along with the ones he didn't use, and put them back in the box, put the lid back on, shook it around a little, and emptied it onto the table again.

"Let's see if we can't resolve this case now," he said. "What is this boy accused of stealing?"

"Mr. Whiting's ring," said Evan Knapp. "And Mr. Whiting also states that a man may have been lost over the side of the *Serelinda*—"

"He's mistaken," said the king. His voice had a hard edge to it that made everyone in the room straighten up a bit. "Oliver Snodgrass would have mentioned something like that in his report. He noted nothing like that, so Mr. Whiting is undoubtedly mistaken. The ship's captain has a better knowledge of who's aboard and who's not than a passenger would. I rule that charge false." He gestured to the Vizier, who thought for a moment, then nodded.

Evan Knapp bowed. "Very well, Your Majesty," he said. "And what of the charge of stealing? The ring that Mr. Whiting described was found in the boy's room at the Crossroads Inn."

The king thought for a moment, then began moving the glass puzzle pieces around again. The room was quiet as he started to form another picture, smaller this time.

"How would Ven have known Mr. Whiting had such a ring?" he asked, examining a red piece of glass.

"Mr. Whiting claims Ven saw it on his hand every day while the two of them were on the *Serelinda*."

"Do you have the ring, Constable?" the king asked.

Evan Knapp nodded and fished the ring out of his pocket. He set it on the table, then bowed and moved away again. The copper gleamed in the light of the lanterns.

King Vandemere took the ring and examined it carefully. Then he returned to the picture he was building in glass, mostly from orange and yellow pieces. Finally he looked up, after glancing at the report from Captain Snodgrass.

"The *Serelinda* picked up passengers in Northland six weeks ago," he said. "That was where Mr. Whiting got on board, according to this report."

"I believe that is correct, Your Majesty," said the constable.

The king fitted a single blue piece into the puzzle, then looked up.

"Well, this ring is made of unvarnished copper," he said, turning it over in his hand. "Copper changes color in salt air. If it had been worn on someone's hand in the salty sea air for six weeks, it would have started to turn blue by now. And yet it is as shiny and orange-brown as the day it was made. Now, how do you suppose that could be, Constable?"

Evan Knapp was silent.

"Perhaps that's because it was just made a few days ago," said Ven excitedly. "Or maybe a few weeks or years ago, even, but certainly it could not have been worn at sea for that long without changing."

The king's smile grew hard again.

"Right. So all I can imagine is that Mr. Whiting is seriously mistaken about the ring, because to accuse someone falsely is a very great crime, one that I am certain he would not want to be found guilty of. What do you say, Constable?"

Evan Knapp looked relieved. "I'd say that there is no need to pursue this matter any further," he said.

"Good. Then you may go," said the king. "Make certain Mr. Polypheme is taken care of and returned to the Crossroads Inn. And release his friends from the town jail as well." The constable bowed.

King Vandemere turned to Ven. "Thank you for coming to clear up these issues," he said pleasantly. "It's an honor to meet someone who has the favor of an albatross. Best of luck to you." He picked up the puzzle pieces and returned them to the wooden box. "I suggest you find out how that ring got in your room."

"Yes, Your Majesty," Ven said as the constable began to usher him toward the door. "But before I go, I believe you owe me something."

The room fell suddenly silent.

Ominously silent.

- 20 -

The Trade of Tales

INSOLENT BRAT," GALLIARD, THE VIZIER, HISSED. "HOW DARE you speak to the king like that?"

I could almost feel the musty walls of the dungeon closing around me again.

I've got to learn to keep things from slipping out of my mouth. I'd been doing so well, but as the charges were dismissed, I got too excited and just couldn't keep my mouth shut.

I really must learn how to do that someday.

The young king, rather than appearing offended, looked at Ven with a spark of interest in his eyes.

"What is it I owe you, Ven?" he asked, waving at the Vizier to be silent.

Ven tried to speak, but no sound came out. He swallowed and tried again.

"Among the Nain, when someone shares the story of his life, it is, er, customary for the other person to return the favor—to trade tales, so to speak. I'm sorry if I was rude, Your Majesty. I've never been anywhere near a king before, much less spoken to one. I seem to have left all my manners in the dungeon."

The king looked intently at him for a moment. Then he turned to the Vizier and the constable.

"Constable Knapp, please go release Mr. Polypheme's friends. Galliard, will you please step outside into the hall?" he asked.

"I'd advise against it, sire," protested the Vizier. His hands were clenched tightly, his knuckles whiter than Matilda's newly sewn sails.

"Of course you would," the king said. "If I need you, I know where to find you."

The Vizier snorted out his breath loudly through his hooked nose, then stormed out of the room, followed by the constable.

King Vandemere waited until the door was closed, then pointed to a chair at the table.

"Please sit down," he said. Then he got up and walked slowly past several of the tables until he came to one which held a small wooden cube the size of an apple. He returned to the table, turning the wooden box over in his hands. He twisted the box in the middle, and out sprang several slats of wood, which opened the box into many odd layers at strange angles.

For a long time the king sat quietly, twisting the box into many different shapes. Finally Ven's curiosity swelled, drowning his embarrassment.

"If I may be so bold, what *is* your story, Your Majesty?"

The young king smiled. "That's a short question with a long answer," he said, continuing to twist the box's parts. "And hardly a fair trade of tales. You only told me the story of your life since you encountered the albatross a few weeks ago."

"That's the entire story of my life so far," said Ven. "Not too much happened to me worth telling before that."

King Vandemere nodded. "Well, I suppose my story is that I was born to be king, but it happened too fast." He closed the box back up into a cube, then put it on the table in front of him.

"My father died two years ago. My mother died when I was born. So I became king when I was sixteen years old."

"You're only eighteen?" Ven asked, amazed, realizing a moment later how rude that sounded. Vandemere was so approachable, so friendly, that it was hard to remember he was a king. "I apologize, Your Majesty—but you look older."

"And you look much younger than you are," replied the king. He reached out and tapped the box, and instantly it flattened into a long, thin sheet of interlocking pieces. Ven blinked. "The first rule of good puzzling—see things as they are, and not as they seem."

The king turned the wooden sheet over, and began spreading the pieces out, though they all remained connected in some way.

"Did you know that there are several other kings on this island?" he asked. Ven shook his head. "And a few queens, not to mention other nobles. Each race, the Nain, the Lirin, the Gwadd, they have their own rulers. But the person born to sit in that throne in the room next door is high king over all of them. So it occurred to me when I was very young that I should go out and see what their kingdoms were like, since I was responsible for them all."

"A good idea," said Ven.

"But I didn't want to go to visit as the crown prince. I knew that there would be a good deal of pomp and ceremony, which I find very boring. I also knew that if people met me as the prince, they would tell me what they expected I would want to hear, and not what they really thought. So when I was thirteen, I told my father that I was going off to learn whatever I could of the world, particularly the part of the world I would rule one day."

Ven nodded eagerly. His eye was drawn to the puzzle again, and saw that the king had assembled each of the corners of it into what looked like little wooden trees, but when he looked at the entire puzzle, it had taken on the shape of a face.

"The second rule of good puzzling—look at the details and the whole picture separately," the king said. "You will see two different things."

He turned the puzzle on its side, then collapsed it into the box cube again.

"So I went traveling. I went alone. And I went in disguise. Not in any special costume, but as a farmhand, a wanderer, a beggar. The sort of person who might live for a while in Hare Warren. A kid, traveling alone. No one noticed me, which was perfect, because then I could see things as they really are, and hear things spoken truthfully and without fear. It was a wonderful time."

"What sorts of things did you see and hear?" Ven asked.

"I saw a forest where the trees protect each other, tall ones growing around ones that are young or fragile to spare them from the wind until they are strong enough to stand on their own. I saw a place at the edge of the sea where giants once walked out to an island off the coast, where you can still see the stepping-stones they used—they're the size of oxcarts. I saw the grave of a star that fell from the sky into the sea, and where it lies still, boiling beneath the surface of the water. I saw a unicorn once, and a lion with wings. But mostly I saw people, my people, people of different races and different types of lives, all of whom had stories that I found fascinating. And I realized what I was really seeing in all of them was magic.

"My father had a court full of magicians and conjurers, as did his father before him, and every other high king in history. I sent them all away when I became king, because I saw what they did as tricks, as amusement. I kept my Viziers—they are advisers who can see things that others can't. The chief Vizier, Graal, is very old, and very wise, and Galliard is his student, also very knowledgeable. But all the men in funny hats making snakes out of silk scarves that used to work in the palace are now out there among the people, entertaining children with their tricks. Because, as king, I only wanted to see the *real* magic in the world, so that I could learn from it, and preserve it."

Ven's curiosity was now itching so fiercely that he could barely keep from scratching his head.

King Vandemere balanced the cube on his palm.

"The problem with seeing a little of that kind of magic is that you gain an appetite for it. Once you know it's out there, it's hard not to look for more of it. I met a few Nain, and learned that they are nervous in the air, preferring to live deep in the earth—but then I wanted to see why, what their world within the mountains was like, where gold runs in rivers, and gems grow on trees, or so I'm told. I met some Gwadd, and found them charming and sad at the same time. They say so little in words—so I wanted to learn their silent language, the language that mice and moles can hear, that speaks not in words but in flowers. I met Lirin, who say very little to humans, but record history in song, and have Singers who swear to tell the absolute truth all their lives so that the tales they sing do not become soiled with falsehood. And I wanted to hear those tales, all of them. And I met Kith, people like Galliard, who have the power of wind in their blood, and can hear what is being spoken on it. I wanted to learn how to do that, too."

The young king stood up and walked to the window.

"But then my father died. I took the throne, as I was born to. And now I'm stuck here. I can't go about the way I used to."

"Why?" Ven asked. "You're the king. Can't you go anywhere you want?"

King Vandemere chuckled. "Because my face is on every coin in the kingdom," he said. "Everyone knows who I am now. They bow to me, and they tell me what they think I want to hear. And there are endless things I have to tend to, grain treaties and armies to supply, shipping laws to follow, and all sorts of boring things. Now all the information about the world I have, I get from someone else instead of seeing it for myself. I have to sort through it, trying to separate out their opinions, their slants, because everyone I know has their own agenda, their own plans. All I really want is—is—"

"The hammered truth?" Ven said aloud.

The king's ears perked up. "What is that?" he asked.

Ven's face grew red. He had interrupted the king again, but the king didn't seem to mind.

"That's what my father used to call it," he said sheepishly. "The hammered truth—facts that are not varnished or hidden, but shaped straight, like steel that has been hammered. He used to say, 'Tell people the hammered truth, and it will ring like steel against an anvil.' "

The king practically jumped across the room. He slapped his hand down on the table, making the box of glass puzzle pieces rattle.

"Exactly!" he exclaimed. He sat down again. "That's exactly what I need—the hammered truth." He picked up the puzzle cube once more. "Fathers. They make us crazy sometimes, but every now and then they tell us great secrets that no one else can. The last thing my father said to me before he died is the most important thing I have ever heard."

"And what was that?" Ven asked eagerly.

The king looked at him, but it seemed like his mind was very far away. "I told him I was beginning to discover the magic that was hidden everywhere in the world, in the people, the creatures, the places. He was very weak, so he could only whisper. He said, 'My son, the magic's in the *puzzle*—collect the pieces, put them together, and you'll have the answer.' And I understood what he meant—that all the things I had seen were like pieces of a great puzzle, and if I could find as many of them as possible, maybe I could understand why the world was made, and what we are supposed to do with it."

"And that's why you have all these puzzles?" Ven asked, pointing at the tables around the room.

"I have them because they remind me to look for the pieces in life and put them together," the king said. "Solving these puzzles teaches me how to think in the right ways. All skills get better with practice." He turned the wooden cube over in his hand. "I'm not sure if I'll ever be able to return to my search for those pieces, however. For the rest of my life I'm expected to stay here and be king, not travel the world looking for interesting places and people and things."

Ven heard sadness in the king's voice, and it made him sad as well. "So what are you going to do, then?" he asked.

The king thought for a long time. "I suppose I am going to keep working on grain treaties and army supplies and shipping laws," he said finally. Then his eyes began to gleam, and a new expression came over his face.

"Unless I can find someone to do it for me," he said.

"What do you mean, Your Majesty?" Ven asked.

"I want to see the kingdom of the Nain when it's not been prettied up for a state visit," King Vandemere said. "I want to see the lairs of dragons and the nests of giant eagles, or what the sunrise looks like at the top of the highest peak of Balatron. But since it is unlikely that I ever will get to, I want to be able to see those things through the words of someone who really has."

The thoughts in Ven's head came bubbling out before he could stop them.

"You need a storyteller," he said excitedly. "There are many of them in Vaarn, where I come from. They travel the world, and when they come to town they bring news, and endless wonderful tales."

The king shook his head. "No," he said. "I don't want a storyteller. I want a *reporter*, someone who will give me nothing but the straightforward report. Storytellers make up many of their stories, and they rely on their own talents to shape a tale. All those tales become nothing more than the storyteller's vision of the world. I want to hear it as I would if I were there myself. I want to see things in my mind as I would have seen them with my own eyes, not as the storyteller sees it.

"I have already tried to find such a person. Many have auditioned, all adults, of course. They have told me a tale to try and gain a position in my court. Until now, they have all been just storytellers. What I need is someone to be my eyes, to go out there, both on this land and in places across the sea I never got to, and see those things for me. And to be my ears, to repeat the tales they have heard in those places."

The king's blue eyes burned with excitement.

"How about it, Ven?" he asked. "Want to audition?"

"I—er—*what?*" Ven replied, his hands starting to shake.

The king made himself comfortable in his chair.

"Tell me another story," he said. "Tell me about something special you've seen."

"I already have," Ven said, embarrassed. "I just told you everything I've seen that wasn't the inside of the ship factory. I meant it when I said the story of my life didn't start until I caught the feather."

"Well, then, tell me a tale someone has told you," the king insisted. "It doesn't have to be especially magical or interesting—just repeat to me a tale you have heard from someone else, someone not at all like yourself. In his or her own words. Try to keep your own thoughts and opinions out of it, as if you are just reporting on what you've been told. Tell me the hammered truth."

"No one talks to me," Ven said. "I'm the youngest in the family—I'm lucky if anyone listens when I ask them to pass the butter."

He glanced out the window, and saw a cloud float by in the shape of a barracuda.

A thought occurred to him.

"Wait a minute," he said. "Maybe I do have a tale or two like that after all."

- 21 -

The Merrow's Tale

So I told the king one of the tales Amariel had used to keep me from falling asleep while I lay on the wreckage, watching the albatross fly in circles above me. She told me stories for hours, and when she grew tired of that, she sang me songs. The songs were mostly soothing, but she grew impatient with my sleepiness, not realizing I was listening to her every word and sound. She would swat me, or pinch me to make me open my eyes.

She started this tale at sunset. She meant to amuse me, I'm sure. But then it grew dark. And the story changed.

When the night came, it didn't really matter whether my eyes were open or not. There were no stars out that night, and except for the sting of salt in my lashes, I could not tell the difference. So seeing nothing but blackness, I listened carefully to her words, because they were the only things in the world except for the darkness.

I still remember the story she told word for word. This is what the merrow said.

⤛ THE SEA BENEATH THE SEA ⤜

Hey! Open your eyes. I know you're tired. I was tired of this hours ago, but I've already wasted so much time on you, you can't sleep. You'll drown. And if you drown, I'll look bad. So stay awake, or I'll pinch you again.

As you can probably guess, now that you've been floating here for a while, it can get very cold in the sea.

Not always, of course. There are rivers of water that run through the ocean, warm currents that make it quite pleasant to be here most of the time.

But sometimes it gets cold. And when it does, there is almost nothing that can be done to escape it.

Merrows have bodies that adapt to the changes in temperature. But when it gets too cold, we go up to the surface and look around for a large rock or even an island to stretch out on in the sun and bask. Basking may seem lazy, but actually it's the way we store up enough heat to go back into the cold depths. And humans shouldn't be criticizing us as lazy anyway. *You* try swimming all day, every day of your life, and maybe *then* you can criticize. Hmmph.

Anyway, it gets cold.

And nobody likes to be cold, even merrows.

Now, merrow females are the most beautiful creatures in the world. Everyone knows that. But merrow men, well, that's a different story. It's probably fair to say that, as creatures of the sea go, merrow men are a little bit lazy. All right, a lot lazy. Very, very lazy. They bask for more than just heat collection—they lie around in the sun on rocks whenever they can to get out of helping with the children or the other work that has to be done. As a result, they are fat around the middle—even fatter than you, Ven. And on top of that, they are ugly. Not my dad, of course, but most merrow men.

They have noses that are flat and round, with big nostrils that sometimes sprout hair. Their teeth are frequently green, and they tend to burp a lot. Bubbles come out the other end as well, which makes them unpleasant to be around.

So maybe now you can see why merrow females are sometimes willing to give their caps to human sailors, marry them, and make lives with them on land instead. Not me, of course. I'm never going to get married. I'm going to be a racing hippocampus rider and win the Grand Trophy at the summer sea festival.

Anyway—

It's dark, isn't it? It certainly got dark all of a sudden. A moment ago I was going to tell you why merrows think the sun is made of rum. But the sun disappeared, and now it's really too dark to tell that story. Are you awake? Because now I can't see your eyes, but if I catch you snoring, I'm going to let you fall into the sea.

Oh, good. You *are* awake.

You're shaking. I hope that's from cold, because you don't seem the type to be afraid of the dark. I hope you're not the kind of person who closes your eyes when you're afraid. Look how dark it is. I guess it's kind of funny to ask you to see the dark; it's sort of like saying "look at all the nothing."

I wonder where the moon is taking us. The moon is the world's pilot fish—do you know what a pilot fish is? It is usually long and thin, striped and spiny, and it swims in the company of a shark, helping it find its way in the depths. The moon does that for the world, too, and when you see its shadow, it's turning the world in a different direction. Maybe toward better areas of the dark universe. Tonight is so dark that I wonder where the pilot fish is going.

It's only dark like this a couple of places down home. In the depths of the sea most all the living things carry their own lights, like your stars, only closer.

I have a story for the dark. I'll tell you about the most terrible place in the ocean.

Did you know that there is a sea *beneath* the sea? I've seen it.

My father wanted to show me never to go there. He knows that if he tells me not to go to a place, I sometimes don't listen, so he took me himself to make sure I never would go alone. And I never will.

When he first told me we were going, I was pretty excited. "A sea *beneath* our sea?" I said. "Below the sand in the ocean there is another ocean? I've *got* to see that."

My father did not smile, but he nodded. "It's something you should see," he said. "But only once. And you will only want to once."

We left home and swam for days. My dad didn't say much the whole way, except that the chain coral, which is the hardest, strongest type of coral there is, had long ago been asked by the Sea King to make a huge wall to keep this place apart from the rest of the world. The coral left one opening. It was not meant to be an entrance, but in case something came out it would have just one way to leave, and the chain coral would be the first line of defense if it was something awful.

The only other thing he said was that the Mythlin, the people who are made from water and live in the sea, built their great city, Tartechor, on exactly the opposite side of the world from it, to sort of balance it out, I guess. That made me a little nervous. Tartechor is a beautiful place, a gleaming city surrounded by a dome made of billions of bubbles, and if they saw it as the opposite of where we were heading, I wasn't sure I wanted to go there. But we did.

Finally we came to a huge path of chain coral. I wasn't sure once I saw it that I wanted to go any farther, because you can get really torn up by chain coral—it can rip right through your scales. But Dad insisted, so in we swam.

At the beginning of the wall there were fish and plants, just like everywhere else, but the closer we got, the fewer and fewer fish there are, until we got to the end, where there's nothing, just sour sea and the bones of coral piled all around. And a hole. Like someone a long time ago rolled a rock away and revealed a great cavern full of evil water. My father told me not to breathe, and we went in.

You probably think because I have gills that I don't know what it means to have to hold your breath, to be afraid to take water in, or to choke on something, but I do. This place, this sour sea, is the one place on earth where I know I could drown. We went into the cave, and it was so dark, not like there was nothing there, but like the light had all been sucked out.

The wider I opened my eyes, the less I could see, and I couldn't speak for fear of getting some of that water in my mouth. I brushed up against some fire coral that burned to the touch, but gave no light, and the whole place felt of something terrible somebody had done, and hidden there.

It felt as if deep at the bottom of that sea, in the darkest darkness, was some treasure somebody had stolen and then broke, or some murder that had been buried. My father says some secrets fester just like wounds, and I think that's the sort of thing that's at the source of that sea. My father had to carry me out of there because I ran out of breath and started to panic. Whenever I have nightmares now, I smell the heat of that water.

When we got far enough away from the chain coral to know that we were truly safe, I asked my father what that horrible place was.

"The beginning of the world," he said. "And its end."

And that's all he would say.

So now you know that, as dark as the depths of the sea may be, as dark as the night gets without a moon, it is really not true darkness. It's just waiting for light to return. There are places that are truly dark in the world, Ven, but this place here, this open stretch of sea where you are floating, is not one of them. It's not really dark here—it's just night. If you hang on and stay awake, in a short while the edges of the sky will start to turn gray, then pink, and the sun will rise, and there will be blue above and all around you again.

- 22 -

The Offer of a Position

Y OU'RE NOT FAT AROUND THE MIDDLE," SAID THE KING WHEN THE story ended.

"Thank you," Ven said. "But I wasn't offended when she said that. She's a merrow. She had never seen a Nain before. And we *are* a little paunchy."

"I can almost hear her voice when you tell her tale," said King Vandemere, standing and stretching his legs. "And I can imagine what it must have been like, lying there, half dead, in the sea, listening to it."

He stood up from the table, walked to the door and opened it.

"Galliard," he said, "will you be so good as to come back in now?"

Once the glowering Vizier had returned, the king sat back down.

"Well, Galliard, I'm satisfied that I have found my reporter—although we will have to find a better title than that," he said.

The Royal Vizier's face turned as purple as an eggplant.

"What? Your Majesty—"

"What is the name of the jailer in the palace dungeon, Galliard?" the king asked, his eyes sparkling with amusement.

The regal man's mouth flapped open silently, like a fish breathing air.

"I really have no idea, Your Majesty," he said disdainfully.

"Of course you don't. Nor did I, and the man has worked in my father's castle since before I was born. And yet Ven took the time to make note of it. He has a natural curiosity and attention to detail that will serve me well, I believe." The king looked at Ven again. "So Ven, what do you say? Are you willing to accept the position?"

Ven's face turned gray, and he leaned forward in his chair, trying to keep from passing out. "Uh—as much as I would love to say yes, Your Majesty—and I would *really* love to say yes—I don't think I can."

"Why not?"

"Because I have to go home," Ven said. "I don't know whether or not my father will want to see me again, but I have to do something about Mr. Witherspoon. My father does—well, *did*—business with him all the time. Witherspoon's one of his best customers. If by chance the family business did survive the sinking of the *Angelia*, it won't if Mr. Witherspoon sets him up again." Ven's face went from gray to red with anger. "And I want to pay a visit to him personally."

"You may be fifty years old and large for a Nain, but you should not take on a human man all by yourself," said the king. "Especially one with pirate connections. That's unwise."

"I wasn't planning on doing it myself," said Ven. "I'm taking my brother Luther with me."

"Hmmm," said the king. "Well, one advantage of being king is that we have some power to deal with matters such as this. I will take care of contacting the authorities in Vaarn myself. I suspect they may take action a little faster on my behalf than they will for you."

"Thank you," said Ven, but he still was unsure about the king's offer.

"Tell you what," King Vandemere said, seeing the doubt on his face, "why don't you think about it? I can imagine you have a lot to figure out right now. You can take some time and consider what you want to do with your life."

"I will," Ven promised. "But can you tell me what exactly a royal reporter would have to do? I understand you are looking for someone to be your eyes and ears, and go to places you can't go to, but what specifically are you looking for? What do you expect to find in this search?"

The king smiled. "I'm not looking for what I *expect* to find, Ven. I'm just looking for what is there. That's all."

"So there are specific places you want me to go?"

"Yes, but eventually I would like you just to explore on your own. Go out and see what's there. Then tell me about it. This is not just a title, it's a job. I will pay you to do this for me, and for your expenses. I will give you whatever you need—soldiers, horses, interpreters, maybe even your own Vizier."

"Your Majesty!" Galliard objected.

"Well, once Graal returns and you are done with your studies, you will need a position, Galliard. I'd hate to see you out of work." The king's eyes twinkled.

"I have to object, Your Majesty," the Vizier said.

"Of course you do, Galliard."

Ven's head was spinning. "I will think about it, as you suggested, Your Majesty. But can you tell me one last thing?" The king nodded. "In the end of it all, what is it you are hoping for? What will you do with all the information your reporter gathers?"

The king considered for a long while.

"I just want to know the answer, as my father said. I want to be the best king I can be, and need to have all the knowledge I can in order to do that. If I can't see those things myself, can't go out and learn about it firsthand, I will have to read it in a book, just as everyone else does. But the book must be the hammered truth. In the end? In the end I suppose I'd like to have a book of all the world's magic. I'd like to have a book of all human knowledge. If I can't be the man who collected that magic, that knowledge, then I want to be the one who commissioned it to be done. I want that to be my legacy. You asked me what my story was. I want *that* to be my story, Ven. Does that make sense to you?"

Ven smiled. "Very much so, Your Majesty."

The king's smile faded slightly in return. "Magic left over from Creation is a very fragile thing, Ven," he said finally. "I need to know as much about it as I can, to have an accounting of where and what it is—because I have reason to believe that it may be in danger of disappearing. There are many people lurking in the world who would see it dead—or try to control it in an evil way. My offer stands, and you should consider this—if you accept it, you might not only be documenting the magic of the world, you might be helping to save it as well. So think on it, and let me know what you decide."

He tossed Ven the box-cube puzzle he had been working on.

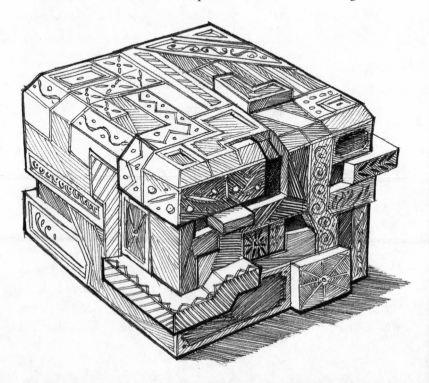

"The last rule of puzzling is this: Sometimes there are many solutions, sometimes only one. But you never know which until you've tried to solve it more than once."

The king pointed to the puzzle in Ven's hand.

"Except every now and then you find one that has many answers, but only one solution. Have you ever seen one of those before?"

Ven shook his head. The box was simple, with no decoration, made from a strange dark wood that had a tint of deep red in its grain.

"That is a practice box made by a Rover master in training," King Vandemere said. "Rovers are an odd people, strange nomads that cannot seem to stay in one place very long. Like gypsies, they travel the world, going wherever the wind takes them, without roots. They have a veil of darkness around them. Little is known about them and their ways, but long ago one piece of lore found its way onto the wind—it was the story of their puzzle boxes.

"A Rover master is a craftsman who learns the secret, and ancient, art of box making from his ancestors. He studies intensely, because in his life he will make only one such box—and it is believed that the box he makes contains his life. The vessel itself is empty—it holds whatever the Rover wants to store in it—but only the one who made it is said to know the combination to the puzzle lock. It would take a very talented thief, or a puzzler of far greater skill than I can imagine ever having, to open such a box. And that is what makes it valuable to a Rover. These rootless people who have no place they call home, who travel the earth in dark caravans and tattered wagons, need an unbreakable vault to hold what is most valuable to them."

"What sorts of things do they store in these boxes?" Ven asked, his curiosity flooding through him, making his skin tingle.

The king shrugged. "I've never seen an actual Rover master's box," he said. "Only this little one, which was made to practice on, to learn the craft. It was given to me by a Rover I met in my travels, a man who had been driven off by his fellows, sent into exile. Imagine that—being exiled by people whose *lives* are a constant exile. He was bitter, and ill—Rovers by nature tend to be thin, withered people, and they share little with outsiders, keeping silent with anyone outside their own clan. This man was more withered than most, but he chose not to be silent. And in doing so, he gave me many insights into people that walk my lands, that know far more of the world than I will ever see, but that no one knows anything about."

"Did he have a box of his own?"

"Yes," said King Vandemere. "He was on his way to go back and find it, alone. When I asked what he was hiding in it—I was young then, and didn't realize I was being rude—his eyes glinted with a mad light, and he began to laugh. He never said another thing to me. He just stood up and left me where we had been sitting, sharing a meal, and laughed as he walked away." The king shuddered at the memory. "I will never forget the sound of it—high and thin, like the whine of the wind in the night when it whips down off the mountains. So the answer is, Ven, I have no idea. Maybe someday you will find one, or more. And if you can figure out how to open them, you will know. In the meantime, you may have that one to practice on."

"Thank you, Your Majesty," Ven said, his eyes bright with interest.

"Well, I've made you my offer. I understand if you don't feel you can accept it. Head back now to the inn, and check on your fellows. Let me know what you decide. If you decide to stay, I will make sure you have what you need to do the job. If you decide to go home, I will pay for your passage. Either way, let me know before the end of the week."

"Yes, sir," Ven said. His stomach turned queasy again.

Never before in my life did I want something so badly, and yet feel at the same time that I should walk away from it. How could I refuse the glory of working for a king, wandering the world for a reason? Feeding my craving for adventure? I'll tell you how—in my mind I kept seeing my teacup sitting empty on my mother's table. I could feel the need my father would have to upbraid me, to yell at me for losing his ship, as he yelled at my brothers on a daily basis. As much as I didn't want to, I had to go back and face my family's anger, and own up to what I had done to their lives.

I just hoped King Vandemere wouldn't be put off if I rejected his offer. I decided to wait before telling him no; it would have been rude to do so right away. Besides, I certainly didn't want to go back to Henry's care any time soon.

Perhaps I could tell the king no in a letter.

The king put out his hand, and Ven shook it again. The Vizier's eyebrows shot up into his hairline once more.

"Best of luck in your decision, Ven," King Vandemere said. "I'll await your answer. And remember, whatever you decide is fine. I promise I will not have your head cut off for refusing my offer."

"Thank you," Ven said nervously.

"And don't forget to look into who set you up. It's important to know who your friends are—and who they're not."

"I have a pretty good idea," Ven said, his forehead wrinkling. He thought about Ida sitting on his bed, pruning her toenails. "But that's good advice. I will look into it, to be sure."

He bowed to the king and was led back down the long hallway, through all the winding corridors, to the base of the battlements where the coach was waiting, this time with only two soldiers.

Ven stared out the coach window as it pulled away, watching the face of the Guardian of the Mountain fade into the shadows that were beginning to fall as the afternoon moved toward evening.

The ride was not bumpy like the one in the jail wagon, and since he was alone, he took the opportunity to nap. He woke when the coach slowed to a halt in front of the inn.

It was twilight.

He hurried down the coach steps as the door opened and watched as it rolled back east toward Elysian, then hurried into the inn.

"Well, well! Look who's back!" Mrs. Snodgrass greeted him as he came through the golden griffin door. "I was beginning to worry about you, laddie. We saved your supper for you, but it's probably cold by now. Let me go warm it up." She squeezed Ven's shoulder and led him into the inn.

Clemency, Emma, and Saeli were clearing their dishes from the table, and all greeted him happily. The kitchen door banged open and Char came flying out, wiping his hands on a white dish towel.

"Gah! I thought you'd never get back," he called to Ven as he hurried across the stone floor. Ida, whose feet were up on the table as she munched on an apple, regarded him sharply but didn't say anything. She finished her fruit, rose lazily and stretched, then made her way slowly over to where Ven stood.

"Glad everything got straightened out, Ven," Clemency said as she herded the girls toward the door. "Welcome home. Come on, ladies, lights out in ten minutes."

Char gripped Ven's forearm and shook it wildly. "Thanks for gettin' us out, by the way," he said, nodding at Ida. "That brig in town is a pretty rotten place, though I've been in a few worse."

McLean called a welcome from across the room, and Ven raised a hand in acknowledgment.

"So what did the king have to say?" Char asked.

"And what's this?" Ida held up the puzzle cube before Ven's astonished eyes. She twisted it twice, the way the king had, and broke it open into two smaller, connected squares. She smiled crookedly, pleased with herself.

"Hey! That was in my pocket! Give it back, you little thief!" Ven shouted, snatching the box from Ida's hand. He walked as close to her as he could without bouncing his belly off hers, and thrust his face into hers so that their foreheads almost touched. "It was you," he said, his eyes narrowing. "You put the ring in my room. That's why you stood up to Whiting—to throw suspicion off yourself."

Ida snorted contemptuously but said nothing.

"Why did you do it? What do you want from me? You've been taking my things, or trying to, from the moment I was unlucky enough to meet you in Kingston," Ven continued, his anger rising along with his voice. "You tried to pick my pocket. You steal any-thing and everything that isn't nailed down. You break into our room. Now you've set me up and had me arrested. Stay away from me, you sticky-fingered brat, or I'll go to Evan Knapp myself and join that line of people in town who want to see you hang."

"*Master Polypheme,*" said Mrs. Snodgrass severely. The rest of the noise in the room faded away at the harshness of her tone. Even McLean's song vanished.

Clemency's head popped in the back door. "Ida—*now,*" she said.

Ida stared at him a moment longer, then turned with a smile that was half of a sneer and sauntered out the back door.

Trudy Snodgrass marched over to where Ven stood and stuck her finger into his face.

"No one is rude to a guest in my inn except me," she said stoutly. "Not even another guest. In the morning you will apologize to Ida. If you have a complaint, or an infraction to report, you know the process. But just because you went to visit the king does not mean you have the right to accuse someone in such an ugly manner. Is that understood?"

Ven exhaled slowly, then felt embarrassment replace his anger.

"Yes, ma'am," he said. "I'm sorry."

"You should be. Now, the two of you, get to bed. The sun has gone down. Get to Hare Warren immediately."

Ven and Char looked at each other in alarm, then glanced out the inn's large windows. The night had come, and darkness had indeed swallowed the world outside the inn.

"Take lanterns," Mrs. Snodgrass said, pointing to two that hung near the kitchen entrance. "To light your way—just to be safe."

Ven and Char mumbled their thanks and good nights, and hurried for the back door.

The lights had been put out already in the windows of Mouse Lodge and Hare Warren by the time they had started across the back meadow. Ven could see pretty well in the dark, being Nain, but even with the lantern Char stumbled several times, tripping over the well pump and dashing his foot against a large stepping-stone on the way.

Finally they reached the door of Hare Warren.

It was locked.

The wind picked up, or perhaps they just noticed it then. In the distance the fog was rolling in, hot steam on a summer's night. The boys thought they could hear the strange sounds they had heard their first night in Hare Warren, the mournful wailing and eerie whine carried on the wind.

Ven banged on the door urgently.

"Cadwalder!" he called, rapping again. "Let us in!"

There was no answer.

Char began to hammer on the door as well. "Come on, Cadwalder—open the bloody door!"

"He must have left for his night watch already and locked it before he left," Ven said desperately. "But why don't the others open it? Can't they hear us?"

Out of the fog at the road's edge shapes seemed to form. Ven and Char both turned, their backs to the locked door, and strained their eyes to try and get a better look.

The gleaming, leaping shapes that looked like ghostly wolves glided silently out of the mist, swirling in circles. The haunting noise grew louder.

And then they lunged, all the same time, toward the center of the crossroads, as if springing into a hole that was opening in the middle of the roadway, in a chorus of inhuman growls.

Then the screaming began.

~23~

The Haunted Night

IT WAS A MOMENT BEFORE EITHER BOY'S HEART BEAT AGAIN.

From the moment they had arrived on the island, and heard the strange whispers and incomplete tales about the haunting of the crossroads, they had no idea what was going on there. For the first time since then, they knew one thing without question.

The screaming from within the mist did not come from something demonic, or ghostly, or from another, more sinister world.

It came from a human throat.

Ven and Char stared at each other for a moment in fright.

Then Ven held up his lantern and looked back into the swirling mist, where mysterious wailing and leaping spirits lunged and dragged away, as if tearing the mist apart.

"Come on!" he shouted to Char, and ran as fast as his legs would carry him toward the crossroads.

"Wait!" Char yelled from the doorstep of Hare Warren, then dashed after him.

"Someone's being killed," Ven gasped as they ran. "We have to help."

As they passed the caretaker's shed, Char stopped long enough to grab two grass rakes that hung on the side of the shed. "No—point—going unarmed," he puffed, tossing one to Ven.

"Somehow I doubt whatever is haunting that road is going to be afraid of a rake," Ven said.

Char looked around quickly.

"Well, the only other weapon lying around here is horse dung," he said, starting off into the mist. "You can take that if you want to and hurl it at whatever is in there."

"No, thanks," said Ven, fighting back his fear and following Char.

Into the rolling clouds of fog they ran, hurrying blindly into the filmy darkness lighted by flashes from the swinging lanterns. The sounds of screaming grew louder as they came nearer to the center of the road, punctuated by the deep growling and unearthly shrieking noise. The boys kept their rakes in front of them, swiping blindly every few feet.

"It's those ghost wolves," Char whispered as they approached. "They're tearing someone apart."

Ven doubled his effort and ran even faster. His hands were slippery with sweat, and he struggled not to drop the lantern or the rake.

They came over the last rise before the road. The boys froze.

In the darkness they could see the white spirits gleaming, their wolf-like bodies huge and muscular, gleaming like ivory in the mist. They were ripping at a body lying in the road, now limp and seemingly lifeless.

A surge of heat rose up from Ven's stomach, racing through him like a fiery wind. Panic, anger, and the need to help blended together and rushed into his mouth like acid, and he let out a guttural scream that was part roar, part snarl.

Then he heaved his lantern with all his might into the center of the crossroads.

The lantern spun in circles and shattered as it landed in the roadway, sending a splash of billowing light skyward.

The beasts reared back, the nearest one yelping as the fire caught it and began to burn.

Ven let out a bellow and rushed forward, waving the rake angrily, Char doing the same half a step behind him.

The shadow-wolves retreated into the darkness.

The boys hurried to the body lying at the center of the cross-roads. When they reached it they stopped. Ven bent down to examine it while Char stood guard, waving his rake menacingly through the mist.

"Oh no," Ven whispered as he turned the victim over. "No. Char—it's Nicholas."

"Gah! Nick? Is he alive? What was he *doing* out here?"

Ven felt for breath, but his hands were trembling so violently that he could not tell if there was any movement in their Warren-mate's chest.

"Don't know—maybe he was sent to town with a message and got delayed. We've got to get him out of here," he said. "Those spirit wolves didn't bolt, they just slunk away. They could come back any minute—come on, help me carry him."

Together they lifted Nicholas off the road, trying not to notice the pool of his blood. They had managed to get his sagging arms around their shoulders when Char looked up suddenly.

"Hear that?" he asked nervously, staring into the mist. "That weird noise? They're coming back."

"We'll never make it back to the inn," Ven said, watching the distant shadows move along the road. "They're between it and us now."

A hideous howl tore through the air, and the ground beneath them began to tremble.

"Come on!" Ven shouted, dragging Nicholas forward. "To the graveyard—it has a fence. Run!"

Pulling with all their strength, they lugged Nicholas's body west across the road to the small graveyard beneath the thicket of trees. Char scrambled over the fence, then helped as Ven pushed Nicholas over before climbing inside himself.

"Sorry, Nick," Char said, wincing, as Nicholas's body hit the soft grassy ground with a thump.

"I don't think he can hear you," whispered Ven urgently. "But the wolves might be able to. Hush."

They dragged Nicholas behind the largest of the Price family gravestones in the middle of the cemetery and settled down beside him, hiding.

"Let's just wait here till dawn," Char said softly. "Maybe if we can make it till morning, they'll go away. Don't bad things go away when the sun comes up?"

"Not all bad things," said Ven gloomily.

"You got another suggestion?"

Ven thought for a moment, then shook his head. "No." He turned Nicholas gently on his side and put his hand in front of the injured boy's mouth. "I think he's breathing—and he needs help." He stood up and looked over the fence. "Maybe I could run for the inn—"

"And then what?" Char demanded. "Who you gonna get to come out and help? Anybody you want torn to shreds?" He exhaled and leaned back against the gravestone, then a wicked gleam came into his eye and he grinned. "Think Ida would come out?"

"Stop it," Ven said, but he chuckled as well. "I guess we just wait and see if they come back."

"Once it gets light I'll run back and get somebody to help carry him," Char said. "I'll see if I can find Cadwalder, if he isn't asleep already. Or maybe McLean."

"Have you ever noticed that McLean doesn't seem to leave the inn much?" Ven mused. "In fact, I don't think I've ever seen him leave the hearth while I've been there."

Char shrugged. "Lots of odd folks in this place," he said. "Never seen so many non-humans in one place before. But that makes it kinda nice." He looked into the mist that was swirling through the graveyard. "At least it hasn't been boring since I met up with you.

Lots to look forward to as your roommate. Assuming you stay, o' course."

Ven sat back down beside a small gray headstone. "I don't belong here, Char," he said tiredly.

"Well, not yet," Char replied, glancing around. "You're still alive, at least for the moment."

"No, not in the cemetery, I mean here, at the inn, in Hare Warren. In Serendair."

Char sighed. "None of us does. It's just that we don't belong anywhere else, either."

"The king wants me to stay, to work for him, but I don't belong here. I have a family, even if they don't want to know me anymore," Ven continued, shivering a little in the mist. "Family reputation is the most important thing to Nain; it's our whole history, everything we are. I soiled our family name *and* caused them to believe I was dead. Even if my mother forgives me, I doubt my father ever will. I can't fix the loss of the factory—but at least I can make sure Witherspoon gets what's coming to him. Even if they don't want to see me, isn't it wrong not to go back?"

Char's face twisted in thought. "It's a nice problem to have, to have to choose between a king that wants to hire you, and a mother to coddle you and a father to yell at you."

He looked out in the distance for a moment, then, seeing nothing, sat down next to Ven. "You make me crazy sometimes, Ven. You're like your beard—you ain't had any cause to grow. You've had more of everything than a lot of folks, more family, more schooling—"

"More good friends to watch out for me," Ven added. "I guess I'm being selfish—you have it a lot worse than I do."

Char stared at him through the low-lying fog. "You know, that's the first time since we've met that you've actually called me a friend," he said. "You think I've only gone through this with you 'cause the captain told me to watch out for you. You feel so guilty about stupid things. You didn't have any choice but to sink those ships—once the Fire Pirates struck, you and those sailors were all dead men anyway. But you still feel bad about it, instead of glad you lived.

"You can't bring my parents back, can't find me new parents, can't seem to understand that some things can't be replaced. You wonder what you can do to make my life better, as if paying for my candy helps. It doesn't. There's some things you just can't do anything about. Stop feeling sorry for me. This is my life, just as that is yours. You have a family, but people pick on you because you're Nain. I have none, and nobody bothers me. We each have our blessings and our curses. In the end it makes us equals. Live with yours, and let me live with mine."

Ven thought for a moment. "You're right," he said finally.

"O' *course* I'm right," Char said smugly. "In case you haven't noticed, I usually am. It probably comes from living so fast." His face lost its grin. "Lives like mine go quick, Ven. Are you really fifty?"

"Yup."

"Fifty years old? Real years?"

"Yes."

Char sighed. "Not to be insulting, but why aren't you more grown-up? Why aren't you as smart as the captain, or any other fifty-year-old person? Are all Nain treated like babies until they're fifty or something?"

"I don't know," Ven said quietly. "This is just what fifty looks like on a Nain."

"Well, I can understand that you don't grow as fast, and that you live longer," Char continued. "What I don't understand is how, if you've had all that time, you're still like me. I mean, you've had fifty years to learn about the world, but it hasn't made you any more, well, *old*. Why haven't you grown up?"

The breeze picked up, twisting curls of fog around the trees, and rustling their sweaty hair.

Over the wind, or through it, they heard a distinctive *SSHHH!*
The boys froze.

At first they saw nothing in the misty graveyard but low-lying
fog. Then in the beat of a heart they saw a form approaching,
growing clearer, before their eyes.

It was a tall boy, a little older than they were, lean and long-
faced, his eyes gazing at them as the haze swirled and parted around
him.

At first they thought it might be Cadwalder on his way home
from work in the mist, but he was taller, slightly stooped at the
shoulder. And he wasn't really coming toward them, he was thickening from the darkness, solidifying, as if he had been there all the
time, but invisible.

"The answer to your question," said the tall boy, "is that he hasn't
had to." His voice was soft like the wind, and it alternated between
being high and low, as if it was just beginning to change. "Nain,
Lirin, Gwadd, merrows, and all those races take a much longer view
of life than humans do. They age more slowly, grow more slowly.
That's because there are so few of them compared to humans. They
have to live long enough to pass along all that they've learned of
their parts of the world. You might want to lie down now."

Ven looked quickly back over his shoulder.

Out of the mist, wolf-like shapes were approaching, low to the
ground, growling threateningly, tracking their scent. The wind carried the weird noise he had heard his first night in Hare Warren.

He lay down on his stomach quickly. Char was already flat on the
ground, his arm covering Nicholas's head.

"You'd best get down, too," he whispered to the tall boy.

The young man smiled. "They won't harm me," he said, looking
into the fog. "They are afraid of me."

Ven raised his head up enough to be able to see. The beasts were
scouring the ground, tracking their scent. They were coming nearer
with each passing moment.

A drop of rain fell on his nose, spattering into mist in the summer heat. Ven blinked as more drops fell on his lashes.

"Great," he muttered. "I can barely see them as it is—now we'll be almost blind in the rain."

The tall boy smiled. "Some blind people see far better than those whose eyes work," he said. "The rain may help you see better, not worse."

"Who are you?" Ven whispered. "Do you live near here?"

The boy turned at looked at him thoughtfully. "This is my home," he said simply. "But I don't live anywhere. My name is Gregory Snodgrass."

- 24 -

The Cemetery Guardian

It's all right," the shadowy boy said after a moment. He smiled wanly at the shock and horror on Ven's face. Char's face was planted into the grass, but his body was trembling like a leaf in the wind.

"You're—you're dead, aren't you?" Ven asked, trying to keep his voice from shaking like Char's.

"Well, yes," said Gregory. "But you don't need to get all quavery about it, as if it were a *bad* thing."

He turned his head toward the road, in the direction of the beasts. "Try and be as quiet as you can," he said.

A moment later he seemed to grow dimmer in the mist, then to expand, as if his body was made of fog itself. Ven's fear turned to amazement as the boy's lanky frame thinned out and spread to almost the size of the cemetery. He opened his now-enormous arms, filmy as haze over the sea, and wrapped them around the small graveyard over which he towered like a cloudy giant.

The sniffing and growling sounds grew louder as the beasts approached. Their milky white forms flickered in and out of the mist as they came nearer, the harsh shrieking growing louder as they picked up speed along with the scent of the boys.

They came to the center of the crossroads, slowing, and as they did, the strange noise became softer. The ghostly wolves stopped in front of the cemetery in the rain, which had grown heavier.

Ven held his breath, hoping that Char's shivering or Nicholas's occasional moaning would not give them away.

A deep chorus of growls filled the wet air.

"Look closer," said Gregory. His voice was softer, more airy, than it had been a moment before, perhaps because he was stretched so thin.

Then I remembered what Gregory had said about the rain helping me see better, not worse.

The first rule of good puzzling: See things as they really are, and not as they seem, the king had said.

I took out my jack-rule and slowly, carefully as I could, extended the far-viewing lens.

Then I looked through it.

The phantom wolves were standing in the rain, the hair on the backs of their necks standing straight up, as if they were frightened.

Their faces were unholy, skeletal, I thought. They looked almost as if they were melting in the rain.

And then I realized they were melting in the rain.

At first, black spots appeared on their milky coats and foreheads. Then those spots began running in great streaks down their sides. The ghostly white color of their bodies ran off the sides and onto the muddy ground of the crossroads, leaving shiny black and brown fur, slick in the rain.

"They're *dogs*," Ven whispered hoarsely. "Whiting's bloody dogs!"

Char's muddy face popped up like a jack-in-the-box.

"*Dogs?*" he asked in disbelief. "Gah! They sound like demons. Dogs don't make noise like that."

Ven wiped the raindrops from the jack-rule and looked closer.

"They have collars on," he said quietly after a moment. "Metal collars—skinny tubes with holes in them—like that sculpture in the square in Kingston! That noise must be the sound of the wind rushing through them when they move."

"All right—so they're not ghost wolves, they're livin' dogs," Char whispered back. "*Killer* guard dogs—they can still tear us to pieces. Like they did to Nicholas."

Through the jack-rule Ven could see that the animals, now black with a chalky film on their coats, were still looking around nervously, as if they could still smell their prey but could not see it through the haze.

The haze that was the shimmering body of the ghost boy.

Gregory's large head floated above them. Ven could almost swear he saw the spirit wink.

Then it leaned out over the road, hovering over the dogs.

"Boo," Gregory said.

The animals reared back, yelping, and dashed off in the direction of the White Fern Inn.

The mist thickened, and the spirit's filmy form shrank back into itself again. He shook his head and sighed.

"That was trite, I know," he said. "But it's such a fun thing to say."

Ven sat up slowly, trying not to notice the terror on Char's face. His curiosity was rumbling inside him again.

"Thank you, Gregory," he said gratefully.

"You're welcome," said the ghost. "You should go now; your friend needs a healer."

Ven reached over and tried to shake Char our of his frightened stupor. "Come on, we have to get Nick back to the inn."

As they gathered Nicholas's limp body, Gregory Snodgrass

began to fade into the misty rain. "How is my mother?" he asked, his outline barely visible.

"Better," Ven said. "Your father sent her some of the Living Water a few days ago, so she is looking well again."

The boy spirit looked sad. "Too bad it's only temporary," he said, his voice hollow.

Char wriggled closer to Ven. "Why?" he asked, his voice still trembling.

Ven swallowed hard to allowed the words to come out. "Is it because—because she's a Revenant?"

The ghost appeared suddenly more solid, as if the question had shocked him.

"My mother—a Revenant?" he demanded, offense in his voice. "Please. Don't be ridiculous. I'm the only Revenant in the family, thank you very much. Wherever did you get *that* idea?"

Char looked blankly at Ven, who coughed in embarrassment.

"Er—Mr. Whiting said that," he admitted. "He told me you and your mother died on the same day."

Gregory was silent for a moment. "Well, I suppose that is true in a way," he said quietly, his voice hollow on the wind. "Certainly a piece of her died when she found out what happened to me—any mother who lost a child would feel that way, wouldn't she?"

Ven could only nod, his jaw clenched. He was imagining his own mother's reaction to hearing the news of the Fire Pirates, as he had done every day since his birthday.

"Maurice Whiting lies through his teeth," Gregory went on. "He always did when I was alive. He doesn't believe in Revenants, or ghosts, or anything else. If he did, he would never come near here at night to send his dogs out to scare the residents at the inn. He has no idea what is going on here. If he knew that the tales of the Revenants buried at the crossroads—as well as me, the one buried in the cemetery—were *true*, he'd turn his sorry tail and run away as fast as his legs could carry him."

Ven and Char looked nervously at each other.

"If Mrs. Snodgrass isn't a Revenant, then why is she sick?" Char asked.

"Because her heart is here, with me," Gregory said. "And with the rest of the family buried here, and in the inn—she loves that place, and the people she takes care of. And because so much of her heart and soul are invested in this ground, this earth, she is being withered by what is poisoning it."

"Poisoning it?" Ven asked, suddenly nervous again. "I thought it was just Whiting's dogs that were haunting the crossroads."

Gregory shook his translucent head. "If that was it, you never would have seen me," he said, his voice light on the wind. "I'd be resting peacefully, but I'm not. The dogs are just a distraction. There is something terrible here, something that I try to stand guard against, to protect my family's inn and the people there. My father always told me when he went to sea to look out for my mother, and that's what I'm doing."

Char poked Ven. "See?" he whispered. "Everyone obeys the captain's orders. You can't escape 'em even when you *die*."

Ven felt sadness overwhelm him. "Does she know?" he asked. "Does your mother know that you're here, and what you are doing?"

The spirit shook its head. "No. That would only make her sadder than she already is. My father doesn't know, either. He spends his time at sea looking for more of the Living Water, but it's his being away from her that really saves her—the last piece of her heart is with him, away from this place, and that piece is safe as long as he's gone."

"I know I'm gonna be sorry I asked this," said Char, "but safe from what?"

The spirit that once was Gregory seemed to grow paler between the drops of rain. "Long ago, something evil was buried here. It was before there was an inn, or a town, just a crossroads. I don't know where, exactly, and I cannot do anything to stop it. It's an old evil, and whatever form it takes, it only comes out at night. It seems to be able to call to the *real* Revenants buried in the crossroads, terrible ones, with angry, destructive natures. That evil draws power from this place, this warm, safe place where the star Seren first shone on the island." He pointed above into the cloudy mist. "If the sky was clear, the star would be right over the inn at midnight. That first starshine made this land magical, gave it special power—and whatever is buried here draws on that power. It sucks the life out of flowers, plants, the wind, people—"

Gregory suddenly stopped and looked straight ahead of him toward the road.

"It walks the earth at night—and you had best be on your way, because it is coming. And it has friends."

Ven's heart flew into his throat and gagged there. He and Char scrambled over to Nicholas and seized him by the shoulders, then wrapped his arms around their necks. They dragged him over to the gate in the little graveyard and pulled him through. Ven looked back over his shoulder.

"Thank you," he called, but there was nothing behind him but swirling mist and dark rain.

"Come on, Nick, wake up," Char urged as they pulled him along the road toward the inn.

Ven said nothing, but continued to haul Nicholas with all his might, hurrying as fast as he could in the direction of the warm lights in the distance.

Over the wet grass to the muddy road they ran, trying to keep from slipping. The tiny hairs on the back of Ven's neck were bristling, and he thought he could feel the breath of something behind him. Whatever it was moved very quickly over the stony road that cut through the dark fields. *It's just the wind*, he thought as the breeze whipped over them. *Just the wind. Please let it just be the wind.*

"Let's not—go through the middle—of the crossroads," puffed Char.

"I'm with you on that," Ven replied, still tugging on Nicholas.

They stepped into the roadway north of where the two roads met, dragging their unconscious Warren-mate. They were almost to the field on the other side, almost to the outskirts of the inn, when Ven stumbled. Then he felt something brush the back of his leg.

He looked down.

An arm, gray and withered, had risen up from the mud of the roadway and was clutching at him.

And then another. And another.

Char screamed as one grabbed his foot and pulled him back.

"*Ven!*"

A dozen more skeletal arms shot up, grasping wildly at them. Five of them seized Nicholas and almost pulled him from their grasp.

A gust of wind kicked up, blowing Ven's wet hair into his eyes. He thought of the first time he had crossed this road with Clemency,

remembering with sudden clarity the words of the blessing she spoke before they stepped into the road.

What does the blessing do?

Makes me feel safe, I guess. Don't know what else it can *do.*

He chanted the words loudly into the wind.

For a second, the grasping hands froze.

"Come on!" he shouted to Char, kicking wildly at the clutching arms.

Char was struggling to break free of a sea of hands that had wrapped around his ankles.

"I'm *trying*," he gasped.

For a moment, panic gripped Ven even more tightly than the hands had. Then he wrapped his arms around Nicholas's waist and pulled with all his might.

"Hold on!" he shouted to Char.

With a mighty heave, he threw himself, and Nicholas, and Char, out of the road and into the damp grass alongside the roadway. He and Char scrambled to their feet and grabbed Nicholas, dragging him toward the hazy lights, not stopping until they were in front of the door with the golden griffin painted on it.

Char banged on the door. "Let us in! Blimey, *let us in!*" he shrieked.

The door swung open.

"Good heavens," Mrs. Snodgrass gasped, standing aside to let the boys in. "The inn door's always unlocked—what happened? What are you boys doing out at night?"

"We got locked out of Hare Warren," Ven said, lugging Nicholas to the fireplace with Char and laying him on the longest bench there. McLean, who had been playing when the door opened, stopped immediately. A chorus of tiny upset voices began to whisper and squeak all at once, and the Singer made hushing sounds in a language Ven had never heard to get them to settle down again.

"What happened to Nicholas?" the innkeeper asked, dunking a rag in the water basin and laying it across the unconscious boy's head.

"He was attacked by Mr. Whiting's dogs," Char said, panting as he sat down on the hearth.

"Whiting's dogs? Where was he?" Trudy asked.

"On his way home, almost at the crossroads," Ven said. "He's been out for quite a while—we couldn't get him to wake up."

"Nor can I, it seems," said Mrs. Snodgrass. "We're going to need Clemency—she's trained in the healing arts. And perhaps you, McLean." The Singer nodded.

"I'll get Clem," Ven volunteered, starting for the back door.

"No—don't go alone," Mrs. Snodgrass said quickly.

"I'll be all right," Ven said. *I hope*, he added silently. "I'll be right back."

He ran out the back door of the kitchen into the rain, which had begun to pelt like angry pebbles from the sky. When he reached the door of Mouse Lodge, he banged as hard as he could, then put his hands over his head to try to dodge the water coming off the roof.

"Clem! It's me, Ven!" he shouted.

He saw a light appear in the window as a lantern was unhooded. The door opened a moment later.

"Ven, what are you doing here?" the curate-in-training asked sleepily.

"No time to explain—Nick is hurt," Ven said, dragging her out the door. "Come on!"

They ran back across the wet field, dodging raindrops, without stopping even to catch a breath until they were back in Mrs. Snodgrass's warm kitchen, with the door closed and bolted securely behind them.

McLean was singing a healing song when they came into the main lobby of the inn. While Clem set about tending to Nicholas, Ven came over to where Char was explaining about the dogs to

Mrs. Snodgrass. Her face was glowing red as her hair with anger and Ven could have sworn he saw steam coming out her ears.

"I'm going to the White Fern right now and haul Maurice Whiting out of his very comfortable bed," she said furiously, stomping over to where her cloak hung on a peg by the door. "When I'm finished chewing on him, he'll know how Nicholas felt. And then some."

"Uh—you can't go out there now," said Char.

"And why not?" Mrs. Snodgrass demanded.

"Mama," Nicholas whispered in front of the fire in his sleep.

Mrs. Snodgrass stopped, her hand frozen in midair. "Oh, the poor thing," she said, her anger disappearing as she left the cloak hanging there and hurried over to the fire where Clemency was chanting words of comfort over the injured boy. "He must have been so frightened. Poor little blighter."

Ven turned around slowly and looked at Char, whose eyes were wide as his own.

Nicholas had called out in Gregory's voice.

"Have to hand it to the ghost—he found a way to keep her from going out when it's dangerous without letting Mrs. Snodgrass know he is there," said Ven quietly.

"Just lookin' out for his mother again, I suppose," Char said when he could speak.

"Char, could you come help us get him into a room?" Clem called from in front of the hearth. The Spice Folk had apparently gathered around Nicholas and lifted him up as a group; he hovered in the air about three feet off the ground, a multitude of tiny handholds dimpling the edges of his clothes.

Char nodded hesitantly, then turned to Ven. "Spice Folk," he said tartly. "You know how I love the Spice Folk."

The orange cat that had been sitting on the hearth rose and stretched.

"I'll go with you," Murphy said.

"They won't bother you while Clem's there," Ven said. He watched as Char took hold of Nicholas's sagging head, and he, Mrs. Snodgrass, Clem, and the cat went off into the deeper parts of the inn. Then Ven went over to the hearth.

"Your song made my headache go away," he said to McLean, who was tuning his instrument. "What was it?

"His name," McLean said over the twanging of the strings. "There's no more powerful magic to a person that his own true name. It is a pattern of musical vibrations and tones that makes him what he is—and if he is injured or damaged, singing his name can make him back to the way he is supposed to be sometimes. True names are the key to the science of Singing."

"That's amazing," Ven said. Nicholas *had* looked better, almost as if he were only asleep. "You not only fixed his wounds with that song, but you made my head feel better as well."

The Singer did not look at him, but smiled slightly as he continued with his task. "Glad to hear it. Tell me the story of your night."

So Ven told McLean about the chase of the demon wolves that turned out to be Mr. Whiting's dogs painted with the same whitewash that gave his inn its white sheen, about hiding in the family cemetery and meeting with the spirit of Gregory Snodgrass, and their terrifying escape through the sea of clutching skeletal hands that sought to hold them captive for whatever was following them.

"I don't know what to do now," he said when he finished the tale. "I'd like to believe that I can help, that before I return home I can make things right here. But this is beyond my abilities. Whatever is out there is far more powerful than anyone realizes, I think. And even being a reporter for the king, with all the troops and all the support he might be willing to offer, still isn't enough to put a stop to what is happening at the crossroads. People will continue to die or disappear, Mrs. Snodgrass will continue to wither away, the captain will sail the sea forever alone, and I can't do anything about it."

" 'Tis a complicated riddle, that's for certain," said McLean. "I don't blame you for thinking it's too much for you—but maybe you are overwhelmed by the large number of pieces to it. If you can solve one part, perhaps the rest will fall into place. You might want to sleep on it and look at it again in the morning."

Ven smiled in spite of his weariness.

"You sound just like the king," he said. "'The second rule of good puzzling: Look at the details and the whole picture separately, you will see two different things.'"

"He's right," said McLean. He smiled again as Ven rose and turned to go. "Good night, Ven. You were very brave tonight, bless your beard."

Ven froze where he stood.

"McLean," he said, "I don't have a beard."

- 25 -

The Singer's Secret

FOR A MOMENT THE STORYSINGER FROZE, TOO. THEN HE SMILED slightly.

"A common Nain expression," he said casually. "I'm sure you're familiar with it."

"Yes," said Ven, walking closer. "Very familiar. And anyone who knows of the expression also knows that it is reserved for older Nain men, those who already have at least a Bramble, and possibly a full Thicket. It's never said to a hairless chin—that's considered an insult."

A quiet chorus of agitated whispers rose from the floor, all but drowned in the crackle of the fire. McLean made a calming gesture at the ground, then turned to Ven and looked at him for the first time that evening. Ven saw a milky sparkle flit through his dark eyes as he turned.

"Sorry, Ven," he said regretfully. "Didn't mean it as an insult, to be certain. It was just ignorance. I apologize."

Ven came slowly over to the blazing hearth and sat down on the chair in front of McLean.

"I think I know your secret, McLean," he said excitedly.

The Singer smiled and looked back at the floor.

"You're blind, aren't you?"

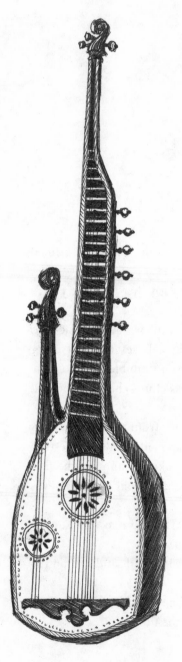

For a moment the only sound in the room was the crackling of the fire.

Finally the Singer chuckled. "Well, I prefer 'sightless.' 'Blind' has a lot of different meanings, and I don't think all of them apply, but yes, Ven, my eyes do not work, if that's what you mean."

"That's why you said you understood what the king wanted, and needed—someone to be his eyes." Ven glanced around the floor at McLean's feet, where all the whispering and fluttering had stilled into silence. "The Spice Folk—they're your eyes. Aren't they?"

The Singer ran his fingers over the strings of his instrument. "I have lots of eyes, Ven," he said as the random music began to form a tune that sounded like the wind. "The Spice Folk do indeed tell me almost all of what goes on in the inn—but they apparently didn't realize your lack of beard was worth mentioning." He made a joking angry face at the floor around his feet, and Ven heard shivering and gasping followed by soft laughter.

"Who and what else are your eyes?" he asked.

"Murphy sometimes, and Mrs. Snodgrass. But most of the time it's the music that lets me see."

"How?"

McLean changed the tune and picked

out a new melody softly, a song that made Ven think of summer grass and wide open fields.

"All of life is at its very core made up of vibrations, Ven, waves of sound that most people hear or light that they see, or so I'm told. But if you don't have eyes to behold that light, and the colors it carries, you can use a different sense to see. I feel the vibrations on my skin, and hear the sounds they make. It's my way of seeing. It can be yours, too, at least for a moment."

Then the tune he was playing changed again, and suddenly in my mind I could see standing around him on the hearth several dozen tiny glowing shapes, some as small as my little finger, the largest ones the size of my hand. They were silver and shimmering, with fluttering wings, and they moved with such grace that they appeared to be floating on the air, the way the wind carries a leaf it is playing with.

He introduced them to me then, one by one—Prilla, Puffball, Rosemary, Fern. As he spoke each of their names, I could see them solidly for a second. Each was as different from the other as the members of Hare Warren or Mouse Lodge were, with hair that was sometimes gold, sometimes brown, or even light gray or lavender. They came in all different shapes, and wore clothing made of blossoms and wood bark. Two mischievous boys, Dill and Fennel, appeared together, whispering evilly to each other; I saw them giggle madly before they faded from sight again. The smallest of the Spice Folk he introduced as Flax, a baby barely big enough to sit up, with hair as soft and silky as the seeds Mrs. Snodgrass had given me. The largest one, the clear leader, was Dandelion, a confident girl fairy with a head of yellow hair and freckles, who shooed the others away from McLean and broke up fights between Dill and Fennel.

Then the music stopped, and the pictures in my mind went away.

"There is much about the world that is unseen to the eye, Ven," McLean said as the song came to an end, and the Spice Folk faded into invisibility again. "That doesn't mean it's not as present as you or I. Remember that."

Gloom returned in Ven's mind as he thought about Gregory and what was stalking the crossroads. "Oh, believe me, I know," he said. "It's my greatest problem at the moment. Whatever evil is buried at the crossroads cannot be seen in the light, and I don't want to be there in the dark with it again. I can't see it. So I can't find it. If I can't find it, how can I do anything about it?"

McLean sighed, then smiled his slight smile.

"The Spice Folk act as my eyes," he said, stretching his arms and moving his hand to work out a finger cramp. "Perhaps you could let them act as yours." He returned to his song. "But after all, this isn't really your problem, now, is it? You can always go home."

"I'm not certain whether I have a home anymore," Ven said.

"Home is where you decide to stay," said McLean. "Where you decide to fight for what matters to you. A man can have many homes, but he has to be willing to stand up and call them his own. Then he is never again uncertain whether he has one or not."

Ven nodded. "May I ask you one thing more?" The Singer nodded. "When you said that Oliver had made good use of me, did you mean to call the Floating Island?"

"Yes," said McLean. "Finding a Nain in the sea, one that can climb a mast into the wind, has got to be a once-in-a-lifetime, miraculous thing—sort of like you finding your albatross feather on the Floating Island. To not make use of that to do something good would be a terrible waste, wouldn't it?"

"I suppose so," Ven said. "But it doesn't feel good to be used."

"Perhaps not. But there is a difference between being ill-used, and being used for a good purpose. Oliver Snodgrass didn't just use you to call the island for his own purposes; he took you there so that you could send a message home, didn't he?"

"Yes," Ven said, feeling better.

"And he showed you one of the wonders of the world in the process." McLean sighed. "How I wish I could go there one day. For a Singer who listens to the wind, there could be no more miraculous place, I imagine."

"I could call it for you!" Ven said excitedly. "Now that we know how, one day we can go out together aboard the *Serelinda*, and I can climb the mast and call the island so you can go there. You would love it, McLean."

"No doubt," said the Singer, "but I don't know if that would be right. Just because one *can* do something doesn't mean one *should*. Something that powerful should only be sought out in a matter of life and death, which is why the captain did it. We will see. If I'm meant to visit the island, then perhaps it will come on its own one day."

Clemency appeared in the hallway. "Ven—Nicholas is awake. Mrs. Snodgrass has made up a bed for you and Char in the room where we took him so you can both get some sleep."

Ven nodded and rose from the chair in front of the hearth.

"Thank you, McLean," he said. "I will think about what you said."

"Good night," said the Singer. He went back to plucking a tune, and Ven thought he could see the flames of the hearth fire dancing along in time to the melody. Ven watched for a few moments, then made his way down the hall to find the room where Nicholas was.

He walked down a dark hallway with walls of polished wood to the only open door. Light spilled into the hall from inside the room.

At first when he stepped through the doorway, Ven thought he had mistakenly walked outside the inn. The room was filled with the light of soft candles and an oil lantern. There was a bed and a nightstand, and a chair in which Mrs. Snodgrass sat. Nicholas lay back against the pillows, a large bandage on his head. He smiled as Ven looked around the room in amazement.

"Some room, eh, Polypheme?"

Ven could only nod. Four slender trees grew up through the floor to form the bedposts, their branches twisted together into a leafy canopy over the mattress. The floor was a carpet of thick grass, and night-blooming flowers dotted it, their colors glowing softly in the candlelight.

Behind the nightstand a little spring flowed in a waterfall over gray rocks. Clemency was filling a pitcher from the spring to refill the water basin next to the bed. And the chair in which Mrs. Snodgrass sat was a wide flowering bush with a cushion on it.

Mrs. Snodgrass saw his amazement and chuckled. "I often have Lirin guests," she said. "This is one of the rooms in which they are more comfortable."

"I can imagine," said Ven. "Glad you're better, Nick."

"Thanks for pulling me out of there," said Nicholas. "Thought I was a goner."

Mrs. Snodgrass rose tiredly. She pointed to the three sets of bedding and pillows on the floor.

"You children should stay in here tonight," she said in a weary voice. "It's not safe for you to go back to the Lodge and the Warren in the dark. Those killer dogs might still be running loose."

"We'll watch Nicholas," Clemency promised. "Get some sleep, Mrs. Snodgrass. I'll call you if there is any change."

"Thank you," said Mrs. Snodgrass. She bent and brushed a quick kiss on Nicholas's head, then left the room, her skirts rustling quietly.

As soon as the door was closed, Clemency turned to Ven and Char.

"All right," she said severely, "what really happened out there?"

The boys related the tale from the beginning, how Cadwalder had left for work early and locked the door, hearing Nicholas screaming at the crossroads, Whiting's dogs, the spirit in the cemetery, the warning it gave them, and their escape through the clutching hands that had risen from the ground. Clemency shivered when they were done.

"There is even greater evil here than I imagined," she said, her eyes gleaming with fear. "I don't know how to keep anyone safe so close to such a thing."

"Well, you have more ability than you know," Ven said. "That blessing you said at the crossroads worked a little, even coming from me."

"That's a blessing of peace we use when we are tending to cemeteries and monuments, old battlefields and the like," Clemency said. "It's meant to bring forgiveness and rest. It won't work in a place where the evil is active, and angry. Whatever is out walking the night can't be contained with a blessing like that."

"Maybe not," Char said. "But we gotta find some way to beat it back."

"If you can find it," said Nicholas weakly. "I've run the crossroads a million times, and I've never seen any sign that something has been buried there. It must have been so long ago that the ground has flattened out completely. You can't dig up a whole roadway."

"Ven can," said Clemency. "He's Nain—they're natural diggers."

"I've never dug a day in my life," said Ven.

"Well, it should come naturally," insisted Clemency.

"We'll go out and have a look in the morning," said Char. "Maybe there'll be some clues in the daylight we could never find at night."

Clemency stretched out on the floor and pulled the blanket over her.

"I'll bring Saeli," she said, her words muffled by the covers. "She has a good eye for things that are unusual or out of place."

One by one they dropped off to sleep, first Nick, then Clemency, finally Char. Only Ven remained awake, trying to find a comfortable position. Something kept nagging at his mind, as if he were missing an obvious clue, and something kept poking into his hip as well. He reached into his pocket and pulled it out. It was the wooden cube, the puzzle the king had given him.

He turned over onto his back in the darkness and twisted the puzzle cube, trying to put the pieces of the mystery at the crossroads together in the same manner as he was solving the wooden one. Finally he drifted off, his dreams haunted by clutching hands and ghost wolves that melted in the rain.

- 26 -

The Puzzle Solved

IN HIS LAST DREAM BEFORE MORNING VEN DREAMT HE WAS BEING stabbed in the back, first by Whiting, then by each of his housemates in Hare Warren and the people in the Crossroads Inn. One by one his friends lined up and took turns plunging a heavy, dull knife into his lower back, handing the weapon to the next person in line when they had finished.

When he woke, his back ached terribly. Ven rolled over and discovered he was sleeping on the puzzle box. He groaned, then sat straight up as a thought occurred to him.

Solving these puzzles teaches me how to think in the right ways, the king had said.

"Char!" Ven gasped, shaking his roommate awake.

"Wha—? Huh?" Char mumbled, half asleep still.

"I need your help," Ven said, shaking Clemency as well. "And yours—and Saeli's. You, too, Nick."

The injured boy sat up carefully in his bed as the others stretched grumpily. "What kind of help, Ven?" he asked.

"Solving this puzzle," Ven said. "Something terrible has been going on for a very long time at the crossroads. We know there is a genuine evil there—not just dogs masquerading as demonic wolves. We know that people have died there, or disappeared, and that something is draining the magic of the place, and the life out of the people who are tied to it. Whatever it is must be something from long ago, so long ago that no one remembers what happened here. And I think it's a riddle so complex that no one person can figure it out or stop it. If it were, Mrs. Snodgrass would have been able to, or Constable Knapp, or McLean, or even all the king's men who have investigated the murders but never found the answer. But those are individuals looking at it. We need to look at it as a—"

"A team?" Clemency interjected excitedly.

"Well, yes, but I was going to say as a puzzle. If we apply the king's rules of puzzling to this situation, we may be able to figure out what is going on there."

"What are the rules?" Nick asked.

Ven looked out the window at the sky, which was beginning to turn a lighter shade of blue at the horizon. "The first one is 'See things as they are, and not as they seem.' The hardest part of this is that everything at the crossroads seems normal."

"All right, then," said Char, shaking his dark hair roughly into place. "Let's go have a look at those crossroads in daylight."

"How can I help?" Nick asked.

"Tell us what you saw before the dogs attacked you," Ven said. "Or what you heard. Have you ever noticed anything strange about the place?"

Nicholas lay back against the pillows and thought for a moment. "I didn't *see* anything—they caught me from behind. But I guess I did *hear* something strange."

"Sort of a weird, windy whine?" Char asked.

"Yeah," said Nicholas. "I had heard that many times before—Albert and I heard it especially loud the first night you guys came."

"The dogs came right up to the window that night," Ven said. "I could hear them growling outside, sniffing around. It was like they were looking for me. I even thought I heard my name."

"When I heard that sound behind me on the road last night, I about dropped," Nicholas. "I could hear it get louder as they got closer, and I kept running faster and faster—and then all of a sudden, just after I ran through the crossroads, the noise stopped. Almost like the sound was swallowed."

"It did?" said Clemency.

"Yes. But then something snagged my foot—it almost felt like somebody grabbed me—then the dogs were on me a second later, and that's all I remember."

"There seems to be a place where the wind won't blow at the crossroads," said Char. "My kite dives smack for the ground whenever it drifts near there."

"That's a piece of the puzzle, I'm sure," said Ven. "Thanks, Nick. You've been a great help. Get some rest. We'll come back and tell you what we find."

Nick's eyes were wide and his face pale. "I hope so," he said uncertainly. "Do be careful, mates."

"I'm going to go get Saeli," said Clemency as they left the beautiful room and headed back into the main part of the inn. "And check in on the girls—Ciara's watching Mouse Lodge for me, but I imagine they are pretty worried."

A chorus of soft whispers and fluttering rose up around Clemency as she headed for the back door.

"Clem," Ven said quickly, "McLean suggested that the Spice Folk might be able to act as my eyes—are they willing to come out to the crossroads with us?"

The inn went suddenly silent.

"Uh—no," Clemency said.

"Hmm. All right," said Ven. He was disappointed, but not particularly surprised.

While Clemency went to Mouse Lodge, Ven and Char went to the stables to find tools for their task. They found Cadwalder there, just finishing up the day's mucking and getting ready to head off for bed.

"Morning, Cadwalder," Ven said.

The tall boy turned around, surprised, and leaned on his rake. "Morning Polypheme, Char." He looked tired. "What are you doing up so early?"

"We were wondering if we could borrow some spades," Char said.

"Sure," Cadwalder replied, nodding to the tack room. "There are a couple over there."

"Thanks," said Ven. "We'll return them when we're done."

"See to it that you do," said Cadwalder, returning to his chore. "I'll be asleep."

Spades in hand, the boys made their way to the crossroads, where Saeli was standing nervously beside Clem.

"You all right, Saeli?" Ven asked gently. The small girl nodded, but he could see that she was trembling. "Good. Let us know if you see or notice anything you think might be important."

The four children walked slowly to the place where the two roads met, searching the area with their eyes. The morning birdsong was strangely quiet; every now and then a chirp or twitter could be heard in the distance, but the area near the road was silent.

"I can feel the evil here," Clemency said, her normally vibrant voice flat and frightened. Ven turned to look at her and saw she was sweating, her rich brown skin dusky.

"Go back if you need to, Clem," he said.

"Not on your life," the curate-in-training retorted.

Ven smiled. "Let's keep together, then."

They circled the entire center of the roadway, stepping carefully in and out of road and grass. Finally Saeli looked up with an urgent gleam in her eye. She bent down and plucked what looked like a blade of grass with some tiny pink-white flowers on it, then held it up in front of the others.

"What is that, Saeli?" Char asked.

The small girl swallowed hard, then spoke. Her voice came out in a crackling whisper. "Yarrow," she said. She handed the plant to Ven.

"What does this mean?" Ven asked.

Clemency shrugged. "It's an herb, a fairly common flower. One of the Spice Folk is named Yarrow, and this is her plant. It's used in medicine to stop bleeding and heal infections, and also as a sign of love."

Ven looked across the fields around the road's edge. "It's everywhere around here."

Saeli shook her head. "Not there," she said in her gravelly whisper. She pointed to a spot along the roadway at the edge of the crossroads.

The four moved slowly closer, and Ven could see that she was right. It was a bulge of dirt beside the actual roadbed where no flowers or even grass grew. There was nothing especially noticeable about the patch, but on closer examination they could see that Saeli was right—there was no sign of the yarrow that dotted the fields elsewhere.

"Can you bring up flowers here, Saeli?" Clemency asked.

Saeli closed her eyes and concentrated, her tiny forehead wrinkling deeply.

All around the road's edge a tiny explosion of colors appeared as wildflowers of every kind suddenly bloomed in the grass. A thick blanket of color spread over the fields, the green grass turning yellow, white, red, blue, and pink in a heartbeat.

"The second rule of puzzling—'Look at the details and the whole picture separately,'" Ven said. "'You will see two different things.'"

"Look," Clemency said, her voice quavering a little.

Nothing grew in the spot.

"Oh, dear," Clemency said. "This is bad."

The wildflowers that had surged up from the grass withered and died away.

"This must be what McLean meant when he said the Spice Folk could be our eyes," Ven said. "If their magic doesn't work here, there must be something terribly wrong with the earth."

"Well, let's get digging," said Char. He started to plant the spade in the dirt when Clemency's hand shot out and grabbed it.

"I don't know if we should," she said quietly. "The evil here is very great. I don't know whether we will be able to handle it."

"It's daylight," Ven said. "Gregory said the evil that was buried here only comes out at night. So we had best get to work."

He and Char began to dig while the girls stood back and kept watch for passing carts. Each time a carriage or a farmer's wagon would approach they would cease their digging, to return immediately to it once they were out of sight.

As Clemency had predicted, Ven was a natural digger. Char had to quit and rest after an hour or so, and traded places with Clem, but Ven kept on, because it seemed as he dug that the earth moved willingly out of the way. Saeli had coaxed a large bush to grow between the hole and the crossroads so that they wouldn't be seen. The pile of dirt from his spade soon grew larger than the bush.

This must be what the Nain who live downworld do, he thought, pleased in spite of the danger of the situation. *It's as if the earth was almost liquid, like swimming through it. No wonder Nain like to tunnel and build roadways, and harvest gems and coal and precious metals. It's easy for them.*

It was long past noon when his spade finally struck something harder than the clay and rock of the roadway. The sun had turned a darker shade of orange and was hanging in the sky, halfway down the welkin, burning ominously.

Even in the summer heat, the four children suddenly felt cold.

Carefully Ven cleared away the dirt. At the bottom of the hole was an intricately carved box, as large as a bench, the many pieces that formed its lid wedged open.

Resting in it was a pile of bones. The skull grinned up at him lifelessly.

At first he could only make harsh sounds at the back of his throat. Ven swallowed, his mouth dry.

"This is a Rover's box,
I think," he said when he
could finally speak. "The king
told me about them."

"Why is it open?" Char asked,
his voice higher than usual.

Ven shook his head. "I don't know, but it would seem that because it's open whatever—whoever—is resting in there is able to get
out at night." He felt his stomach twist into a tight knot. "Gregory
said that what was buried here was an old evil, able to suck the very
life from this place. I don't know how this box got opened, but that
must be why whatever it is can walk the world at night."

Char glanced above him nervously.

"Speaking of night," he said, "the sun's starting to go down."

"What are we going to do now?" Clemency asked. "If anything,
we may have just made it worse. Now we've uncovered the bloody
thing, it can get out without any effort."

"We have to figure out how to close this box and lock it again,"
Ven said, standing and brushing the dirt from his hands. "And
quickly."

"I can't even tell how the bloody lid is supposed to fit together in
one piece," said Char. He reached into the hole and pushed two of
the sides toward each other, but they turned on an angle and sprang
farther apart.

"If this is a Rover's box, it's a puzzle that only the one who made it knows the solution to," Ven said desperately. "That person is most likely long dead—in fact, I bet that's him in the box—except for the bones, it's empty."

"And except for that rubble in the bottom," Clemency said.

Ven looked more closely. Clem was right—beneath the bones were shreds of rotting cloth, some pebbles, a few broken pieces of iron, and a smooth, thin stone, oddly shaped. Nothing of any apparent value.

"The king said Rovers store their treasure in these boxes," Ven said, trying to see around the bones without getting close enough to touch them. "Maybe brigands came upon this Rover while he had it open, killed him, took his stuff, and put him in the box, but couldn't close it, so they just buried it with the top open. No wonder he's so nasty—he's getting revenge at anyone he can catch at the crossroads now. And he's the only one who could have closed the box, because only the person who made it knows how."

"Only the person who made it? Are you sure?" said Clemency, pushing on one side of the lid again, and reeling back when it broke into four separate squares.

Ven thought hard, trying to remember exactly what the king had said.

"It would take a puzzler of very great skill, greater than the king's own, to figure it out," he said. "Or a very talented thief."

The four stopped and looked at each other.

"I'll go get her," Clemency said, starting back toward Mouse Lodge.

"Wait a minute—I dunno," said Char doubtfully.

"That's who I had in mind," said Clem.

"No," said Char, "I mean I don't know if we can trust her. I was in a jail cell with her for an afternoon till they separated us, and she picked me clean. I'm lucky I escaped with my underwear. I'd hate to have her do somethin' stupid."

"The king believes that everyone holds a piece of the puzzle that makes up the world," said Ven. "We need to get this box closed, and I don't know anyone else who has a chance to figure it out. She was able to solve the practice box without a second thought. Go get her, Clem."

Char glowered while they waited, but Ven was too busy watching the sun sink to notice. After some time Clemency returned, Ida following along behind her, an insolent expression on her face.

"Come on, Ida, hurry up!" Ven called.

"Keep your knickers on, Polywog," the girl retorted. She came up to the deep hole and stared down into the bottom of it. "Whoa—bones. I don't do bones."

"You don't have to touch the bones, ya twit," said Char nastily. "In fact, we'd appreciate it if you wouldn't, thank you very much."

Clemency gave Char a sharp dig in the ribs. "Don't you call her names," she said angrily. "She's doing us a favor."

"Right," Char mumbled.

"It's important we get this closed, Ida," Ven said to the girl. "And it can only be closed in one way. The Rover's box is the exception to the last rule of puzzling—there is only one real solution."

The thin girl with colorless hair nodded, then climbed down into the hole directly in front of the box. She stood there with her arms folded, studying it silently.

"How long is this going to take?" Char asked after a long time had passed and Ida hadn't moved. He was watching the sun slip over the edge of the world and the sky begin to turn dark.

Ven shook his head. "As long as it takes, I suppose."

"Hope that the daylight holds out that long," Char replied.

Finally, just as dusk was setting in, Ida unfolded her arms and took hold of two of the four squares that made up one of the lid pieces. She started moving sides and corners together, fitting each piece into place, over and over, layer by layer, until a solid lid to the box had formed. Then she turned the lid sideways, and started to lower it, in two distinct pieces, onto the top of the box.

The last sliver of sun disappeared behind a cloud at the horizon. As it did, the thin stone below the bones in the Rover's box caught the final ray and sparkled in an explosion of a thousand tiny rainbows.

Ven's eyes opened wide. It was the same glitter of color he had seen on his first evening in Kingston, from the tower of the Gated City. He stared past Ida, who was nervously watching the darkening sky, into the Rover's box at the razor-thin stone. In the second when the last ray of sun crossed its surface, a gleaming picture of what looked to be a key appeared with writing below it in a language he had never seen before. The flat surface of the stone glowed with fiery color, then faded immediately to gray again as the light left the sky completely.

The thin stone faded into the darkness again.

"Did you see that?" Ven asked excitedly.

"See what?" demanded Ida, struggling with the lid of the box. The other children shook their heads.

Inside the Rover's box, the bones moved.

Ida gasped.

The sky darkened eerily and the box began to shake.

"Ida, hurry!" Clemency choked.

The wind whipped around the crossroads in a hail of fury, tearing at their clothes and hair. In all places but where the box was, that is—and in that place all was deeply, frighteningly still. A smoky haze rose up from the bottom of the box, thick and blinding.

Ida set her jaw and gave the lid one more turn, then slammed the top of the box down, locking it with a quick turn of three bands of wood carved into the sides. The rim of the box let loose a puff of gray dust, then the lines separating the top from the bottom disappeared, making it solid with no visible cracks. Ida turned to the others and looked up at them from the depths of the hole, then shuddered.

"Bones," she said.

She sighed deeply in relief.

The dust that had escaped the box hung on the wind for a moment, then, as Ida inhaled, rushed in a whoosh into her nose, almost too fine to be noticed. She rubbed her sleeve across her nose, sniffed a few times, and then looked up from the hole again.

"Any day now, Polywog," she said impatiently.

Ven held out his hand to her. "Here, let me help you out of there," he said.

Ida reached up to grasp it, but when she did, her fingers passed right through Ven's palm. Puzzled, she tried again, and still missed.

Then she looked down at her hand and gasped.

It, like the rest of her, was beginning to dim like a lantern running out of oil.

And disappear.

- 27 -

A Desperate Dash

W HAT THE—?" EXCLAIMED CHAR.

"Ida," Ven said slowly, "give me your elbow."

At first the girl didn't seem to hear him; she was staring at her hand, a puzzled expression turning to one of shock. Then she looked back up at Ven, and her pale blue eyes were wide with fear, something Ven had never seen on her face before.

"Come on," he said gently. "Elbow."

Ida crooked her arm and Ven made a grab for the bend in it. This time his fingers wrapped around something solid, and he gave a strong pull, yanking Ida out of the hole and into the pile of dirt beside it.

"What's—what's happening?" Clemency stammered.

They looked around at the crossroads, now swallowed by darkness. The thick steam that had begun to rise from around the Rover's box had disappeared, leaving only the low-lying fog of night. In the distance, warm lights burned within the Inn. Ven saw another, dimmer light traveling slowly from behind the Inn to the stables; *Cadwalder's back to work*, he thought. *We sure have been at this a long time.*

"Polywog, what have you done to me?" Ida demanded in a voice that quavered. She was staring at her hands in the dark, watching as they grew more and more filmy by the moment.

"He's done nothing," came a hollow voice from the cemetery behind them. They turned to see Gregory there, becoming more solid in the dark. "You swallowed some breath of the Rover's grave. Now you are becoming a Revenant yourself. With each breath you take, a little more of your life bleeds away. By this time tomorrow, you will be one of us. I'm sorry."

"No—nobody mentioned that when you dragged me away from supper to help you," Ida said nervously. Clemency reached for her hand and passed right through it; she put her arm around Ida's shoulders quickly.

"What can we do?" the curate-in-training asked Gregory.

The translucent boy considered. "I really don't know," he said finally. "I'm only here to guard the crossroads and look after my mother. Now that you have closed the box, that shouldn't be necessary anymore; at least once you've reburied it. When the crossroads were safe again, I was planning to go on myself."

"Go on?" asked Ven.

"To the light," said the ghost. "Where I am supposed to be. You will see someday." He looked at Ida, who was trembling like a leaf in the wind. "You don't have to be scared. Being dead really isn't all that bad. Neither is being undead."

Ida turned her head and heaved her supper all over the grass.

"All right, we have to do something to fix this," Ven said as Clem bent over Ida and gave her a handkerchief.

"Like what?" Char demanded.

"Maybe McLean can help," Saeli whispered in her harsh voice.

"That's a good idea!" Ven said. "He fixed Nicholas with a song of his true name. Maybe he can do the same for Ida." His excitement waned at the look on Ida's face. "What? What's the matter?"

The thin girl's eyes were wide in the dark. "I—I don't know mine," she said softly.

"Your name? You don't know your real name?"

"Not all of it," Ida said defensively. "Maybe you could lend me one of *yours*, Polywog—don't you have about ten of them?"

"Don't feel bad, Ida," Char said awkwardly. "Lots of people don't—I don't know mine, Cadwalder doesn't know his."

"Thanks—I feel *so* much better now." Ida scowled and turned away.

Clemency was examining Ida's arm. "Whatever is going on here, it seems to be moving from her outer limbs inward. And it gets worse every time she takes a deep breath. So for goodness' sake, Ven, try to keep from upsetting her, and Ida, stop talking." She tore a piece fabric off the bottom of her tunic and tied it around Ida's upper arm. "Maybe we can hold it off for a while."

Char pulled Ven aside and spoke softly. "Ya know, ever since I met her I've wished that Ida would disappear, but I didn't mean like *that*," he said uneasily. "She makes me crazy, but I don't wanna see her die—or worse."

"No," Ven agreed. "We have to do something fast. This is a matter of life and death."

The words rang in his head from the last time he heard them.

Something that powerful should only be sought out in a matter of life and death, McLean had said.

"The Floating Island!" he shouted, causing Char and Saeli to jump. "That's it! We have to get some of the Living Water; that's the only thing I know of powerful enough to counteract this. It was the only thing that kept Mrs. Snodgrass alive—surely it can save Ida."

"You're daft." Char snorted. "That thing was out in the middle of the *sea*, for cripe's sake, and two weeks' sail away. How do you expect to get to it before she vanishes completely?"

"We're not going to it," Ven said, looking around the crossroads. "It's going to come to us. Come on, we have to get to town." He paused, staring at the blank faces in front of him. "Unless anyone else has a better idea?"

A heartbeat later he, Char, and Saeli were running as fast as they could across the fields toward the stable.

Cadwalder had just hung up the lantern and was pulling on his boots when the three children bolted through the stable door, causing the horses to nicker nervously.

"Polypheme! What are you doing here at this hour?" he demanded, gentling the horse in the nearest stall.

"We—we need to get to town, right now." Ven panted, wiping the sweat from his brow. "Please—it's an emergency. Can—you—lend us a wagon?"

Cadwalder blinked, his eyes going from Ven to Char to Saeli.

"Mrs. Snodgrass would hang me by my toenails," he said uncertainly.

"I will hang for you, I promise," Ven said. "Please, Cadwalder, we don't have much time."

The boy considered for a moment. "Do any of you know how to drive a wagon? Or even ride a horse?"

The three children looked blankly at one another.

"I'll take that as a no," Cadwalder said.

"You could drive us," Ven said quickly. "You must be good at it."

"I am, but I'm not leaving my post, Polypheme," the steward of Hare Warren said, picking up a rake. "And I'm not going through the crossroads, let alone to town, at night. Has bad memories for me. I'm sorry."

"*Now* what do we do?" Char asked. "There's no way Ida can walk—all that breathin', she'd be gone before we made it to the White Fern. And those bloody dogs might still be out there. What are we gonna do?"

Ven felt movement behind him. He turned around to see Saeli wandering over to the paddocks of two older draft horses. She waved for Ven to come nearer, and when he did, she motioned for him to get down on his hands and knees. He did, feeling foolish, until Saeli climbed up on his back, holding on to the paddock door, and began whispering into the ear of the nearest horse, a fat white one named Breeze.

"What are you doing?" Cadwalder asked in disbelief, but Char waved impatiently at him.

"Shhhh," he whispered. "Saeli can talk to animals."

With a whinny, the horse lifted its head in what appeared to be a nod.

"Can you do it, Saeli?" Ven asked, feeling his excitement grow as she climbed down from his back. "Can you tell them what they need to know to get us to town?"

The tiny girl nodded, her face uncertain.

Ven turned back to Cadwalder.

"Please, Cadwalder—can we take them? And a wagon?"

The older boy exhaled, thinking. "All right," he said reluctantly. "You can have Breeze and Trillium, the oldest ones here; they're practically dead, anyway. But you are taking the fall for this, Polypheme. I'm not facing the wrath of Mrs. Snodgrass on your behalf. If you don't come back, I'm telling her you stole them."

"Whatever you need to do," Ven said, opening the paddock door.

"I'll tack 'em up for you," Cadwalder said, reaching for the bridles and reins, and pointing to an old, rickety wagon. "And I'll get you a lantern. After that, you're on your own."

Ven nodded curtly. Out of the corner of his eye, he saw an orange shape hovering near the stable door, and turned to see Murphy watching them with what looked like interest.

"Brave lad, isn't he?" the cat said disdainfully, nodding toward Cadwalder, who was busy gathering the tack.

"He's helping, and we need his help," Ven replied. He went over to the cat and bent down in front of him. "Murphy, will you do me a favor?"

"That depends on what it is. I rarely do favors, and I always expect a treat in return."

"A treat?" Ven asked in dismay.

The orange tabby shrugged. "I'm a cat. If I do something for nothing, I get thrown out of the cat guild."

"What sort of treat?"

Murphy considered. "Oh, a nice ball of string, or perhaps a fish head. That would be tasty. I'm not hard to please."

"I'll do my best to find you something," Ven promised. "But please go and tell McLean what's going on. Tell him we are going to take Ida to the island—and that I remember exactly what he said about doing so. He will know what I mean."

The cat sighed. "All right. But there had better be a treat involved."

"Thanks, Murphy," Ven said, returning to the wagon.

It took a very long time to get the wagon hitched to the horses. By the time Ven, Char, and Saeli returned to the crossroads, Clemency was sitting on the ground, Ida beside her with her arms wrapped tightly around her knees. In the dark it was hard to see Clem, even as the light from the lantern hanging from the wagon approached, but almost impossible to make out Ida from the low-lying mist.

"Come on," Ven called, waving to the girls. "Get in!"

The ride to town was agonizing. The wagon Cadwalder had given us was warped and old, barely held together by wooden pins, and the wheels wobbled so much that we were afraid one or more of them would go flying off into the night.

The light from the lantern bounced crazily around the fields and the road as we bumped along in the darkness. Char and Clem stayed in the back of the wagon with Ida, who was fading away more and more by the minute, while Saeli and I sat up on the wagon board with the reins in our hands, me looking useless while Saeli called to the horses in her strange, raspy voice.

All along the way I kept hearing my father's voice as he

admonished me to remember my lessons. I'm not sure what
lesson I ever learned could have prepared me for what we were
doing now—five kids alone in a wagon they didn't know how to
drive, heading for an island they only barely had an idea of how
to find. I didn't know if what we were doing would save Ida, or if
we might all end up joining her and Gregory in the Snodgrass
family burying ground.

I only knew we didn't really have any other choice.

As they came within sight of the White Fern Inn, they could
hear the barking of dogs. The gleaming building glowed a ghostly
white in the darkness, pale as the moon behind the racing clouds.

"Saeli—tell the horses not to worry," Ven said when Breeze and
Trillium lurched to one side as the howling in the distance got
closer. "The dogs are caged unless Whiting lets them out—and I
think by now the ones that attacked Nick are back in their pens."

"That's reassuring," Char muttered.

Saeli urged the horses into a clattering canter as they passed the
inn. All five children tried to avoid looking as they rumbled by the
high fences, where the black and brown beasts snarled and barked
in ear-splitting shrillness, hurling their muscular bodies against the
barrier. Their yellow eyes glowed eerily in the darkness.

"Blow you down!" Char shouted at the dogs from inside the
wagon. "Where's your paint now, eh? Ghost wolves, nothin'."

"Shhhh!" Clem scolded. "Don't tease them—they could tear our
horses to pieces fairly easily."

At that moment, the lanterns at the doorway of the White Fern
Inn were unhooded, filling the night with eerie light.

"What's going on out here?" Ven could hear Whiting shout in
the darkness.

"Hurry," he urged Saeli as the barking grew louder.

The wagon careened down the roadway out of the light from the inn, the barking and howling fading into the shadows behind them.

"How's Ida doing?" Ven called from the wagon board once they were well past the White Fern and lurching down the open road again.

Clemency crawled over to the board and kneeled up beside him.

"Not good," she said in a low voice. "I'm really worried, Ven. Maybe if she had a real curate, a grown-up, instead of just a curate-in-training taking care of her, she might be better off. She needs a healer, and I don't think I'm doing very well by her."

"Hang in, Clem," Ven said, making a grab for Saeli as the wagon swayed and she slid off the board. "You're doing fine. Just remember whatever lessons you were taught, and do the best you can." *That's all any of us can do*, he thought.

After what seemed like forever, the lights of Kingston came into view, a bright haze of burning streetlamps and two large torches that lit the gate into town.

"Drat!" Clemency said, staring at the gate. "I'd forgotten they shut the entrance into town at night. We'll never get past the guard. They never make allowances for kids."

"Maybe we can go around," Ven suggested.

Clem shook her head. "There's no way the wagon would hold together if we go overland," she said nervously. "If we go to the south, we have to drive over a huge levee of rocks toward the fishing village, and if we go to the north, we will have to go all the way around the Gated City. I don't think we want to be anywhere near there, especially at night."

"I'll second that," Char called grumpily from the depths of the wagon.

"Then we're just going to have to find a way to get through the town gate," Ven said.

The gate was an enormous one fashioned in stone and covered with twining ivy, the same gate Ven and Char had passed through

the Gated City

when they first came to Serendair. The man guarding the entrance to the city was barely awake as the wagon pulled up to the gate. He rose sleepily to his feet, blinking rapidly at the sight of two old draft horses, without drivers, pulling a clattering cart full of children.

"What's going on here?" he demanded. "Gate's closed."

From the back of the wagon, Clemency stood on Char's back to appear as tall as possible and tucked her hands into her sleeves, looking very curate-like.

"Good evening, my son," she said solemnly. "Please let us in."

"My *son*?" the guard asked in amazement. "Wha—"

"My name is Clemency, the curate currently assigned to the Crossroads Inn," Clem went on, looking severely at the guard. "I have a very sick passenger, and I must get into the city now, before it is too late. Pray stand aside, my son, and you will be blessed for your efforts."

"All right, get out of that wagon, you kids," the guard replied, pointing to the ground.

"I really don't have time to argue about this," Clemency said, politely but firmly. "Please open the gate."

With a silver *shing*, the guard drew his sword. "I said get out of the wagon," he said menacingly.

Clemency, whose face was now grim, nodded to Saeli.

Directly behind the guard the ivy vines on the gate suddenly stretched, as if waking from a long sleep, then whipped out, wrapping their long tendrils around the man's arms and legs, pinning him to the rocky wall.

"What the—hellpgghfff!—" the man gurgled as the ivy tied itself around his mouth.

Ven and Char leapt out of the wagon and ran to the gate, hauling the portcullis up. Ven tried not to look at the terrified guard, who was now sprouting leaves from every part of his body.

"Heave! Heave! Pretend we're hoisting sails!" he called to Char, who nodded and put his back into the effort. The portcullis glided up easily into the stone of the gate.

"Come on!" Ven called to Saeli.

"May you have a blessed evening, my son," Clemency said as they passed through the gate. The guard stared helplessly as the wagon rattled by. Char and Ven lowered the portcullis again, then ran back for the wagon and hopped in.

The gate guard struggled for a moment, then stopped in amazement.

A large daisy had appeared from within the vines under his nose.

We rumbled and bumped over the cobblestones in the dark, past empty shops and silent fountains. The wind was strong with the smell of the sea, and many of the oil lampposts flickered as it blew through the streets of Kingston.

Our wagon clattered past the twelve-foot-high walls of the Gated City, its guard towers dark for the night. On the other side of the walls lights and music blazed; it seemed as if an enormous bonfire had been lit in celebration of nothing in particular. I could hear the sound of wild laughter and drunken merriment, and it chilled me to the bone.

And in spite of that chill, all I could think about in that moment was the rainbow flash I had seen on that first night in Kingston, and the one in the Rover's box. My head began to itch, but I willed my curiosity to be still—for Ida's sake.

They drove out the northern side of the wharf, where the cobblestone streets were replaced by paths of packed sand and shells. The wind blew in gusts, pushing the clouds along in the sky, rippling over the waves of the dark ocean they could see beyond the sandy streets.

When they came to the same abandoned pier where he and Char had once flown the kite, Ven told Saeli to bring the horses to a halt. The wagon rolled to a stop. While the other children were catching their breath, Ven climbed down onto the beach.

"Stay here a minute," he said, then jogged out to the end of the deserted pier, taking care to avoid the holes in the wood above the water.

Ven looked out into the sea, watching the gentle, constant pattern of the waves as they rolled onto the shore, foaming quietly as they slipped back again into the sea. He reached up to his cap and ran his fingers along the albatross feather, his luck token.

Whether it had brought me good luck or bad was hard to say for certain, but either way, I needed all I could get now.

- 28 -

The *Rescue*

"Amariel!" ven shouted over the rolling sea. "Amariel! are you out there?"

Only the waves answered him, their gentle splashing swallowing the sound of his voice.

Ven waited impatiently for a while, but when there was no sign of the merrow he called again.

"Amariel!"

The silver light of the moon rippled out in the harbor. Ven squinted, but saw no further movement. "Amari—"

The merrow's head popped up in the water directly below him. She looked displeased.

"Stop that!" Amariel commanded. "You're waking everyone up, and since you're using my name, they'll blame me. What do you want?"

Ven sighed in relief. "Who's everyone?" he asked, his curiosity roaring back like a wildfire.

The merrow flipped her hair, showering him with a curtain of salt spray.

"The seals and the sea lions, the pelicans asleep on the buoys and pier posts—and the merrows and selkies, thank you very much. Why are you shouting?" Her green eyes gleamed brightly in the moonlight. "Have you come to explore the depths with me?"

"No," Ven said urgently, "I wish I could, but tonight I need your help. A friend of mine is disappearing, and I have to get out past the harbor and into the open sea. Can you help me?"

The merrow's forehead wrinkled visibly.

"That made absolutely *no* sense," she said.

"I know, I know," Ven said. "But can you help me?"

Amariel thought. "Yes," she said after a moment, "I suggest you find a boat."

"Well, yes, I know that, I meant—"

The merrow dove and vanished.

Ven watched the water for a while, then sighed dispiritedly. He looked up and down the waterfront, then went back to the wagon.

"All along the beach there are abandoned boats, some of them little more than driftwood," he told the others. "We have to find one that will hold us—if we can't, we're going to have to borrow one from the fishing village, and that could get ugly."

"Isn't that also known as *stealing*?" Clem asked disapprovingly.

"Yes, so let's find one nobody wants anymore if we can," said Ven. He turned to the vanishing girl in the back of the wagon. "Ida, stay here with Saeli. Char, Clem, and I will be back as soon as we can."

"Only an hour or so till midnight, Polywog," Ida said nervously.

"I know—we're doing our best, Ida," Ven said. "Try not to worry; it seems to make you fade faster."

"Talkin' does, too," Char added as the three of them headed off down the beach. "You should prolly avoid that as well. Even *after* we fix you."

"Perhaps you can explain to me exactly what your plan is, Ven," Clemency said as they hurried up and down the rocky beach, looking for cast-off boats.

Ven stopped and pointed out into the vastness of the sea along the jetty, where the tall light tower he had seen from the *Serelinda*'s deck stood, its great lantern sending an enormous circling beam into the darkness.

"We need to be out there, past the harbor, in the open sea," he said, brushing back the hair the wind had blown into his eyes. "If we can get out there, I believe I can call the Floating Island—and it should come."

"It took *days* to come the last time," Char reminded him. "And how long do ya think we're gonna survive in a rickety little boat that no one wanted anymore, out on the open sea?"

"Long enough," Ven said. "Come on, Char, we know what we're doing."

"Speak for yourself," said Char, "I'm a *cook's mate*, in case you've forgotten. And a bloody *bad* one at that."

"You're also a sailor," said Ven. "And a bloody *good* one at that." He turned to Clem. "You've been keeping Ida alive and in line for a very long time now—without you as her steward, she would be on the street. You may be a curate-in-training, but you have the wisdom of a real one already. And while I may never have been good enough to merit a specialty in my father's factory, I know what makes a sound ship. We don't have any choice. Ida put her life at risk because we asked her to. The least we can do is risk ours trying to save her."

"Agreed," said Clem, smiling.

Char sighed. "All right. Let's get on with it, then."

The three split up and ran down the beach, checking each abandoned sloop and rowboat they could find. Finally, after looking at every boat the three of them had located, Ven bent down next to a green-bottomed longboat encrusted with barnacles that Clem had located, half-buried in the sand near the abandoned pier.

"I think we found our vessel," he said, ignoring the doubt on Char's face. "It has no oars, but we can gather them from some of the others. The hull is solid, the mast seems intact, once we clear the wasps' nests off it, and the sail only has a few holes. It should get us out of the harbor at least."

"We're gonna die, you know that, right?" Char said.

"Eventually," said Ven, "but not tonight, if we're lucky. Here, help me dig it out."

"Where did this sudden burst of confidence come from?" Clemency asked as she helped burrow the sand away from the sides of the boat. "Last I knew, you didn't even want to face your own family if you went home. What made you suddenly so decisive?"

"Necessity," Ven said, tunneling through the rocks and seaweed around the hull.

When the boat was finally unearthed, the mast lifted and the sail rigged, Ven looked pleased.

"All right," he said, "I think we need to christen her, and then we can set out."

"*Christen* her?" Char and Clem asked in one voice.

"Yes—the only unnamed ship I ever sailed on met an unfortunate end. I think there is something to that naming science McLean practices. If we name our boat something good, something hopeful, maybe it will survive the open sea."

"How about the *Rescue*?" suggested Clemency.

"Good enough for me," said Ven. "Go ahead, Clem."

"Let's get the others first," said Char, heading back to where they had left Saeli and Ida.

When all the children and the horses were gathered on the beach, the boys dragged the sad-looking longboat to the water's edge, and Clemency solemnly poured sea water over the prow.

"Bow your heads," she directed. Everyone but Ida followed her direction. "We name this boat the *Rescue*, because it is going to carry us safely out of the harbor and onto the open sea, to the Floating Island and back in time to save Ida from becoming a Revenant."

"Amen," said Char.

"Hear, hear," added Ven.

Saeli just looked nervous.

Ida, now barely visible, said nothing.

"All right, then," Ven said. "All aboard and I'll cast us off." He caught Char's eye; the cook's mate was nodding at the tiny Gwadd girl.

She was trembling like the wind was running through her.

"Saeli, are you all right?" Ven asked. The little girl shook her head violently. "Are you afraid?" She nodded, equally violently.

She had the same look in her eyes as my brothers always got whenever they drew the short straw and had to do an Inspection. A glassy kind of stare, a terror deeper than regular fear, that comes from a long-held aversion to something. It is a fear that comes from the soul of Nain, so I supposed that Gwadd must have as much of a terror of the sea as my own race does.

I looked out at the rolling waves before me, watching the light tower's beam swing around the harbor, and wondered if I really might not be Nain after all. The sea had a call that thrilled me, and made my curiosity roar. Even after I almost died in it.

He looked around at the dark beach. "Would you feel better staying behind and watching the horses?" Saeli nodded again. "All right, then, hide in the wagon and wait for us. We need the lantern, though—will you be all right in the dark?" Saeli nodded. Clemency helped her up onto the wagon board, and the Gwadd girl slid into the cart, peeking nervously over the side.

"Let's cast off," Ven directed. "Everyone who's going, get in the boat. Clem, you and Ida in the middle, Char, you take the tiller. I'm going to man the sail."

Sweaty with nervous excitement, they climbed in one by one, first Clemency, who made the boat rock violently back and forth as she took her place amidships, then Ida, whose entry did not disturb it at all, and finally Char, who took up his place in the stern, the tiller in his hand. Ven waded into the whispering surf, set the lantern in its place on the prow, and grabbed the tow rope.

"Weigh anchor, Char," he said.

Char pulled the rusty anchor into the ragged boat. "Anchor's aweigh, sir."

"Hold tight," said Ven as he climbed into the bow of the boat. The *Rescue* shuddered as he came aboard, causing the others to grab hold quickly. "Man the oars—let's get out of the surf before I hoist the sail."

The others nodded and reached for their oars. Ida grabbed for one but her hands passed through it. After a moment she set her jaw and looked sternly ahead, no other expression on her face. Together the rest of them paddled, pushing against the incoming tide, bobbing up and down on each wave that came in.

Getting nowhere.

"I—I don't think this is working," Clemency said uncertainly, looking over the side of the boat as it backed closer to the beach.

"Paddle faster," Char muttered, putting his back into it. "The bilge is startin' to leak in already."

Ven struggled with the oar, pulling as hard as he could. Just as he let go and sat back to think, the boat shuddered, then lurched forward with a violent yank. The four children rocked back and forth like bottles tumbling from a shelf.

Ven grabbed the side as the *Rescue* listed forward again, then began to head out of the harbor, without any aid from the oars at all. He rose up on one knee and looked out over the prow.

In the shadows of the lantern on the waves he could see Amariel's head and shoulders, bobbing in the sea in front of him. Ven grinned and opened his mouth to call to her, but the merrow quickly raised her finger to her lips, then dove down into the waves, the scales of her multicolored tail flashing in the lanternlight as it disappeared.

The boat gave one final lurch, and then started to head smoothly out of the harbor.

"I'm going to hoist the sail," Ven said quickly. He had planned to wait until they had rowed out of the harbor, but apparently Amariel did not want to be seen by the other children, so he set about checking the mast, then dragged on the ropes that lifted the hole-filled sail to the wind.

Quietly they glided over the gentle waves, bumping along, heading out of the sheltered harbor past the long, rocky peninsula where the light towers stood, toward the open sea. Char and Clemency sighed in relief when the wind caught the sail, knowing they were done with rowing. Ven looked over the prow at the tow rope stretched tight beneath the water in front of them and smiled to himself.

He turned around to share his smile with the others, and saw that Ida was no longer in the boat.

"Ida!" he shouted, standing up in panic.

Char and Clem looked around quickly.

"Where'd she go?" Char exclaimed.

"I'm right here, you dolt." Ida's voice came from the darkness beside Clemency. The curate-in-training jumped. When the beam of the tower came around again, it fell for a second on their boat, and in its light they could see the thin girl, her arms crossed, sitting where she had been beside Clem, almost transparent. For a moment, she looked exactly like Gregory.

Ven, Char, and Clem exchanged a nervous glance but said nothing. Char went back to bailing the bilgewater out of the bottom of the boat.

The waves got flatter and flatter as they saw the outer edges of the harbor approach. The moon came out from behind the clouds, casting a silver light on the sea almost as bright as the beacon from Kingston's light tower. When at last the circling light was hitting them from behind, Ven stood carefully in the boat and looked back toward shore.

The coastline had faded into the darkness, except for the light tower at the end of the peninsula, from which now only the beacon could be seen.

"We made it!" Ven shouted, feeling the sea wind ruffle his shirt. "We're out of the harbor and away from the land!"

"Now what do we do?" Char called from the stern, holding on to the tiller.

From the water at the bow Ven heard an annoyed cough.

"Ahem."

He leaned forward and looked over the prow. Amariel was floating in the water, her hair glowing silver in the moonlight and pooling all around her in the sea.

"All right, you're out of the harbor. I guess your friend can stop disappearing now," she said, quiet enough so that the others in the boat could not hear her. "So are you ready, *finally*, to come explore the depths with me?"

Ven's face fell. "I'm—I'm sorry," he said, "I have to call the Floating Island now. There are still some things I have to do first. I really appreciate what you've done, though, and—" His words stopped as a tail-slap of cold water hit him in the face.

The merrow's sea-green eyes narrowed.

"I understand. All right, I'm going home. I'm tired of waiting around for you."

"Wait—"

Another tail-slap doused him. When Ven cleared the salt water from his eyes, the merrow was gone.

I don't remember feeling sadder than I did at the moment she disappeared into the waves. Worse things had happened to me—the Fire Pirates, being arrested, being grabbed by the hands in the road—but nothing had made me feel so empty as looking out on the vastness of the sea where she had been a moment before.

Ven continued to watch for a long moment, but there was no sign of the merrow. Finally he looked over his shoulder and called to Char.

"Keep her steady, Char."

The cook's mate grinned. "Aye, sir."

Ven reached into the pocket of his vest, the one on the other side from where he stored the jack-rule. Carefully he removed the conch shell Oliver had given him on the day the Floating Island first appeared. It felt smooth and cold in his hand.

He stood up with the sail to his back, as far forward on the prow as he could get, feeling the sea wind rustle over him, blowing the curls of his hair in every possible direction. Then, with his eyes closed, he lifted the shell into the wind.

At first he didn't hear anything; the wind on the water was brisk, but not enough to swell the waves. A moment later, however, a soft, high pitch caught his ear, a sound that whispered of faraway places and the dance of trees in the breeze. The shell was singing a wind-song unlike any music he had ever heard before, similar to the whistle through the sculpture in Kingston, but more hollow.

He held the shell aloft until his arm got tired, then slipped it back inside his vest and stepped back into the boat to wait.

For a long time, nothing happened. The sea remained peaceful, bathed in silver light. The boat rocked gently on the waves, held in place by the ratty sail and Char's skill at the tiller.

While they waited, the moon set, disappearing beyond the dark horizon. The beautiful silver light vanished, and now the boat was surrounded by darkness, broken only by the tiny lantern on its prow.

"Shouldn't Seren be out by now?" Clemency asked nervously from amidships. "Maybe light from the star might help us to see."

"It must not be midnight yet," Ven called back from the bow. "Gregory said that was when it came out, if the sky is clear."

"Well, it's certainly clear tonight," said Clem.

As if to mock her words, the wind suddenly picked up, causing the clouds in the dark sky above them to race along. The waves started to rise and swell, making the *Rescue* pitch wildly. Clemency grabbed for Ida and found that no part of her body was solid any longer.

In the distance, the area between the sea and the sky began to darken with what looked like storm clouds. The wind, which until then had been whistling a rising song that fell in a tumbling moan, began to whine, and then to howl with fury.

The waves rolled, sending the little boat pitching, the bow rising up, then plunging abruptly. Ven reeled back and clung to the mast, struggling to stand as the wind screamed around them, pelting them with icy hail.

"It's coming!" he shouted to the others, holding up his arm before his eyes to shield them from the sting of the wind and the rain. "Hold tight!"

The spray from the wind splashed over the sides with the waves. Char let go of the tiller and scrambled forward, his bailing bucket in hand, and began tossing water over the side as fast as he could, but the rain was filling the boat faster than he could bail. Clemency helped him, shouting for Ida, but she didn't answer.

"Just our luck," Char grumbled, "she's fallen overboard, and we came out here for nothin'."

Ven kneeled, trying to steady the riggings, which were threatening to snap. He looked up at Char to see the cook's mate staring behind him, toward the bow, his eyes as wide as the full moon had been.

"Uh, Ven?" he stammered.

"What?" Ven asked, turning to look over his shoulder.

"It's here. Only I don't remember it looking like that before."

- 29 -

A Delicate Balance

THE FLOATING ISLAND LOOKED LIKE THE MAW OF A GIANT SHARK lunging out of the dark. The wind swirled all around it, churning the sea, crashing the waves against the island's fragile coast, and causing the trees that lined its curled summit to bend in a horrific dance.

"That's—not the way I remember it, either," Ven said nervously.

"It looks angry," Clemency whispered.

"Well, you might be, too, if you got called away from wherever you were goin' in the middle of the night," said Char, grabbing onto the side of the boat for balance.

"Are you still here, Ida?" Ven called into the shrieking wind.

"Yeah," came a voice on the floor of the stern.

Char scooted away in surprise. "Gah! Where are you? Is it your head that's tickling my bum?"

"My nose, actually," said the voice.

"Ugh!"

"Hold tight to the tiller, and turn the rudder to keep aligned with the island, Char," Ven shouted. "Clem, grab an oar and row." He tried to hoist the sail higher, but the swirling wind caught it and dragged them across the waves, sucking them closer to the unsteady coastline, which was pitching in much the same manner as the *Rescue*.

The rain began to pelt them, strafing the boat in sheets. Ven raised his eyes and saw that there was a pattern to it, currents of air that twisted like a spiral tunnel as they got closer to the island. He trimmed the sail as best as he could, struggling to keep it from falling apart, all the while calling directions to Char, so that he could steer the boat into the wind tunnel.

As they approached the dark island the noise from the wind got louder, a feverish roar that competed with the crash of the waves against the side of the *Rescue*. Ven swallowed hard when he saw the eastern tip of the island sway in the wind so violently that it lifted completely out of the sea, then splashed down again.

"Char! Hard to starboard!" he yelled as another sheet of rain blasted the boat, filling it by almost half with water. "Clem, crouch down as far as you can—er, you too, Ida, if you can hear me."

Char leaned on the tiller, struggling to hold it in the pull of the waves.

With a crash the mast fell over, narrowly missing Clemency, and covering all of them with the ragged sail.

The *Rescue* pitched, then shot forward, spinning wildly in the wind, caught in the tunnel of air currents that were churning around the Floating Island. The sound of muffled screams from beneath the sail was drowned out in the crashing of the waves.

With a thud, the *Rescue* ran aground, coming to a jolting halt.

For a moment, there was no movement from within the battered boat.

Then, slowly, the canvas sail began to bump in places, lift in some and fall in others, as the companions struggled to come out from under it.

Finally Clemency, the tallest of them, let out a growl of frustration.

"Stop moving!" she ordered. When the sail ceased bumping she stood up, like the center pole in a tent, and threw the sail off her head and shoulders onto the sand of the island's beach.

Ven climbed out of the *Rescue* and detached the lantern from the boat's prow, remarkably still lit.

"Char, toss out the anchor," he said, holding the lantern aloft in the wet air. "Ida, are you still here?"

Nothing but the wind, distant and moaning now, answered him. "Ida?"

Clemency and Char took up the call. "Ida? Ida! *Ida!*"

The sound caught the wind and was echoed back to them in a moaning wail.

Ida! Ida! Ida!

"Here," said a weak voice low to the ground. Ven held up the lantern, but saw nothing. He set the lantern down and drew out his jack-rule, extending the lens and peering in the direction from which the voice had come. The image he saw through the glass horrified him.

Pinned beneath the boat was the clear white outline of a girl.

"Oh, man!" Ven exclaimed. "Come on, she's crushed under the *Rescue*. Together, now—heave it off of her!"

Quickly they rolled the boat off of the invisible Ida, who, to Ven's surprise, stood up easily and shook the sand from herself. *I suppose there is something to be said for wasting away,* Ven thought. *It's sort of hard to hurt a body that's not there.* He folded the jack-rule, tucked it carefully back in his pocket, and started across the beach and up the twisted, translucent mountain where the wind made its home.

"Ida—we can't see you at all now, so stay between Clem and Char," he called over his shoulder. There was no answer, but a moment later he heard a loud *ooof!* from the cook's mate. Char went flying and planted his face in the blowing sand of the beach.

"I guess that means she's here," Clemency said to Ven. She offered Char her hand and pulled him up, then switched places with him.

"Remind me again why we're doing this, Ven?" Char said through his teeth as they headed up the mountain.

"Rover's box—bones—she shut it," Ven answered, not turning around as he climbed.

"Oh, right," mumbled Char.

Up the spiraling sides of the dark mountain they climbed, the wind rattling through the trees all around them.

Whatever sense of wonder I had felt when we first came here was gone. The island was dark and windswept; all around us the trees and vegetation danced and writhed as if they were in pain in the grip of the wind. Leaves and hail rained down on us from the misty clouds above, made all the more unpleasant by the alternating blasts of warm and cold air.

I thought back for a moment to the first sight I'd had of the place, the morning sun shining off it, the glistening clouds of fog making it seem like a fairy-tale mountain rising out of the clouds. If the island was able to have a mood, it was welcoming then, if a little timid, and wholly magical. Now, with the black of night broken only by thickening mist, the wind screaming all around us, the rising tone of the voices on the wind as we approached the mouth of the cave, and the total darkness that seemed ready to devour us at any moment, I sensed the island was in a much worse mood.

In fact, it seemed <u>really</u> angry at us.

After what seemed like forever, they finally reached the summit of the shell-shaped mountain. They hurried inside to escape the bitter wind, which had left their skin stinging from its bite.

The inner tunnel of the hollow mountain was even darker than the sea had been. Ven held tight to the lantern, trying not to wince at the large shadows it cast in the trees above. The smell of wet earth filled his nostrils, along with the smell of dread. *We shouldn't have come*, he thought, walking carefully along the downward curve as the mountain curled, the trees and plants thinning until they were gone. *I knew it was wrong when Whiting wanted to call the island, but I didn't think twice about doing it myself.*

He remembered what McLean had said about it again. *Something that powerful should only be sought out in a matter of life and death*, the Singer had told him. The thought made him feel only a little bit better.

They continued down into the belly of the mountain, single-file, listening to all the voices on the wind. When they came to the place Ven thought the wind from Vaarn blew, he called a quick hello to his mother, hoping she might hear.

Finally, in the total darkness at the bottom of the mountain, they stopped beside the tiny silver spring of Living Water in the rich green glen of lichen and moss.

In that place, all the noise from the echo chamber above died away, leaving only the soothing sound of the water's song. Ven bent down beside the stream and gestured to the darkness behind him, in the hope that Ida was still with them.

"Drink," he said. "Just a little; you only need a few drops."

All the sound in the cave around them seemed to die down to a gentle whisper. Clemency and Char watched in silence, holding their breath.

In the middle of the tiny spring a ripple appeared, as if a hand had been slipped into it and a palmful of water removed. Ven's eyes were fixed on the area in front of him, searching for any sign of Ida.

Across the stream from him the air seemed to move, then to shimmer. Slowly, like a spyglass coming into focus, Ida's outline appeared, followed in degrees by the rest of her, filling in colors one by one, her body becoming visible, solid.

Real again.

As soon as Ida had solidified completely, Clemency burst into happy tears. She turned to Ven and hugged him joyfully, released him and turned to Char, who hugged her back. Char turned to Ida, his arms open wide, but the expression on her face caused him to spin back around and hug Clem again.

"You all right?" Ven asked Ida, who was staring all around her in wonder. The thin girl nodded. "Good. We had best get out of—"

Before he could finish his thought, the ground beneath him rumbled.

"What was that?" Char asked nervously. Ven shook his head, but it happened again, this time causing dust and gravel from the walls of the shell mountain to crumble and fall to the floor of the cave around them.

The Floating Island shuddered. In the tunnel above, Ven could hear the sound of trees cracking and rocks sliding.

"Ven—?" Clemency said, her voice trembling. "What's happening?"

Before Ven could answer, the island shuddered again, this time rocking more violently.

"We've unbalanced it," he said, trying to keep from panicking. "Oliver was very specific about the need to keep the place in balance, to not take anything that belonged to the wind." His forehead furrowed in realization, and he winced as if in pain. "Blast! I forgot! Oliver brought something with him, a type of water he said was as rare and special as the Living Water, that came from a well that the wind couldn't reach. It was a *trade*. Of course! We should have brought something to trade for the water, but I didn't."

Dust rained down on their heads from the mountaintop above.

"Do we have anything we can use to trade?" Clemency asked desperately. "The place appears to be crumbling. I don't know if we can even make it up out of the cave, let alone back to the boat or to Kingston, if we don't set it right and balance it again."

"All I have is a jack-rule and a seashell," said Ven, his voice tight and high as he patted his pockets, trying to summon forth something he didn't remember. "Somehow I don't think that will do it."

Beneath them the ground trembled.

Char covered his head as a cloud of dust and grit fell down from the twisted tunnel above. "We're gonna be buried here," he said anxiously. "There's no way we'll make it—"

The ground stopped rumbling, the tunnel stopped moving. The last remaining grains of dust fell. Then silence returned again.

"It's stopped," Clemency said in wonder. "Amazing! How did it balance again? We didn't have anything to trade or—"

She fell silent at the sight that the two boys had already witnessed, joining them in awe.

At the edge of the spring Ida was sitting, staring into the silver pool of water as if it were a mirror. Tears from her eyes were flowing down her cheeks, making their way into the spongy moss at the side of the little well.

Balancing it.

For a long time the other three sat and watched her, unable to speak or move. Ven shook his head in wonder. *The captain traded the island some water from an ancient well that was as rare as the Living Water,* he thought as Ida ran the back of her sleeve roughly over her face and scowled at them. *Ida's tears served as a substitute. They must be as rare, then, too. I bet this is the only time in her life she's ever cried.*

The newly solid girl stood up abruptly.

"Let's go, Polywog," she said, but her tone was not as unpleasant as usual. It was clear to Ven that the Living Water had done more than restore her visibility, but what that effect was, he could not tell. He contented himself with following Ida and the others back up the winding passageway to the air and the trees and the voices and the wind.

When they reached the top of the mountain, the darkness of night was just beginning to fade, giving way to a flat gray that would linger for a few hours until dawn. They scurried down the mountainside, laughing out loud, singing and shouting along with the voices on the wind, past the trees that still were cloaked in night, past the hats and kites and shirts that hung in them, all the way down to the waterfront where they stopped, stunned.

Their boat was not on the shore where they left it.

"I told you to drop the anchor," Ven said tersely to Char.

"I did! I did drop the anchor!" Char protested. "Wedged it into the sand myself!"

"Then where's the boat?" Ven demanded.

Clemency pointed off shore. "There," she said despondently.

The *Rescue* was floating in the middle of the sea, about a hundred yards off the coast of the island.

"Well, *now* what are we gonna do?" asked Char, hysteria building in his voice until it topped out in a squeak.

"We can swim," Ven offered. Clem and Char shook their heads.

"That's the middle of the bloody *sea*, Ven," Char said. "It's gonna keep drifting; we'd never catch it."

"We can try to signal another boat," Clemency suggested. "Once dawn comes, the ships heading for the harbor will start coming in."

"Yes, but we will be somewhere on the other side of the world," Ven said gloomily. "This is a *floating* island, remember? It travels wherever the wind takes it."

"We can try to find a way to steer it," Char put in. "Maybe if we go back down into the mountain tunnel—"

"Or we can wait for the boat to come back," said Ida.

Ven let out a short, harsh laugh that sounded a little like a bark while the other two rolled their eyes or sighed.

"What makes you think it's going to come back, Ida?" he asked as calmly as he could.

"The fact that it *is*," Ida said smugly. She pointed out to sea.

The *Rescue* was making its way directly back to the island under its own steam, or so it seemed.

Ven's panic broke, and a grin of relief spread across his face.

That merrow, he thought happily. *Thank goodness for Amariel.*

Once the boat had returned mysteriously to shore, Ven and the others loaded up, cast off, and sailed for home. Ven turned in time to catch one last glimpse of the island; from just offshore, peace seemed to have returned. The morning air was beginning to twitter with birdsong; the wind that rustled the many and various leaves and fronds that grew on its summit was gentle now, content. The island seemed to be satisfied once more.

And then it vanished into the wind, the same way the Fire Pirates had emerged from it.

I really must learn how to do that myself someday, Ven thought.

Strangely enough, it took them even less time to make it back to the abandoned pier than it had to get to the island in the first place, gliding back out of the sea and into the harbor, almost as if they were being pulled.

Which, of course, they were, even if only Ven knew it.

As Char, Clemency, and Ida were reuniting with Saeli and clambering back into the wagon, patting the horses and chatting in joyful voices, Ven stopped and looked over the end of the pier once more. He waited, watching for any sign of a multicolored tail or glistening hair, until the others started calling impatiently. Then he sighed and bent down close to the water.

"Thank you, Amariel," he said quietly. Then he turned and caught up with them.

The ride back to the inn was much less painful than it had been from there. Ven asked to stop behind the fishmonger's stand and managed to obtain an entire barrel of discarded fish heads for Murphy, a gift he knew would leave him in good standing with the cat.

They took their time passing through the gate so as not to raise the notice of the guard, who was busy by that time talking to the town crier, getting ready for the day that would be dawning in an hour or so. Saeli urged the horses to hurry past the White Fern Inn, but there didn't seem to be anyone there.

They made it back to the crossroads just as Seren began to set. It was the daystar, Ven noted, the brightest star in the sky that glowed in the east as the sun was preparing to rise. It pierced the gray haze that hung in the sky like the light-tower beacon. Seeing its light shining on the crossroads made Ven smile, especially when he remembered Gregory's words about it.

This warm, safe place where the star Seren first shone on the island— that first starshine made this land magical, gave it special power.

Watching his friends climbing happily down from the wagon, chattering with excitement, he had at least a small sense of what kind of magic that might be.

"All right, time to get this Rover's box buried before the sun comes up," Ven said as Char and Ida chased each other around the wagon. Ida tagged Char again, heedless of Ven's words, and then dashed behind the cart, where she suddenly disappeared from sight, letting loose a howl of horror.

Ven ran like lightning around to the other side, to discover Ida had tripped and fallen into the hole with the Rover's box. She glared up at him in a mixture of fury and panic.

"Hmmm, seems I've seen you here before," he said jokingly, offering his hand. "Let's get you out of there before you start disappearing again." Ida grabbed hold and he pulled her from the hole with a nervous yank that sent both of them into the others who had been hovering near. All five went down in a heap.

At the bottom of the pile Saeli began to laugh, an odd, scratchy sound that was so infectious that both Clemency and Ven joined in. Char and Ida struggled to remain straight-faced but eventually lost control, and within a few moments the entire pile of children was laughing uncontrollably.

"What sort of nonsense is this?" demanded a harsh voice above them.

They looked up to see Maurice Whiting atop his beautiful white horse, glaring down at them.

"Nothing, Mr. Whiting," said Ven evenly.

"I cannot believe my eyes," said Mr. Whiting. "You are out of jail? How can that be?"

"By order of the king, that's how," Char piped up from within the pile of bodies.

Whiting's eyes narrowed into gleaming slits in the dusk. "We'll see about that," he said. He kicked the horse savagely and rode over to the front door of the inn.

"Let's rebury this thing and get out of here," Ven said hurriedly. "I don't want to leave him alone with Mrs. Snodgrass."

Quickly they pushed the dirt back into the hole. Ven found that again his Nain heritage helped, as the ground moved easily beneath his hands, so naturally filling in where it had been disturbed that a few moments later it was impossible to see where the hole had been.

"See?" Clemency said importantly. "I *told* you Ven would be a natural at digging."

"Let's get back to the inn," Ven said.

"Wait," said Clem. "Bow your heads—I want to bless the ground."

While Clemency was praying, Ven looked up out of the corner of his eye at Ida. The girl was standing with her head upright, but her arms were casually at her sides, not crossed in front of her or on her hips as they usually were, and her face had lost its insolent expression. She seemed to be listening carefully for the first time he had noticed since he met her.

"Your turn, Saeli," Clem said.

The small girl nodded, then closed her eyes. A moment later a small carpet of forget-me-nots and yarrow appeared, blending in with the rest of the grass of the field in the dark.

And lingered there.

When the flowers did not wither, Clemency turned in the direction of the small cemetery.

"Rest in peace, Gregory," she called.

Then the five of them hurried back to the inn, the light of the bright star Seren, shining down on the place where the box was buried, giving way to the first ray of sun, turning the silver road golden.

~ 30 ~

What Came of It

THE HEARTH FIRE WAS BLAZING INSIDE AS THEY ENTERED, BUT WAS not as hot as the words that were being exchanged between Mr. Whiting and Mrs. Snodgrass, who, though more than a head shorter than he, was standing up directly in front of him, her nostrils flaring in anger.

"You will be payin' for the damage your miserable hounds did to my property, Maurice Whiting," Mrs. Snodgrass was saying coldly as the children crossed the threshold. "Every single hole will need to be filled in, every single gouge, every scratch in every door sanded and painted, every bloody *bush* restored."

"I will be doing nothing of the sort, you shrieking harpy," Whiting retorted.

"We found pieces of dried venison in the gardens outside the windows of Hare Warren," Mrs. Snodgrass said. "You must have put them there to lure your dogs to Ven."

The inn door opened and Vincent Cadwalder entered, followed by Evan Knapp.

"I did nothing of the sort!" shouted Whiting. "I have been at sea for six weeks, and just returned home a few days ago. I have not been anywhere near your bloody inn except in the presence of the constable. And if you slander me further I will have the constable arrest *you*, Mrs. Snodgrass."

"You are making some serious accusations, Trudy," Evan Knapp cautioned. "What Mr. Whiting says is true—he could not have been to your inn until we came together."

In the corner Murphy let out a bored yawn. The old orange cat stretched lazily on the hearth until Cadwalder walked by. Then, with an impressively agile leap, he pounced on the steward of Hare Warren's leg and began clawing at his pocket, yowling hungrily.

"What are you doing, you bloody beggar?" shouted Cadwalder, slapping at Murphy. "Mrs. Snodgrass, get your cat off me!"

Mrs. Snodgrass stopped glaring at Whiting and turned around. "Murphy, stop that at once," she commanded. The cat ignored her, and continued to playfully swat at Cadwalder's pockets until something fell out. The constable stooped and picked it up.

"What's this, then?" he asked, holding it up. It was brown and dried like a thick twig.

"Venison!" Clemency shouted. "It was *you* that planted it outside Hare Warren, Cadwalder."

"And you that must've called Ven's name outside the Warren that night," Char added. "But why?"

"Because he's working for Whiting," said Ida smugly. "His room has all kinds of cast-off stuff from the White Fern Inn—torn handkerchiefs and ratty towels with ferns on 'em and such."

Everyone in the inn stared at her.

"And how do you know that?" Cadwalder finally demanded.

"Because I've been through it," Ida said proudly.

"It's locked!"

"Please," Ida said. She looked at Cadwalder with scorn.

The inn was silent for a moment. Then Mrs. Snodgrass turned back to Whiting.

"You will pay for having my inn restored to its former state, Maurice Whiting," she said. "Additionally, I will just have to go to town and suggest to the judge that he should look into all the problems at the crossroads. So many people have died or disappeared there, it might be good to know whether or not your vicious dogs were responsible. If they are, then likely *you* will be arrested. And I just might file a cause of action against you for all my lost livelihood and the money you've cost me. Faith, I've fed, clothed, housed, and employed *that one* all his life." She pointed angrily to Cadwalder, who shrank away. "Maybe by the time we are done, I'll own *both* inns on this road." Her eyes blazed with anger.

"She very well might at that," said Evan Knapp. "I suggest you do as she asks, Mr. Whiting. I will be asking for another investigation of my own."

Mr. Whiting glared back at her but said nothing.

"Get out of my establishment," Mrs. Snodgrass said. "Go whitewash your inn. Now that you no longer have to paint your *dogs*, there should be plenty left over. I want that building shining like the sun when the judge gives it to me."

Mr. Whiting snatched his hat from the peg by the door and strode over to it. On the way he passed Ven and the other children, and stopped long enough to utter a soft threat.

"This isn't over, Polypheme."

"It's never over with men like you until you die, Mr. Whiting," Ven said with a smile. "Fortunately, as a *Nain*, I will outlive you by four times over."

Whiting stared at him intently for a long moment. "Perhaps," he said finally. "Perhaps not." He stalked up the steps and slammed the inn door behind him as he left.

Ven felt a tickle pass his legs as Murphy walked by, rubbing against him.

"That's two you owe me," the cat murmured, covering the words with a purr.

"Check the wagon," Ven murmured back, covering his own with a cough.

"I am sorry for your difficulties, Mrs. Snodgrass," Evan Knapp said. "How's your young tenant that got hurt last night? That's what I came to find out."

"He's much better," said Mrs. Snodgrass. She pointed to the table where Nicholas sat, eating a bowl of porridge. "Especially now that the shouting has stopped and he can get back to his breakfast. You can speak to him if you like."

As the constable went over to the table, she bent over to scratch Murphy, who was rubbing up against her ankles, preening proudly. "Well, don't *you* look like the cat that ate the canary," she said.

"No," Murphy replied blandly. "If I did, there would be yellow feathers sticking out of my mouth. Excuse me; I think I'll have a look around outside. There's a wagon I have to check on." He winked at Ven, who winked in return, then slipped out the back door.

"Your supper from last night is still waiting, cold," Mrs. Snodgrass said to the five children standing near the door. "Where were you? Why didn't you come for supper?"

The five exchanged a glance. "We weren't feeling much like eating last night, Mrs. Snodgrass," Clemency said quickly. "Our stomachs were a bit unsettled."

"I'll say," muttered Char.

"Oh, you poor dears. Well, Felitza is warming up your soup. I hope you feel better." She bustled away, humming to herself.

Ven, Clemency, Char, Saeli, and Ida waited until the constable had finished talking to Nicholas, then came over to the tables where he sat.

"I really am glad that you are better, Nick," Ven said as Felitza came in, carrying their warmed-over soup.

"Thanks," said Nicholas. "I'm just glad those dogs didn't shred my message packet, since the message in there is for *you*, Ven."

"What?"

Nicholas unwound the cord on the ripped leather bag and reached inside. He pulled out a piece of oilcloth sealed with wax. At the sight of the seal Ven began to tremble.

It was the Polypheme family crest.

"The harbormaster said that some sort of huge bird—an albatross maybe?—had been circling the docks for hours. Finally it dropped this letter on the deck of a ship in port and flew away out to sea again. The captain of that ship gave the letter to the harbormaster, and he in turn sent for me to bring it to you." Nicholas handed him the letter. "It's got your name on it."

Ven nodded numbly. He recognized his father's spidery script.

"Wh—why does this bird keep following me?" he wondered aloud.

His hand trembled as he broke the wax seal on the letter and opened it. His eyes wandered over the words, but they made no sense to his mind over the pounding of his heart. He swallowed, then read each word slowly.

Ven,

First and foremost, our lives have been blessed with many good days, but your mother and I have never been happier than the day your message came on the wind. At first I thought it was my mind playing tricks on me or some deceit of a wandering magician, but when I heard you apologize for losing the ship, I knew it really came from you. Silly lad. As if you had a choice in what you did. We understand, and we are proud that you found a way to fight back in an unwinnable situation. I give you permission to stop worrying about this now. In fact, consider that an order.

Second, you will be happy to know that Captain Faeley and many of your friends from the _Angelia_ were spared from a watery grave. They were able to jump free of the ship before it exploded, and made it to the lifeboats. They believe that it was your actions that gave them this chance. The survivors are safe and well. Lodging was offered to them in Vaarn, but they were in a hurry to get back to sea again — something about chasing the wind or some other such nonsense. Anyway, they lived. So take that off your conscience as well.

You were too young to remember when your brother Alton was little, but he used to be extremely fond of making tin soldiers. Quite talented at it, too. I gave him the position of Chief Modelmaker to put that strength of his to use in manufacturing. Jaymes has always loved to paint, and so now he paints ships. Brendan liked to cook, to boil things until they turned into slag, which is why I put him in charge of making pitch. I've always tried to use my children's talents and interests in the areas that I needed in my factory, so they would be both good at what they did, and happy at it.

Try to puzzle out how I was planning to put your talents to work. I'm certain you will have figured it out before we see each other next.

And _all_ of us, your brothers and sister, your mother and I, we all look forward to seeing you again. But before you jump onto the next ship to sail back across the world, you should take the time to decide what you want to do next.

You're at a crossroads in your life, my boy, a place of decision-making. A moment of truth, so to speak. There are many paths you can choose, many opportunities in front of you. You're old enough now to set out on your own, to make your way in the world, to see its wonders. I wouldn't be much of a father if I didn't realize that might be the calling of your heart. Listen to that call.

Make your way in the world, lad. Do whatever you must, take whatever opportunity comes, but come home and see us when you can.

> With great relief in the knowledge that you are alive,
> And pride that you are my son, I remain,
> Your affectionate father,
> Pepin Polypheme

PS — Your letter came via albatross. The bird appears to be waiting to take a reply back to you. It is sitting on top of the house, making your mother and most of the neighborhood nervous, so I will keep this message short.

PPS — I hope that the jack-rule survived your ordeal. If you see things as they appear through its lens, you are taking measure of the world correctly.

"Well, you children must be exhausted," Mrs. Snodgrass said. "You are also covered with dirt. Go to the well, now, and wash up." She tapped Ven on the shoulder as he walked by, and handed him a wet towel. "And you, young man—you're a terrifyin' sight. Wash that filthy face, laddie."

Ven grinned and rubbed the damp cloth over his face, then handed it back to her and started out for the well once more. Mrs. Snodgrass's brows drew together disapprovingly, and she stopped him again and wiped his face herself. She started scrubbing hard, as if Ven had pitch stuck to his face. Then her eyes opened wide, and she broke into a delighted smile.

"Why, young Master Polypheme, 'tis no dirt that's darkening your chin! Faith, you've sprouted a beard!"

She whirled me around and led me over to the tavern, where there was a large looking glass behind the bar. In my shock I stumbled into Otis, the bartender, but he merely stepped aside and allowed me to stare at myself.

And there it was.

A single whisker protruded from the bottom half of my chin.

From out of the corner of my eye I saw McLean smile to himself. I didn't know if when he blessed my beard the day before he had done so by accident, or had known somehow that it would be coming today. Or perhaps in speaking about it, calling it by its name, he had used some power to bring it forth from deep within my chin where it was sleeping. In any event, I could feel his smile all the way across the room.

I looked back into the looking glass again and couldn't help but grin myself. If a man's beard is the story of his life among the Nain, I suppose this was a sign that my tale was under way.

And even though it was only a single whisker, I think, in all due modesty, that it looked well on me.

"So will you be staying in Hare Warren for a while, Ven?" Mrs. Snodgrass asked. "Or will you be going home?"

Ven remembered what McLean had said.

Home is where you decide to stay. Where you decide to fight for what matters to you. A man can have many homes, but he has to be willing to stand up and call them his own. Then he is never again uncertain whether he has one or not.

It's nice, when you've come to believe that you've lost your only home, to discover that you have two.

"I believe I will be doing both, Mrs. Snodgrass," he said. "But for now, I'm going to stay."

- 31 -

The Royal Reporter

The next morning found me at Elysian Castle once more, standing before the king in his puzzle room. I had come to give him my answer—that I was honored to accept the position of Royal Reporter, and would be happy to act as his eyes and ears out in the world, looking for the magic hidden there.

KING VANDEMERE LEANED FORWARD IN HIS CHAIR. "THE FIRST TIME we discussed this, you asked me what I was looking for out in the world. I need to ask you the same thing, Ven. What are *you* looking for?"

Ven thought for a moment. His mind was still reeling with all that had happened, so he thought back to before his birthday, to what he had been wishing for on all the days before that.

"I'm looking for the Ultimate Adventure," he said. "I want to see the world, too, the way you do, Your Majesty. But, you see, unlike you, I *am* hoping to find something specific out there."

"The Ultimate Adventure?"

"Yes—something that is so momentous, so perfect, so utterly thrilling that it finally satisfies my curiosity for good. Something so amazing that the itch goes away. I have no idea what that would be, or where—but I have this feeling down deep in my guts that it's out there somewhere, waiting for me to find it."

"And then, when you find it, what will you do?" the king asked.

"Be happy, I suppose," Ven said. "Or at least satisfied. And I expect I will have seen enough magic along the way to have stories to tell for the rest of my life, even if my beard never grows in any more than this."

The king smiled broadly. "Well, this works out well for both of us, then. I will pay to allow you to travel in search of that adventure, and in return you can report everything you see back to me."

Ven thought about it. "I'd like that," he said finally.

"Then you accept?"

"Yes, Your Majesty," Ven said, the words still seeming unreal. "I accept."

King Vandemere smiled broadly. "Excellent!" He rang for a page, who entered the room a moment later, bearing a large silver tray on which a book with a blue leather binding lay, its edges trimmed in gold. The king reached out as the page approached and snatched the book from the tray. He tossed it to Ven.

"I thought you might," the king said. "I know that look in a man's eye, the spark that shows he has a thirst to see magical things. I saw it in yours the first time you were here. So I took the liberty of having a journal bound for you. All its pages are blank now, except for the ones in the beginning, which is what you wrote when you were in the dungeon—I think it's rather appropriate that your story begins with a smudge. Fill this book with the stories of what you see when you're out being my eyes—and drawings, too. I want to know exactly what the magic looks like."

"Er—I can't really draw," said Ven sheepishly. "I can do a little architectural drafting, sail and rigging maps and such, and a little bit of cartography—"

"You'll learn," the king said. "All skills get better with practice. When you fill up that journal, come back and I will give you another."

"And you just want to know what is out there?"

"Yes," said the king. "You have an eye for magic, Ven. Find it where it hides—in the people, the cultures, the beasts, in all the places it appears in nature. In the customs, in the stories. You will know it when you see it."

"I hope so," said Ven. "I'd hate to disappoint a king."

"As long as you remember to tell the tales accurately, as they were told to you—the hammered truth—in the words of the person telling them, or as honestly as you can describe them if they are your own observations, then I will never be disappointed," said King Vandemere.

"I promise I will do my best," said Ven.

"Good enough," said the king. "Now we need to discuss what you will need—tools, money, and such. What sort of an entourage would you like? It's important that you remain safe, so we will probably need to assign you some soldiers, and perhaps a few advisers, or a Vizier—"

"If you don't mind, Your Majesty, I think I have everything I need for now," said Ven hurriedly. "I have all the tools I need here." He held up the jack-rule. "It measures extremely accurately, can help me see the details up close or the whole picture from far away, and always reveals the hammered truth." He opened the small knife. "It also peels apples."

The king laughed.

"And as for an entourage, I actually think I have that already, too. I have found a great group of friends who work very well together, like puzzle pieces that fit. I think I could convince them to help me from time to time. And if you're looking for the hammered truth, I think I should be as ordinary as possible, like when you went around in disguise. A kid traveling alone, or with some friends, is better for doing what you want done than someone with a huge entourage of soldiers because they will be less noticeable. No one really pays attention to kids."

The king nodded. "That's true. Well, what about money? I will be paying you well for this. Now that you have money you can move out of Hare Warren, especially if that Cadwalder fellow is going to remain there. You can stay in the part of the inn for paying customers. You don't have to work or do chores there anymore."

Ven sighed. "I like Hare Warren just fine. Cadwalder is a strange fellow, but his life has been really hard. Mrs. Snodgrass has spoken to him, and it's amazing he survived the experience—those scary tales about her are not all wrong. So I don't think I will be having any more problems with him. And besides, Mrs. Snodgrass could use the help with the chores. That's what you do around the house—when you are part of a working family."

"As you wish," said the king, smiling approvingly.

"I thought you might like to have this, though," Ven said, pulling the leather wallet Oliver had given him out of his pocket. He took out a dried piece of yarrow. "This is, as best as we could tell, the first flower that bloomed on the spot where the box is buried. I think I will try to bring you back some memento of each story I collect for you, so that that you can use your actual eyes to see a little bit of the magic as well."

"Thank you very much," said the king, taking the yarrow stalk. "I like that idea. Come and see me in a day or two, and we will decide where you go first. Is there anything else you need from me?"

"Just one thing," Ven said.

"Name it."

"Make certain Mr. Witherspoon pays for what he did."

"Done," said the king.

LATER, AT NOON-MEAL, BACK AT THE INN, VEN TOLD CLEMENCY, SAELI, Nicholas, Char, and Ida the story of his trip to the castle and what the king had said. They sat on the wide porch, sharing a picnic lunch, and asking him all manner of questions about what his new job would be.

"So I hope all of you might be interested in coming with me, at least some of the time," he finished.

"Perhaps," said Clemency. "If I'm not ministering to my congregation."

"I'd like to," said Nicholas. "Let me know ahead of time, so I can make arrangements with another messenger to cover my shift."

"You know I'm in," said Char as Saeli nodded. Only Ida shrugged.

"We'll see," she mumbled, and returned to her food.

"Well, I ain't got no choice, really," Char said, polishing an apple, then placing it on the porch railing while he refilled his glass with cider. "I have to go wherever you go so that I can keep an eye on you. Captain's orders."

Ven laughed. "Yes. And so that I can keep an eye on *you*. That's what friends do—they look out for each other."

Char nodded and reached over to pick up the apple he had carefully polished.

It was gone.

So was Ida, but the sound of loud munching could be heard inside the inn, fading away as she ambled toward the kitchen.

"Gah!" Char snorted in frustration. "There's a bloody *dozen* apples right there on the table! Why does she always have to take mine?"

Ven chuckled. "She's trying to get you to take notice of her," he said. "And me, and Clem, and all the people she steals from in Kingston. She's good—you saw her lock that Rover's box. She could take anything she wanted and no one would ever know—but she likes getting caught. She must be alone in the world."

"We're *all* alone in the world," Char muttered grumpily. "You don't see us stealin' each other's things, do ya?"

"No, but that's because we're *not* alone," said Ven. "I have a family, no matter how far away they are. You have the crew of the *Serelinda*—and we both have each other. We're not alone. But Ida—I bet she has nobody."

"Maybe," agreed Char. "Well, I have to get back to work. Mrs. Snodgrass says a large number of people are coming for a party tonight, and the inn is going to be full again. Lots of work to be done in the kitchen."

"What a hardship," Ven said. "We all know what you like best about being in the kitchen."

"Yes—Felitza," Char said dreamily.

Clemency raised an eyebrow. "Why is that, Char?"

"Look at this cornbread," Char said, waving it in front of her nose. "It's perfect—not an ounce of ash, not a burn mark anywhere. Buttery, with a touch of honey. That girl is a *goddess*."

Ahead of them they heard a giggle. Both boys looked up to see Saeli watching them over her small shoulder, a twinkle in her eye. She turned quickly and hurried into the inn, followed by Clemency.

"Come on," Ven said, rising and brushing the crumbs from his shirt. "Let's go see if Mrs. Snodgrass needs help with anything. I need to go to town later. I have to tell someone about my new position. She deserves to hear it before anyone else."

Char crammed the rest of the cornbread into his mouth and stood up.

At his feet the grass suddenly flattened, and a patch of daisies sprang up in front of him.

"Whoa," Char said, stopping with one foot in midair. He put his foot down, then called his thanks to Saeli into the inn. "What do ya think she's trying to say with this?" he asked Ven, squatting down to examine the delicate white petals.

Ven coughed. "I think it's a reference to your kitchen goddess," he said.

Char's eyebrows knit together. "What? 'She loves me'? Or 'she loves me not'?" He looked embarrassed.

"Maybe she just thinks you should pick them, give them to her, and tell her how much you admire her skills with cornbread," Ven said.

"Hmmm." Char considered for a moment. "Not a bad thought at that." He snatched the flowers from the ground and followed Ven into the inn.

As the door with the golden griffin closed behind them, the flower boxes at the inn's windows swelled with greenery, then exploded with bright blossoms of white and red.

No one was there a moment later to see the flower beds and gardens that lined the pathway to the inn's door erupt in color, a living rainbow of flowers blooming across the wide green lawn and all the way to the crossroads.

And remaining.

- 32 -

The Second-to-Last Chapter

The waves rolled under the abandoned pier.

Ven had been staring out into the sea since late afternoon, but there was still no sign of the merrow.

I don't know why I expected to see her. I suppose I just hoped I would. I know she was disappointed the last time we saw each other. There really was no reason for her to come back.

Just when the sun had finally sunk below the horizon, leaving just a little orange arc at the edge of the sky, a tail broke the surface of the water, waving.

Ven scrambled to his feet and ran to the edge of the broken pier.

"Amariel!" he shouted into the wind. "Here!"

The merrow appeared a moment later in front of him, water streaming from her hair and face.

"Did you stop your friend from disappearing?"

"Yes, and I am *so* glad to see you," Ven said, kneeling down at the dock's edge. "I wanted to thank you for everything you did for us. I have so much to tell you. And I brought you a treat. A friend of mine assures me that every favor should be rewarded with a treat." He reached out and handed her what was left of the boiled-sugar guard tower he bought his first day in town.

"Well, you do owe me some stories," Amariel said, smiling slightly as she took it. "After all, I told you hours' worth, and all you did was lie on your back and shiver." She popped the candy into her mouth, and Ven had to struggle not to laugh at the look on her face.

"Those stories brought me a great deal of good luck," Ven said. And he told her about what had happened since he had seen her last.

"It doesn't surprise me that the merrow tale won you the job," she said when he had finished. "Our stories are so very much more interesting than yours, I imagine. So, are you ready to come *now* and visit the deep? We can go see Asa the fisherman in the morning and have him cut you some gills. You will see things that no other land-liver has, and learn stories that will make that king glad he hired you."

Ven sighed, then shook his head sadly.

"I want to," he said, "but I can't today. I have so many things to do first—so many places I know the king wants me to go here on the land. But one day, maybe."

He thought of the tales she told him while he floated on the broken hull of the ship, and suddenly an idea struck him. "But *you* could come with *me!*" he said excitedly.

The merrow blinked. "How?"

"Didn't you say that a merrow can grow legs and walk on the land if she entrusts her cap to a human man?"

"Yes," Amariel said. "So?"

Ven coughed, suddenly embarrassed. "Well, I realize I'm not human, exactly, and not really a man yet, but we could see if it would work. You could give me your cap, and I would keep it safe. And then you might be able to grow legs, at least for a little while, and come and explore the dry world."

"What happens if I go all *human*?" Amariel said disdainfully. "I told you, merrows who stay in the dry world lose their personalities and become dull and boring."

"If I find that is happening, I promise you I will drag you right back to this pier, put the cap back on your head, and toss you into the sea," Ven said, only half joking.

"Hmmm," said the merrow.

"So, what do you say? Will you come?" Ven asked anxiously.

The merrow considered for a moment, then shook her head, swimming backwards.

"I want to," she said, "but I can't today. One day, maybe. Good-bye."

"Wait!" Ven called as she drifted over the crest of a coming wave, preparing to dive. "Will you come back, at least? Will I ever see you again?"

Amariel's smile widened.

"Maybe," she said. "Maybe not. One never knows."

With that, she dove into the next wave and disappeared into the endless blue of the sea.

Ven watched for a while, knowing that he would not see her again that day, but waiting anyway until the sun had disappeared beyond the horizon completely. Then he headed to the city gate to catch the wagon back to the Crossroads Inn in the twilight.

When he arrived, Ven could feel a difference in the place, and in the crossroads. He climbed out of the wagon, thanked the driver, then stood in the middle of the road, just watching for a little while.

Beyond the darkness of the crossroads, the inn itself was full of light and noise, with music playing, the sound of dancing and laughter, and lanterns shone in most of the windows. *Mrs. Snodgrass has a full house again*, Ven thought, pleased.

But even more than the inn, the fields around the crossroads had changed.

The little cemetery was peaceful.

The night was quiet and dark, and the stars shone almost as brightly as they did at sea.

~ 33 ~

The Last Chapter—
and the First Chapter

So now I am sitting in my new home, in front of the fire, listening to McLean singing quietly to an invisible audience, and writing in the journal that the king gave me.

I am trying to put down on paper all the things I can remember since my adventure began. I've tried to draw the things that I can't describe well in words, but I am even less of an artist than a writer. I guess the king is right—all skills get better with practice.

On the morning of my birthday, I was sure I would never have a beard, a life, or a story worth telling of it. I still don't have a beard, though it's coming along nicely. And I'm not sure how much of a life I will have; no one ever is. But I do have a story. And that's coming along nicely, too.

My father always said that any letter or tale should be written from beginning to end with the same quill pen. I suppose the message there is that one should keep a story brief and to the point. But some tales are longer than others. It seems to me that the more excitement a story holds, the larger the feather which is sharpened into the quill that writes it needs to be.

So you can probably guess which feather I decided to use to pen this one.

And I sharpened it with the knife in the jack-rule, so that the words it writes might be as measured and as accurate as possible.

All of this wondrous, terrifying, amazing adventure began with a birthday gift from an albatross. I have come to believe that she didn't just lose the feather by random accident, but rather dropped it on me to make me see that sometimes it is the little things in life that carry the most magic.

I owe that bird a lot. She saved my life by catching the eye of the _Serelinda._ The feather she gave me both spared me from Ida's itchy fingers and brought me a new, if somewhat reluctant, friend. Her actions made the king want to meet me. Everything good that has happened to me since my birthday began with her gift.

I have also come to realize other things since that morning. For a long time I believed that my father never thought I was good enough at any one thing to become a master of it. Now I realize what he was really doing when he sent me to train in each of the manufacturing areas.

He was teaching me to be the Inspector.

That's what he was trying to tell me in his letter. He knew my strength was in looking at _everything._ He found a way to put my curiosity to work.

My father, who is superstitious but does not believe in magic, is the one who trained me to see it. Maybe I can show it to him someday.

I miss my family very much. Hard as it is for me to believe, I especially miss my brothers teasing me, my mother fussing over me, my sister treating me like a baby—all the things I hated when I was with them. I wish I could show my father that my beard is finally growing in. And I will go back home one day.

But for now I have a job to do—and it's as perfect a task as I could ever hope to be given.

I have a whole world full of magic to explore, a whole lot of pieces of the magic puzzle to find.

And I have a book or two to write.

ACKNOWLEDGMENTS

I would like to thank the many archaeologists, anthropologists, language experts, and museum curators who assisted in the restoration of the first of the Ven Polypheme journals, especially:

Dr. Winifred Biggles Frumpton, for sharing her secret recipe for removing sand stains

Mrs. Pickles Butterworth-Smythe, for granting me access to her wonderful collection of Gwadd art

Sir Ambrose Dillwopper, for his kind encouragement

Godric Meanfilly, Esq., for his research into the legalities of reprinting ancient Nain texts

Ms. Susan Persimmon Chang, Project Director, for her exquisite management of the archaeological dig, as well as the publication of these historic findings

Mr. Brett Helquist, for his superior expertise in art preservation, without which all of Ven's sketches would be nothing more than old, dirty confetti (smelling of stale seaweed)

Dr. Parsifal Booh, documentarian, as well as his wife and her twin sister, cultural researchers Beatrice (Bea) Biddie and Barbara (Barb) Biddie-Booh, Department of Nain Studies, University of Vaarn, Professors Emeritae. As they came out of retirement to consult on this project, I want especially to thank the old Biddies

Betty Senwod, Artist-in-Residence, Lirin Conservatory of Native Art, for her expertise in tribal drawing and rituals—with thanks for bailing me out of jail that time after the Toockus Ruckus ceremony

Joe Fish, for, well, whatever he feels he deserves thanking for (there, happy now??)

S. Uther Twaddle, Ph.D., research scientist, Marincaer Maritime Institute

Infamous archaeologist and Site Director Samot E. Snave, for all his inspiration

And you, the reader, for helping to keep the magic of the world alive.

Elizabeth Haydon is currently working to
restore the recently discovered second volume of
The Lost Journals of Ven Polypheme,
The Thief Queen's Daughter.

Here's a sneak peek for your eyes only.
Check behind you before you turn the page.

The Stolen Alleyway

"TRY THE STOLEN ALLEYWAY."

The three children followed her finger with their eyes. She was pointing to a dark side alleyway off the main street, where a thin vapor of mist appeared stuck between the buildings. At the opening of the alleyway there was a sign.

Steal A'way, it read.

The old woman wiped her nose with the back of her tattered sleeve. "If yer looking fer somethin' that was stolen, ya best check there first, laddie," she said, her black teeth glistening in her mouth beside the holes where there were no teeth at all. "That's the place where stolen things are sold."

"Isn't everything in a thieves' market stolen?" Clemency asked.

The ragged woman drew herself up as tall as she could and snorted in contempt.

"That's a lie," she said angrily. "Not everyone in the Gated City's a thief. Some of us's just the kin o' thieves from long ago. Many honest folk works here in the market." She seemed to reconsider her statement. "Well, maybe not *many*, but there's some here and there. Now, git." She shooed them away with her fingerless-gloved hands.

"I-I'm not sure about this," Char said nervously. "That place looks even creepier than the rest of this creepy city."

"Come on," said Ven impatiently, starting for the alley. "We don't have time to waste—if Saeli's in there, we have to get to her before she's sold. Let's go."

Clemency nodded and followed Ven, with Char catching up a moment later.

As soon as we stepped onto the cobblestones of the Stolen Alleyway, I could understand why Char hesitated. It was almost impossible to see the buildings in the mist, but what I could see looked dark and abandoned, even in daylight. The street itself was winding, and curved off into the fog.

People were walking along the alleyway, stopping at the booths and tents that lined the street, just as they did in other parts of the Gated City. But these shoppers were different. Unlike the people wandering the brighter parts of the Outer Market, glancing at all the different wares, these people seemed as if they were looking for something specific. They also seemed much more nervous, much more desperate.

We understood how they felt.

The booths of this alleyway were not as brightly colored as the ones in the main streets. Instead of the carefully painted banners and the carved boothplates there were simple signs above each stall made from ragged gray cloth, each bearing the name of the goods offered, printed on them in ink.

Char and Clemency both stopped in the middle of the street as Ven approached the first booth. He squinted to read the sign.

Kisses

Ven's eyes moved down from the sign to the person sitting beneath it.

A white-haired woman, or what appeared to be a woman, grinned back at him toothlessly, the wart on her chin sprouting hairs as long as the ones on her head.

Ven backed away in alarm.

Clem grabbed his arm and led him deeper into the alleyway.

"Might want to avoid that one," she said.

"Er—yes," Ven coughed.

"This is the oddest place I've ever been, and I've been in some doozies," Char muttered as they made their way past the huddled shoppers, looking at the strange booths and the signs above them.

"What can this possibly mean?" Clemency asked as she read more of the signs on the booths.

Thoughts

Moments

Glances

"They're all things that can be stolen, just like actual stuff," said Ven, passing a gray rag banner reading Dreams. "Stolen thoughts, stolen moments, stolen glances, stolen dreams—I've heard of all of those things, but I never thought they could be resold."

"Well, if you ever had a kiss stolen, you can go back an' get it from her," Char said, pointing over his shoulder at the booth where the warty old woman had been. "But she can *have* the one Lucy

Dockenbiggle took off'a me when I was nine, thanks anyway. I can't believe anyone would buy that one—it was pretty awful."

"Who is Lucy Dockenbiggle?" Clemency asked curiously.

"Keep moving," said Ven under his breath. "I don't think we want to linger long here."

They continued down the Stolen Alleyway, past signs for Youth, Knowledge, and Time. Some of the booths were empty, while others had a single person sitting within them, waiting for customers. Ven slowed down for a moment in front of one reading Shirts. Within the drapes of that stall they could see shirts of all sizes and colors hanging, flapping gently in the foggy breeze.

"This one doesn't make sense to me," he said, coming to a halt. "Shirts? What is this doing in the Stolen Alleyway? Shouldn't it just be in the Outer Market with all the rest of the goods?"

"No," Char said quickly, tugging at his arm. "Haven't ya never heard of someone losin' his shirt? It means he got taken for *everything* he had. I don't think we want to be near this booth especially."

"Yes, my guess is that the residents of this place could steal the shirts from our backs and we might not even notice," added Clemency. "Keep moving."

"I only see three more booths anyway, and no sign of Saeli," said Ven anxiously. "It was probably a mistake to come here."

They hurried down to the end of the alleyway, passing booths for stolen ideas and futures, until they came to the last stall on the street. The ratty, gray sign read:

Childhood

"Saeli!" Ven shouted, looking up and down the street. His word seemed to be almost instantly swallowed; it did not echo as it should have.

"Let's get out of here," said Clem, glancing around. "She must be somewhere else. I think we should look for a flower seller—that's the kind of person who might make use of a Gwadd."

"Yeah, let's go," Char urged. "I wanna go back to the normal part of the market, where everyone is just a thief looking to take your money. This place is givin' me hives."

Ven nodded, and turned to head back out the way they came. Just as he did, he and the other children heard a soft female voice behind them call out.

"Char!"

The three turned around in shock.

There was no one in the street looking their way, just the same shoppers with their heads down, their eyes averted, milling through the alleyway toward the booths they sought.

"Saeli?" Char called.

"Over here," replied the voice. It was coming from within the last booth, the one labeled Childhood.

"Saeli!" Ven shouted again as the three ran toward the booth.

Just as they came to within a few feet of it, the drape in front was pulled back. Inside the booth was a young woman with dark eyes and hair, and a bright, warm smile. Her eyes never glanced at Clemency or Ven, but rather went directly to Char. Her smile widened.

"Char," she said softly.

Char's face was as white as snow.

"How—how do you know my name?" he stammered.

I thought back to something McLean once told me when he called me by name even before being introduced to me. He said that once I had spoken my name in the inn it was on the wind and could be heard by Storysingers and other people who know how to listen to what the wind hears.

The young woman in the booth might have been part Lirin, though she seemed very human. Perhaps she was a Singer, but my guess was that she was not. Singers take an oath to always tell the truth, and I had my doubts that anyone behind the gates of this city could have ever made good on that promise.

The young woman looked for the first time at Ven, then at Clemency. Then she shook her head.

"No, I'm sorry, I have nothing for you two," she said briskly. "You must both have had happy childhoods—or acceptable ones." Her attention returned to Char. "But you, now—you were robbed of yours fairly early, weren't you, Char?"

Ven glanced at his friend. Char was trembling violently.

"Let's go," he said, taking him by the shoulder.

"Wait!" said the young woman quickly. "If you leave now, Char, you may never get the chance to find it again."

Char's eyes were focused straight ahead. He shrugged off Ven's hand and walked slowly up to the booth.

The woman within the stall smiled again. She reached under the counter and pulled out a tiny glass box with a purple oval stone set in the top.

"How—how much?" Char asked, his voice shaking.

"Char—don't," Ven said, but his words seemed to be swallowed again by the mist in the alley.

The woman's smile grew brighter, and her cheeks took on a rosy glow. "For the whole box—one thousand gold crowns," she said sweetly.

Char's face went slack. "I—I don't have that kind of money," he whispered. "I prolly won't see that much in my whole lifetime."

The woman nodded. "Some people are willing to spend everything they gain in a lifetime to recapture their lost childhoods," she said. Her voice was as smooth as caramel candy. "That's a high price to pay. But for a single gold piece, I would be willing to let you see a moment of yours."

"I—I—"

"Leave him alone," said Ven angrily. "You're a cheat and a charlatan! Nobody can buy back childhood. Come on, Char, let's get out of this place."

"Shut up!" Char snapped; his eyes were glowing with interest and fear. He fumbled in his pockets and produced the single gold piece the moneychanger had given him, then held it out, his hand quivering, to the young woman.

Her hand shot out quickly, like all the other hands of the sellers in the market, and snagged the coin. Then she slid the box with the purple stone forward on the counter.

"Go ahead," she said softly. "Have a peek."

Slowly Char took hold of the top of the box and raised it.

Ven looked inside. There was nothing in it, just a velvet-lined bottom the color of a cloudless sky.

"You tricked him," Clemency said accusingly. "Give him back his gold piece."

The woman's smile grew brighter still. She looked at Char, who was staring into the box, his eyes glistening.

"Do you want your coin back, Char?" she asked, amused.

"No!" Char gasped, his voice harsh. "Shhhhhh."

I have no idea what he was looking at. The box was empty; I could tell from Clem's expression that she was seeing it the same way I was. But Char continued to stare into it, his eyes gleaming, until the young woman slammed the top down. Then he looked as if he had been slapped across the face.

"That's all one gold piece buys you, I'm afraid," she said to Char regretfully. "But you can take it if you want."

She opened the box again. Char reached in quickly and pulled his hand back as she closed the top again, gently this time.

"I—I could work for it," Char said. Ven was alarmed by the intensity in his voice. "I can cook, an' I have experience as a deckhand—"

The woman nodded thoughtfully. "I suppose we could arrange something like that," she said casually.

"No! Char, snap out of it!" Ven shouted, shaking his roommate by the arm. With Clem's help he dragged Char, struggling, away from the table, away from the woman with the warm, black eyes, down the street of the Stolen Alleyway, and back into the bright light of the late morning in the open air of the Outer Market.

Ven did not stop until he had reached the well in the center of the street. He pushed Char down onto the well's rim, then hauled up a bucket and splashed the water from it on his friend's face.

"What happened?" he asked as Char shook his head, spattering drops of water everywhere. "What did you see in that box?"

Char looked down at the cobblestones of the street.

"I can't explain," he said finally. "Happy times, the warm grass— maybe a picnic. Images of things in my memory that didn' make no sense at the time, and don't now. But they were *real*; she wasn't fakin' me. Especially this." He opened his hand.

In it was a red glass bead.

"I remember this," Char continued. "I'm not sure how, but I remember being held and playing with this. Maybe a whole string of 'em." He turned the bead over in his hand. "And the smell of lemon and roses. I remember that still, too. Whoever was holdin' me smelled like lemon and roses."

"Did you see anyone's face?" Clem asked.

Char shook his head.

READER'S GUIDE

The Lost Journals of Ven Polypheme

THE FLOATING ISLAND

ELIZABETH HAYDON

Illustrations by BRETT HELQUIST

ABOUT THIS GUIDE

The information, activities, and discussion questions that follow are intended to enhance your reading of *The Floating Island*. Please feel free to adapt these materials to suit your needs and interests.

WRITING AND RESEARCH ACTIVITIES

I. Real-World and Magical Entities

A. In the course of his journey Ven Polypheme sees, meets, or is told about many intriguing creatures, places, and things that the king eventually describes as pieces of the magical puzzle of the world. Some of these entities come from the real world, such as Megalodon, or from real-world myths, like the merrow, while others are totally products of the author's imagination. Make a list of the wonders Ven sees, and divide the list into three columns—real, myth, and imaginary. Then look them up on the Internet to see if you are right. You may be surprised how many of the "magical" things that Ven sees actually have a basis in real life.

B. Oliver Snodgrass tells Ven a story about how some people say the world was made when he explains the origins of the Floating Island. Do you know any other stories about the way the world came to be? Most cultures have their own explanations of how the world was made. Go to the library or the Internet and look up some of the cultural tales about creation. How are they similar? How are they different?

C. Dill is the tart spice that is used to make rye bread and pickles. When McLean introduces some of the Spice Folk to Ven, they seem to have personalities that mirror the name of their spice, like Dill and Fennel, who are mischievous. What sort of personality would a fairy named Rosehip have? How about Mustardseed? Make a list of spices from your spice rack or from the Internet, and decide what kind of personalities their fairies would have. Taste some of them. Choose one and draw that fairy.

II. Different Races and New Families

A. Ven explains the way Nain name their children. He is proud of being named for Magnus the Mad. Were you named for anyone or for a special reason? Write down your name(s) and look up the meaning on the Internet or in the library. Does it fit you? See if you can figure out what Polypheme means by looking up the parts of the word (*poly* and *pheme*) as well as the whole name on the Internet.

B. Throughout the book, we see people of different races being suspicious of one another. The merrow is very distrustful of Ven when she thinks he is human; the woman on the road is horrified to hear that there are Nain nearby. Why are people suspicious of those who are different? Examine your own thoughts. Have you ever been suspicious of someone of a different race? Why?

C. Some of the races that are mentioned in *The Lost Journals* are the Gwadd, like Saeli; the merrows and selkies, like Amariel; the Lirin, like McLean; the Kith, like Galliard; and, of course, the Nain, like Ven. Make a list of the different characteristics of these races. For instance, the Gwadd are shy and don't like to talk. Could this be because they are so much smaller than everyone else and feel vulnerable? Which races have things in common? And which of the Five Gifts of the Creator—wind, water, fire, earth, or starlight (ether)—does each race seem most like?

III. The Sea

A. Doing something "to the bitter end," being left "high and dry," or "on an even keel" are all expressions from the sea that are used in everyday life. Research other sea-based expressions and see if you are using any that you didn't even know were from the sea.

B. The sea has served to inspire a vast amount of poetry throughout time. Read some of these famous poems about the sea: "Sea Fever," by John Masefield; "Break, Break, Break," by Alfred, Lord Tennyson; "Christmas at Sea," by Robert Louis Stevenson; or "Casabianca," by Felicia Hemans. What sort of images do they all have in common? Then write your own poem about the sea, whether or not you have ever seen it.

QUESTIONS FOR DISCUSSION

1. The story opens with Ven writing a letter from jail. Why do we sympathize with him instead of thinking he's a robber or murderer? We start the story in the middle, before we know who everyone is. Does telling a story while looking back allow us to change our opinions of people in the story as we read?

2. The sense of not belonging is shared by many individuals. Too tall, too short, too thin, too big, too young, too dark, unfortunately our sense of being unique bumps right into our wish to belong to a group. How do you cope with that conflict? Ven is a Nain, and therefore an outsider, but in the human city his family is almost its own colony. What kind of group within a group do you belong to? Are there times when we belong in groups we might not want to belong to?

3. Ven receives two gifts early on—the albatross feather and the jack-rule. The idea of "a feather in his cap" usually means an accomplishment, something to be proud of. The feather is one of those details that might have been overlooked if the story just unfolded from beginning to end. Is the reappearance of the albatross throughout the story what makes his first meeting important? The jack-rule turns out to be a kind of graduation gift. What kinds of gifts do you think Pepin gave his other children?

4. Whose fault is it that the ship was lost? Later in the story we discover that it was a planned, not random, attack, but at the beginning, who do you blame for the loss of the ship and crew? Ven refuses to let Amariel or the captain make him feel better about the ship and men he thinks he destroyed. We, the readers, understand both that he had no choice and that it's likely they would have been destroyed by the pirates anyway. What about Ven makes him hold onto the feeling of being responsible?

5. Amariel says, "You're welcome. Good-bye," several times. If she leaves, it's likely Ven will not survive. Why is she so eager to leave? How does Ven convince her to stay? Which of Ven's friends has the most curiosity besides himself?

6. Notice how the stories Amariel tells are very different from Ven's. It's not just because they come from different places, but because they see the world differently. Would someone from a snowy place and someone from a very hot place have the same difficulty? How hard is it for people who have very little in common to be friends?

7. A number of children in the story—Char, Ida, and Cadwalder—don't know very much about themselves because they are orphans or abandoned. What would it be like to have no idea where you came from? Or when your birthday is? Or what your real name is?

8. If you had the chance to be the king's Reporter, would you take it? Where would you go?

FREE CURRICULUM

Available September 2006 at www.venpolypheme.com

A free curriculum with integrated subject areas will be available for download upon publication of the book. The series-specific teachers' materials are cross-curricular, with customizable exercises and lesson plans in varying degrees of difficulty for different grade levels. Subject areas covered include Language Arts, Math, Social Studies, Geography, Science, and Art, with mini-curricula in Nautical Studies, Mythology, Environmental Science, and Music. The curriculum also includes comprehension and discussion questions listed chapter by chapter.

FIC
HAY

Haydon, Elizabeth.

The Floating Island.

$17.95

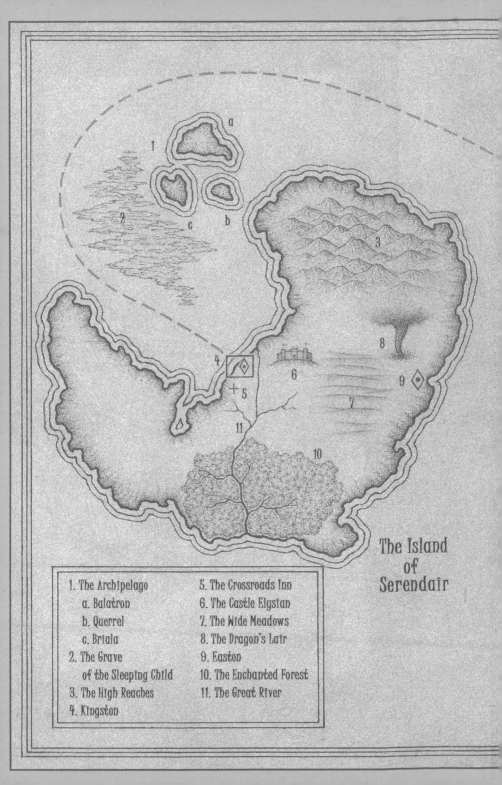

The Island
of
Serendair

1. The Archipelago
   a. Balatron
   b. Querrel
   c. Briala
2. The Grave
   of the Sleeping Child
3. The High Reaches
4. Kingston
5. The Crossroads Inn
6. The Castle Elysian
7. The Wide Meadows
8. The Dragon's Lair
9. Easton
10. The Enchanted Forest
11. The Great River

Fodor's 2010

ALASKA PORTS OF CALL

Where to Stay and Eat
for All Budgets

Must-See Sights
and Local Secrets

Ratings You Can Trust

Fodor's Travel Publications   New York, Toronto, London, Sydney, Auckland
www.fodors.com

FODOR'S ALASKA PORTS OF CALL 2010

Editor: Kelly Kealy

Editorial Contributor: Stephanie Butler

Writers: Teeka A. Ballas, Jessica Bowman, Linda Coffman, Heidi Johansen, Sue Kernaghan, E. Readicker-Henderson, Tom Reale, Laurel Schoenbohm, Sarah Wyatt

Production Editor: Astrid deRidder

Maps & Illustrations: David Lindroth, Mark Stroud, *cartographers;* Bob Blake, Rebecca Baer, *map editors;* William Wu, *information graphics*

Design: Fabrizio La Rocca, *creative director;* Guido Caroti, Siobhan O'Hare, *art directors;* Tina Malaney, Chie Ushio, Ann McBride, Jessica Walsh, *designers;* Melanie Marin, *senior picture editor*

Cover Photo: (Humpback whale, Frederick Sound): John Hyde, Wild Things Photography

Production Manager: Angela L. McLean

ISBN 978-1-4000-0869-8

ISSN 1520-0205

SPECIAL SALES

This book is available at special discounts for bulk purchases for sales promotions or premiums. Special editions, including personalized covers, excerpts of existing books, and corporate imprints, can be created in large quantities for special needs. For more information, write to Special Markets/Premium Sales, 1745 Broadway, MD 6-2, New York, New York 10019, or e-mail specialmarkets@randomhouse.com.

AN IMPORTANT TIP & AN INVITATION

Although all prices, opening times, and other details in this book are based on information supplied to us at press time, changes occur all the time in the travel world, and Fodor's cannot accept responsibility for facts that become outdated or for inadvertent errors or omissions. So **always confirm information when it matters,** especially if you're making a detour to visit a specific place. Your experiences—positive and negative—matter to us. If we have missed or misstated something, **please write to us.** We follow up on all suggestions. Contact the Alaska Ports of Call editor at editors@fodors.com or c/o Fodor's at 1745 Broadway, New York, NY 10019.

PRINTED IN THE UNITED STATES OF AMERICA

10 9 8 7 6 5 4 3 2 1